Painter Place

PAMELA POOLE

Pamela Poole
Ephesians 3:20,21

eLectio Publishing
Little Elm, TX
www.eLectioPublishing.com

Painter Place
By Pamela Poole

Copyright 2015 by Pamela Poole
Cover Design by eLectio Publishing, LLC featuring original art by Pamela Poole

ISBN-13: 978-1-63213-079-2
Published by eLectio Publishing, LLC
Little Elm, Texas
http://www.eLectioPublishing.com

Printed in the United States of America

The eLectio Publishing editing team is comprised of: Christine LePorte, Lori Draft, Sheldon James, and Jim Eccles.

For my husband, who proposed a secret engagement in shimmering moonlight on a South Carolina Beach in 1985.

Thanks to all the prayer warriors who blessed me. The Lord is faithful!
Special thanks to my son Andy for encouraging me to write a story that I'd want to read
and to Michelle Castro for being the first person to read the early manuscript and encourage me.

Painter Place

This story is about a fictional family who lives in a fictional setting along the South Carolina coastline. They will interact with real places, people, and history of the times, but those interactions are imaginary.

PART ONE
Changes

Chapter One
1985

"I shall be telling this with a sigh
Somewhere ages and ages hence:
Two roads diverged in a wood, and I—
I took the one less traveled by,
And that has made all the difference."
—Robert Frost

"'Painter' was an occupational name in Europe for someone who painted, especially a craftsman who painted stained glass," began Caroline Painter. "In the Middle Ages, the walls of churches were often covered with painted decorations. There's a record of someone named Hugh le Peyntour who was hired in 1308 to do the painting on the pavement at a church called St. Stephen's Chapel, Westminster. Some families who came to America with the name Peyntour—and all of the other variations of it— changed it to the spelling as it is today."

Caroline paused as the visitors drew closer to hear her soft Southern accent. "As for how this island got its name . . . Well, my ancestors were creative people who loved entertaining other creative people, so the locals off-island referred to the property with a double meaning as 'the Painter Place.'"

She smiled at the couple wearing shorts and flip-flops in her family's gallery. This was a common question from visitors to the island, and she grew up hearing the response as often as if someone were talking about the weather.

"Do you mean that the original owner of the island didn't give it that name?" asked the husband. His wife looked from him to Caroline, and both looked at her expectantly with raised eyebrows.

"That's right. My ancestor officially named it 'White Island,' the translation for *u ne ga*, the Indian name for it. White symbolized 'south' and denoted peace and happiness. They said that the White spirits lived in the south. The town that sprang up on the mainland here adopted the island as part of their namesake, Whitehaven, symbolizing a haven of peace and happiness."

Caroline paused before elaborating. "Though my ancestor Patrick agreed that it was an idyllic name for a place to live, he never forgot why he came here, or why he never saw his father again. He settled here before North and South Carolina were separated, and he referred to himself as a 'Carolina Castaway.' He signed his name as Patrick Painter, including his paintings, but his friends and family usually called him by his nickname, Castaway."

The couple was completely caught up in this history of Painter Place. The husband removed his hands from of his pockets to put one set of knuckles under his chin and the other under the elbow of the arm he crossed over his Hawaiian print shirt.

"What happened to make him think of himself that way?" asked his wife. They waited for her answer with a look that reminded Caroline of her little sister Marina's face when she used to read stories to her.

"Patrick Painter's family was in England at around 1680, and his religious beliefs were a point of conflict among the people and government," she began hesitantly. "Though his father precariously held a high political office and they were a well-respected noble family, their faith could be their ruin and bring about their death. Reputation or character didn't count for much in those times. His father decided to use some personal connections to sneak his mother, his wife, and his only living son, Patrick, away to the colonies. Patrick was a young adult given the charge of looking after his mother, grandmother, and the family fortune, which had been discreetly liquidated and invested by a trusted friend, a descendant of the Gregory family, who would leave with them. Arrangements had been made to settle them onto this island estate in Carolina, thus Patrick's self-imposed nickname."

"His nickname is the inspiration for Caroline's name," added Shelly, who had seen her customers and walked over to join them. "Though it doesn't have the 'a' on the end, when you add her middle name, you hear it—Caroline Amanda!"

The couple was clearly delighted. Shelly smiled back at them and then over to Caroline, affectionately pushing a stray strand of Caroline's long blonde hair into place, keeping the attention on her. Then she raised her arm gracefully to indicate a group of paintings hanging nearby under soft spotlights. "Here, see for yourself in her signature on her work." Shelly began walking, leading the couple to the paintings.

Standing to one side of work hanging on the wall, she looked from the paintings to the young artist. "Caroline is her uncle's star protégé, though his students come from all over the world."

The wife fished out her reading glasses from a straw purse decorated on the front with bright appliquéd summer flowers. The flowers coordinated with the appliqués around the neckline of her tank top, and Caroline wondered if she had made them herself. She put pink cat-eye-shaped reading glasses onto her nose and joined her husband as he leaned closer to see the signature on the paintings.

"Caroline A. Painter!" The woman repeated it, pronouncing the initial with an "ah" sound as if it was added to the end of her first name. She laughed, and her husband chuckled.

"So your legacy from a Carolina Castaway is to be a Carolina Painter!" The husband announced this as if savoring the answer to a riddle.

"The Painter family's creativity extends to how they name their babies." Shelly's rich, deep auburn hair was shining with red highlights from the summer sun. She leaned her head slightly over to him as if sharing an insight that not many people knew about. Her hair always reminded Caroline of the color of burnt sienna when she squeezed it from the tube onto her palette.

"So now you know my name, but I don't yet have the pleasure of knowing yours," said Caroline, extending her hand to the couple.

"Oh, that's right—I'm Ken, and this is my wife Kim," said the man. "We're from Darlington. Just here for a day trip."

After chatting about how closely "Kim" sounded like "Ken," some of the misadventures that their similar names had caused, and whether they knew any of Caroline's mother's connections in Darlington, the couple purchased the painting that Shelly had shown them and promised they would be back next year.

Seeing them out the door, Caroline checked the clock. She wanted to leave on time today and looked around to see what might need to be done before closing up the gallery. Stable stall doors served as counter fronts and bookcase doors, and overhead, the skylights were framed by exposed ceiling beams. All were preserved from the estate's old stables. Even the wood plank walls were part of the restored structure, which now included a gallery, two art studios, and indoor classroom space. It was opened after World War II because of popular requests to display and sell her family's creative and diverse work, though they were represented in other galleries, even internationally. People had begun to travel more by automobile after the war, bringing visitors to Painter Place who wanted something to take home to remember it by.

Shelly was recording the sale of Caroline's painting into the account book at the counter, so Caroline didn't begin a conversation as she replaced some empty displays with new items. Two of her dad's driftwood carvings, one of her sister's unusual baskets, three of her aunt's jewelry designs, several art prints, and one of her grandmother's books had sold on this busy Friday that would end the month of May, 1985.

She turned to the empty spot on the wall, wondering which of two paintings would best replace the one sold to the happy couple who had loved the stories about Painter Place. It had been a large painting of the marsh at twilight, her favorite time of day. She had one similar to it from a different view, and another of a Great Blue heron fishing in the same marsh, glowing in the blush of the morning light.

She walked back to the storage room. Looking over her inventory, she noticed that there were only a handful of originals left. She really needed to get back to painting right away. Occasionally, The Painter Gallery would feature a temporary show for an accomplished student of her uncle's or one of the many well-known artists who came to spend time on the island, or it would host a retrospective show of paintings created by her Painter descendants. But mostly, it was up to Caroline and her uncle to keep original paintings on the walls.

Caroline chose the painting with the heron, remembering that her bird paintings sold well. People liked birds. She had been told that some of her collectors named the birds in their paintings, and even talked to them as if they were pets. Setting the painting aside to take into the main gallery to hang, she carefully put back the other marsh scene. She remained standing there, again considering the reality of her inventory. She felt a little overwhelmed.

Turning to pick up her painting, she caught Shelly looking at her with those deep brown eyes that seemed to read her mind and confront her with it. She couldn't hold Shelly's gaze.

"When will the paintings in the show in Atlanta come back to the gallery?" Caroline asked as she carried the painting of the heron over to the blank space on the wall. She didn't want to ask but needed to know how to plan for time in the coming weeks. She had not been very responsible about her commitment to the gallery since graduating from junior college a few weeks ago. She meant to schedule days to get over to the studio but had decided that she just needed a break before starting to work again.

Shelly opened the cash drawer to begin the closing process at the counter. "Not for three more weeks—if the delivery arrives on time. Don't count on that. Five of the paintings have already sold."

This wasn't the answer she had hoped for, despite the great news about the sales. "Oh," she said lamely. She would need to get into the studio tomorrow and next week, and really needed to set a routine again for working. But there was so much happening at Painter Place in the summer months, such as the Island Summer Dance tomorrow night at the pavilion.

Satisfied that the painting of the heron on the marsh was settled, Caroline placed the label in the clear pocket on the wall and looked at the antique clock behind the counter. Five minutes to closing. She needed to get home to change and eat dinner before her date with Chris.

Shelly didn't miss how Caroline had checked the time. She closed the envelope with the bank deposit inside.

"Maybe you didn't hear me. I just told you that you've sold five paintings, plus one here today. Any thoughts on how many artists that happens to?"

Caroline blushed. "Of course—it's great news! I'm just a little distracted."

Slowly, almost as if she was talking to herself, Shelly said, "You know, not every Painter family member chooses to live on this island."

She placed the receipts in a file box before continuing. "The world across that bridge is full of people from off who are enchanted by Painter Place. They love the idea of it, love to visit it, and love the Painter family—but they could never commit to what it takes to be a part of it." Shelly gathered her things onto the counter.

Just as locals on the mainland in Whitehaven called the island Painter Place, they also had a word for anyone who didn't live on the island or have close ties to it. They were said to be from "off."

Like Chris. Caroline knew Shelly was referring to him. She didn't look at her as she walked to the counter to gather her purse and lunch bag. "Sometimes a life decision hinges on another person," she ventured. "Waiting to see what they will do affects your own road."

"If you're waiting on someone else's choices to determine your life's course, you don't know your own mind or your heart," Shelly returned as they walked to the door.

Caroline exaggerated a sigh of resignation and smiled weakly, pausing at the open door when the South Carolina afternoon heat wrapped itself around them like a blanket. "Okay, I'll bite—apparently you have something on your mind."

They locked up and walked toward their cars. Shelly took a deep breath and turned to look directly at Caroline. "You have a date tonight with a nice young man you've been serious about for months. This young man has spent the last week in another state—another state, Caroline—to look into things that will decide the direction his future will take him."

Shelly paused for effect. "You have a kind of love for him, but you're not sure if it's enough—that much I can tell. And in the distraction of your emotions, you haven't really considered how this can mesh with who you are or how this affects your family. You're thinking of what it might be like to trade your life and goals to follow his."

Shelly paused again. Caroline didn't say anything, but she wore an expression that hinted at defiance.

"Caroline, you're missing the big picture. You have an exceptional opportunity in life, a gift, and the best possible place to nurture that opportunity and gift. You don't understand it yet, but here at Painter Place, you'll have a lot of influence for good, carrying on your uncle's legacy."

She grasped for a way to reach her friend, trying again. "You can't stop painting to live an ordinary life—the kind of life that's satisfying for most people. And you shouldn't think you can just paint somewhere else. There's no other Painter who meets the requirements to inherit Painter Place if you decide to leave the island. Chris would have to find a career here in Whitehaven for this relationship to work."

They were standing in front of Caroline's restored '65 Mustang, a gift from her dad on her sixteenth birthday to celebrate the year she was born. It was painted Twilight Turquoise. As she looked at it now, she put her hand on the convertible top. "I don't want to lose him." A vague feeling of uneasiness formed inside her.

Shelly turned to walk away and didn't answer until she got into her car. "Girl, what you're in danger of losing is you," she said through the open window before starting her little yellow Beetle. With a sad, somber look at Caroline, she backed up and drove out of the parking lot. She turned right onto Pavilion Avenue out to the causeway bridge over the Intracoastal Waterway that was the only drivable link from the island to Whitehaven.

Caroline stood looking after her. Many reactions flashed through her mind. First, she felt misunderstood, and then resentful, annoyed, and uneasy. Why did Shelly have to ruin her excitement at seeing Chris tonight? She'd been counting the days until he got back, praying that he now had a clear direction for his career path and a place in it for them to have a future together. In the few minutes of time that it took to reach the driveway at home, she understood why Shelly's words bothered her so much. She was always right.

Chapter Two

"I unconsciously decided that, even if it wasn't an ideal world,
it should be and so painted only the ideal aspects of it—
pictures in which there are no drunken slatterns or self-centered mothers . . .
only foxy grandpas who played baseball with the kids
and boys who fished from logs and got up circuses in the backyard."
—*Norman Rockwell*

"I know I can do this—I just need a chance to try." Caroline heard her older brother Patrick protesting from inside the house as she walked up the back steps of the porch. Lady, Marina's collie, was on a leash at her favorite spot instead of in her kennel under a sprawling oak. The pet loved to be near the door at dinnertime when the family was all together.

Caroline's hands were slathered in Lady's kisses before she opened the screen door, trying not to divert her parents' attention from her brother to herself. She quietly put her purse and car keys on the little table at the door. Her family glanced over at her, and her mom got up to take dinner out of the oven while Caroline walked over to the sink to wash her hands. Dad and Patrick continued their intense conversation.

"They've already got the property right there at the bridge. Dad, if I can get legal permission to use the name 'Castaway,' and permission to duplicate some of the architecture and décor similar to Painter Place, I'll be a partner and the manager with no financial investment. Since my namesake is the original Carolina Castaway, I'm important to the plan, and surely this is a huge opportunity for a guy who's fresh out of college looking for a job!"

Marina came bounding into the kitchen, exaggerating the act of inhaling a savory scent. She grabbed a stack of plates that had pretty magnolia blooms painted on them and gathered the napkins and forks to pile on top before carrying them to set the table. She practically danced over, a slow and graceful rhythm that included using the table settings as her partner, and the men sat back to allow room for their plates. Patrick was working on adjusting his attitude about his conversation being interrupted by dinner.

Caroline couldn't help but smile at her sister. Marina never seemed to just walk, like other people. She danced. It was common to have music filling the house, especially the 60's music that her parents favored because that's when they dated and married, but the radio wasn't on. Marina didn't need it since there seemed to be perpetual music in her head that influenced her movements.

"Mamma, I need to hurry," Caroline said, making her way toward the table with the mashed potatoes.

"Oh, okay, sure. I guess Chris is home?" Caroline's mother and Marina carried more steaming dishes over to the table.

"Supposed to be, but he didn't call," answered Caroline as she pushed back her chair. "Sherrie did. He called home last night and said he'd be traveling in today. I'm supposed to meet him at 6:30 at the chapel." Talking about it revived her anticipation. She missed him.

"Goin' to the chapel and we're gonna get ma-a-arried," sang Marina, bobbing her head and snapping her fingers. Caroline rolled her eyes but couldn't help smiling.

Andy Painter cleared his throat and looked around at his family, and everyone bowed their heads while he blessed dinner. Three sets of arms reached for the mashed potatoes just after "Amen."

"Let Caroline get started first," Valerie Painter said firmly with raised eyebrows.

"Why the chapel?" Her dad watched her as she finished getting a serving of the potatoes and passed them to Marina. "Sounds like an unusual destination for a date."

Caroline shook her head with her mouth full, shrugging.

"Maybe he's going to ask her to marry him!" chirped Marina, setting the last platter down in front of her full plate. She used her hands to pull stray brown waves of hair back behind her ears as if they would get between her and her food. None of those beautiful magnolias on the plate were visible anymore, hidden by a hearty Southern meal. "Every Painter gets married in the chapel," she commented before putting a forkful of the potatoes into her mouth.

Caroline didn't miss the looks passing between her mom, dad, and brother. They didn't mean for her to see it, and she quickly looked back down at her plate. First Shelly, and now her parents and her brother—that knot of tension somewhere in her middle grew tighter.

"Yeah, and we have our funerals there, too, which is the same thing, right?" Patrick quipped back at Marina as he leaned closer to her over his plate. "There really needs to be something about that engraved on one of those plaques."

"Yeah, try and get Gran Vanna to approve of that!" Marina laughed as she tipped a shaker in the shape of a seashell to sprinkle some salt on her green beans.

"But if she would, who better to compose a profound way to express it—one that would end up becoming some famous quote or something!" Patrick exclaimed before putting a bite into his mouth that was so big that it would insult the table manners of their genteel Southern belle grandmother.

Caroline rose from the table.

"Don't you want dessert?" Marina asked incredulously. "Patrick made his famous chocolate éclair!"

"Yum! No kidding?" Caroline asked as she put her plate by the sink. Patrick's creative talents were his culinary skills, and they looked forward to his recipes. "Cut a giant piece for me and put it in the fridge. I'll have it tonight when I get in. I need to change clothes and get out of here."

Coming up behind her mom's chair on the way out of the kitchen, she put both hands on her shoulders and kissed the top of her head. Valerie Painter's dark hair was cut in a cute longish bob with fringey bangs, like a fashion model, and smelled vaguely like island flowers. Her mom held a fork in her right hand, but reached up the left one to pat her daughter's, waiting for the request for a favor that usually followed this gesture. Andy Painter looked up from his plate at them, also recognizing the familiar gesture and slowly chewing his last bite while he waited for what would follow.

"Mamma, I've been thinking today about your blue sweater and how it really brings out the color of my eyes," Caroline began.

"I haven't even worn it yet—you and Marina keep it in the laundry basket!" protested her mom half-heartedly, looking at her husband, who was smiling as he shook his head. She sighed. "I just washed it, and it's on a hanger on the doorknob to my room—it hasn't even made it to my closet!" She finished her sentence over her shoulder as her daughter headed toward the master suite.

"You're the best, Mamma! I'll wash it for you myself this time," Caroline's voice trailed. She grabbed the sweater and rushed toward the huge, gracefully spiraling staircase at the heart of the house, stepping onto the gorgeous colors that the stained glass dome above her splashed onto the steps.

Andy looked at his wife and swallowed the bite of roast he'd been chewing. "Maybe I should take you shopping for another one so I can see it on you," he suggested before putting a forkful of green beans into his mouth. "That sweater must be something else!"

"No, Dad!" exclaimed Marina. "It's special because it's hard to get. Kinda like Patrick's chocolate éclair—if we had it every week, we wouldn't look forward to it so much."

Chapter Three

Could you tell me the way to Somewhere—
Somewhere, Somewhere,
I have heard of a place called Somewhere—
But know not where it can be.
It makes no difference,
Whether or not
I go in dreams
Or trudge on foot:
Would you tell me the way to Somewhere,
The somewhere meant for me . . .
—Walter de la Mare

Often, there wasn't a lot of point in putting too much time into a hairstyle on the island. But the humidity was low tonight with little wind blowing. The styling gel that Caroline used to hold a gentle wave of volume in her hair was going to work for a few hours. She kept her straight blonde hair trimmed to just past her shoulder blades so that she would have the best range of styles to wear to tame it in island weather. Today, she'd been able to wear it down, the way Chris liked it. Her feathery bangs were cut like her mother's, in diagonal layers so that they didn't run in a straight line across her forehead, and they ended just below her eyebrows in a way that drew attention to the fringe of her eyelashes. She knew the blue sleeveless sweater with her white jeans really brought out the best of her features and shoulders.

Confident that Chris would love how she looked, she felt her mood buoyed again.

She checked her pink lip gloss in the rearview mirror before she pulled the car out of the driveway onto Castaway Drive. She dared to consider— what if Chris actually did propose? Why had he chosen the chapel for a date? She hadn't even told him she loved him, but was there a chance that he was ready for a big step?

***

19

At home, Valerie Painter got up from the table to go to the kitchen counter to answer the phone, interrupting Patrick's conversation with his parents again. Frustrated, he lightly tapped his hands on the table and tilted back in his chair, looking up at the high ceiling. His dad sighed and rubbed tanned hands back through his sun-bleached blonde hair. They looked at Valerie to see who she was talking to—it would matter a great deal in how long this conversation he had started would take.

"Well hello, Sherrie! You left your photos over here on Wednesday—they must have still been on the table when you packed your overnight bag, but we'll get them to you at church on Sunday. What? Oh, honey—I can't understand what you're trying to say."

Valerie turned from the counter back to the table to signal a look of alarm toward the guys. "Sweetie, why are you crying? Is there anything I can—well, yes, he's here. Hold on."

Valerie's eyebrows were raised in a silent question to Patrick as she pointed the receiver at him and briskly motioned for him to come.

Patrick jumped up to take the phone, and his dad instinctively pushed his own chair back and stood up expectantly, as if ready to do something if someone needed him.

"Hi, there, Sher," he greeted her, using her nickname. He held the phone to his ear, looking out of a kitchen window at a sky that he could tell was going to make a dramatic transition into night. But he only noticed it for a moment.

"Oh. Well—uh, I didn't see that coming. Obviously you didn't, either." He turned around to look at his mom and dad, whose eyes never left his face. "Sher, please don't cry . . ."

In Patrick's experience, one never knew what direction things would go with a crying female. He gave his mom a look that begged for help but resigned himself to his situation and did the best he could.

When he hung up the phone about five minutes later, Patrick had forgotten about finishing the conversation with his parents about his future. Caroline's future was the one foremost on his mind. Marina danced with bare feet down the stairs to get a glass of lemonade to take to her room, but she stopped short at the kitchen door, seeing that something was wrong. Patrick began to quickly explain to all three of them what Sherrie's call was about.

Moments passed as they all stood silent. Then Valerie jumped into action. "Andy, call Wyeth. We've got to get her out of here!"

***

The sky overhead was the kind that promised a spectacular sunset and twilight. The ever-changing attributes of the sky as a day ended fascinated Caroline. What a blessing to live here, where there were no city lights to compete with sunsets, starlight, and fireflies. She felt an overwhelming sense of peace and belonging, and that squeeze of her heart that she'd come to think of as a "hug" from God. She knew beyond any doubt that it was one of those moments shared only by the two of them.

"Thank you, Lord, for—well—for my life," she whispered. It's all she could think of to say that would cover everything.

Passing the marsh, garden areas began to appear on the left side of the island road, groomed for the historic Painter family chapel. Shadows with exaggerated shapes lay long from the flora and fauna at this time of the evening. In a few minutes, the chapel would come into view.

She turned on the radio. "If you're not headin' out to that there shindig on the Island t'marra night, just put on your shaggin' shoes, or kick 'em off altogether, and join me right here for the best Carolina beach music!" boomed the deep voice of Shaggin' Pirate, the boisterous DJ across the bridge in Whitehaven. "Here's a request as we continue dancin' to those Friday night Sounds of the Sixties. Bill says this is for Tammy—they're celebratin' somethin' special tonight!"

She recognized the song in the first several notes. Her dad would often stop whatever he was doing when it came on the radio at home, grabbing her mom to dance, hug, or just sing it to her. The Temptations cooed "My Girl."

> *"I've got sunshine on a cloudy day*
> *When it's cold outside, I've got the month of May*
> *I guess you'd say, what can make me feel this way?*
> *My girl, my girl, my girl, talkin' 'bout my girl . . ."*

Caroline pulled up and spotted the little orange Triumph that had once been Chris' dad's car. His dad was sentimental about it—and had kept it long after getting a family car—until finally he gave it to his son to drive. Chris was waiting for her in the open door of the chapel, leaning with his right shoulder on the door frame, arms crossed from elbow to elbow.

He jogged lightly over to her car to open her door for her while she tucked the keys into a pocket on the outside of her purse. She drank in the sight of his wavy, light brown hair, cut in a short, preppy style. The tail of his polo shirt was tucked into khaki jeans. The muted olive green color was his favorite and really suited him—so earthy and natural, even with the little alligator logo in a different green, looking like it would bite anyone sneaking up on him from his left side.

They smiled at one another through the window, and she jumped out to hug him before he had a chance to close her door. "I missed you!"

He hugged her tightly, letting out a deep breath and responded, "I missed you, too." They stood there like that for a few sweet moments, swaying side to side as if barely dancing.

Finally, Chris lightly brushed a kiss on her forehead and began to pull away to close her car door. "Let me look at you!" he exclaimed light-heartedly, standing back and taking in the full effect of all that planning she'd done earlier just for him. He slapped his right hand up onto the little alligator logo over his heart as he took an exaggerated deep breath, rolled his eyes skyward, tilted back his head, and let his knees buckle, staggering back a little.

Caroline laughed at his antics, but then played along. She moved into what she hoped was her best model's pose for a runway.

She could see that Chris appreciated the pose, looking at her as if memorizing the sight. "When I saw you drive up, it hit me that you're the kind of girl guys write poems to, sing songs about, and paint pictures of. There's nothing in all the beauty of Painter Place that can hold a candle to you."

She was surprised and touched by this, delivered in such a serious tone of voice and expression, but kept playing along as if he were joking. She moved gracefully from the pose of a model into what she hoped was a pose depicting a princess accepting compliments from her subjects,

22

holding out her left hand for a kiss. "In that case, there's no competition to be vanquished," she said in her most regal tone.

His expression became thoughtful. He took her extended hand and did kiss it, then held it in his own. "Let's go for a walk," he said, using her hand to lead her.

Usually, when they walked on the island, it was along the beach. "Here?" asked Caroline in surprise.

Chris had taken a step toward the path in his Sperry Docksiders, pulling both of their arms straight since she stood rooted to the spot beside her car. He stood still, too, looking at her in a way that sent a stab of worry flashing through her mind. She was suddenly aware again that the weird knot of tension was back in her stomach.

"By the way, why are we meeting here?"

He continued to hold her hand, but turned to look at the old chapel. She never took her eyes off of his tanned, clean-cut, all-American guy profile.

"I knew it would be open until dusk, and it wasn't likely that there would be visitors at this time on a Friday evening," he finally said. "I wanted to come here to be alone inside for a little while before I saw you."

Her mind was racing now. She knew he'd been praying—why else would he come here like that, to be alone inside? Was this a good sign, or—not?

"Something important must be on your mind," she ventured. "Maybe something to do with your trip?"

"Come on, walk with me," he coaxed in a pleading tone, turning back to look at her and pulling lightly on her arm. This time, she reluctantly stepped forward, and they began walking down a sandy path that led away from the chapel.

Every sound seemed magnified as they first began walking in silence, swinging their arms slightly in rhythm as they held hands. The distant roar of perpetual crashing waves, palm leaves rustling in an occasional slight breeze high overhead, seagull calls, insects rubbing wings together, and serenading songbirds all contributed to the symphony that was the island.

"I'm really glad I attended the career conference, and I met a lot of great people. It was . . . life-changing," Chris said after a little while. He didn't seem to have finished his thought, so Caroline waited for him to say more.

In a few more steps, he did. "Do you know the story of Jim Elliot and Nate Saint?"

"Sure. We learned about them several years ago when I was still in youth group at church. Before your dad came to be our new pastor. They had unforgettable conviction and courage."

"I met some people who knew both of them this week," Chris said.

She didn't think he was waiting for a response from her since he seemed to be thinking.

They took a few more steps before he said hesitantly, "Caroline, while I was at the conference, I finally came across the missing puzzle piece that put things together for me. I know now what my next step is, what I'm supposed to do." Caroline looked over at him, and saw that Chris was looking ahead instead of at her.

She waited for what he would say next, but when he was quiet for so long, she looked down at her sandals. This date wasn't going at all the way she had hoped. She couldn't anticipate what he was going to say, but she sure didn't like the way he was saying whatever it was. One thing was very clear—he didn't expect her to embrace this new revelation about his future.

She looked back up as they kept strolling along the path, which was beginning to curve in a meandering way back toward the chapel. The stained glass windows would be beautiful from the inside of the building, where they would be glowing from the late rays of the sun. Strong shadows in the shapes of semi-tropical surroundings splashed across the stucco. Her mind wandered as her artist's eye imagined which purple and blue would be the right mix for the shadows as a complement to the warm glow on the stucco.

Chris stopped at a low sculpted marble bench beside the path and pulled her to sit on it, interrupting her mental plans for a painting. Unexpectedly, he sat down cross-legged on the ground facing her, taking both her hands into his and resting their joined hands on the knees of her jeans. He looked up and held her gaze intently with green eyes that had dark green rays fanning out into them, like a palm, and she was lost for a few moments, breathless. Something really big was getting ready to happen.

"Caroline," he said in a gentle tone. "I can't take you where I'm going, and you can't wait for me to return. It's breaking my heart, and I'm miserable that it may break yours."

The symphony of the island sounds magnified and took over the silence again. Chris waited while Caroline sat speechless. She looked at him in astonishment, and then looked down in confusion at their clasped hands, trying to gather her wits. She was too stunned at this turn of events to know how to respond. Guys got on the ground in front of you to propose, not to break up with you. Breakups happened to—other people—and definitely were not what guys like Chris did. This was all wrong. This couldn't be happening.

Chris broke the silence first. "I've always suspected that I would end up in some level of ministry, but I never told anyone except my parents. Once we moved here and I finished college, I wanted to be with you so much that I looked desperately for options with my degree, knowing that I could be a teacher or something at church on the side instead of having a full-time ministry. I wanted to have a life that included you, though I suspected it would be difficult to do that without taking you away from here. Now I see that I was running from what I was meant to be, and I wanted you to run with me, away from what you are meant to be. This week, I finally had no excuses and no room for doubt anymore. I know what I'm supposed to do, and I'll never be the same if I don't do it."

He had become more animated as he talked, and the firm conviction in his voice reminded her of hearing his dad in the pulpit as he preached on Sundays. She could not help but admire him, even though she felt abandoned and insignificant, cast aside for a higher calling. In a flash of certainty, she knew that this man holding her hands would do great things—not famous things, but things that really mattered. She also realized suddenly that it was important for his reputation —now more than ever—that they had dated differently than most people their age. When they began seeing one another, they'd agreed to be mindful of what they had learned in youth group and from their parents about dating relationships, trying not to be alone together anywhere that could leave open any speculation that they were intimate.

"Where—" her voice broke and she had to stop to clear her throat. "Where are you going?" she tried again. She felt like she was being forced to play a part in a dreadful dream until it was over and she could wake up to a different reality.

Never one for drama, and raised to behave like a lady in any unpleasantness, she was uncertain what to do next. She wanted him to think well of her whenever he recalled this conversation in years to come, or told the story to other people, or—or changed his mind and came back for her. She didn't know why, but how she handled this was important.

Chris still held her hands and looked directly at her. She felt self-conscious that he was most likely seeing a rush of different emotions cross her face.

He sighed. "I can't tell you specifically where I'll be. I'm not sure myself, and only our team's families will know. It's potentially dangerous, so the mission board is looking for single men in this case. I leave for training immediately—in the morning, in fact. Once in the field, I'll rely on mail whenever the plane is scheduled for a supply drop. My family is driving me to training so that I can leave Sherrie my car, and Dad will have a guest speaker fill in for him at church on Sunday."

"How long will you be there?" asked Caroline in a small voice.

Chris bit his lip, looked away, and then looked back at her. He let go of her hands to stand up and brush the sand from his jeans.

Caroline stood up, too. He looked intensely into her eyes for a few moments as if struggling with his answer, then took her face in both his hands to make her look right at him. "Don't wait for me," he said thickly.

He let go of her face and pulled her into a tight hug, and she understood. This part of her life was over.

She suddenly felt desperate at the thought that everything before tonight was like approaching the end of a great book. She gulped a few deep breaths to hold back a rising feeling of panic at having no control over what was slipping through her fingers like water, never to be captured again. Something she knew instinctively dawned on her then with light and clarity, something her family had taught her in many little ways as she was growing up in order to prepare her for life. No matter what songs, poems, or romantics say, love does not conquer all.

The emotional hug intended to soften the blow had to come to an end eventually. Caroline decided that she should be the one to pull away first, signaling that she would be okay. She glanced away when Chris's eyes quickly searched hers. As she began stepping away on her own, he grabbed her hand before strolling slowly alongside her, back up the path. She couldn't help but feel comfort in the fact that he now looked miserable and still wanted the connection of holding her hand. But he also seemed relieved, and it hurt to know that she was already a part of his past.

She roughly shoved back all of the feelings rising inside of her. There would be time for them to overwhelm her later, when she was alone. Right now, she needed to just savor these last moments together and end this well.

The stroll up the path to their parked cars was a quiet one. They stopped, awkward and unsure about what should happen next.

Tears stung Caroline's eyes again, but she furiously blinked them into submission. She just stood there, looking away.

She noticed that Chris's Adam's apple bobbed as he swallowed hard a few times. He couldn't disguise the catch in his voice, his words tumbling out now. "I don't know how to tell you how sorry I am. You know you're the only girl I've ever loved. If you can forgive me, I'd cherish being able to remain friends—we're good at being friends. I hope you'll write to me—I need for you to write to me. I don't know how to stop thinking about you being my girl, or how to be without you anymore."

His last word broke off in a choked voice. He looked away, pressing his lips together, but seemed to decide to look straight at her and let her see his pain.

She closed her eyes to clear her head and prayed silently, *Lord, help me get this right.*

"I'm really hurt and disappointed," she finally began. "But you've never been anything but good to me, even now, when you're breaking up."

She tried to smile, and he smiled back just as weakly. Caroline was whispering when she regained her composure and continued. "As you spoke about your calling, it was obvious that it's right for you. Shelly tried

27

to tell me today that I was gifted for another path, but—I suspected it might mean losing you."

"She's right. You belong here, at Painter Place," stated Chris firmly.

As he was speaking, they heard running footsteps. They both turned to see Patrick jogging down the road toward them with Lady keeping pace on her leash. As if on cue, they looked at one another, in a rush for a final private moment to say goodbye. The question was still in Chris's eyes.

Caroline blurted, "I'll try to write to you, but it will be awkward to act as if—as if we aren't a couple anymore."

"Hey," called Patrick, throwing up his free hand as he drew closer. Lady somehow managed to wag her tail at the sight of them as she struggled to run faster than her leash would allow. Chris dragged his eyes from Caroline's to greet him.

Chapter Four

So much of what is best in us is bound up in our love of family
that it remains the measure of our stability because it measures our sense of
loyalty.
All other pacts of love or fear derive from it and are modeled upon it.
—Haniel Long

"Hey," Chris called back as Patrick rapidly came closer to them. He took a deep breath and smiled tensely. He had known that telling Caroline's family about his plans would be awkward, and he didn't feel ready for this.

If Patrick noticed that his response lacked enthusiasm, he disguised it well. His faded blue tee shirt promoting the church softball team was sweaty, and he was panting nearly as hard as Lady was when he reached his sister. They could tell that he wasn't just out jogging with the dog. He'd been running hard. He took a minute to catch his breath while Chris and Caroline greeted the ecstatic collie and waited awkwardly.

When he could breathe well enough to talk, Patrick ran his fingers through hair the same color as his sister's. Like his dad, he did this when he was thinking over something he was getting ready to say. She suspected now that somehow, he knew something was wrong.

Patrick stepped toward Chris to shake hands. "So—I hear that you'll be leaving us again tomorrow, for much longer this time." He looked at Chris with an earnest expression in his blue eyes.

Chris' brows shot up in surprise.

"Sherrie called and told me about it," explained Patrick. "This is huge, man. Sounds like it's not a call for the fainthearted." He stood directly in front of Chris and briefly put out his hand to touch his upper arm. "We'll be praying for you, you know that. Keep everyone updated at church, okay?" His voice sounded much friendlier than his serious expression.

"Uh, sure," Chris said almost absently. He scowled. "My sister called you?" He adjusted his weight, settling into a stance with legs slightly apart and thumbs hanging from his front jeans' pockets.

Caroline picked up on this change in his body language and tried to hide her interest in this code talk between the guys by quietly commanding Lady to sit. Lady immediately obeyed, leaning against her leg and looking adoringly up at her, then at Patrick, and back to her. Caroline pretended to be distracted by the collie, but her mind raced. Sherrie and Patrick had often hung out together since he'd come back from college recently, when they happened to be in the same places. They acted like good friends who were comfortable with one another's company, but Caroline suspected Sherrie would like to be more serious.

Patrick handed Lady's leash over to her, and then casually put both his hands on the hips of his gym shorts. This motion pulled his still-damp tee shirt across his shoulder and torso muscles. He shifted his weight to one running shoe, looking deceptively relaxed. Caroline knew this stance. More body language. She forgot to feign disinterest as she watched them.

"Yeah, she did." Patrick's drawl always stretched out the word "yeah" a little, but it sounded like he might not be finished with it. Then he seemed to change his mind about saying anything more.

"So your family already knows?" asked Chris.

Patrick nodded slowly but otherwise didn't move.

Chris said flatly, "I was going to follow Caroline home and tell them myself. Sherrie was crying and said she was too upset to talk about it before I left to drive over."

Patrick looked at Chris steadily for a moment, then over to a nearby palm that was waving gently in the sea breeze. He inhaled deeply and exhaled slowly as he looked back at Chris. "I think she feels better now that she's talked it through. No need to come by. Just head home and spend time with your family tonight. My parents wish you well. They sent me to fetch Caroline, who has her own packing to do. She's headin' to Europe."

Caroline blinked in surprise. Her brother broke up the body language challenge with Chris and reached over to lightly slap him on the shoulder in a friendly farewell gesture. "The next time I see you, I expect to hear about some amazing adventures, man!"

Chris was speechless and hesitantly nodded his head.

Patrick turned to his sister. "Mama and Daddy are waitin' on me to get you home, princess." He began moving toward her car. "I need the keys to your carriage."

"Look in the outside pocket of my handbag." She turned her head to speak over her shoulder but remained in the same spot she had been standing in with Chris before her brother's unexpected arrival. Lady stood from her sitting position at Caroline's feet, ears perked up and eyes on Patrick, ready to run to him.

Chris and Caroline looked at each other, feeling awkward under Patrick's supervision.

"Europe?" Chris asked quietly but incredulously.

"It's news to me, too," Caroline answered. She heard Patrick open the passenger door of her Mustang and knew he was waiting to escort her in. He whistled again, this time to call Lady, who leaped delightedly into action. Caroline let go of the leash, and Chris immediately reached out to take that empty hand.

"I didn't mean for the evening to end like this." He drew in a deep breath of resignation and smiled at her sadly. "Goodbye, my Caroline," he whispered.

"Bye, Chris," Caroline whispered in a choked voice. Though tears stung her eyes, she didn't want to take them off of his. She wanted to remember the way he had always looked at her—as if there was nothing in the world more important. But, of course, there was now. There had to be. She never could be first in his life—and never wanted to now that she knew his path.

Patrick was still waiting with her door open. She let go of Chris' hand and slowly turned to walk to her car. She didn't look back.

Chris flinched at the slam of the car door when Patrick closed it. It sounded so—final. As the Mustang disappeared into the palm trees that lined the sandy road, he stood looking after it. Noticing the sky and shadows, he realized that soon the estate caretaker would come to lock up the chapel for the evening. But he couldn't bring himself to leave yet. He plopped right down to sit on the sand where he'd been standing. For a minute or so, he sat quietly, listening to the sounds of an evening on the coast. He would miss this.

It was a relief that breaking off his relationship with Caroline was behind him, since he seriously did not think he could do it. So many things about how it had unfolded had to be an answer to his prayers. He didn't know how he would have faced Caroline's parents. When he'd asked them to court her, it was understood in good faith between them that he was thinking about a future with her. But at least if he'd gotten to explain this new life direction to them himself, he'd have had more time to be around Caroline tonight, with a private goodbye. He hated that his last memory of her was of her back to him, walking away. Suddenly, a dam inside of him broke, and he sobbed uncontrollably with his head in his arms, crossed over the knees of his jeans.

It was a good time for a figure in the shadows to slip away unnoticed — the first chance since Chris had unexpectedly arrived at the chapel. Quiet footsteps stayed in the cover of trees near the path and walked away from the chapel gardens toward the north beach at Dog's Head.

The short ride home for Caroline and Patrick began in silence. Patrick hoped he looked relaxed. He pretended to be intent on driving, but out of the corner of his eye, he was watching his sister with a mix of fascination and dread. Her expression looked stricken and dumbfounded, but he could tell that she hadn't been crying, as Sherrie had. She'd always seemed pretty sensible to him, but he'd learned that girls are a mystery best handled with caution.

In his mind, he saw again how Caroline had walked away from Chris without looking back. She didn't cause a scene, act like her life was over, or beg him to change his mind, like ladies in the movies did. Standing at the car waiting for her, he realized that he admired her dignity and grace. His sister was — cool. Yeah, cool.

He felt a little vindicated at Chris' tortured expression when Caroline walked away. He wanted Chris to hurt because he'd hurt Caroline, an eye for an eye. But he had to admit this wasn't like any breakup he'd ever heard of, and he wasn't sure how he was supposed to feel about a breakup because God had called someone to the mission field.

He suddenly realized that the drone of the commercials on the radio had been replaced by music. He glanced over at Caroline, who was hiding her face by looking out the window. Peter and Gordon were lamenting a breakup in "Go to Pieces."

> ". . . I tell my arms they'll hold someone new
> Another love that will be true
> But they don't listen, they don't seem to care
> They reach for her but she's not there . . ."

Good grief! Where are the party songs when you need them? Patrick forcefully punched the next set button on the radio to hear "One" by Three Dog Night.

> "It's just no good anymore since she went away
> Now I spend my time just making rhymes of yesterday
> One is the loneliest, number one is the loneliest
> Number one is the loneliest number that you'll ever do . . ."

He quickly jerked the knob of the radio toward him to turn it off. Out of the corner of his eye, he saw Caroline's shoulders shaking gently. He turned his face toward her, but she was still looking out of her window. *Oh, man, here it comes,* he thought. *Good thing we're near the house.*

He was surprised when it became obvious that Caroline was stifling giggles. Soon she gave up and doubled over in her seat in waves of uncontrollable laughter. Lady was joining by happily yapping from the back seat with her head out over the console to the front. Baffled but unable to help smiling, he pulled into the driveway. Circling around to the back of the house, he deftly pulled the little car into the garage created in the raised foundation and turned to his sister. Her laughter was contagious. "What?" he asked between chuckles.

She had begun to recover a little. "You," she gasped, "trying to protect me from the radio."

But by now he also noticed that the tears in her eyes were not just from the laughter. He guessed that the giggling fit was a reaction to the emotions she must be holding back.

"Come on, before someone else gets that chocolate éclair I promised to save for you. Mom will have that hazelnut coffee to go with it to keep us awake for a while, since Uncle Wyeth, Aunt Chrissy, and Gran Vanna are on their way over."

Caroline instantly sobered and shook her head. "Oh, Patrick. No. I just want to be alone. I don't want to talk about this."

Her expression was so vulnerable, her eyes full of pleading. All he could think of to do was reach across the seat to touch her hand. "No worries—no one else wants to talk about it right now, either. But they need to plan your trip because you leave in a couple of days."

He tried to keep his voice cheerful and nonchalant as he opened his door. Lady jumped out, and he went over to open Caroline's door while she gathered her purse and wiped under her eyes with the visor mirror down.

"That's another thing—why did this trip come up out of the blue yonder?" she mumbled.

He closed the door after her and put the keys to the Mustang in her hand. She just stood there, hesitating. He took her arm. "Come on! You still need to show off Mom's sweater, and I need a quick shower."

They had just put their forks into some dessert when the door chimes played the notes to "Joyful, Joyful, We Adore Thee." Caroline's parents opened the big double front doors to greet family guests. Everyone began making themselves at home, gathering around the huge dining room table. Gran Vanna asked to sit next to Caroline and settled into her chair with a small pillow to help her back.

The familiar buzz of several people laughing and talking at once to one another filled the house with cheer. The main topic of conversation among them during dessert was the dance tomorrow night at the pavilion. Caroline inwardly winced at the thought of attending, imagining that friends who would learn of Chris' new plans would be looking at her and feeling sorry for her.

As they were clearing away the pretty magnolia blossom dessert plates and getting more coffee, the phone rang. Valerie had asked Marina to answer the phone and take messages. But when Marina took this call, she covered the receiver with her hand and motioned for Patrick to come take it, whispering, "Chad insists on talking to you. It's about tonight."

Patrick left the table, saying he'd only be a minute and waving his hand for everyone to carry on. He moved as far away as the phone cord would let him so that he could hear.

Chad was home. After four years away in college, without a word. She wondered if he'd brought a girlfriend home with him, and strained to see if she could pick up on any of Patrick's phone conversation while still following the plans for travel on the large calendar and sketch paper outline that her uncle was showing her family.

"I know you just got in, man, and I'd love to ride, but I really need to be here for my family right now. I can't always be your excuse for not being around to talk to Gloria—it's high time you handled that situation, Chad. You've never been anything, she just—I know, I know, and she's followed you like a puppy for years. I can hear your frustration, and she needs to find another gold-digging opportunity."

So he didn't bring a girlfriend home and was still dodging Gloria, thought Caroline. Maybe a girlfriend would be visiting soon, or he'd be leaving again.

Patrick listened briefly before interrupting. "Look, I think you'd better be ready for her to turn up the heat now that you're back. We'll just show up together tomorrow night, and then, you know, we can dance with anyone we want to." Patrick ran his left hand through his blonde hair, the habit that always reminded Caroline of their dad, and then slid it into his jeans pocket and leaned his back against the wall.

"Hey, Joey is going to be the DJ. Big Mike had some kind of surgery and had to send Joey. If you want to request anything special, give him a call. Don't forget ancient tradition—you're supposed to dance with my sister if you're around. You two will show 'em how it's done." Patrick leaned with his free hand against the wall for a push-up. Then he switched the receiver to the other hand for another one. "Yeah, my family expects me to be social, ha-ha. Sherrie can't come because she will be with her family as Chris—uh, her brother—leaves for training for the mission field."

He listened for a moment. "Uhhh—well—" he hesitated, and she saw him turn to glance up at her. Their eyes met before he smiled at her and winked. She smiled weakly, looked away, and tried to focus again on the family's chatter.

"She's okay. Look, I need to get back. They're planning a trip to Europe for Caroline with Uncle Wyeth to film an art series. They'll be leaving early next week." He headed toward the cradle for the phone, glancing again over to the dining room. "Yeah, it's sudden, but Wyeth's planned this for a while. My parents think Caroline needs to get away. Aunt Juliette is working on getting someone to film it. Yeah, she's in some pirate movie they're shooting in Florida right now, so she may get to swing by when it's over. Hey, look, I'll call you in the morning, okay?"

Patrick hung up and came back into the dining room, where everyone was gathered around the map that Uncle Wyeth was spreading out, smoothing his hand over the creases. His uncle had insisted on keeping the location of the filming a surprise until dessert was over, and was just putting his finger on a spot on the map.

Caroline came to life. She shot up like a jack-in-the-box to her feet to see the location at his fingertip, as if she didn't believe she had seen it.

"Mevagissey?" She gasped in disbelief, momentarily forgetting the heaviness that had settled in her heart. She locked her blue eyes, full of surprised hope, to Uncle Wyeth's kindly brown ones. "Mevagissey — we're going to England?" she asked again.

Uncle Wyeth was smiling broadly. No one else said anything, enjoying Caroline's obvious delight. Her mom and dad exchanged looks. She sat back down, looking at the mark on the map again, then back to her uncle.

"Yes, Mevagissey," Uncle Wyeth said quietly. "Have you finished *The Dark Is Rising* yet?"

Chapter Five

*"It is never good dwelling on good-byes ...
it is not the being together that it prolongs,
it is the parting."*
—Elizabeth Bibesco

"I know this is an early evening for you youngsters, but I need a little more beauty sleep than you do," said Gran Vanna in her soft Georgia drawl.

"So that's the secret!" quipped Patrick to his grandmother, following her down the stairs of the front porch, glad for conversation to mask being at her back for quick support if needed. "Girls, did you hear that beauty tip from the most beautiful woman on the island?"

Marina had remained up on the porch so that she could run back inside for her turn to do the dishes, and Caroline had only descended half of the stairs. As Gran Vanna reached the solid footing of the brick walkway, she turned to look back up at Caroline with the soft brown eyes that Uncle Wyeth was blessed to have inherited. "Sweet Caroline, you come up to the Big House around lunch time and see me tomorrow," she said. "Maggie Jane is cookin' something special just for you, and I've got somethin' I want to talk to you about. You'll still have plenty of time to get ready for the pavilion."

When the grand lady Savanna Painter spoke in her soft accent, everyone within hearing distance stopped to listen. It had always been that way. Savanna Painter had a presence about her that commanded respect. Her manner made everyone want to please her because they liked her.

The awkward moment had come. Caroline was looking down the rest of the stairs at her beautiful Gran Vanna. Soft, wavy brown tresses brushed her shoulders, always reminding her of a heavily carved Renaissance frame designed to show off her grandmother's classic features. The lantern lights on the veranda highlighted the gray touches in her hair, much as the buffed metallic accents on a beautiful frame added interest and depth without detracting from the painting inside.

Caroline had held her feelings back for a couple of hours now. She sighed and her eyes filled with tears despite her tight smile. "Oh, Gran Vanna," she choked.

Her grandmother set her mouth in a pretty pout and opened her arms. Somehow Caroline made her way down the steps with tears streaming down her face and made it into her grandmother's embrace.

***

Marina was swaying in her characteristic way of continual dancing as she was washing up the coffee cups. Her brother had the wooden lid of the console stereo up, trying to tune in to a radio station that catered to a Friday night crowd that liked rock music. He wasn't sure he had the right station yet because he needed to wait for a car dealership commercial that was promising not to be undersold on convertibles this summer.

"Patrick, honey, keep it down—we're heading to bed," said his mom over her shoulder on her way to the master suite on the first floor.

A sultry swaying beat from Credence Clearwater Revival began blaring through the big front speakers of the console and Patrick reached down to adjust the volume.

Caroline began making her way to the rotunda staircase. Marina rushed from the kitchen to stop her, putting a soapy hand on her arm. "Let's have a pajama party in my room tonight, just girl talk, popcorn, some music—or we could stay up and watch the late-late movies? I need some help deciding what to wear tomorrow to the dance!"

Caroline smiled at this gesture by her sister to want to make her feel better. "Great idea, but I'm really tired. I promise to help you tomorrow. I just want to be alone right now."

Marina's eyes searched her face. Patrick had come over to join them with a dish towel flung over his broad shoulder and hands on his hips. He saw the soap drips on Caroline's arm and deftly swept the dish towel off of his shoulder to dab it dry.

"Then come to my room if you wake up and want some company," Marina pleaded.

"Yeah, and be quiet so you won't wake me up while I get my handsome sleep," said Patrick sternly. Marina rolled her eyes and slapped the back of his hair lightly.

"Ow!" he yelped as if he were in pain. "I mean it, now, don't make me have to come to Marina's room to crash the girly party or I'll commandeer the popcorn for a more worthy cause. Besides, you both should get a lot of beauty sleep. A *lot*. Seriously."

Marina exaggerated a gasp, then reached out as if she would slap lightly at him. He easily dodged her hand with an athletic move and hurried into the kitchen, anticipating a chase.

"What?" he was asking, shrugging and holding out his hands. "I just don't want to be embarrassed tomorrow in public by my sisters, who are heedless of their poor grandmother's beauty advice."

Caroline couldn't help laughing as she shook her head and went up to her room. Their voices faded off as they continued to discuss the repercussions of making him join in the sisters' pajama party.

When her makeup was off, she put on some jogging pants and a tee shirt instead of pajamas. If she couldn't sleep, she thought she might sneak out to sit on the porch with Lady. She looked a long time at her mom's blue sweater, lying across the curving chaise lounge sofa where she'd taken it off. Would she ever want to wear it again, or would it always be a painful reminder of the date when Chris broke up with her?

Shaking her head, she told herself this was silly and she was being dramatic. It was not the sweater's fault. Funny how people associated sights, smells, and places with pleasant or painful memories.

She lay down across her bed, pulling back the bedspread but otherwise not bothering getting into it. She wasn't just making an excuse when she told her siblings that she was tired. She really felt exhausted, but assumed she would not sleep regardless. Her head was spinning with all that was happening to her, and she didn't feel secure that the rollercoaster she'd been on had come to a stop yet. She closed her eyes to keep from seeing the blur of the ceiling fan blades.

***

With palm trees behind his head, Chris's green eyes looked intensely into hers, and he took her face into his hands to keep her looking right at him. "Don't wait for me," his voice said thickly. "Don't wait for me . . ."

She became aware of tears running down the side of her face onto her arm, and both the bed and her tee shirt sleeve were damp with tears from her dream. She used the back of her hand to dry her face, sniffed, and moved onto her back to gather her senses. She had fallen asleep.

Rolling over onto her stomach, she craned her neck to see that the alarm clock was at 11:11. She had slept only about an hour. Her head hurt from sinuses swollen from crying, and her eyes felt hot. She would need to get her head up on a pillow and get some tissues to blow her nose.

She padded across the room from the bed to the bathroom, grabbing a tissue from a pretty box. She hated the tight feeling in her throat and chest. When she saw her reflection in the bathroom mirror in the soft night-light, she just stared, still a little disoriented from sleep and dreams. She was struck by how tragic she looked in the eerie light, a young woman with disheveled hair who'd obviously been crying, and who had little dents on the side of her face from sleeping on the stretched fabric of her tee shirt sleeve.

When she went back into her darkened room, she walked past the bed over to the window seat. *The Dark Is Rising* lay there. Glittering ribbons hung where a beautiful handmade bookmark that her mother had given her was tucked into it. Reading might take her mind off of her dreams, memories, and misery.

Her window was open slightly to catch the soft coastal air, and moonlight streamed in through the fanlight glass over the top. She took a deep, ragged breath to calm herself, undecided about whether to sit down in the darkness or turn on a lamp to read. Reflections of the moon outside were dancing across the waterway, setting off the dark silhouettes of the Adirondack chairs and swing.

"Caroline," she heard Chris say softly in her mind, "I can't take you where I'm going, and you can't wait for me to return. It's breaking my heart, and I am miserable that it may break yours."

This unexpected and vivid memory startled her. Restless, she stood up and went to quietly open a dresser drawer, pulling out a worn sweatshirt to replace the tee with the damp shoulder. She pulled her hair into a ponytail and pulled the tail through the adjustable hole in the back of a Braves baseball cap. She put athletic socks and tennis shoes on her feet and insect repellant on her neck and ears, then she grabbed the tissue box and pulled a beach towel from the narrow linen closet. There was a flashlight in the closet, and she tested it to see if the batteries still worked before carrying it with her.

She tiptoed out of the house on her way to the Adirondack swing. As an extra safeguard against mosquitoes, she rolled the bird of paradise print beach towel into a scarf shape to drape from around the back of her neck, pulled her hands into her long sweatshirt sleeves, then settled in, letting the soothing rocking motion of the swing calm her.

Sitting there, she was peacefully lulled at first with the familiar cacophony of night sounds. But more memories quickly jarred the peaceful setting, as if someone was taunting her with the replay button on a recording.

"I know what I'm supposed to do, and I'll never be the same if I don't do it," she heard Chris say again.

He had moved on. She was part of his past.

And—what if he never came back? What if something terrible happened to him in a dangerous place?

The tears came now. "Why? God, why did You let us ever begin this if You had another plan?" she mumbled out loud. "Why did You let us go down a path that led to nowhere? What a waste of time—of life."

She sniffed and reached for a tissue. "I should have been creating an inventory of paintings or—whatever—while I waited for the guy you'd picked out for me, if You had only let me know." She blew her nose. By now, she had talked herself into feeling annoyed with God.

"You know you're the only girl I've ever loved . . . I don't know how to stop thinking about you being my girl, or how to be without you anymore."

Memories flooded her mind, making her whole body ache with the tension of grief. An empty spot slowly yawned open inside of her, one that had opened years ago, but hadn't been so empty since she'd met Chris.

41

"I can now see that I was running from what I was meant to be, and wanted you to run with me, away from what you are meant to be." Caroline wished she could stop the memories and pulled up to sit cross-legged on the deep seat of the swing, hugging her stomach with her sobs.

"Chris is in My hands. Nothing is wasted." She heard this in her heart and mind, but there was no question it was not her own thought. She caught her breath, sitting up straight.

***

"Are you sure she's okay?" whispered Andrew Painter to his wife. They watched the silhouette of their daughter by the water from their bedroom bay window. He'd been pacing back and forth on the soft rug in his gym shorts, tee shirt, and bare feet, characteristically running his hand through his hair.

"Yes." His wife Valerie's voice was soft. "She needs to do this. Holding back her feelings and grief would've changed her inside. She's had enough of that the last four years."

"How do you know she needs to cry that way?" Her husband whispered back as he came up to stand behind her for the hundredth time.

Valerie Painter smiled sadly at a memory, but continued to watch her daughter. "Remember the night we met? My friends had taken me out to distract me from a break-up. England will be Caroline's distraction. She needs some time to work things out, away from Painter Place."

Her husband snorted quietly and began pacing again. "The guy you cried over wasn't worth all the fuss if he'd miss a chance with you. Hope you didn't take it as hard as Caroline is," he muttered.

"Worse. Hers isn't personal, just a change in life. Mine was from being left behind for another girl, just like my dad did to my mother. I felt terrible for weeks. I had to cry it out several times like this before I could move on—I wasn't free to be myself again until I got it out of my head and my heart. I was still sad when my friends insisted on taking me out, and then—then the most ruggedly handsome guy I'd ever seen drove up in a really hot car, with my favorite song booming out of the stereo speakers."

Andy Painter laughed quietly and came up behind her, planting a kiss into the crown of her hair and glancing out of the window again. "It was

42

love at first sight. The other guy would have had to get out of my way if he'd been smart enough to stick around, 'cause it was time for us," he said in a low voice.

***

Caroline had no more tears and was exhausted. Remarkably, peace had replaced the tension as if a turning point had been rounded. She blew her red, sore nose again on her last tissue, then stuffed the pile of used ones back into the empty box.

Standing up, she took the front edge of the beach towel around her shoulders and wiped her face with the corner. As she stood there silently, looking out over the inland waterway to the sparse lights of homes on the outskirts of Whitehaven, another memory came to mind. "Thank You for my life," she had prayed on her way to the chapel to meet Chris.

Now she said it out aloud again, though her heart was as sad this time as it was full. "I still thank You for my life," she said to the starry night sky. "Thank You. Please—show me how to live it."

***

Patrick moved away from the window in Caroline's room. It looked like his sister finally stopped crying and was heading back up to the porch, carrying a tissue box and a beach towel. He quickly made his way to his own room at the front side of the house, which had views of the beaches of Brush Point.

Before he could cage a thought it flew from his mind—he was angry with Chris for hurting Caroline. But it should've ended by now and it was only a matter of time before she'd have been the one to hurt him. This turned out to be perfect timing. He had to keep up the face of a decent relationship with Chris, though, because of Sherrie. He didn't know where things might or might not lead with her someday, but they would be awkward for a while.

He heard Caroline's footsteps faintly on the stairs through his open door. Marina's room was the twin for Caroline's, balancing out the back corners of the house like bookends, and he didn't think for a minute that she was not awake and watchful. Probably even his parents were doing the same in their room beneath Marina's.

He tiptoed silently toward his bed and saw a movement in the woods from the adjacent window. Someone had been leaning against a car just down by the side of the road from the driveway, toward Brush Point, parked within view of the inlet and backyard. Alarmed at first, he froze in his steps. Then he relaxed—in a car, the house could only be accessed by someone who knew the gate code. The security guard at the bridge would not have allowed anyone over onto the island at night unless they belonged here or were on the guest list. The shadowy figure got into what looked like the silhouette of a sports car though the shadows of the trees, without making much noise with the door, and he heard an engine start. The back of the car was toward the house, so someone had driven in earlier and parked—and waited.

The mystery was solved when the driver slowly made the turnaround and headed back up the road, not turning on his lights in front of the house. He recognized the model in the moonlight. Patrick grinned from ear to ear. Things were about to get interesting.

Chapter Six

"All the world's a stage,
And all the men and women merely players.
They have their exits and their entrances,
And one man in his time plays many parts . . ."
—Shakespeare, As You Like It, act I, scene vii

There was something going on in the parking lot at Painter Place. It would have been more than half full on a Saturday in early June anyway, and more so today because of preparations for the annual Island Summer dance at the pavilion. But there was a small group standing around.

As Caroline pulled into the lot and then into a designated space for family members in front of the gallery, she noticed her brother Patrick, a couple of guys she didn't know, a young couple who looked like tourists—and a more grown-up version of Chad Gregory. They were standing near a very futuristic-looking car, but all turned to her.

Feeling self-conscious that they were watching her as if she was the topic of conversation, she got out of her Mustang. She was glad she had put on that blue sweater of her mom's that she'd taken off last night with a question as to its fate. It had been easy to pick up this morning to wear to see Gran Vanna for a lunch date. She'd added a cute white tennis skirt and strappy little white sandals that laced up at the ankles to tie in a bow in the back. When she was getting dressed, it hadn't even crossed her mind that she might run into Chad Gregory here. She wasn't used to thinking of him being around anymore.

She couldn't help thinking in clichés. Whatever he'd majored in at college, he must have made straight A's in "impossibly handsome" and "working out."

Patrick interrupted her train of thought by calling for her to come over, motioning with his hand. It was so much to take in at once—the car, and Chad.

She just stood still beside her door. Sadness weighed on her heart this morning, and she felt strangely as if she was watching herself in a detached way.

She wondered which rich summer guest had driven this here. She'd grown up learning to appreciate cars, and there weren't many like this one in the world.

"You're embarrassing me," teased Patrick. "You're supposed to be my way cool sister, and I'll have to stop bragging about you now. If you're that impressed, you can ride in this anytime. Come on!" He beckoned her with a wave of his hand.

She shook her head a little, laughed at herself, and began walking over shyly. Where had this awkwardness come from?

"Is she the one?" asked one of the guys she didn't know. He had turned to look up at Chad.

Chad looked a little taken aback at being asked this, glancing at the guy then back at Caroline. "Uh—yeah. Yes, she's the one. This is Caroline Painter," he said as she came up to stand beside her brother. His voice nudged sleeping memories. "And yes, she's my—inspiration."

Caroline's mouth dropped open just as another guy in work clothes looked around from the side of the house, calling to the ones standing with the car, saying break was over and he needed them. They trotted off in that direction, muttering something about being glad to meet her and how they admired the car.

Chad's deep voice and slow Southern accent hadn't changed. Memories began rolling in like the surf. She closed her eyes for a moment and took a deep breath.

"You must have told that story before we walked out of the gallery," commented the young lady in the couple left standing there. They were in the shade of an ancient oak that spread moss-laden branches over the cars. She wore her sunglasses on top of her head like a headband, sleekly holding her long black hair from her pretty face and showcasing sparkling earrings. "How did she inspire you to get this car?" she asked eagerly.

Great question, Caroline thought. She had closed her mouth and opened her eyes but was too confused to say anything. She stood there trying to grasp too many things at once. She hadn't had enough sleep and wasn't sharp this morning anyway. Her heart ached and her throat was still a little tight from so much crying and sitting by the water in the night air. This was too much like last night with Chris—she felt like an actress on a stage where suddenly everyone had forgotten their lines and were improvising with no direction. She might just go home and stay in her room if this was how things were going to be.

Chad smiled at the young lady then looked over at the car. "When I saw this design, I felt overwhelmed. It was so beautiful, unexpected, creative, and exciting—far and away beyond any other that I'd seen. And I immediately thought of Caroline."

He turned to Caroline, meeting her eyes with an unwavering gaze. He wasn't smiling anymore, and his expression held no teasing. She remembered this look and couldn't breathe.

The young lady gasped. "My word! That—that is the most romantic thing I've ever heard!" she exclaimed in awe. She looked over at the guy with her, putting her hand on his arm. "It's the stuff of legends!"

The guy laughed and put his sunburned arm around her. Caroline noticed that he wore a college ring on the hand in which he held a bag from a gallery purchase. She glanced over at Chad's hand. If he had a new college ring, he wasn't wearing it.

"Caroline, there you are." Gran Vanna's melodic voice floated down from above them. They all looked up at her. "Come on up soon, honey. Lunch is ready," she said from her position on the porch that ran the length of the second floor above them. "How do you like Chad's new car?" she called down.

Caroline recovered herself. "Oh, well, uh—it's quite something!" she stammered.

Gran Vanna chuckled and called back down. "It's something, all right! Have him open the doors for you before you come up!" She disappeared into the house.

Chad sprang into action, and seemingly in an instant, the red doors were in the air, and it looked as if the car would take flight. Chad stood by expectantly, and Patrick stood with his arms crossed, a huge grin claiming the width of his face.

The couple admired this view of the car before moving toward their own. "Miss Painter, and guys, it's so nice to have met you," said the young man. He extended his hand to the guys. "We've been here too long already and need to get to lunch ourselves."

The young woman whispered to Caroline, "If you keep a journal, this is worth writing about today! And I love your paintings in the gallery."

Caroline nodded slightly and smiled at her. "Thank you," she whispered back.

A motorcycle thundered in behind the launching Lamborghini. Chad, Patrick, and Caroline waved to acknowledge Joey, their friend and tonight's DJ for the dance. He shut off the motor and pushed the kickstand on the cycle, deftly pulling his bike helmet off in one swoop and releasing brown hair to his shoulders. He whisked out a pale yellow envelope from his back pocket. He whistled appreciatively at the car and was now the one gawking.

The profile of the red 1985 Lamborghini Countach was stunning. Caroline was more comfortable now that Joey was here and joined him to peek inside. She looked up in Chad's direction but intentionally didn't meet his eyes. "Your chores pay a lot more than mine do. Where's the Porsche 944?"

He laughed. "At home in the garage. This is for Sundays and special occasions."

He came around to stand beside her, shoving both hands into the frayed pockets of his bleached-out jeans, which sported a frayed 2-inch rip in one thigh and a small worn hole in the other knee. He was clearly at the Big House to help with the pavilion preparations, wearing a worn Carolina tee shirt that was frayed at the hem on the right side. His blonde hair already had the nearly white streaks he always got in the summer. Some of them fell over his tanned forehead almost to his eyes.

She wished he wouldn't stand so close. She was losing focus.

"Seriously, I'm still in shock," he said, apparently either oblivious to the effect he was having on her or pushing it. She would know which if she looked at him, but she couldn't.

"When Dad asked me on the phone what I wanted for a graduation gift, nothing came to my mind, so I just joked off the cuff and said 'a new

48

Lamborghini Countach.' And then I forgot about it. But you know my dad . . . he's never met a financial challenge he didn't want to conquer, and he had some favors owed to him by someone in the financial arena with Lamborghini. I didn't get a color or option choice—but the joke was on me when I came home yesterday to see the Countach tied up with a big bow in the front yard!"

This made perfect sense to anyone who knew the Gregory guys, Caroline knew. It was all about investment value. Depreciation wasn't a problem with a Porsche or a Lamborghini. If you had the money, why invest in an ordinary car that would be worthless in less than a decade?

Joey slid into the driver's seat and put one hand on the steering wheel when he remembered the envelope in his other hand. Holding it out, he said, "Oh, Patrick, I promised to play postman this morning and bring this to you. Take this, will you, so I can figure out how Chad's going to back this thing out without hitting anyone. How do you see around that spoiler?"

Caroline started backing up toward the house. "I'll let you good ol' boys talk cars while I have some lunch. Congrats, Chad. It's—ah—good to see you." She turned quickly and hurried to the stairs to go visit her waiting grandmother.

***

Caroline bounded through the door to the kitchen of the Big House from the garage nestled underneath. She entered the rotunda that was the heart of the mansion and the inspiration for the smaller, less grand version in her home. She always looked up in reverence at the stained glass dome before ascending the stairs. It was a stunning portrayal of the Genesis account of Creation, with a sunburst of light in the center as Christ. Encircling the center in six segments were the Six Days of Creation. She looked back down at the stairs and glided her hand along the carved railing, going up as fast as she dared.

Her grandmother's beautiful voice was coming from her sitting room to the right, and Caroline found her talking to Mr. Paul, the grounds supervisor. Mr. Paul was saying that the new torches and Japanese lanterns had come in late but were expected to be ready for tonight. "I'll go down and round up the boys to help," he concluded, nodding to acknowledge

49

Caroline's entrance into the room. His tanned, rough hands clutched a safari hat in front of his work uniform with "Painter Place" and his name embroidered like a small logo over his heart.

Gran Vanna stood up in her usual stately manner to hug her granddaughter as she continued her conversation with Mr. Paul. "Very good, Mr. Paul. Where would we be without you? The DJ is new and will need to be pointed in the right direction to set up. Those boys will be very distracted this afternoon, I'm afraid."

She smiled at Caroline and the groundskeeper. "I realize there will be things that need my attention, Mr. Paul, but if possible, please tell the staff that I'd like the next half an hour undisturbed for lunch. Ask them not to interrupt Wyeth as well. He'll be handling many long distance calls as he plans his upcoming trip."

"O' course, Mrs. Vanna," said Mr. Paul, smiling and turning toward the door to leave the room.

Caroline saw a place setting for her at the little table where her grandmother was sitting. She walked over to it.

She loved this room. It was like an enclosed porch, with mock French doors that took up most of the two outside walls. Shutters were folded like accordions and hung at the corners beside the doors. They were painted a beautiful sky blue so that even if they were closed against a storm, they would be a reminder of the sky on a clear day. When open, the marsh was visible in the distance. High tide had created a lot of water to reflect the beautiful blue in the sky right now.

It suddenly occurred to her that it was also the direction of the chapel. She was surprised to have that thought cross her mind, and realized that while she had a persistent sad feeling in her heart today, she had temporarily forgotten what had happened last night.

"Chicken and dumplings may be more of a cold weather meal, but it's always appropriate as a comfort food," commented her grandmother, following her gaze with a knowing smile. "Let's enjoy Maggie Jane's little contribution toward mending a broken heart."

Caroline bowed her head as Gran Vanna thanked the Lord for providing their lunch. Then her grandmother lifted the lid from her shell-decorated soup crockery. The smell of the rising steam made Caroline's mouth water, and she eagerly did the same.

She took a dainty bite and closed her eyes, savoring the flavor. They ate together without much conversation, content to enjoy one another's company and the view of the marsh.

She took the last bite of her dumplings, and her grandmother looked over at her empty bowl. Smiling, Gran Vanna took the lid from an extra bowl on the table, saying, "I love your mother's handiwork, but I always wondered if these soup bowls might have been just a little too small for times when the contents are the meal instead of just the first course."

She spooned most of the steaming chicken and dumplings into Caroline's empty bowl, in the tradition of southern hospitality and gracious manners. "Eat up, child, or Maggie Jane will be disappointed and might even accuse me of upsetting your appetite." She spooned the remainder of the food into her own bowl.

"Caroline, as a little girl, you've shared some of your dreams with me over the years. Do you remember little Sabrina?"

"Of course! She's still on the shelf in the upstairs storage room," Caroline answered. She took the last forkful of her second helping of dumplings, then put her utensil down while she chewed slowly in the ladylike way her grandmother had trained her to do. She had not thought of her favorite doll for years and was curious about why Gran Vanna had. She could see Sabrina in her mind, with her beautiful little dress the color of sunshine and a bonnet adorned with butterflies.

"You carried her everywhere, pretending to be her mother. You always had crayons and paper or coloring books in your 'baby' bag. You told me that when you grew up, you were going to be a mommy and teach your babies to draw pictures like Uncle Wyeth and Poppy Noble." Her grandmother paused and smiled. "Once, I heard you talking to Sabrina as you sat on the steps, pretending that there was a storm outside. You told her never to be frightened because you would both always live here at Painter Place, and that God was here."

Caroline was startled. She sat speechless for a few moments, her hands clenched in the embroidered seashells on the linen napkin in her lap. "I remember," she whispered.

"Child, I just wondered—will you share with me today what some of your dreams are now that you've grown up? Do you still want to have babies that will always live at Painter Place, and is God still comforting you here?" asked Savanna Painter gently, her brown eyes looking steadily into her granddaughter's blue ones.

Caroline gasped and raised her right hand to cover her trembling mouth, using her left one to absently pull her hair behind her ear. She looked out the window through tears that blurred the marsh and the distant direction of the chapel. Gran Vanna sat completely still and waited.

"Yes. Yes, of course I do. How could I have forgotten?" Caroline whispered.

***

Later, the girls were working on designing Marina's beautiful wavy hair into a style that would behave on the beach for a summer evening. Caroline had come home after lunch for a nap and a cool pack for her eyes, and she felt much better. They had decided to try out some homemade beauty treatments from a magazine, giggling and making the most of time spent together before Caroline's trip.

Her sister's excitement was contagious. "I know you'll like Danny," she cooed. "Are you sure we chose the right thing to wear?" Marina's voice was a little anxious as she smoothed the fullness of a ruffle on her soft purple skirt.

Caroline gave her a little smile in the mirror, working a fancy pewter comb into her sister's hair. It was encrusted with little crystals that looked like amethysts, and the wrapped French braid made her look like inspiration for a sonnet.

"It's perfect," Caroline assured her. "The skirt is the color of a gentle twilight evening. It's great on you. Remember Mamma's rule—always wear something that swings when you'll be dancing!" Marina had joined in to repeat the rule with her sister, ending at the same time.

"What are you wearing?" chirped Marina in a singsong voice. She was holding up two different dangly amethyst earrings to decide between them. "I want to do your hair, so you need to start getting ready soon."

"Well, it's a surprise!" teased Caroline. Marina swung around on her vanity stool, eyes sparkling. Caroline laughed. "Aunt Juliette called me this afternoon during lunch with Gran Vanna, and she insisted that I run up to her storage closet in the attic and find a specific outfit. All I can tell you is that it reminds me of waves and surf on the beach. Come to my room after I have a shower, and you can see it."

Marina sighed. "I wish I were built a little more like Juliette," she said in a voice full of longing.

They heard a car drive up. "That must be Chad bringing Patrick home!" exclaimed Marina. "I want to look out the window. I'm the only one who hasn't seen his car yet." She sprang from the vanity bench to her large bay window seat.

Caroline smiled and followed after her, answering her questions about the raised door when Patrick got out. Chad did not get out or turn off the engine, and after Patrick waved at him, he backed up so that he could face the driveway out to the road.

He saw Marina open her window and wave enthusiastically at him, and he waved back. Realizing that he could see her, too, Caroline waved shyly from behind the window. He waved again and flashed a big smile, then put the car in park and opened the door. He pulled off his Ray-Ban sunglasses and stood there in his dirty work clothes. The hole in the knee of his jeans was bigger now.

He looked up, calling, "Princess Marina of the Painter Dynasty, will you entreat your sister of legendary beauty to be merciful and dance with a frog like me tonight?"

Marina giggled and looked back at Caroline, who nodded at her. It was the first time she could remember him asking her to dance with him. He'd always just told her to.

Marina called back, "Chad the Frog of the Red Lily Pad, she has agreed to honor your request, but there will be no frog kissing on the island, for it is forbidden. If you are indeed a prince, you must find another way to prove it."

"Rightly so, princess—well spoken! You are as wise as you are beautiful. Your challenge is a worthy quest, and I shall set out at once. Please convey to your sister that I live to be at her beck and call."

He bowed at the waist, sunglasses still in hand. He put them on his face as he got back into the Lamborghini, and waved up again before easing the car forward.

They waited to hear Patrick come inside but didn't hear the door open. Caroline told Marina she would check back in with her later. She wanted to tell Patrick about her visit with Gran Vanna before she began getting ready.

She went downstairs. "Patrick?" she called.

He wasn't in the house. She went to the back door and saw him sitting with his head in his hands on the top step of the porch. Lady was lying down on the wood planks beside him.

Caroline felt a stab of concern as she opened the back door and stepped out. Her brother raised his head and looked out at the water but didn't acknowledge her as Lady did. She went to sit down beside the collie, rubbing her ears. She noticed the yellow envelope and an open note in his hand.

"I thought you might want to know about my visit with Gran Vanna today, but it looks like perhaps you've moved on from my troubles to your own," she ventured.

She was just wondering what to say next when he finally lifted his arm from his thigh and handed her the note. "Our troubles are related—quite literally related," he said flatly, never taking his eyes off of the waterway where a handful of fishing and sailing boats were filled with people enjoying a summer weekend together.

There was no doubt who had written the note. Sherrie's curly, up-and-down cursive letters filled the small page. Caroline raised her eyebrows in surprise and with some dread. This must be about Chris, and she didn't want to think about that before the dance tonight. But how could she understand how to help her brother if she didn't read it?

"Dearest Patrick," it began. "You were so great at making me feel better when I called last night. It meant so much to me. We had to leave early this morning, and I assumed you'd be sleeping in, so I called to ask Joey if he'd pick this up on my front porch chair and bring it to you when he came out.

"I will not be returning with Mom and Dad after they drop us off, but will spend the summer away. We made some phone calls early this

54

morning about a job opportunity as a secretary's assistant at the camp where Chris will train for the mission field, and I was accepted. Now I will get to spend more time with him before he leaves. I'm afraid it will be hard on my parents to have both of us gone.

"Chris and I talked and cried together late into the night, and some important things that I should have understood became obvious to me. In hearing him share his heart, my perspective became clear about my own goals for the future.

"How can I say this without embarrassing myself? I'll just be forward. I hoped that someday we'd be more than friends, Patrick. It was not my motivation in my closeness with Caroline and your family—it was just born in knowing them, and especially you. In fact, as Chris finally realized, your family is so down-to-earth that it's easy to lose sight of what it would take to live as one of you. I see now that I dream of a simple future while the Painter family is larger than life.

"Having a summer away will help me settle into this new perspective of knowing myself better. Caroline must feel very hurt about my brother's decision, and rightly so. I'm afraid he should have been better prepared before asking to do something so serious as to court her, so he hasn't exactly acted with chivalry, and he regrets it very much. I pray that, in time, it won't come between any of us as friends. I will write to her soon, once I'm settled, so that she can have my address here. May the Lord bless all of our paths this summer so that we have lots of things to share when we meet again. Warm Regards, Sherrie Shepherd."

Caroline reread the letter, her eyes filled with tears. With a sigh, she looked out over the water. "Do you remember Sabrina?" she asked.

Patrick was so startled at the question that he looked over at her. "Yes. She was—very well looked after," he said with a hint of a smile.

"And endured kidnapping at your hands and Chad's on a regular basis, for which I had to come up with many an unusual ransom," she added. She looked down at the letter in her hands, then out toward the shore of Whitehaven again.

"Gran Vanna reminded me of something I told Sabrina once. I was imagining that I was comforting her in a scary storm, and I said, 'Sabrina, you never have to be frightened because we will always live here at Painter

Place, and God is here.'" She was quiet for a minute, taking a deep breath to calm the emotion that threatened to sting her eyes again. A deep part of her soul was touched by this memory. "Gran Vanna asked me if that was still part of my dream. In that instant, I knew beyond a doubt that it always has been. I don't know how I lost sight of it, but I know that it will guide me from now on."

"God is everywhere," said Patrick. She could tell that he was still trying to grasp what she was saying.

"Of course He is. He's at work everywhere and anywhere that He has led someone who loves Him to be. But I knew then—and know now—that ultimately, for me, He is here—at home."

Chapter Seven

Brightly patterned Japanese paper lanterns lined the roof beams and railings of the huge wooden-decked pavilion, glowing gaily down on the dancing couples with smiles on their faces. Crowds were laughing and talking, gathered around torches on the beach. More lined the sides of the long pier that jutted out into the Atlantic. The annual Island Summer Dance was in full swing at Painter Place.

People would soon draw in closer to the cheerful lights as a protection from insects, but at this moment, anyone paying attention was not looking at the lights and torches. They were admiring a twilight that defied description. Those on the pier had the best view, for they did not have nearby lights to interfere with the colors.

"Is it yellow, peach, or pink?" asked Marina's date, Danny. He stood with Marina and Caroline near the end of the pier. "It's changing even as I name 'em. Look, the pier is glowing!"

Above the horizon line of soft plum water, a Carolina blue sky faded into golden yellow, pale orange, peach, pink, magenta, purple, and indigo—and some of them all at once. The surf carried this remarkable palette on the crests of waves that deposited them onto the crushed shells of the sandy shore.

Caroline and Marina were delighted at Danny's first experience with an Atlantic Ocean sunset. The pier was situated with the west to the right and behind it, and the clouds and moisture in the eastern sky captured and exaggerated the volleyed hues from the opposite direction.

Danny was unguarded, unassuming, and open. His family had recently moved to Whitehaven when his father had taken a job there last winter. It was a difficult time for a high school senior to be moving. He had met Marina on his first day in the cafeteria, and she and her friends, all juniors, had taken him under their collective wing. Soon they had become close friends. But Caroline saw more than friendship in her sister's eyes when she interacted with Danny.

Joey, the DJ, had been playing some pop music, so it wouldn't be long before he mixed it up with some oldies. She turned to look around. Her parents were walking toward the pavilion hand in hand to be close by when the older songs came on. The Painter mansion loomed as a large dark silhouette against the backdrop of twilight colors, with welcoming lights in all the windows.

She leaned against the railing on the pier and turned to Danny and Marina. "Danny, do you dance? My sister seems to have perpetual music in her head and dances instead of walking."

He laughed in his gentle way, looking at Marina. His manner was unhurried and respectful. "Yeah, I've noticed that about her. I haven't had many chances to dance, but I'm willin' to learn. I like different kinds of music, but for dancing, slow songs are just easier. I saw your parents heading up to the pavilion. Do they dance together?"

Marina and Caroline looked at one another and laughed. "Come on, see for yourself!" exclaimed Marina, pulling him along by his arm. "And, by the way, most people here like dancing to the slow songs, too. Joey will be playing a lot of them."

"And every song played is screened," Caroline added in a conspiratorial tone, leaning her head slightly his way as they made their way to the pavilion. "You should know this about our family. There are no lyrics allowed that celebrate drugs, drinking alcohol, or other dark behaviors, just as none of those are allowed on the premises. We don't worry about the reputation of the bands, though, since God uses unbelievers to bless believers all the time."

"That's cool by me." Danny wore an earnest expression as he looked over at Marina. "I love that about the Painters."

In a flash, Caroline understood that a girl like her sister was exactly what Danny was looking for.

From somewhere to the side of them, Carly Hammond ran up, her sister Cassie following closely behind. They were the pretty dark-haired daughters of the mayor of Whitehaven and had been friends with Caroline and Marina for as long as they could remember. They had the slightly exotic Polynesian look of their mother.

Carly clutched Caroline's arm and took it into hers as she matched Caroline's stride. Looking at her face as they walked, she said, "Oh, Caroline, I have to hear what happened with Chris! You must have cried all night." She stopped Caroline to look into her face, her soft dark eyes stern. "Trust me, this was for the best."

Caroline made a "humph" sound with her breath. "I know, I know," she agreed. She headed again toward the pavilion, pulling Carly's arm straight. Her friend rushed to catch up.

"And Chad is back in town," chimed in her sister Cassie, peeking around from the other side. "Oh, my word—have you seen him yet? He reminds me of a taller version of Don Johnson in Miami Vice!" Cassie made a little squeal of delight, then looked at the sky and fanned her face as if she would faint. They all broke out laughing, and Danny rolled his eyes.

"What? Don't act like it's not true!" Cassie exclaimed. "Sure, Chad's hair's lighter and longer and falls down on his face more—so exciting!— but otherwise he could be Don's taller double."

Caroline corrected her. "Chad's eyelids aren't heavy, so you can see his eyes more, and his nose is shorter."

Cassie was undaunted. "See, you've thought about it, too! I half expect him to hop out of a convertible Ferrari without opening the door and pull a badge out of his Armani blazer pocket!"

Her sister Carly stopped dead in her tracks, now pulling Caroline's arm back. She let out a low whistle, and they all followed her gaze to see a man standing with Uncle Wyeth, Aunt Chrissy, and a pretty young woman wearing a simple little black dress.

"Who is that divinely tall, dark, and handsome creature with your uncle?" Carly asked breathlessly.

Cassie gasped at the sight, as awed as her sister, but the others looked at one another and burst out laughing. Caroline answered that she honestly didn't know. Marina guessed that he was the guy she had overheard her parents saying had flown in this afternoon in his own private plane.

"He's the filmmaker that'll be working on the painting documentary that Uncle Wyeth and Caroline are doing in Europe," Marina explained. "Come on, Carly, we'll introduce ourselves!"

"Ohhh, Caroline! Honestly, it is sooo hard to be friends with you!" lamented Carly as she kept her arm through Caroline's and walked toward Uncle Wyeth. "Who else do I know who could have a summer like yours fall right into her lap!"

***

Patrick and Chad were standing by a clump of palms at some park benches near the parking lot, trying to remain in the shadows so that they wouldn't be interrupted while they worked out some last minute plans. Gloria had called Chad's house several times, leaving messages. She was upset that he had not asked to be her date now that he was home. There would be no avoiding her tonight. Patrick just hoped he could help Chad with his social skills to keep it from being unpleasant and embarrassing. He didn't want anything negative between Chad and Gloria to happen before the meeting with his dad.

"Come over tomorrow after lunch. Tell my dad your plans now that you're out of college, and ask if you can start seeing Caroline now. From there, we can lead into telling him about the restaurant. He's resisting because of having Painter Place influences attached to my partnership. If you're really willing to clean that up and help me, I think he'll give us his blessing—and maybe even pitch in."

Chad looked directly in the face of his best friend. "Okay, but—I just got back. Will your dad think I'm schmoozing you and your sister?"

Patrick ran his fingers through his blonde hair and sighed. "Of course not! Do you have the ring?"

Chad put his hand into the pocket of his tailored and cuffed khakis, mumbling, "You must know something you haven't told me." He pulled out a masculine, expensive-looking gold chain, dangling it with a finger so that a ring on the end swayed.

"I do. But even if I didn't, I know this—she's never looked at anyone like she looked at you today in the parking lot." He let out a low whistle. "I'd have been chilled to the bone if I'd seen her look that way at another guy—sisters shouldn't be sizing guys up like that, it's hard on brothers. I can't let myself even imagine what she was thinking about."

Chad couldn't hide a huge grin, relieved that Patrick had noticed. His confidence had soared when he recognized 'the look' from Caroline, but as the afternoon wore on, he wondered if it had been just wishful thinking.

"I thought I'd dreamed it," he said under his breath.

"It wouldn't take much on your part to influence her to get to know one another again, now that you aren't kids anymore," Patrick encouraged. "As for what else I know—I know that Caroline has suddenly remembered her focus." He paused significantly, letting his statement sink in. His friend's eyes were alert as they watched his face in the dim light and waited on him to elaborate.

"Her life calling is, and always has been, to live here at Painter Place and continue what our family's always done. She just got distracted. She told me herself this afternoon. And you told me that you've figured out your focus, too—which is to live here at Painter Place and do what your family's always done. Sound familiar?"

Patrick paused again, hoping to create a dramatic effect that wouldn't be lost on his friend, who looked at him intently, but said nothing.

"You're both committed, and no one else is. It's just right, man." Patrick shrugged matter-of-factly and reached out to the chain and ring, holding them up out of the shadows into the light. It sparkled. "The chain is a little heavier than she wears, but I think you have a great idea."

"It was the best I could do at the last minute," Chad said with some concern in his voice. He slid the ring and chain back into his pocket. "There was no time to get to town once I thought of it, so I had to use one of mine." He looked back up at Patrick. "By the way, buddy—are you okay about the letter?"

Patrick shrugged again and frowned, a little embarrassed. He stuffed his hands into his khaki pockets and looked over at the palm tree silhouettes. "Sure, man. Just glad we weren't where Chris and Caroline were when she figured it out."

"I could have used a warning about Chris before I came back," Chad said. "I hope you aren't keeping anything else that huge from me."

"I thought it would blow over before now. It was only a matter of time. It would've ended this morning, that's for sure," Patrick said.

They stepped out of the shadows and began walking slowly to the lights. Patrick stopped short with another low whistle, and Chad turned to see why. Caroline, Marina, and the Hammond girls were laughing with a couple that was standing with Uncle Wyeth. The guy was looking down at Caroline and taking her hand.

"Want to tell me anything else—like something about a movie star coming to Painter Place?" Chad asked sarcastically.

The dark-haired man was leading Caroline to the pavilion floor to dance, and the others moved closer to watch. Marina's date led her closely behind her sister. Patrick and Chad reached a spot where they could watch without being part of the group.

"You're not far off! That has to be Cameron Fisher, and his assistant, Natalie. Get this—he flew his own plane into Whitehaven this afternoon. All I know is that he's Aunt Juliette's friend and a filmmaker who's in between jobs and working with Uncle Wyeth on this video series he's doing as a favor to Juliette. Oh, and he's a widower. I thought the guy would be old, gray, and pudgy. He only looks about thirty."

He ran his hand through his hair, then put both hands on his hips. He looked over at Chad with a distracted expression, then back to the group. "I wonder if Natalie is his girlfriend. She looks much younger."

"Gee, Patrick. Thanks for the heads-up!" Chad sputtered. He stood watching as the filmmaker and Caroline laughed together, clapping in rhythm with the others in a line dance as Kenny Loggins sang "Footloose."

The wispy fringe of her bangs and fine fringe on her white blouse swayed and snapped with her movements, and the blouse and fluttering short turquoise skirt were like waves rolling onto the beach. Her hair reminded him of a waterfall in the back, with a kind of braid traversing the crown of her head, separating her hair into silky strands, the way water would look running over rocks. The contrast of the sun-highlighted top layer with the darker blonde below the braid was beautiful, like where the sun hit the water and made it glow.

This was not the picture of a heartbroken young lady. This was a young lady having a lot of fun. With some guy she didn't know.

"Here's a heads-up for you then—incoming!" Patrick hissed, unconsciously copying his friend's defensive posture by moving his hands from his hips to cross his chest. "Gloria's at your right, and she's locked on target. Whew, there are missiles in her eyes, man! Don't push the launch button."

The *Footloose* soundtrack was still the popular theme as the DJ slid in a slow song to let everyone catch their breath. The muscles in Chad's jawline clenched as the filmmaker easily caught Caroline by the waist and led her masterfully into the beat. The guy was a great dancer, and she was graceful in a low dip that nearly brushed the tips of her fingers and her long blonde hair to the floor as the music played.

> *"It seems like perfect love's so hard to find*
> *I'd almost given up*
> *You must have read my mind . . ."*

"Weren't you even going to ask me to dance?" snapped Gloria, interrupting Chad's thoughts. She stood facing the pavilion but turned her head his way to look him up and down.

Chad's arms were crossed over his white shirt, open a few buttons down to show some of his chest. His long sleeve cuffs were rolled back, revealing the Rolex Submariner that his grandparents in Charleston had given him for graduation. He hated it when she looked him up and down like that, and he didn't take his eyes off of the dance floor.

"New watch to go with your new car?" Gloria asked.

"It was my granddad's," said Chad, his voice even and flat, and his eyes still on the pavilion. "I always wanted to wear it when I went to see him as a teenager. He had it cleaned and engraved for me for graduation."

An idea flashed into Patrick's mind. "Gloria, see that tall guy dancing with Caroline? He's a filmmaker who flew his own Cessna Golden Eagle into Whitehaven today. Would you like to meet him?"

Gloria sniffed, tilting her chin up, and turned her eyes to the dance floor. "He's a really good dancer," she observed, shrugging her bare shoulder and pursing her beautifully painted lips. "He seems a little young to own a plane. Did you say he's a filmmaker?" Her mood was getting lighter.

"Yes, he's a friend of my Aunt Juliette, the one who's an actress. Come on, we'll take you over. Chad, ask Caroline to dance so that Gloria can meet Cameron."

Chad followed them, playing off of Patrick's lead. But he was shaken and continued to glance back at the dance floor. If he had expected Caroline to be sad and pensive tonight, he was mistaken. He hadn't been expecting competition for her attention, either. He and Patrick reached the group just as the song finished and Cameron and Caroline were coming down toward them.

As they rejoined the others, the filmmaker took her hand to his lips again in a gallant gesture and looked into her eyes. "Thank you, Miss Painter, for the privilege of dancing with you," he said in a deep, rich voice. "I was—enchanted."

Chad bristled, and Caroline blushed, nodding her head in acknowledgment of the compliment. Patrick deftly made introductions in his easy way. He was clearly taken with Natalie, and his face lit up with delight when she was introduced as Cameron's sister.

Chad politely waited a moment before taking Caroline's hand—the one Cameron had not kissed. "Dance with me."

He tucked her hand around his waist, holding it against his stomach muscles as he led her single file through the gathering around the pavilion. He felt Cameron watching and hoped he'd note the familiarity between them.

Joey shook shaggy brown hair out of his eyes and looked up to see Chad. He nodded. Whistling notes opened a song by Gary Lewis and the Playboys, and he spoke over them. "This is a special request tonight to Caroline, from Chad."

Caroline was already in Chad's arms when she heard her name, dropping her mouth open. He freed his hand a moment to point from his heart to hers. He joined most of the crowd in singing along. He inhaled the smell of the ocean and simply enjoyed every moment, every breath.

> *"Walk along the lake with someone new*
> *Have yourself a summer fling or two*
> *But remember I'm in love with you and*
> *Save your heart for me.*

When the summer moon is on the rise
And you're dancin' under starlit skies
Please don't let stars get in your eyes, just
Save your heart for me.
When you're all alone, far away from home
Someone's gonna flirt with you-ou
I won't think it's wrong if you play along
Just don't fall for someone new
When the autumn winds begin to blow
And the summertime is long ago
You'll be in my arms again I know, so
Save your heart for me
Darlin', save your heart for me . . ."

Caroline also sang along with the irresistible, happy-go-lucky tune, and her eyes sparkled when he looked right at her and sang, "Darlin', save your heart for me." But she apparently had more control over "the look" tonight than when she was surprised this morning, and he wondered how he could break down her guard so he could experience it again.

He took a moment to glance around the dance floor. Patrick had secured Natalie and was talking in that easy way that made him so likable. Marina was giggling as she showed Danny a turn for the slow dance steps. His own parents were laughing about something with Valerie and Andy Painter, and Chrissy was smiling up at Wyeth as she traced her finger down his cheek in front of his ear. The mayor and his wife were cutting up the dance floor with some showy moves. Everything seemed right with the world, and at that moment, with a pang in his heart, he wished for it to always go on this way. He wanted this to be his life. He always had.

"Dance with me the rest of the evening," he said huskily into Caroline's hair near her ear. "Just tell everyone you have a date."

Gloria was smiling up at Cameron until she glanced around, her hazel eyes meeting Chad's. She narrowed them before she turned up her pretty nose and looked away, her red hair smoothed into flipped ends on her shoulders, which flashed in the light of the paper lanterns.

The first notes to another romantic oldie in this set continued the happy mood in the pavilion and encouraged a lot of singing along from those who'd enjoyed many Island Summer Dances. Chad smiled to himself. This one might be a way to tease Caroline and break down her guard. He knew she was looking away from him on purpose, and he put his hand on her chin to turn her face to his.

"Remember your part? You stand in for Marie, and I'll cover for Donny. Blondes have more fun anyway." He already had her in a side-by-side step that followed a turn in the dance they'd created for this song years ago.

She followed him without singing, and when she got close enough for him to hear, she said, "I've grown up—I'll only sing it for fun, not for the message."

In a flash, he understood that the lyrics about cherishing the memory of someone who wasn't around bothered Caroline. It wasn't because of Chris, or she wouldn't avoid his eyes. She didn't want Chad to think she was singing the words to him.

Intrigued and more determined than ever, he encouraged her. "Okay, just for fun then—here's your part, are you ready?"

She smiled tightly and gave in, speaking Marie Osmond's part in "Deep Purple Dreams" before joining him to harmonize with the ending.

> "When the deep purple falls
> Over sleepy garden walls
> And the stars begin to twinkle
> In the sky
> In the mist of a memory
> You'll wander on back to me
> Breathing my name
> With a sigh.
> In the still of the night
> Once again I hold you tight
> Though you're gone, your love
> Lives on in moonlight beams
> And as long as my heart will beat
> Sweet lovers will always meet
> Here in my deep purple dreams . . ."

As the song ended, he made sure she was facing him. He searched her eyes quickly and found them melancholy before she looked away.

The next song began, and Chad quickly looked over at Joey with raised eyebrows. Joey winked and grinned, obviously enjoying his little joke on Chad by playing "Time Won't Let Me" by the Outsiders.

Chad took a deep breath and decided to make the best of it. He put on a smile and tried to put himself in Caroline's line of vision so that it would be awkward for her to avoid looking at him.

> *"I can't wait forever*
> *Even though you want me to*
> *I can't wait forever*
> *To know if you'll be true.*
> *Time won't let me (oh, no)*
> *Time won't let me (oh, no)*
> *Time won't let me . . . ee . . . ee . . . ee . . ."*

Chad watched Caroline glare at Joey, who winked back at her with a grin before Chad dared to reach out for her face to turn it to him as the Outsiders sang the last words of the song.

> *". . . Hear me baby, waitin' that long*
> *Take me back, I'm comin' back right now*
> *Hear me baby, sayin' I'm comin' home*
> *I'm comin' home, oh hear me talkin', pretty baby . . ."*

Caroline's mouth dropped open, and she rolled her eyes. "Did you two plan this?" she demanded just before he led her into a turn. He looked at Joey, who had thrown his head back laughing.

"Absolutely not. But I wish I had."

She huffed, and the song ended. Joey announced the next segment into the microphone. "It's Madison Time! Line up—guys on the far side and gals over here."

Chad reluctantly let go of Caroline as those who understood what was happening gathered on two sides. Danny moved as far to the back of the men's group as he could to learn this popular dance from the '50s and '60s.

"Experience in the front, beginners in the back, and you shuffle things around if you get the knack," Joey barked out. Chad positioned himself across from Caroline to keep Cameron from matching up with her. "Now give me a strong line," called Joey, and everyone began crossing a toe to touch from one side to the other.

From the Madison, they moved on to the Stroll. Caroline and Chad matched again, and he signaled to her across the space in line as they moved up to their turn. Laughing, they brought out some of their old favorite moves from their teen years down the line, and everyone was clapping along and hooting.

The line dances changed to a set of shagging music, and Chad was glad to be able to talk to Caroline again. Shagging was done mostly with the lower body, leaving the upper body still except for advanced moves like turns. Couples began the characteristic pendulum moves toward and away from one another, attached with one arm, singing the familiar words.

"With this ring, I promise I'll always love you, always love you," sang the Platters.

Caroline easily followed every new collegiate shag move he'd learned, though she would have been more accustomed to the State Dance of South Carolina, the Carolina shag. He wondered if she'd learned from Chris or her own college experience. Her parents danced next to them in their signature turn, and after four years away he still thought they were the best couple on the floor.

Soon, Bruce Channel was belting out "Hey, hey, baby, I want to know if you'll be my girl." Even people along the sides of the pavilion who weren't dancing were singing along and clapping.

The first notes of a new popular love song were so distinctive that the crowd reacted instantly, scurrying for a place to slow dance. Those who did not make it onto the pavilion floor danced barefoot in the sand around it. Chad and Joey exchanged glances, and Joey winked. Chad put his arms around Caroline's waist, and he closed his eyes at the feel her hands close to his shoulder blades. They swayed to a love ballad by Three Dog Night.

> "Just an old fashioned love song playin' on the radio
> And wrapped around the music
> Is the sound of someone promising they'll never go . . ."

According to his plan, it was time. He spoke quietly, close to her ear. "When I was about your age, I went through a bit of an identity crisis. But I worked through it and made a decision that my life is here at Painter Place, just as someone in my family has always lived here. My brother will work in the London office."

Taking Caroline's right hand with his left and not missing a step, he easily reached into his right pocket. The next time he grasped her left hand for a turn, he put something firmly into her palm. She blinked and looked surprised but poised, as he had expected, and she didn't stop.

"I want you to have this while you're away this summer," he said, looking directly into her questioning eyes. "It's a promise."

"A promise?" she asked. She followed through a turn and faced him again, their noses only inches apart.

"I want you to keep my college ring as a pledge that I'll always take care of your home." He had stopped dancing in the middle of the dance floor, looking at her. Everyone else kept moving with the music as the song ended.

Caroline blushed and looked around to see who might be watching. "Let's take a break," she said. His heart skipped a beat. He wasn't sure if this was a good sign. He nodded and led her through the crowd. He noticed that Cameron was watching him with a cool expression and was now dancing with Carly, who beamed over at Caroline with that knowing look that girls with a secret shared.

"Let me guess," he said over his shoulder as they stepped off of the pavilion floor. "Carly wanted an introduction to Cameron."

Her laughter was like cool water, always soothing. He brought her up to walk beside him, heading to a large booth where volunteers were working shifts to hand out refreshments.

"And Cassie was fanning herself over you—you would make her whole summer if you'd ask her to dance."

Chad laughed. "Well, I'm honored, but I have a date tonight, remember?"

They were each handed a cup of some tropical punch with a long stick spearing a pineapple chunk and a cherry, and Caroline picked up an iced sugar cookie. She held it in a napkin with her forefinger and thumb as she kept the other fingers wrapped around the ring in her palm. They headed toward the beach, kicking off their shoes along the sand dune into a puzzle of too many other pairs to count. Chad sat down their cups in the sand to roll up his khakis from the ankles so he could walk along the water's edge.

"She says you look like a tall version of Sonny Crockett. I bet you get that a lot," she teased before swallowing some of the punch.

Chad shrugged. "Hmmm. Well, I suppose the show has been a new conversation starter in my life. I say he looks like me, not the other way around." His eyes scanned the beach for a quiet place to walk.

Caroline bit her cookie and hesitated as she chewed and swallowed. "To the pier?" she asked, looking around before taking another bite. Two little crescents cut into the cookie as she ate around the edges to create a design with her teeth marks. He reached for her hand to admire her progress. They smiled at each other over the cookie before he looked around.

"Na, too crowded," he answered, bringing his face closer to her ear so that she could hear him over the surf and music. Joey had cranked things up. "Come on," he said, nodding his head to the right, toward the south beach at Brush Point.

Strolling along the side of the pavilion to be close to a trash can for their cups, Caroline stuck out her arm to show off her cookie design. "Want to guess?" she asked over the music.

"A sunburst, or maybe a starburst," he answered without hesitation. "If you tossed it up into the air, it would hang there and sparkle." She smiled and put the bite-sized sunburst into her mouth. He laughed. "On the other hand, if you swallowed it, the sparkles would make you glow. And you do."

Patrick and Natalie were walking on the beach ahead of them. She nodded her head toward them, dropping her empty cup into the trash can. "He seems to like her," she said, eyebrows raised conspiratorially.

Chad followed the direction of Caroline's nod and took his last swallow before tossing his cup in after hers. "Things happen for a reason. That letter from Sherrie was timed just right to set him free." He looked up to see pain cross her features. He instantly wished he'd thought before he said the first thing that came to mind. *Stupid*, he berated himself. Of course, she'd think of Chris.

"Uh, what I meant was—"

"It's okay, you're right," Caroline cut him off. Chad linked his arm through hers and pulled her toward the water, where they let foam roll in over their toes. The moon was nearly full and stretched itself out in a moving band of its reflection on the ocean. Caroline had a faraway look.

Chad reached down to her hand. He'd always thought she had an artist's or a pianist's hands, with long, graceful fingers. He closed his eyes in a brief prayer, then turned the palm up and started opening her fist at her pinky finger. She didn't open the next one, so he pried it up, too. She was pressing her lips together, trying not to smile, and didn't open any other fingers. Looking up and rolling his eyes, he exaggerated a sigh and decided to play along until her palm was open. The ring and chain had left impressions in her hand.

Caroline looked down and gasped. "This is not a college ring!" she said. There was no school mascot or colored stone set into the carved gold, silver, and black metal ring in her hand.

"Not in the traditional way," agreed Chad. "It's carved with the family crest to represent why I'd gone to college and engraved with a verse from scripture to remind me of who gets the glory. That's where my allegiance lies, not in a school color or mascot." He picked it up with both hands and placed the chain over her head, letting it rest around her neck. "The verse inside is from Psalm 1:3, about a man who seeks God. It says, 'He is like a tree planted beside streams of water . . . whatever he does will prosper.'"

She looked down at the ring where it held a few strands of fringe on her blouse. The rest blew gently in the ocean breeze. When she looked up, she said thoughtfully, "The promise you're making is only about Painter Place, right?"

"Well—yes. For now," he began hesitantly. "I just felt that you needed to know there's someone who understands all that it means to live at Painter Place." He pulled her arm into his to walk on the beach, farther from the din of the pavilion crowd.

"I came home to begin a career here. I'll stay when Dad retires. But—I want to get to know you again, too. I hope it's alright with you that I'll be asking your dad tomorrow if I can see you."

She glanced over at him. After walking a few more steps in silence, he said, "I never saw you with anyone but me."

Caroline stopped in her tracks to face him. "Why haven't you said anything before?" she asked incredulously.

When he'd been rehearsing things to say tonight, this was one he kept bumping into. He couldn't tell her the real reason yet.

"You know, I learned when doing a school project that my name means 'warrior, watchful, and alert.' It struck me right then how well my name suited me because I've watched over you since we were kids—from the background. I stopped things from hurting you as you lived without you knowing there was ever a threat. I waited in the shadows when you were hurting or facing a challenge to see if you needed help. Just ask your brother."

Chad looked out at the water, memories playing with expressions on his face. "I was growing up two years ahead of you, Caroline, and that was a big difference for me, going to college while you were only just starting to drive that little Mustang. There were a lot of expectations for me to live up to for the last four years before I could come back."

He looked at her gravely and shook his head. "I expected you to be sheltered here until I returned. When I went through an identity crisis and panic at the thought of becoming my father, I didn't see it coming."

Caroline raised her eyebrows. Chad said quickly, "Look, I never did anything that was illegal or immoral to taint my connection to Painter Place or embarrass our families. I—you know—dated once in a while for group school events—but I never felt free enough from you to have a girlfriend. And I sure didn't count on you having a boyfriend."

"Chad, when you went off to college, it was like you just disappeared," Caroline reminded him. Her tone had an edge. "It was really confusing for me. You even spent summers away for internship credits. When you did drop in a few times, I always happened to be gone, so I knew it was planned."

She looked away to the sea now, replaying her own memories. "I knew you'd leave Painter Place someday for college, but I'd secretly hoped that when I turned sixteen, you'd ask Daddy if you could see me sometimes, or at least stay in touch and come home on holidays. Patrick was gone, too, so

I didn't know what was going on and was embarrassed to ask him over the phone. It seemed obvious that you'd met someone and dusted Painter Place off your feet. By the time I graduated, Chris' dad came to be our pastor, and we had an instant connection. After a year or so, we started going out when he was home from college and stayed in touch when he was at school."

Chad looked away. The breeze off the ocean blew strands of sun-streaked hair over his brow to the other side of his face. "I thought of you every day, and counted on things working out when we were ready."

Patrick and Natalie had walked up to them on their way back to the pavilion. Patrick instantly saw the ring around his sister's neck and searched Chad's face for a hint of how things had gone, but it was unreadable. Natalie seemed to sense that they had interrupted something. "We're just heading back to the house," she announced, pointing her hand up the beach. "My brother will be looking for me."

"We should do the same." Caroline nodded at Chad, and he reluctantly nodded back. They all waded through the water's edge toward the cheerful lights of the Island Summer Dance, then laughed together at their struggles as they stumbled around to fish out their shoes from piles of them on the sand dune.

Chad was determined to keep Caroline with him. He headed toward a palm tree where they could watch the dancers on the pavilion floor without her being accessible to Cameron for another dance. He leaned back on the trunk of the palm, putting her in front of him and pulling her back against him, daring to put his arms across hers on her waist and hoping her dad wouldn't see them. The waterfall of her hair tumbled onto his shirt, and he momentarily closed his eyes at the scent of it. They watched everyone for a few minutes, not saying anything. Chad felt overwhelmed by being close to her again and by the memories of summers gone by.

Caroline shivered slightly. "Want to dance some more to warm up?" he asked, bending his head close to her ear so that she could hear him over the music.

Impulsively, Caroline broke free of his arms and turned around to look up at him face to face. Chad was taken off guard, pushing his back deeper into the slender trunk of the palm tree and looking down at her in surprise.

"Remember when we kids were supposed to leave the Island Summer Dance early to camp out with our sleeping bags on the veranda of the Big House?" Caroline asked.

Chad nodded, speechless, not knowing where this was going.

"And remember what we did instead of going to sleep?" she asked.

A boyish grin flashed across his face. "We danced. And you always picked me."

"It's late, and there's no one on the veranda. Let's go dance." Caroline's eyes challenged him in the torchlight that made her blonde hair glow. "I pick you."

He gazed at her for a few moments, held captive by the old familiar thrill of being mystified around her. Nothing was spoken, but he hoped she caught what he was saying with his eyes—she always had. Then he put one arm around her to keep her warm as he led her across the road to the Big House.

When they climbed the steps up to the wide veranda on the old French Colonial mansion, they looked back over the railing at the romantic lights of the pavilion, just as they did when they were much younger. Summer on the island always felt magic, but events at the pavilion made it seem like living in a fairy tale.

The crowd was thinning now, and soon Joey would wrap up with a summer-themed song. At the moment, there was a slow dance. As Little River Band began singing "Reminiscing," Chad took her hand and they turned away from the sight.

> *"Friday night, it was late*
> *I was walking you home,*
> *We got down to the gate*
> *And I was dreaming of the night.*
> *Would it turn out right?*
> *How to tell you girl*
> *I wanna build my world around you*
> *Tell you that it's true*
> *I wanna make you understand*
> *I'm talkin' about a lifetime plan."*

74

Chad kept Caroline in the shadows on the veranda, away from the lights in the windows. He touched the side of his face on her hair.

> "... *Hurry, don't be late*
> *I can hardly wait*
> *I said to myself, when we're old*
> *We'll go dancing in the dark*
> *Walking through the park and reminiscing ...*"

She melted into the familiar instinct of following Chad, there on the same boards with the same view of the Atlantic that they'd grown up with. But he was holding her a little closer than he would have when they were kids.

Chapter Eight

"Each man should frame life so that at some future hour,
fact and his dreaming meet."
—*Victor Hugo*

It was going to be another unusual day in Caroline Painter's life. She didn't sleep in on Sunday mornings, and it was usually an afternoon for relaxing, not packing.

When she had first opened her eyes, she lay still, disoriented from a very deep sleep. Her room seemed too dark, but then she realized that it was cloudy outside. She remembered what day it was and felt a sudden ache hit her heart. This first Sunday with Chris being gone was now something to be faced. She squeezed her eyes shut and a tear ran down her face. It was a goodbye to something familiar, and she imagined there were more to come in the process of untangling herself.

She took a deep breath and rolled over. She saw Aunt Juliette's clothes on the chaise lounge where she had thrown them last night, too tired to hang anything up. Fully awake now, she sat straight up and looked around. Where was Chad's ring?

Throwing back the pale turquoise sheets, she looked over onto her dresser. The turquoise drop earrings and the sterling bracelet that she'd worn were on top of her jewelry box. Beside it on the dresser lay the gold chain and ring that Chad had given her as a promise.

She fluffed her pillow and put the extra one behind it, reclining back again into the soft bed. Feeling off-kilter from the crazy turns her life had taken this weekend, she rubbed her hand over her brow as if she could brush away the cobwebs from her mind. She wanted a few moments of peace and quiet before the busy day ahead. She felt confused and needed time to think. Why was everything happening at once? And how could she be so interested in Chad's attention when an unguarded thought of Chris could hurt so much and make her cry?

The aroma of coffee wafted in from under the gap in her door—something like hazelnut and vanilla. And eggs. And sausage gravy.

She lay still a few luxurious minutes more, praying for guidance through this time when she was feeling so vulnerable. She opened her eyes and began to plan a packing schedule. She also needed to call Shelly, run by the studio to gather some supplies for the trip, and go to the Big House for dinner.

Ummmm . . . the smell of cinnamon rolls . . .

In a hurry to eat now, she got out of bed and made it up. She headed to her bathroom for a very quick shower, then pulled on some fringed cut-off jean shorts and a jade sleeveless baby-doll top that she didn't plan to pack. With hair combed but still wet, she headed downstairs.

Patrick was the breakfast chef this morning, and he had a warm plate in the oven for her.

"Yum, I'm so going to miss this while I'm away," said Caroline, coming to stand beside him and patting his back where his name and number were emblazoned on an old jersey.

He smiled and filled the warm plate, then put it on a small tray. He nodded over to some mugs. "Grab one of those—Mom and Dad took the carafe out onto the porch."

"Where's Marina?" asked Caroline as she picked up a mug, one of her mom's creations with gorgeous palm trees painted in the glaze. She also grabbed a fork and spoon wrapped in a napkin.

"She got up to go to a worship service with Danny, so she had to make do with cereal and toast. He goes to a new church plant in Whitehaven, but he came to pick her up." He gathered things onto his own tray and followed behind his sister out to the porch.

Valerie and Andy Painter were cheerful this morning. "Love the crushed pecans in the topping, honey," Valerie told her son, using her fork to point at the cinnamon roll on her plate. Lady lifted her ears and bobbed her head as she watched the fork, sitting a respectful distance away as she was trained to do, licking her mouth occasionally as if she could imagine the taste of the family's breakfast.

"And there's my lil' sunshine on a cloudy mornin'!" Andy said brightly when he saw his daughter. His broad smile crinkled little lines at the corners of his blue eyes. He wore the short-sleeved white safari-style shirt that she liked with some khaki shorts, looking like he was heading out with Indiana Jones on an adventure. He was so fit he could have kept up with Jones, too. She smiled back at him and settled her plate on the marble top of the wrought iron table.

"Sweetie, Uncle Wyeth said not to worry about coming by the studio to pack for the trip," said her mother between dainty bites of her second cinnamon roll. The dark background of her blouse really brought out her hair, and the foliage in the flower stems highlighted her eyes. "He said to let you know that you only need to decide on a new travel sketchbook and pencils to take in a carry-on for the plane—the sketchbooks that you and he make with both the heavy sketching and watercolor weight papers inside."

Caroline let the light, fluffy taste of the egg fill her mouth, savoring it before crushing it with her teeth. She smiled at her mom and nodded her head to indicate that she had heard her. She enjoyed a bite of the spicy sausage gravy over a piece of toast and made a yummy sound, lightly kicking Patrick's leg with her bare foot to get his attention. He looked up from his own plate, smiling absently as if silently saying "thanks for the yummy sound."

Caroline swallowed and took a sip of her grape juice. "Uncle Wyeth has saved my day! Honestly, I'm sort of shell-shocked this weekend and don't feel confident about making any decisions."

Valerie set down her empty coffee mug. Her eyes told Caroline she understood on a level that was more than just sympathy. "Uncle Wyeth said this was his job. He has some plans for you on this trip that he thinks you're ready for."

Caroline was fleetingly curious but continued to eat while her food was warm. She could talk to her uncle later.

Her mother went on. "Marina and I will help you pack some clothes, but Aunt Chrissy said to pack light because she is going to take you to boutiques around Mevagissey to support the locals. She also talked to Aunt Juliette and is packing a suitcase with a few special occasion items from her wardrobe at the cottage. Just in case . . ." Valerie emphasized the last three words. She was smiling and raising her eyebrows as if to imply all sorts of possibilities.

"Okay, so let me get this straight." Caroline twirled her fork as she spoke. "I'm taking a business trip to Great Britain with an internationally known artist, who is packing my art supplies. A former fashion model and a movie star are collaborating together to pack a suitcase full of clothes for me, which will be appropriate for special occasions that I don't know about."

Her parents nodded. "It couldn't happen to a nicer girl," her dad confirmed.

Caroline watched her brother eat the last bite on his plate. "Patrick, you are one distracted fellow this morning. What did you do with my real brother?" Waiting for his reply, she began unrolling her cinnamon roll, eating it from one end.

Patrick looked up sheepishly. "The real Patrick is just tired this morning from such a wonderful evening. And he's distracted by the gears turning plans over in his head." He reached for his palm tree coffee mug and took a long sip.

"I wonder if one of those gears is named Natalie," speculated Caroline slyly. She looked over at her parents, who glanced at one another curiously but remained relaxed.

Patrick flushed and ducked his chin. "Well, I have other things on my mind, too." His chin came back up with his usual confidence. "Chad's coming over after lunch, Dad, and we'd like to talk to you about a couple of things."

Valerie pushed her chair back, saying that they'd better clear things away before Chad came over. Caroline's dad caught her eye as Patrick got up and stacked some things on his tray to follow his mom.

"Before you get all caught up in the rush, I want to ask you something." He leaned up to the table and folded his arms across the veins of color in the marble top. "It looked like you were able to move on a little and have fun last night." He cleared his throat. "Phillip Gregory tells me that Chad has come back to Painter Place with a single-minded purpose. Have—uh—have you thought about getting to know him again now that he's all grown up and planning to stick around?"

She sat still for a few moments, looking out at the water before turning to her dad. "He gave me his college ring last night as a promise that he's dedicated to doing his best for Painter Place and carrying on his family's tradition. It's not a typical college ring because he said he's not committed to a school. He said his commitment is to what he went there to prepare for. It's a signet ring with his family crest and a Bible verse engraved inside from Psalm 1:3, about a man who seeks God."

"'He is like a tree planted beside streams of water . . . whatever he does prospers,'" quoted her dad, looking out over the water as a sailboat glided by. "Yes, very appropriate." His voice trailed off.

"But why would a man who seeks God drop off the edge of the world and not even acknowledge a friendship for four years? Perhaps this is a new commitment for him. I don't know, but until he reveals what really happened, I can't trust him. He was holding something back last night about why he had avoided me for so long."

Andy Painter knit his brows as if troubled. "But you both have the same basic goal at Painter Place."

"Yes. But that's not enough, Daddy, and nothing seems straightforward anymore—not even dependable Chris. I'm feeling really vulnerable and wary of being deceived, and I just can't make any important decisions right now. Time will tell whether Chad and I will work together as friends or—something more. That's not to say I'm not—interested in more, you know. I'm very—flattered."

Andy Painter laughed now, and Lady wagged her tail at the sound. "Okay, you just start packing, and I'll handle Chad."

His eyes became serious again as they stood up with their trays in hand. "Both you and Patrick have learned something about what it means to be a Painter this weekend, in a way that me and your mamma couldn't have explained. Most Painters come with strings attached. When you get back from this trip, there are some things you and I will have to talk over. The good news is that so far, the Lord always sends along someone who embraces the strings."

She couldn't hug him with her tray in hand, so she took a crab step over to come beside him and laid her head on his shoulder. He tilted his head over to touch hers in return.

***

Up in her room a few minutes later, her large suitcase yawned, ready to swallow up whatever she decided to feed it.

81

Intimidated by the suitcase, she decided to pack her carry-on bag first. She put in her Sony Walkman and a handful of music cassettes, choosing the early hits of the Beatles and a collection of other British bands she liked. She packed Toto and Kansas in case she got homesick for an American sound. *The Dark Is Rising* by Susan Cooper was tucked into the side pocket to finish on the plane. The other two books in this series were the ones set in Mevagissey, which the author renamed Trewissick, and were on her bookshelf.

She heard Marina come in downstairs and chat with her parents and Patrick before hurrying upstairs to Caroline's room. She popped her head in the open door, holding a grilled cheese sandwich with two bites taken out of it nestled into a napkin. She was glowing with excitement and looked pretty in a simple yellow dress. "I'll be right back—let me change, and I'll help you."

Seeing her sister dressed for church reminded Caroline that she had not gotten ready this morning before chasing her appetite down to breakfast. She turned from packing and put on some makeup so she would be ready for dinner in a few hours. She was trying to figure out what to do with her hair when Marina popped back in. "Here, let me," she said, grabbing Caroline's brush and pulling out a chair.

They chatted about the trip as Marina deftly worked Caroline's long blonde hair into a fat French braid that swept asymmetrically from the right side to the left at her neck, ending just over her left ear to escape from a braid into a ponytail that sat on her shoulder. The braid was entwined with a black leather ribbon lacing studded with silver beads, which looked like a slender headband across the top of her bangs. The ribbon ends became part of the fringe of her ponytail, and the effect was both classy and sassy at once.

Their mother came up when Chad arrived, and they closed Caroline's door to pack. They were just closing the suitcase when there was a light tap on her door.

"Come in," sang Marina, picking up two pairs of shoes to put back into the closet. But the door opened only slightly.

"Caroline, do you have a minute?" It was Chad's voice.

Marina clamped the back of her wrist over her mouth in surprise, her fingers still wrapped around leather ankle straps on a pair of Caroline's sandals. It looked like shoes were sprouting from her face. Her eyes were wide and danced with excitement.

"Go ahead, we'll pick up." Valerie nodded her head toward the door. She and Marina raised their eyebrows, exchanging knowing looks and smiles.

Caroline stepped out into the open hall near the stairway. She half-smiled self-consciously at the way he was looking at her.

"Can you walk with me out to my car?" he asked, tilting his head toward the stairs. "I'm leaving, and I'd like to talk to you."

"Sure."

The sun had come out, and the stained glass dome overhead was throwing a myriad of colors like a kaleidoscope on the stairs. Chad walked down the wide staircase beside her on the enchanted path created by the glass, and she had the strange sensation of walking through a fairy tale with him. She could hear her dad and Patrick talking in the living room, and it sounded like they were discussing the new restaurant that her brother wanted to be part of.

As they reached the bottom of the rotunda, Chad waved over to her dad and brother. "Thanks. See you both later at the Big House."

Chad always used the back driveway instead of the front semicircle drive for guests. He and Caroline walked out the kitchen door to the back porch, where Lady reigned. She looked up at them but didn't leave the spot where she was having an afternoon nap.

"It turned out to be a beautiful day," commented Caroline when they stepped out into the sunshine and walked to his car. She lightly brushed the sleek, sparkling finish of the Lamborghini with the fingertips of one hand.

The corners of Chad's mouth curved in a broad smile as he watched her gently touch the red paint. He rested one arm on the top of the car, leaning his right side against it. He looked very relaxed as if to assure her that it was no big deal. "I told you I drive it on Sundays."

She laughed. "And on special occasions," she added, pointing at him with the hand that had been touching the car.

"I'm glad you remembered that because today is both Sunday and a special occasion."

"What are we celebrating today?" Caroline raised her brows and waited, crossing her own arms and tilting her head a little to the side to listen.

"Do you want to hear the best first, or save it for last?"

Caroline sighed and looked out at the distant shoreline of Whitehaven, taking her time as if this was a tough decision. "I think—I will save the best for last," she announced.

"Well, one thing we're celebrating is that I'm going to be your brother's business partner."

"Does this mean he can be part of the new restaurant?"

"Well, we're asking for a meeting tomorrow evening to discuss it with the guys he's been talking to, but I think we have a deal they can't refuse. If not—well, maybe we can buy the property from them and get our own investors." His expression became serious once the conversation had turned to money.

She looked at Chad with eyes shining. "You're a terrific friend. You two will figure something out. This is definitely a celebration!"

He laughed, standing up from his position against the car and hooking his thumbs in both pockets. "We've been in some tight spots, so we can work together and keep our sense of humor. We'll have to hang on for this adventure."

They were quiet for a few long moments. He looked out over the sparkling water as it slapped against the pier in the wake of passing boats. Then he took one hand from his pocket, raking the back of his blonde hair with it, much the way her dad and Patrick did with the top of theirs. The sign, she thought. It happened when they were thinking through how to say something.

Chad took a deep breath. "And now, the best for last!"

His mouth was shaped into a smile, but he didn't have his usual easy air of confidence. He moved a step closer and reached out to take her hand in one of his, using the other to point over his shoulder and behind him. "I don't suppose you noticed those charred marks on my back—the ones I got from getting grilled by your dad." He did a little half twist as if to show her. "But he has given me his blessing to chase you around to convince you to hang out with me." Chad took her other hand now so that he was holding both of them.

"So as a reward for my bravery, I'm asking you to see me tonight. After the family dinner at the Big House. Nothing is open on Sunday in Whitehaven, and dinner keeps me from being able to take you somewhere nice for a first date—but we could watch the sunset from the pier, go hang out at the pool at my house, watch a movie at either my place or yours, or go walking on the beach. I don't care what we do—I just need to spend some time with you before you leave the country. And I hope we can stay in touch while you're gone."

Caroline looked down from his eyes to the little polo player logo on his cobalt blue shirt, then back up. "Sure," she nodded. "But I don't know yet what I want to do. Let's think about it, and I'll see you over there later."

He unconsciously started swinging their clasped hands a little in approval. She cleared her throat. "Hey, listen, Chad. I told Chris that I'd try to write to him."

Chad stopped swinging their clasped hands, and his expression became inscrutable. He pursed his lips a little as he stared into the distance with unseeing eyes. His tone changed only slightly. "Of course. You're friends. I imagine he'll need one."

He let her go and raised the car door. As he slid inside, he grinned and said, "Let's celebrate tonight." He started the car, and the radio came on.

> "Life would be ecstasy, you and me endlessly . . .
> Groovin' . . . on a Sunday afternoon . . ."

Chad looked up at her in surprise, and they laughed at the irony of the Young Rascals song. "I have special requests with all the local DJs," Chad quipped. He winked and pointed from his heart to hers, just as he had at the dance last night. She was beginning to think of it as "their sign."

***

85

Leaving Andrew Painter's estate, Chad punched in the gate code to close it to road traffic. Visitors to the island could ignore the "Private" signs on the beach at Brush Point and walk along it to the house, but they couldn't use the road to drive in and satisfy their curiosity.

Sure enough, there was a car heading slowly toward him whose driver hesitated at the sight of the gate. The car's inhabitants were pointing and gesturing excitedly to one another about the Lamborghini as Chad drove by and tipped his hand. Then the driver turned left to see where Unega Trail led, and Chad knew the car would have to turn around at the dead end just past the beach cottages. He had looked around the whole island on Friday evening to scout out which cottages were being used by summer guests who were seeking a retreat, a break in a creative block, or just inspiration.

He slowly drove up to the Gregorys' gated drive and pressed the code to get in.

Chad needed to discuss how his meeting with the Painters had gone with his dad and then do a few laps in the pool to release some energy. He felt keyed up, despite running up to Dog's Head and back this morning.

He found his dad on a long distance call with his grandfather, so he motioned that he'd talk to him later. He changed into swim trunks and grabbed an extra-large beach towel and his Wayfarer sunglasses. He walked out to the pool, ignoring the outdoor stereo—he wanted to be quiet and think.

Diving in with almost no splash, he made powerful strokes to clear the length of the pool quickly, and turned back. After a few strong laps, his muscles relaxed, and he swam easily, enjoying the silky way the water slid over his skin. His head was clearer, and he began to mull things over.

From the pieces that Chad was putting together, it looked like Chris had been trying to create a future with Caroline as he went along for these past months, based only on his feelings for her. Not having a plan for what he was supposed to do in life, or how he would provide for a wife, he had tried to just work Caroline into wherever he ended up. Andy Painter had seen too late that it had confused Caroline.

Though Chad was once like a son to him, he was very stern today and had made three things abundantly clear: Chad was not to encourage her with any romantic intentions unless he knew for certain that he was either going to take his father's place as administrator at Painter Place or live in the Big House someday and work from here; he was not to come near her with romantic intentions unless he was seriously considering her as his future spouse; and finally, if they decided that marriage was not right for them, Chad must be able to continue to work with her to run Painter Place with no hard feelings. No Painter before now had married into the Gregory family—they had always kept love and business separate.

Caroline would be the heir to the Big House and most of White Island, replacing Wyeth someday according to the carefully laid out rules for how the family passed on the estate. Her father had warned Chad to consider all the implications of his daughter's position and talk it over with his own father to be certain there was nothing in the prenuptial contract that would take him by surprise. Painter Place itself could never be split. She would keep the Painter name as an artist for the business, though legally her name could be her husband's. Chad assured Andy that he had already had that conversation with his dad, so Andy relaxed and gave him his blessing to court Caroline.

Chad swam to a ladder to climb out of the pool and shook the water out of his hair. He stood beside the pool for a minute to let gravity pull the water from his body, turning his head up to the sky and soaking in the warm sunshine.

He walked over the textured pavers to a chair in the sun and stretched out all six feet one inch of himself in it, putting on the Wayfarers lying on the small side table. The knots of tension were nearly unraveled now, but not quite. He took a deep breath of the hot island air. He decided that the tension would not go away until he stopped avoiding the fact that he needed to deal with jealousy.

If he was honest, it was jealousy that kept him from having peace. He had no claim on Caroline, just permission to pursue a relationship. It didn't matter that he'd waited four years to get the chance to date her—being near her again was making him feel possessive.

His jaw and neck muscles flexed at the memory of her sobs by the water on Friday night. He knew he couldn't expect Caroline to just forget that her feelings for Chris had ever existed. This would take some patience.

She'd always have some bittersweet memories that he was powerless to erase.

He clenched his fists at the thought of dating her while she and Chris were writing letters to one another. He was going to brainstorm an end to that. He took a deep breath and relaxed, stretching out his hands. Sherrie's letter to Patrick had indicated that there were no romantic ties left for her or her brother. There was no threat from this former boyfriend—only ghosts that needed to vanish.

He sighed, closing his eyes behind the sunglasses. He didn't know how to size up this older Cameron fellow that was getting ready to spend a lot of time with Caroline, and she could meet other guys on her trip or even at Painter Place. She had been in a relatively sheltered world before graduating from a Christian junior college last month. This trip was like her coming out season, and he had only just sneaked in under the wire at the last possible minute to be a part of it. This had to work out, or he'd have to drop back to Plan B, the one where he promised her dad that he could just be friends if things didn't work out.

Though he'd agreed to it, there was no Plan B. All his life, there had only ever been Plan A.

He sat up, putting his legs out to either side of the wooden lounge chair and combing both hands through his drying hair to get it out of his face and off his neck. He pushed the sunglasses up onto his head and rubbed his temples and forehead as if to stimulate his thinking. He was going to have to keep his eyes focused on the big picture.

***

Sunday lunches or dinners were not private family affairs at Painter Place in the summer months. Guests who were staying in the rooms in the mansion were welcome to eat with them in the dining room. Maggie Jane and all the staff had Sundays off, so Valerie, Chrissy, Camellia Gregory, and Savanna took turns planning the food.

This week, dinner was at 6:00 sharp, and it was Camellia Gregory's turn to bring the food. She had a live-in housekeeper who cooked two meals a day, but she also had Sundays off. This week, Camellia had asked her housekeeper to skip cooking for the family on Saturday and instead create trays of deli meats, cheeses, breads, crackers, olives, and salads.

Home cooked mustards, sauces, and dressings filled little ceramic pots created by Valerie Painter. A little tray of fancy cookies was intended to go along with the contents of two ice cream freezers of homemade fare out on the porch.

Wanting to dress up a little bit for her first official date with Chad, Caroline decided to play up the ribbon that her sister had braided into her hair. She put on a short white denim skirt and a black sleeveless knit top with a V neck that pulled into an oval of hammered silver metal. She wore only one hammered silver earring, set with black onyx and designed by Aunt Chrissy, on the side where her ear and neck were bare. It swung gracefully as she moved her head, and a slender matching bracelet slid lightly up and down her forearm and wrist.

She was hoping for the reaction she saw in the unguarded expression on Chad's face as she entered. He recovered and flashed a charming smile at her before continuing to listen to something Gran Vanna was saying.

Caroline used her best Southern Belle manners, resisting re-sculpting cookies or unrolling things. Then she spent a few minutes with each person, beginning to feel the first pangs of missing her family—perhaps brought on by the reality of packing today. She often just stopped and took in all the conversations and interactions with the people she loved among all the things in the house she loved.

Guests at dinner included Cameron and Natalie Fisher and a mystery writer who was staying in one of the upstairs suites for two weeks. The writer asked to be called by his pen name, Wolfe Lyons. He was on retreat to brainstorm a new novel with a beach setting. Caroline didn't want to think about where the murder would take place on the island.

Patrick had strategically positioned himself near Natalie after the meal so that he was included in most of her conversation.

Caroline found her Uncle Wyeth in the library. "Don't stress over inventory right now," he told her, reaching out a hand to her shoulder. "You know Shelly—she'll be playing up the fact that you're on this trip and will be coming back with fresh work from England to hang. She'll have visitors jotting a trip back to the gallery on their calendars and buying Beatles and U2 albums in the meantime!"

Caroline loved his infectious, jovial laugh. He had described Shelly exactly.

"It sounds like she'll have her hands full with this new guy you're bringing in to cover classes and help her in the gallery," Caroline said. "She thinks that with his credentials, he's going to either take over her job or tell her all the things he thinks she could be doing better."

Uncle Wyeth laughed again. "They'll get along famously! By the way, we'll talk some shop on the flight about the plan for the film."

"Thanks a million for doing the packing for me!"

He waved nonchalantly that it was nothing, and she began to walk around to see Gran Vanna and the Gregorys. She had fun watching Gran skillfully draw out the things she wanted to know from Danny, who was delighted with her.

While she was talking to Camellia and Phillip, Chad came up beside her and stood close, his shoulder touching just behind hers and his hand on the small of her back. She got the impression that he was showing her off to them. She noticed Cameron walking by on his way to the kitchen and doing a double-take when he saw them. She covered his awkward moment by smiling quickly at him and glancing back at Camellia, who was talking about Chad's little brother Cole, currently living in London with Phillip's brother and attending a university nearby. Caroline glanced up at Chad to find that he was coolly watching Cameron, who was now talking to her mom and dad.

"We're going to say goodbye to everyone and head to the pier to watch the sunset," Chad told his parents. "Will you be home soon if we decide to watch a movie or something?"

Camellia nodded. "Sure, we were just getting ready to tidy up the leftovers and say our goodbyes, too."

Chapter Nine

"If you do not change direction, you may end up where you are heading."
—*Lao Tzu*

Caroline and Chad sat on a big roll-up mat from her straw beach bag, spreading it over the boards of the pier. It was difficult to imagine that only last night it had been crowded with guests at the Island Summer dance. The sky was promising to show off with a full moon as it had the night before, and the ever-present rolling surf was soft enough to talk over in a normal voice if you were side by side.

Caroline's siblings had left the Big House when she and Chad did, flashlights in hand for coming nightfall as they took off in different directions on the beach. Natalie had agreed to walk for a while with Patrick. Her camera hung on a cord around her neck since part of her work for her brother was to photograph the island. He was always scouting potential locations for filming, and Painter Place was being added to his file. As Natalie and Patrick headed up the northern side of the beach, toward Dog's Head, Caroline thought that her brother would probably recount to her the legend of King's Ransom. Marina and Danny took the southern side to Brush Point, and she imagined that Marina would tell him the legend of the lost treasure. Sunsets were a treat that most of the residents and guests on the island took a delight in, so all rocking chairs on the porches at the Big House were occupied tonight. Cottage guests were roaming here and there along the shore, and two artists stood down the beach at easels, getting the beach scene on canvas so they could be ready to capture the sunset colors.

"What are you thinking about?" asked Chad. "You have a faraway look, and I was hoping you'd stick around with me tonight."

Caroline took a few moments to answer. "Do you know if the coast of the English Channel is as pretty as this?"

"Never seem to make it out of London when I'm there," said Chad, shaking his head and gazing out at the horizon. "I'm looking forward to seeing it through your eyes in your paintings. But I can say unequivocally that there couldn't possibly be a more beautiful place than this. You need to hurry back to Painter Place—and me."

She was quiet, taking in the view. Other than the gentle surf, there was no sound except for the gulls calling.

Chad stretched out to lie back and look up. The first stars were beginning to reflect the setting sun. Caroline did the same.

"While we're on the subject of things that are beautiful, you should know that I think you are. You always were, but I've been amazed all weekend at how you've grown up."

Caroline smiled and couldn't help blushing. "Thank you. I was pleasantly surprised at how my brother's dashing best friend turned out, too. There's clearly a trail of broken hearts behind you."

They were both quiet for a few minutes. She noticed that he didn't disagree with her.

"Who are you, Chad Gregory, now that you're all grown up?" asked Caroline earnestly. "Is that something you can just tell me, or is it one of those things that I have to discover a little at a time?"

He turned his head to look at her, trying to gauge how serious she was. "I knew I was coming on too strong this weekend, trying to muscle my way in between your boyfriends. Now it's too late—I've set the tone for our whole relationship."

She burst out laughing, looking over at him so that they were face to face. Their smiles faded as their eyes became honest.

"I told you about myself last night," Chad began. "I'm still the friend you grew up with, just a much-improved model. Ask me whatever you want to." *Except for one thing,* he thought.

"I want to know what your weaknesses are," she said. They were still face to face while stars were becoming visible overhead.

He didn't blink. "Wow, you're really serious. But the answer's easy. My main weakness has always been you, and you've always known it."

This was obviously not the answer she had expected. She glanced away and then back, trying again. "What I mean is—there has to be an Achilles' heel on the person everyone considers to be a golden boy."

He looked at her in genuine surprise, caught off guard once again. He made an attempt to joke about it. "As far as I know, only my mother and my grandparents think I'm golden. And if it weren't for my sweaty running clothes, the housekeeper might make that list."

Unrelenting, she kept her gaze locked on him. He tried again. "Okay, okay. I have a secondary weakness, a jealous streak that taps into an attitude and brooding. It surfaced this weekend, due to some challenges with my main weakness. I'm not proud to admit that I have a problem with pride. But—it would be kind of fun if you'd checked my heels, too, just in case."

Caroline rolled her eyes and sat up. He propped himself on one elbow, facing her, and reached out to touch her arm, lightly running his fingertips up and down it. "Hey, I know. I've been hanging around your brother too long. Show me how this is supposed to go by answering first. Is there anything I should know about you?"

She was thoughtful for a few moments, looking out at the darkening horizon and biting her lower lip before answering. "I recently got off track, kind of like what you described last night. I'm disappointed in myself and embarrassed, and it's shaken my confidence." She paused, but he could tell she wasn't finished so he remained quiet. "I've regained my focus, but I'm not really sure that I'll recognize 'distractions' from 'directions' in the future."

Chad whistled. "So that's what you mean." He sat up now. He was in dangerous territory and needed to be careful of his response.

They were quiet for a while before he finally spoke. "Then you should know that I have a protective—even possessive—attitude toward Painter Place and the Painter family. During my own time off track, I wasn't sure that was healthy. I started trying to see myself somewhere else. I prayed a lot about it and talked to my pastor on campus. Finally, I came to realize that it was all part of who I am. Like a calling."

He looked over at her and leaned his shoulder to tap hers. He didn't want her to remember Chris and his calling. "Hey, maybe we can agree to talk to one another when we see a 'distraction' or a 'direction.'"

Still looking serious, but with a small smile on one side of her mouth, she looked over at him and nodded. "Sure. That makes sense." Putting both arms behind her now to rest on her palms like an easel, she looked up at the night sky. "I see Polaris."

"A star to guide the sails of a tall ship," he commented. Then he looked across his shoulder at her. "Let's lighten up and go do something. Did you decide how you want to spend the evening as you discover and exploit my weaknesses?"

"Well, it was a process of elimination," she began. "I don't feel like walking on the beach or swimming, and if we watch a movie, we won't get to talk. So I think we should play ping pong and then sit by the pool and listen to some music." She raised her brow and looked at him for a reaction.

He turned around as he rose to his feet. "Hey, wait a minute! Ping pong wasn't on the list!"

Caroline took his hand to pull herself up. "Has your new improved version gotten good enough to beat me after all these years?"

Chad leaned over to roll up the mat. "Oh, is that how it's going to be? Okay, just remember this is a distraction, not a direction."

Part Two
Confusion

Chapter Ten

"I have never been lost, but I will admit to being confused for several weeks."
—Daniel Boone

Even as the art documentary crew was landing in London to change planes, a shock wave was reverberating there in the offices of Gregory Global.

A phone call alerted Justin Gregory, who was at home in Kensington recovering from a mild heart attack. Justin called his brother Phillip in South Carolina. Phillip Gregory called Andrew Painter and then his father-in-law and his daughter in Charleston. After that, he arranged a flight out of Charleston for himself, his wife, and his son Chad. When Chad arrived back at home from his meeting about the restaurant partnership, he called his friend Patrick and packed his suitcase.

***

Caroline awakened in a room that was not her own, to seaside sounds that weren't like the murmur of the surf at home. Salt, seaweed, and fish gave the air in the room a faint but pungent aroma.

Rolling over on a small bed, she saw that Natalie was asleep on another bed like it a few feet away. Her luxurious dark hair spilled over her face, and Caroline couldn't help thinking what a wonderful portrait this sight would make. She smiled, thinking that Patrick would appreciate it.

Their suitcases were stacked near a dresser in a pretty room with walls painted a stormy blue color. She and Natalie weren't going to unpack much of their things because they would be getting private rooms when some guests at the bed and breakfast checked out tomorrow.

A look at her watch told her that they'd slept for hours. She felt lazy from what amounted to more than a day of traveling, and unlike her watch, she hadn't adjusted to the time difference in Mevagissey. Fortunately, Uncle Wyeth had scheduled the first two days of this trip to rest and plan.

She shifted slightly to lie on her back. Looking up at the ceiling, she silently thanked the Lord again for this trip and for the people He had put in her life. She asked Him to give her a teachable spirit, to guide her to be salt and light, and to help her be ready if there was some way that He wanted to use her in His work here.

A week ago, all she knew was that her uncle wanted to film a teaching series overseas. It was a blessing when he made the decision to go ahead with it on the night that Chris broke off their relationship, choosing a location he knew she'd love. So much healing had happened in her heart already.

This led to thinking of Chad. Her mind's eye saw the newspaper clipping from the Whitehaven Register that he had brought her when she was leaving yesterday morning, telling her to look at it every day while she was gone. She had tucked it into her sketchbook for safe keeping. As usual, the paper had devoted a whole page to the Island Summer Dance at Painter Place. Chad had cut out a close-up picture taken of them dancing together in the pavilion. It was like one of those posters that promoted a movie, with the hero in a captivating pose with his heroine love interest. She was surprised at the way they were looking at one another. The caption underneath read, "Caroline Painter and Chad Gregory celebrate his return home to Painter Place."

Wide awake now, Caroline rolled over toward Natalie to see if her eyes were open yet. She remained in the same pose. Quietly, Caroline propped herself up on her left elbow and reached over the side of the bed to her carry-on travel bag. As stealthy as a whisper, she eased her sketchbook out of the bag, then the pencils.

She would need to work quickly. Opening the sketchbook to see the news clipping of her and Chad safely secured in the inside cover page, she hesitated only a moment to look at it. She didn't need to—it was burned into her memory.

She chose to use a whole sheet of sketch paper and refocused her thoughts. She looked for the main shapes in Natalie's pose to get her proportions right. After a few light marks on the page, she began filling in the facial features. If she couldn't get them right, the rest of the portrait wouldn't work, so she didn't waste time on the hair and background yet.

Natalie's vulnerability and long hair tumbling in abandon were the main attraction in this pose. Caroline was glad that the features worked out so that she could add the hair. She switched to a pencil with softer graphite to get darker values and began shading in the stronger lines and shadows. She used the side of the pencil to sweep lost edges onto the curve of hair and a kneaded eraser to lift out highlights. She decided to fill in what was left of the page with the suggestion of fabric draping on her model's shoulders, pillow, and sheets. Underneath her signature, she noted: "Natalie Fisher, June 1985, Mevagissey, UK."

She hoped to fill the book with many vignettes of this trip to inspire future paintings. She placed it on the table that separated her bed from Natalie's and rose to get dressed without waking her roommate.

***

The sun cast late afternoon shadows through the lace curtains in their room when Caroline and Natalie left it later. They looked for their travel partners to see if there was a plan for dinner. Uncle Wyeth, Aunt Chrissy, and Cameron were gathered on a sofa in the sitting room, where the artist and filmmaker had pens in hand and were looking at one another's notebooks. The photographer and two apprentice cameramen sat in chairs near large bay windows overlooking the harbor.

Everyone stood when the young ladies entered the room, greeting them and quickly sharing jet lag stories before leaving the bed and breakfast together through a heavy, ancient-looking front door with weathered jade paint. The door handle was a fascinating sculpted diving mermaid, and Caroline made a mental note to photograph it or sketch it.

The group was charmed by the quaint architecture of the village and the way the houses opened up into the streets. Views of the harbor were everywhere. Overwhelmed by her first experience of all that there was to see, Caroline would have tripped on a doorstep if Natalie hadn't caught her arm.

"If you can't look where you're going, someone else needs to." Natalie linked arms with Caroline. "Don't worry—I'm used to it. Walk with me. My brother will be on his own tonight."

She inclined her head toward Cameron and his crew. The men were bumping into one another as they took in their surroundings. Sometimes

99

they would just stop abruptly and put up their hands to form a frame around a scene.

"Creative vision," Aunt Chrissy pitched in from behind them, where she had Uncle Wyeth's arm. They glanced over their shoulders to see Uncle Wyeth peeking through space between buildings at some fishing boats in the harbor. Aunt Chrissy rolled her eyes when they looked, smiling as she guided her husband in step with the others.

Caroline was glad they understood. Cameron looked back at them, and Natalie pointed just two doors down at the sign they were looking for.

"Wyeth's creative vision is mainly why I gave up modeling," continued Chrissy to the young ladies walking in front of her. "He needed a handler."

Everyone crossed the threshold of a door that Cameron held open for them. They were greeted by delightful aromas wafting out into the street. The establishment had a few patrons but wasn't crowded yet. There were paintings of ships and fishing boats on the walls, and the place had the general atmosphere of being inside a ship captain's quarters.

Natalie came up beside Chrissy while the men helped a waitress pull several tables together. She said in a low tone, "Cameron needs an assistant or handler of sorts, too, but someday I hope to have a reason to stay in one place. I don't like traveling. I want a home."

Caroline raised her eyebrows. It crossed her mind that her brother might be a good reason for Natalie to settle in one place. This trip would be a way to learn more about the young woman that Patrick had been so quickly taken with.

Chrissy replied to Natalie in a low tone as well. "I come from a sad family background, and Wyeth's family was irresistible to me. I fell in love with the Painters almost as much as I did with him. It was the family I'd always dreamed off, and the home I never knew."

Cameron had come up and placed his hand on Caroline's back, asking her to sit with him at dinner. She nodded and sat in the chair he pulled out for her while the waitress placed a centerpiece back onto the table. It was shaped like a ship's lantern with gold tinted panes of wavy glass.

Uncle Wyeth introduced himself to the friendly waitress.

"Your surname is 'Peynter'? Did you visit here because you have relatives in the area?" asked the waitress as she opened the centerpiece and lit the candle. She wore a name tag that said "Patty." Caroline loved her British accent. She used an "r" sound on words that ended with "a".

"No, though our ancestor did travel from England to the United States in 1680," said Uncle Wyeth. He explained the spelling of his last name and told her that his group was visiting to film an art documentary and teaching series, choosing her village for the picturesque setting.

"A film? Smashing! Well, you may have some very distant relatives here. My cousin just married a Peynter descendant—that's spelled P-e-y-n-t-e-r. The Peynters have been around here since about 1120 and are an important part of history. O' course, some were scallywags like buccaneers and lawyers. But others were respectable, like priests." She grinned broadly. "Cornwall's history is full of honest professions like fishing—and dishonest ones like smuggling."

"Which category would artists fall into?" asked Wyeth with a wink at the waitress.

"Ask me at the end of your visit here—that's a new one for the locals," she quipped back.

"Well, in the meantime, I've heard that Cornwall has a fantastic history of food, and we're hoping you'll help us with the menu tonight. We've missed a couple of meals in travel and sleeping and plan to make up for it. We're interested in anything nonalcoholic to drink and whatever you recommend for dinner and dessert."

Caroline and Chrissy chose to try a "squab pasty" of mutton and apples with Cornish Fudge for dessert. Wyeth and Cameron chose from several versions of fish, and Natalie chose a pasty of beef and onion with ice cream for dessert. Caroline shuddered at the idea of Stargazy Pie, which the young camera guys and the photographer ordered. She could not imagine eating a dish in which fish heads were looking up at her.

Caroline noticed that Patty, the waitress, couldn't keep her eyes off of Cameron, though she made no attempt to flirt and seemed to assume that he and Caroline were together. She brought the group a wonderful assortment of small cheese wedges and home baked breads as an appetizer, explaining that the Cornish were famous for their dairy products. After Uncle Wyeth said a blessing for the food, there were sounds of appreciation for the cheeses as the group tasted the samples and recommended them to one another.

When the main courses arrived, Cameron and Caroline decided to share a few bites of their different orders. Natalie asked if she could also swap a bite of pasty with her brother's fish, and suddenly the whole group was sampling one another's orders. Caroline staunchly refused the offers of Stargazy pie and endured a lot of resultant teasing from the crew.

With the main course over, they enjoyed coffee and dessert. Chocolate was just what Caroline needed, and she closed her eyes as she enjoyed the bite of fudge she had taken. She opened them again to see that everyone except the camera crew was watching her. Cameron wore an amused expression. She blushed at being the center of attention and asked if anyone would like to try the fudge.

"We wouldn't dream of taking a single morsel away from you," said Aunt Chrissy. "Everyone can sample mine instead since I'm too full to eat it all."

Uncle Wyeth swallowed a bite from his wife's fork and nodded approval. He looked at Caroline. "I hope you'll savor every experience here, paying careful attention and really seeing with your eyes and senses, like Leonardo da Vinci did," he said. "I heard a quote about that once— 'Wherever you are, be all there. Live to the hilt every situation you believe to be the will of God.' I don't remember who said it."

Without hesitation, Caroline answered, "It was Jim Elliot."

Suddenly Chris' voice filled her mind. "Do you know the story of Jim Elliot and Nate Saint?"

Shaken, she put down her fork and sat back in her chair. There was an awkward silence as her uncle and aunt looked at one another.

Her uncle cleared his throat and said, "So it was. And such a man would have understood how to live life to the fullest every second." He reached for his coffee cup and swallowed some before looking back at his niece with sadness in his brown eyes.

Cameron caught the undercurrent of interaction between the Painters. "The name sounds familiar. Will someone remind me of who Jim Elliot is?" he asked.

Chrissy answered. "He was a missionary to a native tribe who murdered him. One of them later claimed that there were angels surrounding the missionaries as they died."

The solemn moment was interrupted by Jesse, one of the camera crew sitting at the next table. "Hey, no one is smiling down there! We're wondering if anyone else has a messed up inner timetable and will be up for a walk down to the lighthouse after dinner."

They accepted his offer and finished dessert while Uncle Wyeth handled the check with the waitress. Patty insisted that they come back often as she placed the unfinished part of Caroline and Chrissy's fudge in a little box stamped with a tall ship for them to take with them.

After enjoying a walk in the fading light of day in the harbor, they headed back to the bed and breakfast. Before reaching the brass mermaid diving into the jade door, the crew was trying desperately to convince Caroline to accept their private commissions for paintings of Stargazy Pie.

***

Behind closed doors in his uncle's house in Kensington, Chad paced the length of Justin's library. His uncle was sitting in a chair behind a massive desk with a palladium window behind it. His little brother Cole was in a nearby wing chair answering his father's questions, and no one in the room liked the answers.

"Dad, I swear, I didn't give away any client information. I just wanted to check a few accounts for personal reasons for a project that my study group is working on, and I found Uncle Justin's password to get into them. It was wrong, and I'm sorry. I meant to destroy the notes but hurried to a party where we were going to talk about our project. I forgot about it once I put the paper in my shirt pocket. It—uh—disappeared at the party." Cole looked down at the pattern on the Oriental rug.

Philip Gregory stopped his own pacing and stood directly in front of his son. "Cole, how would anyone have gotten the piece of paper out of your pocket?"

Chad paused and turned to see what his brother would say. Cole didn't look up. "I don't actually know. I passed out for a little bit," Cole finally answered in a small voice.

All three men looked at him and blinked as if they couldn't believe what they had just heard. When no one spoke for a few moments, Chad took a deep breath and raised both hands to clasp behind his neck, looking up at the ceiling. Cole ventured a glance up at his father before he looked back down at the rug. "I only had three drinks. That's all."

Justin and Chad exchanged glances, but Phillip Gregory's eyes did not leave his son's face, and his voice was like steel. "When did you start drinking?"

"I haven't started drinking, Dad. This was only the second time. I—don't handle it well," he said haltingly. "I know what scripture says about it, and that story about Noah, where it's not even a good idea in private—and that you've always told me it's stupid for anyone who handles other people's money to drink—but this isn't Whitehaven, Dad. I'm just about the only guy I know here who doesn't drink. I'd seen Uncle Justin in restaurants with a drink sometimes when he was with clients and thought it would be okay if I just had one. But after I have just one—it's harder to decide that it's not a good idea to have another one."

Justin's mouth dropped open. He recovered quickly and snapped it shut, meeting Philip's scowl before looking at his nephew. "Cole, have you ever seen me take a drink?" he asked.

He waited, but Cole didn't answer. "Sometimes when I go out to dinner with a client who doesn't know me, they order a glass of wine or champagne for me before I arrive. I simply let it sit there without touching it. From now on, I'll ask the waiter to take it away so I won't influence anyone else."

Cole's blue eyes widened as he looked at his uncle. "Oh," was all he said. He studied the pattern on the Oriental rug again.

"What is this project you were working on, and who would benefit from the client information that you looked at?" asked Phillip.

"I can give you names of everyone who was there when I was conscious, but George is the one I suspect most of taking it. He was asking a lot of questions about Global clients instead of our project model. I can see now that I should have been wary, but at the time—well—you know. I wasn't—thinking." Cole leaned forward and rubbed his head with his

104

hands. "I'm so sorry, Dad. I'm sorry, Uncle Justin. I'd give anything for a do-over."

Phillip stopped pacing and put the fingertips of both hands on his temples. Eventually, he lowered them and looked at Cole. "I know you're sorry, son. But that won't be enough for a judge if an investigation doesn't clear you of criminal activity. Do you know if anyone there had a camera?"

Cole looked startled. "No—I don't think so" he stammered. He blew out his breath and wiped his hands across his face.

"Someone outside the company has tried to look at some accounts. Why did you choose those particular clients?"

Cole's eyes were frightened now and pleading as he looked at his dad. "I was concerned about how those accounts were impacted by a new regulation that was passed while Uncle Justin was in the hospital. I wondered if there was anything the company could have done to have sheltered the investments somehow if only Uncle Justin had been there."

Phillip shook his head and blew out a deep breath. After a few moments, he said in a weary voice, "Cole, you've brought a scandal down onto Gregory Global that might damage your family, the employees, and some clients for years to come. I'll do everything possible to get you through this, but it will cost me and Justin dearly, and you'll have to find another career. As of today, it isn't going to be with Global."

Phillip motioned to his younger brother Justin to follow him out of the room, leaving his sons in the library. Cole looked stunned and miserable, rubbing his face in his hands before standing up and slowly walking toward the window behind Uncle Justin's desk. He stood looking out with his hands jammed in the pockets of his designer jeans. Chad went to stand at the front of the desk to confront his brother.

"Which accounts?" Chad asked. Cole was looking out the window with his back to the room, his dark wavy hair flipped up around the collar of his pink polo shirt.

"My best friend's family, my girlfriend's family, and the Painter estate," he answered in a flat tone.

"You've got to be kidding me!" Chad exclaimed incredulously. "You've put the Painter accounts in jeopardy?"

105

Cole's attitude became defiant. He shrugged, replying over his shoulder. "They're just clients, Chad. The one that matters is my girlfriend's family. Her dad's a banker, and if he finds this out, I'll never get to see her again."

Chad was furious. Cole jumped when his brother slammed his fist down on the desk and leaned over toward him, raising his voice. "You're clueless if you're choosing which client's money is more important than another's! Dad's right. This is the wrong business for you."

He took a deep breath and lowered his voice to normal volume again, though his tone was tense and sounded like his dad's. "The Painters are like family. Their London accounts may not be the big ones, but they depend on us. When I promised to protect Painter Place, I didn't know I'd have to protect it from my own brother!"

"Oh yeah? Then maybe you'd like to sell that red Lamborghini to pay a new tax they've been hit with this year!" Cole shot back, turning to face his brother with clenched fists.

Chad didn't move from leaning with his palms down on his uncle's desk, his dark green eyes narrowed and flashing in anger. After a standoff of glaring at one another for a few moments, Cole's expression suddenly crumpled from its defiance. He walked toward his brother and sat heavily in the leather swivel chair at the desk. He reached up to rub his forehead again with one hand, leaning on his elbow on the chair's armrest.

"Who did you make the promise to?"

Chad stood up straight, crossing his arms over his chest. "Caroline. I'm going to marry her."

The room was silent except for the ticking of an antique grandfather clock, a Gregory family heirloom.

Cole looked up at his brother, tears brimming in his eyes. "I didn't mean what I said about the Painters, Chad. I was trying to make my mistake seem less serious than it is. The truth is that I checked because I was worried about them."

Chad continued to face his little brother. The anger in his eyes cooled and became thoughtful. The grandfather clock ticked on in a measured rhythm that soothed his tension. "Okay," he finally replied. "Okay, show me. I'll give you a chance to prove it." He set both hands on his hips. "I'll get access to the Painter accounts tomorrow at the office, but right now, I want to hear what you're thinking about how they might have been sheltered."

***

On Wednesday, Wyeth Painter and the film crew went back to the quaint bed and breakfast after having lunch with the ladies of their group, who were now shopping. After spending the morning with a map of Mevagissey, exploring for filming locations, the crew would use the time in the afternoon to make sure all of their equipment was in working order. Then they would gather again in the sitting room to map out the new scenes they wanted to add to the schedule. Tomorrow, filming would begin.

Their host's name was Mr. Holmes, and he caught Wyeth on his way upstairs. Mr. Holmes told him that he had settled Caroline's things in a private room with a balcony overlooking the harbor, just as Wyeth had requested. Then he handed him a message on a folded piece of paper, saying that Andrew Painter had called and wanted his brother to call him as soon as possible.

Wyeth nodded and thanked the host, who led him to an antique desk where there was a phone for guests to use. A London newspaper lay on top of the local news beside the phone, and a cheerful vase of fresh flowers sat on the top of the desk.

Wyeth reached his brother's marina in Whitehaven, where Andy was working late to handle a summer rush of boat repairs. After an update on how everyone was enjoying Mevagissey, the tone of the conversation became serious. Cameron had come out of the kitchen with tea to take to his room, but he stopped at the bottom of the stairs when he heard Wyeth's voice in the foyer.

"Well—let's see—yeah, there's a London paper right here. The financial section? Okay, wait a minute." Pages rustled as Wyeth searched through the newspaper on the desk.

Cameron heard a gasp, then Wyeth's voice again on the phone. "Yeah, it's today's headline all right. It's—well, uh—hearing you say it didn't have the impact of actually seeing it in bold black letters. I'll bet Phillip went through the ceiling." Wyeth was quiet while he listened to Andy. "But as

107

far as Phillip can tell, there's been no harm done to the accounts, and they're protected now. Oh, I see, I see." Wyeth sighed.

The newspaper rustled again as he refolded it and put it down. "That's too bad. Does he expect the investigation to clear Cole?" He touched the petals on the flowers in the vase absentmindedly as he held the phone receiver to his ear. "Well, about that tax—we'll have to do something because we budgeted for that income, and it's tight. Chad's working on it? So he's in London, too?" Wyeth put his hand on his hip. "Andy, look—do I need to go to London?"

Some boards in the floor creaked as he took a few steps in front of the desk. "He will? Okay, I'll let the host here know that we may get some important phone calls. If you and the Gregory family are handling this, I'll try to just focus on what I came here for. But let me know if you need me. Yes, yes, she's doing great so far. Love to everyone! Goodbye."

Cameron ducked back into the kitchen. After Wyeth went up the stairs to his room, the filmmaker went into the foyer to the desk where the guest phone was. He set down his teacup and opened the newspaper, searching for the financial section and catching his breath as he whispered the headline, "London Financial Giant Under Investigation." He looked at the subtitle. "Gregory Global May Have Leaked Client Information."

After reading the article, Cameron put down the newspaper and picked up his cup of tea. He stood at the desk, sipping it and staring out the window. When finished, he set the cup on the desk and picked up the phone.

***

"Look here, I'm the brains, and you're the beauty. Just do what I tell you. You'll get the publicity you need, and I'll get credit for the pictures."

Inside the café, a man in a flat plaid cap picked up his coffee cup and put it to his mouth. The beautiful woman he was sitting with rolled her brown eyes at him and turned to look out the cafe window at Threadneedle Street. It was raining, but the weatherman said it would clear up soon.

"It'll be tricky to catch one of the brothers when they're coming out," said the young woman. "We may have to wait around all day."

"And you have something better to do?" asked the man sarcastically, setting his cup down. "It's not any trickier than when I got photos of the Princess. I have a partner who will let me know when they're coming out. I've arranged for the cab driver."

"Are you sure the financial scandal is the right story to use? I don't want to be associated with anything negative," said the woman, turning from the street view to look at the dark-haired man in the cap.

"Trust me. This will blow over in a week. But while it's a headline, it's the biggest thing going. By tomorrow, it'll be on the front page, not back in the financials. You know why? Nothing else interesting besides sports is going on in London right now, so the press has to be creative. Until the Bond movie comes out next week, or unless there's some sort of sensational murder, all we have to do is attach you to a Gregory prince, and you're gold." He gulped the last of his coffee.

"Well, which brother would do me the most good?" asked the young woman.

The man looked thoughtfully out the window again. "Hmmm. Well, one is here in university and is a bit younger than you—seems very approachable. The other is a year older than you are. He's aloof and just comes in for business now and then. Both are American."

He turned back to her with a smirk. "I suppose the Gregory money has bought the men in the family some beautiful wives over the generations to contribute to the gene pool. Either of these kids would be great to show you off in the photos. The older is blonde and looks enough like a popular actor in America for people to look twice. The younger looks more like his dad and reminds me a bit of the young photos of our own Timothy Dalton, minus the chin dimple."

"My word! You don't say!" exclaimed the young woman, eyes sparkling. "I prefer the younger for my purposes. It might even turn into something. We'll have to trust fate to decide which one gets to propel me to fame."

From across the street, the photographer noticed his contact waving frantically. Laying down money on the table for the bill, he exclaimed, "That's the signal. They're coming out. Let's go!"

Chapter Eleven

"If thou rememberest not the slightest folly
That ever love did make thee run into,
Thou has not loved."
Shakespeare, As You Like It, act II, scene iv

Chrissy had an instinct for snooping out some great boutiques. They selected souvenir gifts for family members and friends and had them shipped directly from the store. They also found hats to protect them from the upcoming days spent in the sun. Caroline had fun picking out some new clothes that Chrissy and Wyeth said they wanted to give her to wear for the filming. The local shop owners appreciated the business, and they spread the word around the village that their goods would be worn during filming of an art video.

The film crew had set up according to plan in the sitting room back at the bed and breakfast, and when packages began to be delivered before the ladies returned, Cameron raised his eyebrows.

Wyeth noticed Cameron's expression and smiled tightly. "Chrissy calls this reaching out to the locals on behalf of the Painters. She's my ambassador this afternoon. She assures me she's making me look good."

"Then Natalie's an ambassador for the Fishers. She has my credit card, and she knows how to use it. I may have to spring for another suitcase to get all this home." Cameron eyed the stack of packages with a tag saying "Fisher" taped to it.

When she returned in the late afternoon, Caroline was thrilled with her new room. On the dresser, a tall ship sailed motionlessly in a huge glass bottle with a frothy lace doily sea underneath. She smiled, remembering how Chad loved tall ships. She should take a photo of this for him.

She parted the lace curtains and opened some weathered French doors with watery glass panes, stepping out onto a balcony with a curly ironwork railing and flower boxes spilling over with colorful blooms. Sunshine warmed her face, and the view was amazing. There were cliffs in the distance. The air was filled with the faint rattle of rigging and the shouts of fishermen to one another. She wished that she could set up to paint.

Going back inside to unpack her suitcase, she began putting things into the dresser drawers and found hangers for her new items in the old mirrored wardrobe. She pulled her jewelry case out to put a few new items inside and saw the chain with Chad's ring on it. Holding it in her hand for a moment, she decided to put it on. It slipped down under the neckline of her blouse so no one could see it.

Natalie knocked at her door, and they walked downstairs together to the large dining room, where Wyeth had had a meal catered by another local restaurant so the group could focus on work. He invited Mr. Holmes and his mother to join them. The Holmes duo identified the more unusual dishes, and white-haired Mrs. Holmes had interesting stories to tell about the old traditions behind some of the recipes. She enjoyed having Caroline take such an interest in the food and ask so many questions.

"My brother Patrick would love to be here for this. He wants to be a chef and is working on managing a restaurant back home. I need to sketch some of these and make notes for him," said Caroline.

After dinner, they gathered in the sitting room again to finalize the schedule for the following morning. Caroline noticed that her Uncle Wyeth looked haggard as he handed out a schedule outline to the ladies. She wondered if her own weariness was showing.

"Cameron tells me to expect tomorrow to be a tough day," began Wyeth as he looked at them. "We'll have to be flexible and patient. We can't control noise issues, wind, weather, and curious bystanders." He paused and glanced around the group. "After tomorrow, we'll have a better idea of how to work with one another, so this *will* get easier. Our second artist will work with me the first couple of days to understand what my expectations are. By next week, Caroline, I want you to be on your own. Jesse will go along as your cameraman, and Natalie will also be a part of your team."

Caroline looked up at her uncle to nod that she understood. She glanced at Jesse, who wrinkled his nose and smiled crookedly at her.

"This weekend, we'll have a special visitor coming in to sponsor us. He's an artist acquaintance of mine named Dante Kent, and he has invited us to a formal reception in our honor. He couldn't book a venue on such short notice, so he's borrowing a friend's yacht to travel here to the harbor. We'll have three decks for a dinner party. I approved a guest list of gallery and museum representatives. Everybody clean up nice and act respectably."

Everyone but Chrissy looked surprised by the unexpected event. She smiled indulgently at Caroline. "Juliette has you covered on this one," she said with a smile.

Wyeth told them they were free to go rest but to be down at 7:00 in the morning for breakfast. He asked Caroline to stay behind.

After the room had cleared, Wyeth quietly told Caroline about the phone call he'd received earlier in the day from her dad. His voice was weary and concerned as he explained that Cole could be in serious legal trouble. His eyes were stinging as he took Chrissy and Caroline's hands and they prayed together, first for the Gregorys and next for their own witness on this trip.

Back in her room, Caroline sat down cross-legged on her bed, thinking about the how the Gregorys and Painters' lives and businesses were so intertwined. From the time of their narrow escape from England together, the Painters had trusted the Gregorys and relaunched them when everything had been taken from them. She spent some more time praying about their current troubles. Then Chris came to mind. She prayed for him as well, and it seemed to help her continue to untangle romantic feelings.

Rubbing her tired eyelids with her fingertips, Caroline sighed and got up to arrange what she would need early the next morning. The small box with her leftover Cornish fudge sat on the dresser, and she put it into her tote bag for tomorrow. If the day was anywhere near as hard as Cameron warned, chocolate therapy might come in very handy.

Glimpsing her sketchbook on the lamp table beside her bed, she remembered that she was behind on things she wanted to note inside of it. She couldn't resist glancing at the newspaper photo of her and Chad together at the dance, then turned a few pages past the portrait of Natalie. She drew off several squares and rectangles to format sections of the page, like a comic book, and then quickly drew some foods, unusual items in shops, and other things she had encountered during the day. She jotted down notes, and within fifteen minutes, she closed the book and turned out the light.

***

Mr. Holmes didn't get a chance to read the *London Times* or the local paper the next morning until after his guests left in a rush, carrying all kinds of equipment with them. When he finished them later, he folded them neatly for the foyer desk beside the phone and put fresh flowers in the vase.

***

Cameron hadn't been kidding about what a tough day the film group would face, but at least the weather was made to order, in the high 60s with little wind. Caroline felt both stressed and blessed as she fetched painting supplies and made notes to help her uncle. She was now seeing his genius and gifted teaching skills through a new lens.

Cameron's crew wasn't fazed by interruptions and changes the way she was. Cameron was very hands-on and huddled around one or the other of them constantly when he wasn't helping Wyeth follow their outline. Caroline found herself watching him a lot, admiring the respectful way he worked with people. He was totally focused, and no matter what went wrong, he was suave and professional in his white polo and khakis. He sported his Ray-Ban aviator sunglasses on top of his head most of the time so he could look into the cameras, and they controlled his straight black hair in the breezes. He caught her looking at him once. He did a double take to look back at her and smiled.

When they stopped for lunch, Jesse asked her to come over to rest on a folding stool in the shade beside him. Handing her a cold thermos of herbal lemon tea and a sandwich from a small cooler, he squatted down in front of her to look at her face to face. He was in his mid-twenties with an impish smile, and the freckles sprinkled across his nose made Caroline think of Tom Sawyer. She felt like an adventure was imminent when she was around him.

"You're pulled in a lot of directions on the first day," he said. He searched her eyes as if trying to read whether she was discouraged or overwhelmed. "I want to tell you something from the other side of the

114

camera that might help you understand what we're capturing with your uncle."

He put his hands down on the ground to settle into a cross-legged position beside her and gestured with them to help illustrate some aspects of being behind the cameras. She ate her sandwich and then the piece of fudge while he told her that they were shooting from a Direct Cinema approach. He explained that this left out the interaction of a producer and put the emphasis on the subject. He also explained that photographs and voice-overs would be used to fill in, so some of the noise interruptions would not be the problem she imagined. Editing would be a huge part of how the film turned out.

Caroline was the first of the tired group to walk through the jade door into the foyer late that afternoon, and she gasped at the sight of the photo on the front page of a newspaper on the desk. She stopped dead still. Chrissy bumped into her, unable to check her steps to the sudden halt. Caroline used her free hand to grab the paper and ran up the stairs to her room with her things.

She didn't bother to close her door as she dropped her tote bags along the way and threw off her hat. She laid the newspaper out on her bedspread. The headline said something about a scandal at Gregory Global, but Caroline barely saw it. Underneath it, there on the front page, was a large photo of Chad looking down and smiling at a stunning young woman, who was looking back up at him. The woman was sultry and sophisticated, and her expression was coy as if they shared a secret. They were outside of a building in the city, with glass reflecting ghosts of signs, people, and traffic. The caption underneath stated *Phillip Chadwick Gregory III is seen leaving the offices of Gregory Global with fashion model bombshell known as Tippy.*

Caroline put her hands to her mouth and backed away from the newspaper, but her eyes were locked onto the photo. She bumped into the dresser and stood frozen there. Chrissy and Natalie reached her door with bewildered expressions. Seeing Caroline's reaction, they came in to look at the newspaper lying on the bed.

Chrissy turned quickly to her. "It can't be what it looks like."

Natalie snatched up the paper as if she needed to see it up close to check for a mistake. She looked up at Caroline, shaking her head. "I know a playboy when I meet one, and Chad is not even close. There's more to this."

Caroline took her hands from her mouth and braced herself with them on the top of the dresser that she was leaning against. The pale, stricken look on her face was beginning to grow into a flush of anger.

"There's more to it alright. A picture says a thousand words. He sure didn't waste any time looking her up when he got to London. He just didn't count on getting caught when I'm in the country to see the papers. One girl for Painter Place, and others tucked away wherever else he spends time. No wonder he stayed away so long."

Chrissy and Natalie glanced at one another with concern. "Honey—" began Chrissy.

Caroline put up a hand in front of her to stop her. "Don't worry, it's not just that he's with someone else," interrupted Caroline. "It's that I suddenly understand who he is, and who I am. Look at the cut of his suit and her clothes. For heaven's sake, look at her!" She pointed at the paper, and then she looked down at herself.

Natalie looked at Chrissy in alarm. Caroline put her hand back on the dresser behind her and shook her head.

"I don't belong in his world. All that glass and stone surrounding them—I couldn't breathe. I was so naive when he showed up a few days ago on my sheltered little island."

She closed her eyes and reached up a hand to rub her temple as if a headache was beginning. "And anyway, if it wasn't Tippy looking at him like that, it would be someone else. There will always be *someone*—just like it was with my grandfather. Chad is too handsome to be taken seriously— and apparently much wealthier and important than I realized. He's not— safe. This photo is a much-needed reality check and I'm walking—no, I'm running as fast as I can—away from Chad Gregory."

She took a deep breath and let it out in a long sigh but didn't open her eyes. "I don't want to be rude, but I'm goin' to get a shower now," she said flatly. "I'm okay. But I'm stayin' in my room to paint tonight. Would you bring me a little something back from dinner?"

Chrissy nodded mutely before she and Natalie reluctantly left the room. Natalie still held the newspaper and closed Caroline's door behind her. "I'm going downstairs to call Patrick," she whispered urgently to Chrissy.

"Good," whispered Chrissy. "I don't care what she says, she's not okay, and she's scaring me. I'm staying here. Just bring me some dinner back, too."

***

Sherrie knocked on Chris' bunkroom door. She didn't have to wait long before he opened it, and he came out with a smile to greet her. She smiled back weakly and looked down at a large manila envelope in her hand.

"Do you have a few minutes? I don't want to interrupt if you're in your group," she asked.

"No, I'm free right now. What's up?" He could see that she was troubled, and the space between his eyebrows creased with a little scowl.

He followed her out into the heat of the day as she went to sit down on the porch steps. He settled in beside her. She opened the envelope and pulled out some papers.

"Mom and Dad wrote, and they sent something from home," she said as she sorted the letters from a newspaper page. She handed him a sealed envelope with his name on it. "This letter's for you. And this," she said, "is the *Whitehaven Register*." She unfolded it. "They did a full page feature of the Island Summer Dance last Saturday."

She watched Chris' reaction. He drew back like someone had slapped him, and he grabbed the page from her hands. His eyes were wide and confused.

"Your concern for Caroline was unnecessary. She rebounded quickly when her childhood sweetheart came back to Painter Place." Sherrie's voice was bitter. "It would have gotten messy if you'd stayed around. I'm glad you left before she broke your heart." She pointed to a photo of Patrick and Natalie dancing in the crowd. "Look at Patrick's face. He's dead gone on this woman. I made a fool of myself by sending him that letter the same morning."

117

Chris looked over at her angry expression and sighed. He folded the paper back up again, handing it back to her as if it was repugnant. "Yeah, well, I understand that you're upset, and I'm sorry that you're hurt. But remember that you walked away before the girl arrived, and I walked away from Caroline before the Gregory's son came home. We shouldn't want them to pine over us—that's just our pride."

Sherrie didn't respond, so he continued. "In the scheme of things, what does it matter? I don't know about Patrick, but I do know Caroline, and she never looked at me like that. Good or bad, Chad's the one." His voice broke off. "She couldn't have hidden it and would have had the pain of telling me."

They sat silent for a few minutes before Chris sniffed, shifted, and put his arm around his sister. "I've seen how some of the guys here look at you. It won't be long before you move on. You need to get past this and stay in touch with the Painters."

He stood up, holding the unopened letter from his parents. He reached down to help his sister stand. "Are you okay?" he asked.

She nodded and put papers back into the envelope. "Are you?" she asked. "Will you still write to her?"

He shrugged and turned away to hide his feelings. He'd never tell her he was crushed. "It really hurt to see her with him. I wish I didn't have that memory to live with. But it only proves that God's timing is perfect. It wouldn't be appropriate for me to write. I'll just keep up with her through you."

Chapter Twelve

"I have sometimes been wildly, despairingly, acutely miserable . . .
But through it all I still know that just to be alive is a grand thing."
—Agatha Christie

A soft, salty breeze played with the lace curtains on either side of the doors that opened to the balcony in Caroline's room. She let it blow her silky hair dry. She gazed at herself in the mirrored wardrobe door thoughtfully, remembering the model in the newspaper photo with Chad. She opened the wardrobe and chose some flattering jeans and a pretty baby blue sweater. The sweater had three-quarter length sleeves to stave off the cool evening air that she expected on the balcony soon. She put on makeup as if she planned to go out to dinner with the group and, as a final touch, she put on some of her new boutique earrings. Being dressed to be seen made her feel better.

Painting might take her mind off the turmoil of her feelings. She was wildly all over the place and couldn't even seem to pray about it. One moment she'd be trembling in anger that Chad dared to treat her with such disregard after the commitments he had made last weekend, and the next she'd feel cold and impassive, wondering what she'd expected from a guy who'd been avoiding her for four years. Then she'd think of Chris and how she had hoped he'd take Chad's place in her life, and she felt desperate with loss. Chris would never in a million years have been seeing other women after asking her dad to see only her.

On the balcony, she set up a light folding travel easel and camping table with her canvas, palette, and water. She used a thin brush and paint to sketch out proportions for some distant sea cliffs. She knew she would have plenty of photos of the area, so her goal was not realism. She felt angry, rebellious, and on edge—something bold would suit her mood. If she were at home, she'd go do something unexpected and reckless to release her emotion.

Satisfied with the space and outlines on the canvas, she turned to color decisions. Thinking only in terms of the light or dark value of the shapes, she chose light or dark acrylic paint colors that she liked together. She needed to work quickly while she had light.

As she began painting, she listened to the sounds of a harbor tucking itself in for the night. Only a few people passed on the street now and then, so she could sing something low to herself. "Never Been to Spain" by Three Dog Night came to mind because it mentioned England.

> "... Well, I've never been to England
> But I kinda like the Beatles ..."

At first she kept trying to stick with the soothing measures of the few words she knew of the song to soothe her inner turmoil, pausing as her train of thought changed with a color or stroke on the painting. But "Owner of a Lonely Heart" began to shout in her mind instead. She sighed and gave in. At least Yes was a British band, she thought. She couldn't remember all the lyrics, but one part and the chorus came to mind as she related to it.

> "Owner of a lonely heart
> Owner of a lonely heart
> (Much better than a)
> Owner of a broken heart
> Owner of a lonely heart
>
> Say, you don't want to chance it
> You've been hassled before
> Watch it now, eagle in the sky
> How he dancin' one and only ..."

The cries of calling gulls joined the music in her mind. The distant cliffs fell off into the white foam edges of the English Channel. She became completely lost in her canvas, where her turmoil seemed to spill over. She was calming down.

"Mind if I see what you're working on?" asked a man's voice. Caroline looked around in her surprise.

"Down here," the voice guided her. She looked over the edge of the curly ironwork to see a young man looking up at her with amusement.

"Well—sure." Caroline put down the brush she was using to sign her name at the bottom right of the painting. She was glad she had just finished. Taking it from the easel, she turned it so it faced the street where the young man stood.

"I've never thought of the cliffs that way—smashing! Is it for sale?"

Caroline was taken aback again but managed to say that it was. She recovered enough to remember to smile at him and introduced herself.

"Is that how you signed the painting? I can't read it from here." The young man on the street tossed his head to shake the longer side of his straight dark hair. The other side was buzzed short over his ear.

"Well, almost. I add my middle initial on all of my work." She shrugged. "It's a long story."

The young man grinned. "I'd like to hear it. Can we talk over coffee or tea? My grandmother and uncle run this place, and you're stayin' in the room that used to belong to my parents. I got in this afternoon to visit." He gestured down the street to a sign over a bicycle leaning on a stone wall. "There's a little café just down here. I'll wait in the foyer."

"Well—okay," Caroline agreed haltingly. "Give me five minutes to clear my things away. And I have to let someone know where I'm going."

"O' course!" he replied, heading toward the jade door down on the street. "I'll wait."

Caroline quickly washed her brushes. She looked in the mirror and asked herself if she had gone crazy. Then she decided that if she had, she was going in style. She put on the coordinating necklace and bracelet that matched her earrings, then picked up the painting and rushed downstairs.

***

Wyeth was on the phone in the wide foyer where the young man he had met as Mrs. Holmes' grandson came back through the door and now seemed to be waiting. He raised his eyebrows and stammered to the other person on the line when he saw Caroline meet the young man with a painting in her hand. The young man looked it over appreciatively and then smiled at her and nodded. He propped it on top of a narrow bookcase on the opposite wall of the foyer and gestured with his head to the front door.

Caroline pantomimed to her uncle that she was going out, pretending to drink something from a cup. Wyeth's eyes opened wide. He silently mouthed, "Not late." She nodded understanding and stepped out of the open door to join her new collector.

"Uh—I'm sorry, Phillip. Would you repeat that? Something surreal just happened, and I'm a little sidetracked." He tested the length of the phone cord, but it would not reach the door so that he could look out and see where his niece was heading.

"Well, Caroline just walked out the front door with the grandson of the landlady here." He gestured with his arm as if Phillip Gregory could see him. "Well, I don't know. As I was telling you earlier, she was really upset about that photo and was staying in to paint on her balcony tonight. The next thing I know, she came down dressed to go out—with a finished painting and a new collector. Apparently the young man is buying the painting and taking her out."

He took a few steps over to the painting. "Are you sure it's the same guy? I've never heard of Public Parking. Well, I mean, I know about public parking, but not as a British band. Do these guys tour with the Cars?"

He listened a moment and smiled. "Tell Cole to stop laughing at me."

He glanced again at Caroline's work resting on the bookcase. "This isn't a painting like anything I've ever seen her do. It looks like therapy, or—venting. It could be a good album cover for a rock and roll band if they wanted to sing about tellin' someone to jump off a cliff. Maybe that's what Baker has in mind—inspiration."

He turned the canvas around with his free hand to look at the back as if there were some hidden clue there. "Cole just told Chad?"

Wyeth was pacing now, dreading this. He could hear Chad's incredulous and angry exclamations in the background. He rubbed his forehead before responding into the phone. "Tell him I'll talk to her when she gets in, but when she left, she believed he's seeing other women. And she is free. Chad's got a much deeper problem than her dating a rock star if she'd jump to a conclusion like that without talking to him first."

***

Tippy walked in and sat down in the same cafe where she had met the photographer on the previous morning. This time, the view from the window was getting dark enough for the street lights to come on. "So who is she?" she asked without ceremony.

"You won't believe it," he exclaimed. "It's some little Pollyanna from the States, and of any place in the world that she could be, it turns out she's in the UK doing a film with her famous artist uncle."

The model's eyes narrowed as she looked first at him, then out the window. "I knew there was a girl. We're lucky that you got that shot of him being polite enough to smile when I bumped into him. He didn't even notice me!"

"Well, he notices her. Take look at this." He slid a photo over to her. "This was in a newspaper back home on the continent, only last Saturday."

Tippy's eyes popped before she slid the photo back over to him. Her voice raised an octave. "This is hopeless. We can't get any more out of him. If that's your Pollyanna, this guy's hooked on the 'glad game.' It's just my luck that I didn't get the other brother."

The photographer shook his head. "Now you underestimate me," he replied. "This could be better. We just have to get creative. I've got a guy working on it. I'll call you in the morning."

***

Caroline and her new acquaintance sat down across from one another at a very simple little wooden table in the front window of the coffee shop. They settled their steaming mugs and dessert plates.

"Thanks for ordering something authentically Cornish for me," she said, unwrapping a fork from its napkin cocoon. The little cafe was playing upbeat music from British bands, and the music lifted her mood. She'd sung enough about moving on tonight.

When he didn't respond immediately, she looked over the table at him. He had a very slight smile and looked directly at her with expressive large brown eyes. His directness left her uncomfortable.

"Are you sure I shouldn't have ordered somethin' with onions so you could cry?" he asked.

Startled, she blinked before tilting her head. "Why would I do that?"

"Because it doesn't look like you have, and you might need to. I heard the chaps in the sitting room at my gram's. You must be the one they were talkin' about. Then a dark-haired young lady phoned some guy named Patrick, and I couldn't help but overhear her from my room in back of the kitchen."

Caroline held his eyes with a steady gaze of her own that flashed sparks. "When and if I'm ready to cry, it won't be on a stranger's shoulder." She dismissed him with a look and picked up her fork.

He burst out in a hearty laugh, clapping. "Touché, Miss Painter, touché! There's more to you than meets the eye." He lifted his coffee cup to her as if toasting in her honor. After taking a sip from it, he sobered.

"Oh, well, then. It seems you don't need my shoulder, but maybe you'll lend me yours. I need a stranger for that." He glanced around absently before lifting a bite from his small plate.

Puzzled, she followed his lead on taking a bite of her dessert. After swallowing, she ventured a question. "Is that British code for saying that you need someone to listen to your problem, but you're incognito?"

Over his coffee cup, Baker had a serious look in his lively brown eyes. He put the cup down. "Yeah."

She chewed her next bite thoughtfully before shaking her head. "Listen, if this is about a romantic relationship, I've crashed and burned twice in less than a week. I'm so bad at this that I'm ready to go it alone for a while." With a gloomy look, she put another forkful of chocolate into her mouth as if it would help.

"It's not about a girl." He looked around again to see if anyone in the shop was listening, but they were alone.

Caroline had to smile when she figured out that he meant "girl" when he said "gull." She was enjoying the sound of his accent, but it was a bit of a challenge to carry on a conversation.

"Since you bought me dessert, I'll listen to your problem. Sometimes just talking about something has a way of helping people to see it more clearly, so you may be able to work it out on your own. But can you speak slowly, without local slang? Remember, I'm not from around here." She allowed one side of her mouth to hint at a smile.

He smiled back. "You, on the other hand, speak with a gentle, soft swish of words that's easy to understand. Your accent and voice are mesmerizing, like music. I heard some of what you were singin' to yourself on the balcony. You move with it as if you're feeling it deep down."

She blushed and thanked him for the unexpected compliment, then took another sip of the warm coffee dwindling in her mug. "Music is a big part of my life back home. So tell me about your problem."

She sat back in her chair to listen and to study him. He wore a silver stud earring shaped like a tiny link of chain. His eyes were soft with long lashes any girl would beg for. The bridge of his nose had a slight arch, but not enough to be a distracting feature. At first she thought his mouth was too large, but when seen with his entire face at once, it worked out somehow. His face had the unshaven shadow that guys thought was so tough.

He began talking about a dilemma he was facing, being vague about the details—something that would cost him his job if he refused to do it. He was scowling when he ended, saying, "I only know that I wouldn't want my gram to know about it."

Caroline sensed that this situation was bigger than she had expected. Moving to sit forward with her forearms on the table and hands clasped, she asked, "How did you determine that what you were told to do was wrong? Are you a Christian?"

It was his turn to look startled. "My mum and gram took me to church since I was a wee one. I learned about things that were right or wrong back in the Bible times, and now I try not to do the worst ones. I wear this. It was my mum's." He pulled up a chain around his neck to free a plain silver cross from under his open shirt.

"Who is Jesus—to you?" asked Caroline. She kept her gaze steady, but his eyes were darting around.

"He's God's son. He's part of the Trinity." He crossed his arms over his chest and looked relieved that he knew this. He tossed his head, shifting his long bangs away from his eyes. "What does that have to do with my problem?"

"So you don't know or follow Him, personally?" asked Caroline. Her new acquaintance was squirming a little, which sent the cross skipping across his shirt.

"I don't know what you mean. I'm not much for prayin' and don't go to church unless I'm visiting Gram, if that's what you're getting at."

"If you loved Christ, you'd want to spend time with Him. So there has to be another reason why you're struggling with this decision. Is it fair to say that it's because you don't want to do something that will let down someone that you love dearly—someone who has a deep conviction about it?" She sat back to give him some space. "Do you suspect that she has a good reason for her convictions?"

"Well—yes. But it's more than that. If it really *is* wrong, I don't want to be a bad influence."

"This will be something public?"

"Very," he replied with distaste, looking away as if she might guess what it was by looking in his eyes. "But it's part of my new contract. And if I refuse, it affects my—my friends, too."

Now he leaned forward, arms on the little table. She noticed that he unconsciously tapped his fingers to the beat of the music. The speakers were playing an upbeat song she didn't know from a band she hadn't heard before, but it was clear that he did.

He continued to look out the window, tapping his fingertips. Caroline leaned forward again, drawn by a look of desperation that swept fleetingly across his face. She reached out her hand to put it on his arm, and he turned to look at her. Their faces were only about a foot apart now at the little table.

"Nothing in life is worth losing your self-respect and peace of mind," she said softly. "Don't set a price on something that's priceless. Once the bad influence is let off the leash, you'll have no idea how far-reaching the consequences could be. But you'll still have to pay them."

He looked at her for a long moment. "Thank you," he finally said. He looked down at the table and then back up at her again. "Would your answer have been different if you thought I was a Christian?"

"Yes. You'd have had a different point of reference for the authority in your morals."

A group of young adults burst through the café door, laughing with one another. Caroline and her friend sat back in their chairs, and she glanced at her watch.

"I need to get back. I have a long day tomorrow," she said.

He nodded, and they rose to leave. Before they reached the door, a petite young lady rushed over to grab his arm. "Baker! You're home!" She was beaming up at him.

He grinned at her and introduced Caroline to Beth. "I'm walkin' Caroline to Gram's. Stay 'til I get back?"

"Sure. Nice to meet you, Caroline!" said the young lady with a warm smile. She waved as they walked out into the summer night.

Baker stopped abruptly just outside the weathered jade door, looking intently at Caroline. To her surprise, he pulled her into a hug. "I don't know what to say," he spoke over her shoulder with his arms around her. "You gave me a lot to think about. You still owe me a long story about your artist signature."

He let her go as suddenly as he'd put his arms around her. He grabbed the brass mermaid to open the front door for her, and she stepped inside. He said good night and turned back around as it closed, noticing someone slipping between the buildings across the street. He scowled. It looked like the photographers had found him.

***

When Caroline reached the top of the stairs, she saw that her uncle and aunt's door was open. She tapped on the doorframe before peeking around. "Come on in," said Chrissy, who was sitting propped up with pillows on the bed and a novel in her hands.

Uncle Wyeth sat in an armchair in a corner with his sketchbook. Caroline let the familiar look of focus on his work clear from his face before she began talking.

"I just wanted to let you know that I'm back. Can I see?" She nodded at the sketchbook.

Her uncle turned it around as she walked toward his chair. "It's Chrissy reading."

127

Caroline studied the drawing. "The glow of backlighting in her hair from the lamp is amazing, even as a sketch. I'd love to see you paint this."

"Maybe I will. Speaking of painting, they tell me to expect a heavy fog in the morning. Sleep in a little, and we'll plan to leave around ten if the fog has cleared."

Chrissy patted the other side of the bed to indicate that Caroline should sit down. "Sweetie, we'd like to talk to you."

Chrissy exchanged a meaningful look with her husband, and he cleared his throat. "I was on a call to the Gregory family as you were leaving tonight," he said. "Someone used their current trouble as a platform to get publicity by manipulating a photo for the papers, and Chad is upset that you saw it and believed the implication. His family was just outside the photo's range and assured me that he had never seen that model before. She came up and bumped into him, and he just smiled that it was okay when she apologized. Then the family got into their waiting limo, which was held up by a taxi."

Chrissy said, "Chad asked that you call him tonight when you get in. Obviously, he was—concerned—to hear that you went out with Baker Holmes."

Caroline had a blank look. Her aunt and uncle glanced at one another. "Do you know who you were with tonight?" asked her uncle.

"Mrs. Holmes' grandson," Caroline answered. "He saw my painting from the street while I was on the balcony and wanted to buy it. He told me his grandmother ran the inn and asked if I'd go with him to get a cup of coffee. He had overheard some of the family talking about Chad's photo and thought I might want someone to talk to. When I told him I didn't, he said that he could use someone who doesn't know him to listen to him. He has a serious decision to make about work. I prayed for discernment and said what came to mind. As we were leaving, someone came into the café and called him Baker. I didn't even know his last name was Holmes."

A huge grin spread across her uncle's face. "Caroline, you just counseled a British rock star on whether to renew his contract with a big record label. Cole told me it was in the news that Baker is hedging on signing because they want him and his band to appear in some racy music videos for the new music channel on television."

Caroline looked dumbfounded. "Are you certain it's the same guy? What's the name of his band?"

"Public Parking, and he's the lead singer," answered her uncle. "He writes their songs and plays guitar in some of them. They haven't released anything in the States yet, but Cole follows them." He looked at her intently. "What advice did you give him?"

"Well, I asked some questions that led me to know he isn't a Christian, so I couldn't use that point of reference. I told him that nothing in life is worth losing your self-respect and peace of mind, and not to set a price on things that are priceless. He had mentioned that he didn't want to be a bad influence, so I reminded him that once the bad influence is unleashed in a public way, the price of the consequences can't be calculated—but he'd still have no choice but to pay them."

Chrissy wiped a tear from her eyelashes.

Wyeth cleared his throat again. "Very wise advice from such a young lady. I hope he'll heed it."

He held out a card for Gregory Global to her with Justin Gregory's number jotted on the back. "Give Chad a chance to explain."

Caroline hesitated, returning his pleading look with one that said she didn't want to do this. He continued to hold out the card, and she finally took it and nodded. She got up from her seat on the bed. "Will you please be praying for Baker's salvation?"

Caroline closed her aunt and uncle's door and stood looking down the flight of stairs into the foyer. She bit her lower lip and slowly descended to use the guest phone.

Chapter Thirteen

"Eternal life is knowing God, not just believing some true things about Him."
John 17:1-3

Caroline wished she could have a night's rest before dealing with Chad, but it wouldn't be right to make him wait when he hadn't done anything wrong. Though she now understood that he hadn't been caught stepping out with the model in the photo, Caroline was still bothered by seeing them together. It opened up some things inside of her that she wanted to think about.

She picked up the phone from the desk and sat it on the floor beside her, where she could lean back against the wall. After dialing Justin Gregory's number, she held the receiver to her ear, closed her eyes, and ran the fingers of her free hand through her long hair.

Chad picked up before the first ring finished, as if he'd been holding the phone. She sat up and opened her eyes at hearing his voice on the line. "Hello," he said a second time.

Caroline remembered to speak. "Hi, Chad. I got your message to call."

He spoke in a rush. "It's great to hear your voice. I miss you."

She smiled to herself. "It's good to hear yours, too. I'm surrounded with captivating British accents that I'm having a hard time making conversation with. People here talk about girls, and I thought they meant gulls."

Chad's spontaneous laugh in his deep voice reverberated in a sweet spot in her heart. She still wasn't used to hearing it again after so long. She leaned back against the wall and closed her eyes to savor it.

"What are *you* complaining about? Around here, they're putting gulls in photos with me." Chad's voice wore a grin.

She couldn't help doubling over in laughter sitting there on the floor. It felt good.

"I'm glad we can laugh about it now. I have to admit, I experienced a moment of high ego when you didn't like seeing me with a—uh, gull—in the newspaper. But then Patrick told me everything else you were thinking, and I crashed. We've got a deep problem if you'd even imagine that I could do what you're thinking. Please, Caroline, tell me it was only because you were upset. Give us a chance."

Caroline leaned her back against the wall again before speaking haltingly. "I don't know how to talk about this, and I'm too tired and emotional to trust myself. I don't want to say something stupid. You just materialized back into my life a few days ago, Chad—I don't know who you are anymore, or where you've been, or who you've been with. Maybe now you'll take Cole's place in that steel and glass cage in London. And the model—she's the kind of woman who seems to fit into the circles you live in, and many more like her will always follow you around, just like Gloria. I don't want that kind of drama. I'm not going to fight other women over someone who's strong enough to set boundaries around both him and me."

Chad's voice broke in over the line in a rush of words. "I know you need time to get used to me being around again, but I've only been at college and internships, and I told you last Saturday night that I haven't been with anyone more than having an expected date for an unavoidable event. What you see at Painter Place is who I really am! Last Saturday night at the Island Dance—on the beach, on the veranda in the shadows, on the pier at sunset—that's me. That's us, Caroline. All the things I told you there—that's me."

He paused, but she was silent. "I travel to London once or twice a year. My cousins here can take Cole's place. That model is shallow and manipulative, trying to profit from my family's trouble. That's not the kind of people I surround myself with. If you assume that I live and think like people in a soap opera just because my family has an international business, it's insulting, and you're acting like a snob."

For a full minute of long distance charges, neither of them spoke. It was Caroline who broke the silence.

"You're right, Chad. I'm sorry. But it looked so real and brought out something serious that I need time to think about. "

"Apology accepted. I know where this is coming from. What I'm asking you for is really as easy as it looks. Somehow, I'm goin' to prove to you that I'm a safe place. You're exclusive, Caroline—you've never had any competition, ever, and I'm not playin' around. I'm waitin' on that same commitment from you, and I'm still on the quest that Marina sent me on to convince you that I'm your prince."

A smile teased the corner of Caroline's mouth at the memory of last Saturday afternoon, when a filthy, sweaty Chad in torn work clothes had asked Princess Marina if her sister would dance with a frog that night.

Her voice was soft now. "This was easier at Painter Place."

Suddenly, the front door opened, and Baker Holmes walked in. He took a step backwards in surprise when he saw her sitting on the floor.

"A while ago I was looking up to you. Now you're looking up to me! I'm glad you're still awake—can we talk?"

He took a couple of steps to where she was sitting on the other side of the desk and saw that she was on a call. "I'll make you some tea for when you're finished," he said, pointing to the kitchen.

"Who is *that*?" asked Chad. The way he asked told her that he knew.

Realizing that Baker might overhear her conversation, she didn't want to say his name. She told Chad that she needed to hang up now. Still holding the receiver to her ear, she picked up the base of the phone to put it back on the desk. Baker was humming in the kitchen and drumming on a table.

"Caroline—he's a distraction." Chad was using his voice of steel.

"He might be a direction. I don't like ending our conversation this way, but I have to go. I'm glad we got things straight about the newspaper. "

"Caroline," Chad said quickly. "When you go back to your room, look at our photo and my ring. Remember what I said tonight."

"Okay. I will. Good night, Chad."

***

Baker popped his head out of the kitchen door. "Do you like honey in your tea?"

The absurdity of the situation hit her, and she began laughing.

"What? Inside joke or something?"

She began to walk toward him. "Not at all! I'm just mulling over how impossible it would be to tell anyone that the leader of Public Parking is in the kitchen making me tea. Yes, I'd like a teaspoon of honey."

"Aha, now I see where you're goin' with this. You found me out." He was nodding his head and smiling as he motioned over to a pub table with stools in the center of the kitchen. "Chamomile," he said with a nod at her steaming cup. "You'll sleep."

"Thanks, Baker. I'm really tired, though. I shouldn't have any trouble. It was a long, hard day, and tomorrow looks only a little better from a filming standpoint."

"This'll only take five minutes. And answering a question for me will only take two or three."

She took a sip from the fancy china cup to see if the tea was too hot to drink. He reached into his pocket and pulled out some cash. "Will this cover the painting? I'd like to put it in my room." He tilted his head at a door off of the kitchen.

She reached out to count the money on the table. "It's too much, Baker. The painting's a small experimental piece that I released some of my feelings into." She began to separate part of the money.

"That's what makes it so valuable to me! It's like you knew my feelings, too, about the problem I told you about." He reached across the table and pushed the rest of the money toward her, his hand pressing hers down on it. They locked eyes in a battle of wills.

She nodded. He finally took his hand away, and she put the cash into her jeans pocket. "I really appreciate the compliment—that you want to own one of my paintings," she said. "I'll have a receipt for you tomorrow."

Baker abruptly changed the subject and looked levelly across the table at her. "Tell me what you would have said tonight at the café if you thought I was a Christian."

She tried to look calm, but her heart raced. She silently prayed, *Lord, I'm too tired to handle this. Help.*

"Another time, in another mood, I might have said something different, but anything I'd say at any time would have come from scripture. We'd have that in common if you were a Christian—it would be our foundation for truth, our authority, instead of our opinions. Do you have anything to write with?"

He looked around and saw his grandmother's market list. He stood to reach for it, pulled off a fresh page, and picked up a pencil. Without a word, he sat back down, looking at her expectantly.

"I think the book of Proverbs has a lot of general guidance for life in it. You've probably heard Proverbs 3:5. 'In all your ways, acknowledge Him, and He shall direct your paths.'"

She waited while he scribbled down notes. His long asymmetrical bangs obscured his eyes when his head was bent over the page.

When he looked up again, she continued. "To acknowledge Christ, you have to believe that He really is who He claims to be—the Way, the Truth, and the Life. He has to become your Savior if you're going to acknowledge and follow Him as His friend."

She paused a moment, seeing understanding dawn in his eyes. "The guy I was on the phone with when you came in is a lifelong friend. He recently—he gave me a token to show his promise to always look after my best interests at Painter Place, an island that I live on. He had his life verse inscribed on it, Psalm 1:3. The passage is about a man who seeks God, so read the verses around it. It says he is like a tree planted beside streams of water. Whatever he does prospers. Taken in context of the whole of the Bible, that doesn't mean that the selfish things the man might do will prosper. Only the things he does while walking along with the Lord."

Baker's expressive eyes were hungry when he glanced up at her after writing down notes. She felt a deep humbleness at how crucial this moment was. How could God possibly trust her with it?

Her voice was soft when she said, "Baker, all the wisdom in the Bible may help people who follow those general principles to make better decisions, but it will not give them peace or secure their eternity. Salvation is more than that. I have another verse for you. Don't write it down yet— just listen." She leaned forward with her hands around her tea cup, and her blue eyes looking into his brown ones.

"The Lord, your God, is with you, He is mighty to save. He will take great delight in you, He will quiet you with His love, He will rejoice over you with singing."

Baker closed his eyes, dark lashes veiling his thoughts. He swallowed hard.

"That's from Zephaniah 3:17," she said finally. "Can you even imagine hearing the Lord sing over your salvation, anticipating an eternity ahead with you?"

He didn't move, so she stood up quietly. "Thanks so much for the tea. You're really a remarkable guy, Baker Holmes."

She went over to take the notepad and pencil from in front of him on the table. She wrote down the verse and drew a heart with a little cross in the middle of it. She lightly brushed his shoulder with her hand before going up to her room.

Chapter Fourteen

"LOVE: The irresistible desire to be irresistibly desired."
—*Mark Twain*

The London fog hung like layers of sheer draperies in front of the windows of Justin Gregory's home on Friday morning. It didn't matter that there was nothing visible in the fog. Chad wasn't standing there for the view. His mind was planning the weekend.

He turned his head to the grandfather clock as it chimed the hour. Soon everyone else would be up and ready to ride to the hearings, which were scheduled to end at noon. Unless something unusual came up, this would be the last day. Next week, they would know the ruling.

His father came in first, and stopped short, taken aback by Chad's presence in the room. "You're up early, Chad. Had breakfast?"

"Not yet. I wanted to talk to you, Dad. Is it possible for us to travel to Mevagissey tonight or tomorrow?" His eyes were hopeful. Even his tan couldn't disguise the dark smudges under them.

Phillip Gregory looked at his son thoughtfully. The telltale signs of a restless night were not lost on him. He cleared his throat. "Well," he said. "I think we could all use a change of scenery after a harrowing week here in the city. If Justin's family can get away, too, we could invite them."

He stopped near Chad. "I can have my secretary get to work on the travel arrangements. Shall I call Wyeth? They have a formal reception planned in their honor on some yacht or something for tomorrow evening, and we'll need to get on the guest list."

"Sure." Chad looked distracted. "Can I talk to your secretary first?"

Phillip cleared his throat again and nodded as he said, "Of course. But before we make any plans, you ought to see this morning's paper."

Chad's heart froze. "Oh, no. More photos of me and Tippy?" He reached to take the newspaper out of his dad's hand.

He unfolded it and gaped at the front page, splashed with photos of Baker Holmes and Caroline. Chad looked up at his dad's grave expression, and then walked over to sit down in Uncle Justin's chair, putting the paper on the desk in front of him.

With a pang, he understood now what Caroline might have felt when she saw him in the news yesterday. But this was much worse, and he fought a twinge of panic. The photographer had caught her and Baker through a café window with their faces close together, walking down a darkened street side by side, and hugging outside a door. Stunned, Chad scanned to read the captions.

Baker Holmes Flees London Over Contract, claimed the headline. A paragraph underneath said, "Under pressure to sign a contract that he doesn't like, Baker Holmes, leader of the British rock band Public Parking, evaded the media to travel to his hometown, where he met Caroline A. Painter. She is a young American artist traveling with her uncle, who is creating an instructional art film. Miss Painter's American boyfriend, Phillip Chadwick Gregory III, was caught by a London photographer with the British model Tippy and published in the news headlines on Thursday. That same evening, Miss Painter was seen in the arms of Baker Holmes, whose London girlfriend broke up with him on Monday."

Chad fumed inwardly. This was what Caroline was doing before she called him last night, when she was so upset that she closed the book on him, according to Patrick. This was when she thought there was something going on between him and Tippy. Maybe she actually *was* finding solace with Baker, as the reporter claimed. After all, she was in his arms dancing at the Island Summer Dance the night after Chris broke up with her. Were both she and Baker reacting on the rebound, as the news implied?

Chad closed his eyes for a moment, reminding himself of Sunday afternoon by the pool when he resolved to be patient and keep his view on the big picture. Even if she were attracted to Baker, he would never fit into Painter Place. When this trip was over, she was going home.

Dreading to look closer but unable to tear his eyes off the photos, he studied them. In the one taken through a café window, she and Baker seemed to be looking intently at one another. Their faces were close enough to have leaned in for a kiss. Her hair was down and her lips parted as she looked intently at the young man across the table. It looked like she may have had one arm forward, as if reaching out to him. What could possibly be that important for two strangers to discuss?

He looked over at the photo of the two of them walking close together down a quaint, narrow street, silhouettes in the streetlights. But it was her—he'd know Caroline's figure anywhere.

It was the last and largest photo that was hardest to take. The paper had played it up for the best possible effect, and Chad was certain every copy had sold out early. This photo was art. Baker held Caroline in an embrace in front of a large wooden door. Light from nearby folded over them like drapery, creating dramatic shadows on one side that made the scene look like it was straight from an old black and white movie like Casablanca. Her hair was a lustrous glow entangled in his hands behind her back. Over her shoulder, his eyes were closed. His expression was solemn, so whatever Baker's intentions, he definitely wasn't fooling around.

Chad wavered between feeling sick and wanting to throw something. He glanced quickly up at his dad, who was watching him. Throwing something wasn't an option.

He took a deep breath and looked back down at the photo. Caroline's arm was by her side, not around Baker. He could only see her left arm at this angle. He decided to give her the benefit of the doubt as to the position of her right one. The caption was as hard to bear as the photo: *Baker Holmes and Caroline Painter find comfort in one another's arms, and Public Parking fans wait to see how this relationship with Miss Painter will affect his record contract.*

At that moment, Cole came in, dressed for the hearing. Realizing he'd interrupted something, he stopped, as his dad had done earlier. Phillip gestured to him to come on in. Hesitantly, Cole came toward them, curious about what Chad was looking at so intently. He came over to the desk to peer over his shoulder, and he let out a long, low whistle.

"Well, well. Congratulations, big brother." He slapped Chad on the back. "Thanks to your little diversion with the infamous Tippy, you've just made Caroline Painter the most well-known artist in the UK—maybe in the whole world, at least for today. You can't buy publicity like this—man, you can't even dream it up!" He leaned in closer to read the article.

Chad got up brusquely, giving Cole his chair. "Dad, can you call your secretary now?" His voice was businesslike and clipped. He shrugged briefly to set his shoulders and straightened his suit as he headed toward the door. "I'll take it in the next room."

Phillip dialed the phone. "I'll check with Justin about this weekend. Let me know when you're finished," he said to Chad's back. He looked at Cole, who was reading and grinning. "Cole," he said to his son.

Cole looked up absently in acknowledgment of his dad.

"Cole, would you like to invite Shannon to spend the weekend with us in Cornwall? We'll be attending a formal reception, so she'll need to dress appropriately."

Cole whooped in a very non-British response, pumping one fist. "I'll call her on the other line as soon as I finish this caption." He stood up slowly, keeping his eyes glued to the paper lying on his uncle's desk. He reluctantly pulled himself away to leave the room. "Wait until she sees the paper today! Can we take this with us?"

***

Phillip phoned in an attempt to catch Wyeth before the group left for the day. He asked if it was too late to add up to ten more to the guest list for the reception after dinner was served, telling him that they had no definite travel agenda yet. He asked that Wyeth not tell the rest of the group in case things didn't work out.

"Oh, and Wyeth," said Phillip. "For the record, Chad asked us to travel before he saw today's paper."

"Today's paper?"

"A very good photographer followed Baker and made the most of his outing with Caroline. The photos are remarkably dramatic, and I admit I was almost convinced myself. It's been turned into a romantic rebound between him and Caroline, fueled by Baker's London girlfriend with the same record label breaking up with him on Monday and the photo of Chad yesterday with Tippy. The paper is stirring up Public Parking fans with speculation on how the beautiful young artist from America might influence Baker in signing the contract here."

"Well, they don't know yet how true this is. She's had a dramatic influence on him that I suspect will end with him not signing." Wyeth reported what Caroline had told him and Chrissy when she came in the night before and asked that Phillip pass along that information to Chad.

"Caroline hasn't come down yet, but if you don't get to Mevagissey tomorrow, let's try to get these two on the phone. It's not what it looks like. And it wasn't payback. She's struggling, but not over Baker Holmes."

After he hung up the phone, Wyeth heard Mr. Holmes come in from the back porch. He walked through the kitchen to the foyer, where he saw Wyeth. He tentatively held out a newspaper in his hands.

"Beggin' your pardon, Mr. Painter, but there's been a misunderstandin'. You see, my nephew, he's—well, often photographed, you might say. These reporters only get about 'alf what they say right. The rest is—improvised."

Wyeth looked back at him with a grim smile, taking the folded paper but not looking at it.

"It's all right, Mr. Holmes. I've already had a call about this and understand."

"We—don't want any bad experiences for our guests," stumbled Mr. Holmes. "Baker's a good kid. We're ever so grateful at how your niece took up with 'im. He rose early with us before he headed out to see our pastor. He told us he's a Christian now. My mom has cried for joy on and off all mornin'." He beamed at Wyeth.

Wyeth stood speechless for a few moments, taking Mr. Holmes' words in. He finally spoke quietly. "Praise God . . . thank you for sharing that with me, Mr. Holmes."

"We're having a party here tonight, and there'll be lots o' food. You and your group are invited to have dinner and celebrate with us. We hope you'll stay."

"We'd be honored, Mr. Holmes. You're very gracious."

Mr. Holmes nodded and left to get back to running the inn. Wyeth took the newspaper into the sitting room to open it. Scanning the page, he groaned out loud. He wished his brother would never see this. After reading it more carefully, he looked absently out of a window into the

141

swirling fog. Could this publicity be a blessing in disguise? A knock on the foyer door interrupted his thoughts.

Someone must have tucked their head inside because he heard a voice say, "Holmes, a delivery if you please!"

Mr. Holmes was already on his way to the door, greeting the person he apparently knew. They exchanged pleasantries, talked about the upcoming storm expected tonight, and said goodbye. Then Mr. Holmes peeked into the sitting room at Wyeth.

"Mr. Painter, someone's gone and sent flowers to your niece," he said. "Shall I leave 'em in the foyer, or take 'em upstairs?"

Wyeth looked at his watch and then rose from his chair. "I'll take them." He picked up the newspaper and walked into the foyer. A bouquet of cheerful sunflowers in an expensive-looking porcelain vase sat on the desk with an envelope bearing Caroline's name.

The vase was truly a piece of art, and Wyeth whistled appreciatively before he squatted down to look levelly at it on the desk. It reminded him of an antique Canton style but with modern stylized images on it. Each section had a painting of something that could represent Painter Place. Palm fronds were creatively designed into heart shapes, and a couple of herons were unmistakably a pair of lovebirds.

Wyeth grinned and straightened to stand again. He had no doubt who sent this.

It would take two hands to handle. He folded the paper so that it would tuck into his belt at the small of his back. Then he carried the bouquet upstairs. At the top, Jesse and the other cameraman were just coming out of their rooms. Wyeth craned his neck to see around the profusion of flowers.

Jesse said, "Mr. Painter, can I open a door for you?"

Wyeth asked him to knock on Caroline's door. There was an excited murmur as the photographer, Cameron, and Natalie heard the others and opened their doors to see what was happening.

Jesse knocked and said, "Caroline, it's me, Jesse. Your uncle has something for you, if you can open the door."

Jesse looked over at Cameron and whispered, "What if she's not—you know, dressed yet?"

"Then she won't open the door, knucklehead!" shot Cameron, rolling his eyes. "You told her who it was."

The other cameraman hissed, "Forget it—you'd never be that lucky."

By now, Chrissy had also opened her door. "What in the world?" she exclaimed at the sight of all of them in the hallway.

Caroline opened her door wide, fully dressed and brushing her hair, to find everyone gathered there. She looked down at her watch in confusion. "Am I late?" she asked.

Her uncle moved up to the door behind the sunflowers. "Someone sent you these," he said.

"Seriously? They're beautiful! And that vase! Okay, set them over here." She moved out of the doorway and pointed to the dresser.

As her uncle moved past her, Caroline saw herself in a photo in the paper tucked into the back of his belt. She snatched it up, opening it to see the other side while he found a place for the vase. Her eyes were almost as wide as the centers of the sunflowers when she wailed, "What kind of girl will people assume I am? Will Chad see this newspaper?"

"He already has," said her uncle solemnly. He rubbed his hand over his face. "Your daddy's gonna kill me, but I honestly think this will turn out right."

From her room door, Jesse had a glimpse of the subject matter in the photos. He pumped his arm, squeezed his eyes tight, and wrinkled his nose. "YES!" he burst out. Looking around at their astonished faces, he said to the others, "Man, I love working with this family! There's more drama than a Saturday afternoon marathon of B-rated sci-fi flicks!"

Natalie and Chrissy gently pushed Jesse out of their way to enter Caroline's room.

"What's in the newspaper?" Natalie reached Caroline first and stood beside her to take one side of the page into her hands. She gasped. "Caroline, I thought you said you'd be in your room last night!"

Caroline explained that she'd been at her easel on the balcony when Baker had come up on the street and asked to buy the painting and to take her to get coffee.

Jesse mimicked static and a voice-over in a movie, holding his hand to his mouth like a microphone. "A good man who walked away still lurked in Caroline's heart when Chad came back home, ready to sweep her into his arms and live happily ever after. Chad found that two in her heart is one too many, and it quickly became three, which is a crowd. When we reach four, somebody's gonna die!"

Guffaws came from the hallway.

Wyeth was trying not to smile, leaning back onto the dresser near the sunflowers, his arms crossed. "Listen up, guys. Something amazing came out of all this mess. Baker Holmes came to know Christ last night after talking to Caroline, and he's meeting with his pastor this morning. No matter how this looks at the moment, God is working it all for good. With this kind of publicity, you can bet that God's going to get some glory when Baker begins telling his reasons for the change in his life."

Caroline looked thoughtfully at her uncle. They all seemed to be mulling this observation over.

Wyeth cleared his throat. "Be ready to get a lot of attention when we go out anywhere, and keep an eye out for journalists, photographers, and Public Parking fans. Try not to be caught in a way that makes you look like that fourth guy with Caroline—the one who's gonna die."

Jesse grinned and reached out his arm. "Hey, can we see that paper? The photo at the door just made someone's career. Whose name is on the photo credits?"

Natalie handed it to him while Chrissy asked, "Who sent the flowers? The vase reminds me of Painter Place."

Caroline hesitantly stepped forward to take the envelope. She looked at it as if gathering her courage for another unexpected turn of events. Then she slid the card out, opened it, and read the inside.

She looked up at her uncle. "Did Chad send this before or after seeing the photos?"

"After," Wyeth said solemnly.

144

"Can you tell us what the note says, or is it too private?" asked Natalie. She would normally never dream of asking such a question, but she wanted to tell Patrick about this, and Caroline didn't seem upset by the contents.

Caroline said, "It's from a song he dedicated to me at the Island Summer Dance last Saturday. It says,

'When the summer moon is on the rise
And you're dancin' under starlit skies
Please don't let stars get in your eyes, just
Save your heart for me.'

From my heart to yours,

Chad"

Chapter Fifteen

"A work of art which did not begin in emotion is not art."
—*Paul Cezanne*

The fog lifted in the late morning, giving way to a slightly overcast day. The Painter group set out to get some filming done. Caroline was glad she was still Uncle Wyeth's retriever, following directions. She was embarrassed to be the cause of so much distraction for the last couple of days.

She enjoyed the creative aspect of filming something like an art demo, which could be boring if not handled well. She'd seen enough of those and cringed for the artists. The perspective that Jesse shared with her expanded how she imagined the presentation in the film. Sometimes, he'd motion for her to work with him.

When they took a break in the early afternoon, Cameron pulled her and her snack aside with him. He looked around for photographers and was careful not to stand close to her as he drained about half of a bottle of water. She was eating a small apple, making a row of bites all around the top before beginning another row parallel to it.

"Juliette doesn't know that when I agreed to take this job on short notice for her big brother, I actually delayed another job to take it. I decided that it was time to get to know her family." He looked over at Caroline. "The kind of publicity that you and Chad are getting reminds me of why she and I have kept our relationship a secret."

Caroline almost dropped her apple core. With an effort, she swallowed the bite in her mouth without choking while her mind scrambled for something appropriate to say.

"Are you trying to tell me that you and my—you and Juliette—are a couple?" she finally managed to stammer.

Cameron nodded. "It's not easy to have a typical relationship when we both travel so much. She's a little more than two years older, but she plays roles as young as a college kid. I'm older than I look."

He grinned. "That skirt and blouse you wore at the dance last Saturday—she knew I'd remember it. You and Juliette look so much alike that she thought it would be fun to remind me of a date spent with her." He kept his grin as he looked out over the water momentarily, lost in a memory. "She is a breath of fresh air to a serious guy like me. Now I see that most of her family has the same positive outlook and playful personality. There's never a dull moment."

Caroline laughed. "It's a way to cope with all of the drama we don't mean to create," she quipped, recalling Jesse's comment earlier that morning.

After a pause, Cameron's face grew serious again. "In the circles that Juliette and I work in, if the media found out that we get together sometimes, it would be a mess. I don't want her to be portrayed as doing something she'd never do to try to influence her way into movie roles."

Caroline was thoughtful about this before she said, "Wow. You two have a complicated relationship."

He drank more from his water bottle and smiled wryly at her. "You have no idea."

He shook his head as if to clear it. "We have a common mindset, though. Imagine being successful in our business when you're a Christian. It's like walking a tightrope, and you have to let a lot of things go." He paused to look around before he continued quickly. "I wanted to tell you that I was wary of Chad when I met him last Saturday. Juliette adores you, and I felt like I already knew you when I came to Painter Place. I sort of appointed myself to keep my eye on the unexpected turn of events when he showed up. I warned her that she wasn't there to see Chad's resolve from a male perspective. She laughed and assured me that everything was fine, and she expected you two to get together someday. She explained something about how my being from 'off' was going to affect how I process this. In the week since then, Chad's really grown on me." He shrugged. "I admire how he handles himself."

"Thank you for telling me this. It explains a lot of things," Caroline said.

The crew was heading back to their equipment. "It's time to get back, but I hope we can talk sometime. I'd like to hear some of the legends about

Painter Place and see what you and Wyeth think about shooting some scenes there for a movie I'm working on."

"No kidding? Sure," she agreed, walking with him as far as the cameras, which were set to overlook the harbor. Wyeth had been teaching the illusion of how to create a representational view of rigging on fishing boats with a minimal number of actual marks in a painting. Caroline got out the sketchbook she'd been carrying around, filling in another quick study while her uncle didn't need her.

At first, they weren't sure if the increasing number of bystanders was due to the weekend tourists coming in or curiosity over the newspaper report. Visitors came up to the light barricade, where a sign prohibited crossing into the filming area. Many were young adults, and all were respectful, murmuring among themselves when they talked, as if spectators at a golf tournament.

Wyeth finished his painting session much earlier than scheduled. He removed his microphone and walked over to Cameron, who had just finished talking to his photographer.

Wyeth and Cameron held their heads close together, and the artist gestured to the cliffs that dropped into the water in the distance. Cameron crossed one arm over his waist and propped the other at a right angle to it, putting his fist to his chin as if in deep thought. He glanced over to the bystanders. Finally, he nodded at Wyeth, and they took a few steps toward Caroline, who was chatting with Natalie and Chrissy about the reception the next evening.

"Caroline, can we speak to you?" asked her uncle, motioning for her to join them.

She hesitated in surprise at being singled out. As she walked over, it occurred to her that if Cameron ever married her Aunt Juliette, these men would both be uncles to her, and she couldn't help but smile at the sight of them working together with such intensity.

The rest of the crew watched, whispering to one another, trying to guess what this could be about.

"Caroline, would you like to do a painting on site here of the distant cliffs, similar to the one you did last night for Baker? It's a different view and time of day, and you'd have to improvise with my brushes and colors.

It could be a trial run for being on your own next Monday, with me here to fall back on. We'll film it just in case it works."

Her uncle waited and searched her face. "You can reveal it at the barricades, and include it in the exhibit at the reception tomorrow night."

Cameron quickly added, "If you're not ready for this, just say so. There's no pressure. We can pack up and go."

He tilted his head to indicate the crowd. "They're here because of you and Baker, and you have a chance to deliver something positive to the feeding frenzy. My photographer told me a few minutes ago that he spotted reporters trying to blend in. It would be great publicity if the painting is a success."

Caroline looked from Cameron to her uncle and bit her lower lip. "I don't feel the same way as I did when I painted the cliffs last night, so it will turn out differently. But—I trust your instincts. I'll do it."

Wyeth nodded and put his arm around her shoulders, leaning his head down a little toward her ear to talk as he led her toward his empty easel. Cameron jogged over to his crew and drew them into a huddle.

Caroline was used to painting in public, so she didn't feel shy. But she couldn't help feeling off balance about how to approach this unplanned painting. There was going to be a struggle. She would naturally lean toward painting this in her typical style, but she felt that her uncle was hoping to see something like the painting that Baker had collected.

She and her uncle switched roles. He helped her choose the tubes of acrylic paint that would blend closely into the color scheme she used last night.

As she stood under the canopy that shaded the easel, Cameron attached her microphone. Natalie discreetly fussed with freshening up her makeup and taming her hair. She handed her a water bottle and some lip balm and gloss to put on before filming, in case her mouth felt dry from talking in the salty breeze.

Taking a deep breath and smiling, Caroline indicated to Cameron that she was ready. Standing straight with head held high at the easel, she tried to speak clearly into the cameras as much as she could. The crew adjusted to filming or photographing over her shoulder when needed, or coming around to her side and in front of her. She improvised her mental organization of her usual process to explain the technique of using values instead of realistic colors for the subject.

It helped that she had painted a similar scene in a similar way the night before—blocking in the main shapes went very quickly and didn't require much concentration. She was easily able to stop and make points about the composition. But she felt the most important key to recreating the mood of last night's painting was going to be when she started painting with her back to the cameras.

She had decided to dare to let herself remember something that had fleetingly crossed her mind when she woke up this morning. She'd pushed it away then, but now she would face the pain from what had happened to her exactly one week ago when she showed up for a date with Chris.

As she painted, his face flashed into her mind. He was sitting cross-legged on the ground, looking at her. He took both of her hands into his and rested their joined hands on the knees of her jeans. He held her gaze intently with green eyes that had dark green rays fanned out into them, like a palm. "Caroline, I can't take you where I'm going, and you can't wait for me to return. It's breaking my heart, and I'm miserable that it may break yours."

She felt breathless at the intensity of the memory and paused with the paintbrush in mid-air. Instinctively, she wanted to grab something to break her sudden fall backwards into a hole where feelings had not yet healed, like the adventure movies where someone fell and caught a root or vine before they hit the bottom where the deadly vipers were.

Gulping and forging ahead with her brush, she painted in quick, powerful strokes of movement the sea where it slammed into the base of the cliffs, breaking apart into a zillion pieces that fell back harmlessly as spray. She created more spray by pulling back on bristles of her brush.

Now that she'd opened the door to memories, they flooded in. She heard Chris' voice again in her head. "I can now see that I was running from what I was meant to be, and wanted you to run with me, away from what you are meant to be."

She pressed her lips together and looked down at her palette, loading her brush with the color she'd chosen for the sky. She painted it as a free, open space over the scene.

"What you are meant to be." Chris' words repeated in her memory. Unexpectedly, something she couldn't define opened up inside to free her. She stopped painting and stepped back when she felt it.

She hoped it was only for an instant that she stood there like that. A passing boat full of fishermen looked at her curiously over the back of the easel, reminding her of where she was. Regaining her composure, she turned to comment on the progress she had made on the painting, as if nothing had happened. A glance at her uncle told her that he was studying her reactions.

She gathered her thoughts and did a quick evaluation of her progress for the benefit of the cameras, then turned back to the canvas.

She mentally searched for unresolved tension that might carry her to the completion of this painting. Brush in hand, she kept her eye on the distant cliffs and thought about why she was doing this in the first place.

That led to the photos, resulting in a quick stroke that gave personality to the focal point of the painting. Then she imagined what Chad must have felt when he saw her with Baker in the newspaper, which led to her imagining what she'd have felt if she'd seen him wrapped up with Tippy like that.

The last thought pushed a stroke over the cliff in a blurred, lost edge. Anyone walking there would have fallen into the tumult below.

Standing back, she decided it was finished. She told the cameras that at this point, anything more she could add would only get her bogged down into details that would detract from the impact of the painting. She signed her name, and the crew took the photos they needed.

She looked at her uncle, who was standing like a proud father wearing a broad smile of satisfaction.

They all began to efficiently pack up the equipment, save for a camera on a strap that Jesse could handle on his shoulder. He would be filming the interaction with the bystanders.

Wyeth put her dry painting into her hands to carry as they went over to the barricade, where he greeted everyone before trying to walk through. "For many of you, this harbor is an everyday sight, and perhaps you even take it for granted. We're seeing it with fresh eyes, and my niece and I will be capturing it in both paintings and teaching films. We're enjoying the views, the villagers, and, of course, the food."

The group clapped. "Can we see the painting that Caroline just finished?" someone asked, and others joined in to agree. Uncle Wyeth nodded to Caroline with an encouraging smile. She held it in front of her, and cameras began clicking.

"Tell us more about the painting," a young woman said.

"Why did you choose those colors?" Now people were asking several questions all at once.

Caroline's confidence chose that moment to make an appearance again after a week of wavering. She felt it surge, and she took a step toward them. They grew quiet.

"This painting is an experimental direction for me—one of my two deviant works, if you want to think of it that way." She paused and smiled at the positive response from the young adults before she continued.

"This painting was born out of some recent painful experiences. We don't have cliffs where I live on the Atlantic, and yours drew me in as a visual representation of the abrupt changes that happen in life. Those changes can distort our perspective, so I distorted the colors in my painting, keeping them in the same value tones as the scene—an art technique I don't have time to explain here."

"Was this painful experience from seeing your American boyfriend cheating on you with Tippy?" asked someone in the crowd.

"Will you be giving this painting to Baker Holmes?" shouted someone else in the crowd at the same time. Suddenly, the group was more animated.

Cameron and the photographer stepped forward, but Caroline put up one hand to the crowd and held her painting in the other.

"If you're really interested in my response, you'll have to be quiet. I don't have a loud voice," she said with her eyebrows raised.

Wyeth bit his lips in a line to keep from smiling. The old Caroline had returned, and her manner was so much like her grandmother Savanna.

When the only noises came from the harbor itself, Caroline spoke again. "Yes, I was very upset about the newspaper photo of my friend

Chad Gregory and Tippy yesterday, but it was not the first of my recent painful experiences. My comment about it, for the record, is that I believe the explanation given to me by Chad and the Gregory family. They have a track record of impeccable integrity that dates back hundreds of years with my family—all the way back to their friendship here in England. They've never met the model who appeared in the photo, and Chad was simply being polite when she bumped into him on the street. Clearly, he was someone's target, to their own ends. It's a shame that so many people have a creed of living for themselves, at the expense of others. If more of us lived by the Golden Rule, the world would be a better place."

Caroline paused as the crowd murmured, and there was some applause. She turned her painting to look at it herself.

"As for whether I'll give this painting to my new friend, Baker Holmes, it's presumptuous to assume that he'd even want it. He collected the first one last night. This one will be part of a private exhibition at a reception tomorrow evening here in the harbor."

"Did anything happen between you and Baker Holmes that will affect his contract decision?" shouted a man with a notepad and pencil. Another man beside him had a camera in front of his face. Everyone seemed to hold their breath, waiting for her answer.

Caroline looked levelly at the reporter. "I hope so" she answered, nodding her head slightly. "But I didn't know who he was at the time, and what happened wasn't of a romantic nature."

The gathering became animated again, and this time, her uncle and the crew surrounded her as if on cue. They pushed the barricade aside, and the babbling crowd parted to let them through.

***

"Chad, come here, quick!" urged Cole, shouting from across the hallway as the family was finishing dinner at Justin Gregory's home in Kensington. Chad was already leaving the dining room and crossed to the family room in two athletic strides of his long legs. He felt like he'd been walking in a mine field since he'd arrived in London, so every muscle was ready to spring into action.

He heard Wyeth Painter's voice before he got into the room and knew it had to be coming from the television. Chad came closer, not certain if he

154

dreaded this or welcomed it. His family was gathering behind him, everyone trying to find a spot where they could see the screen.

The cameras panned out so that the harbor setting appeared behind Caroline, and his heart jumped into his throat. He was tense with wariness, trying to brace himself. She was holding a painting in front of her at waist height.

Sleek, sporty sunglasses worn on top of her head tamed back the long blond hair that played gently around her bare sun-kissed shoulders in the sea breeze. She was wearing a snappy sleeveless knit top with a squared-off, ribbon-trimmed nautical sailor collar.

Bystanders were asking her questions all at once. Chad watched in fascination as Caroline took a confident step toward them, in charge. He warmed at the sound of her voice—the sound of home.

Caroline's voice continued, and the reporter broke in with the cameras zooming closer to a painting in Caroline's hands. Chad's brows shot up in surprise. It was really good, but it wasn't—her. Some of the strokes had obviously come from a passionate energy.

"Was this painful experience from seeing your American boyfriend cheating on you with Tippy?" asked someone in the crowd.

Chad gasped. He desperately searched her face in that instant for a clue as to how she was going to handle this one. She blinked, but he saw her characteristic poise kick in, and she responded coolly to express confidence in him and his family.

The television studio reporter did a voice-over while the photo of Chad and Tippy flashed across the screen. The reporter explained that this was the photo in the news the day before. She pointed out that although the question from the crowd used the term "boyfriend" for Chad Gregory, Caroline used the term "friend" in her response. Chad had painfully noticed the same point.

Then the images of Baker and Caroline from today's paper were flashed on the screen in succession. The reporter said that these photos had attracted a growing crowd of fans into Baker's hometown today, and that they were gathered at the harbor barricade to see Miss Painter and ask her about her relationship with Baker.

The screen went back to Caroline's interview at the harbor. "Did anything happen between you and Baker Holmes that will affect his contract decision?" asked a reporter on the scene.

Chad braced himself.

Caroline kept looking directly into the reporter's eyes and replied, "I hope so. But I didn't know who he was at the time, and what happened wasn't of a romantic nature."

A new photo was splashed onto the screen. It was of Baker Holmes looking up and pointing at either Caroline or the painting she was holding. It seemed to be in the last light of the evening. She was on a balcony a few feet over his head. She was looking at him, blonde hair hanging down, returning his smile. The painting looked like another scene of the cliffs, similar to the one she showed today at the harbor.

The reporter wrapped up the segment with the last photo by saying, "Miss Painter's statement that she hopes she has influenced Baker Holmes' contract decision added fuel to the fire of intrigue for fans of Public Parking. Despite Miss Painter's denial, the photos of her and Baker Holmes last night make this one as remarkably romantic as a scene from *Romeo and Juliet*. The resemblance of today's painting to the one she's holding in the photograph, which he appears to like, makes his fans wonder if she painted a second one for him today. One fan voiced this comment for all of the rest after she left the harbor."

And then a young lady's face appeared in a screen full of other faces getting close to the camera. "Perhaps Caroline Painter didn't need to know who Baker Holmes actually was to fall for him and decide that Phillip Chadwick Gregory III is just a loyal friend after all."

Chad felt his breath knocked out of him. He didn't see where the gasps in the room came from because he couldn't tear his eyes from the television. The screen then filled with images of his family leaving Gregory Global this week.

"In a related story tonight, the Gregory family's woes are not over. Private hearings have been conducted this week to determine if their international finance corporation, Gregory Global, leaked private account information about several of its investors. Threadneedle Street watches and waits for the decision, which will be made early next week. When asked for an official comment, Justin Gregory, who lives here in London and manages the firm for his family, stated that all of the accounts at Gregory Global are safe."

Justin abruptly walked out of the room while the news moved on to the weekend weather. Phillip strode over to the television and turned it off just before the phone rang. He picked it up while the rest of the family remained where they were. There was an air of confusion and urgency that kept everyone quiet.

Gregory Global's publicity manager was on the phone, and Justin came back in after Phillip answered. He went over to stand beside his brother, indicating that he needed to speak to him. Phillip nodded but let the manager finish whatever he was saying before telling him to hang on. He covered the mouthpiece and paused for Justin, who looked at him and then at the family.

"The house is staked out by the press right now. The security we hired this week is keeping an eye on things, and I let them know that the formalwear delivery is the *only* thing that gets through tonight," Justin said.

Phillip nodded agreement while Cole, Chad, and their cousin protested. Their cousin had a date, Cole wanted Shannon to come over to stay and leave with the family tomorrow, and Chad said he needed to go running.

Phillip's voice was firm. "No one is leaving this house tonight, and no one is coming over. They would follow you around and ask questions. Chad, do you really want to answer the one about your thoughts on the fan's comment in the interview tonight, or show up in a photo in the morning paper jogging on a Friday night with a melodramatic caption about being lonely and heartbroken? Cole, do you really want to draw *any* attention to yourself or your girlfriend right now?"

Phillip raised his eyebrows and waited for his sons' responses. Chad began pacing with his hands on his hips, and Cole blew out his breath and shook his head.

Their cousin grudgingly nodded in agreement at Justin, but muttered, "I didn't even do anything."

Phillip took his hand from the phone to return to his phone call. "Justin says they're set up outside the house now. Security is handling it."

He looked around the room at everyone while he listened, then said, "We agree, but we have some tense young adults locked up in here—there may be an explosion."

He allowed a tight smile when he caught Chad's eye, then said into the phone, "Yes, I think her comments about us will go a long way, too. She's very poised, and it was great timing. Tell me what you found out and what we can do about it."

Cole got up and went to open a door on the cabinets built into one whole wall of the large den. He pulled out a box for the board game Risk and headed toward a table. "Come on, let's choose up teams and try to take over the world. That's what everybody thinks we do anyway."

Chapter Sixteen

"The world cannot hate us, we are too much like its own.
Oh that God would make us dangerous!"
—*Jim Elliot*

The inn was crowded and noisy in a happy way on Friday evening, ringing with laughter and stories as the Holmes family celebrated Baker's upcoming baptism and career decision. The petite girl that Caroline had met in the café the night before was there, looking very much at home.

A soft summer rain was just beginning to come down when large saffron buns and tea were served for dessert, and Baker nodded his head at the back door as an invitation to Caroline to come out to sit on the porch with him. They took their plates outside to some rocking chairs and settled in.

"I saw the paper and heard about what happened at the harbor," said Baker as he watched her sample a bite of one currant-filled teardrop on her saffron bun. "I've been trouble for you, eh? But admit it, the photos were smashing!"

"They were artistic," she agreed. "I'm afraid to think of how many years and in how many places they'll be showing up. I'd have been convinced if I hadn't been there."

She looked into the distance while she enjoyed another bite, then she said quietly, "Am I just naïve, Baker? Are you ever surprised at the way people's lives are manipulated by the media, just for a payoff in creating a sensation? Aren't there enough real issues in the world?"

Baker's hearty laugh lightened her brief moodiness. "Absolutely not! 'Real' happens any day, and people get used to it. They miss out on their own lives thinkin' everyone else is more interesting."

"They're throwing away a gift," Caroline said with conviction. She put her plate down and sat back in the rocker. "Life happens while they aren't even paying attention, and soon it's over."

They sat looking out at the rain on the garden without speaking for a few minutes. Leaves danced with each pelt of a raindrop, and water trickled into the centers of blooming flowers. Eventually, Baker said, "Can I mention your name in my personal testimony? When you asked me about Jesus—you made Him sound like someone I wanted to know because you thought so much of Him."

He moved up to the edge of his rocker with excitement in his voice. "I just—I feel like I want to shout about it to everyone in the world! Two guys in my band are Christians—they just weren't vocal about it because they knew I wasn't, and they didn't want to rock the boat. The other one was like me, and when he heard my story today, he made the same decision I did. The members of Public Parking all agreed to call our agent and turn the offer down. We don't know what's goin' to happen to us, but we feel free, like we've walked away from a huge burden. I wish they could've been here tonight—maybe you can meet them sometime."

Tears stung Caroline's eyes. "Baker—I don't know what to say. This had to happen because of other people's prayers and influence in your life, not just talking to me. It's a blessing and a lesson I'll never forget. I learned that I can miss what the Lord is doing all around me in much more important matters than my own hurt feelings. I'd be honored if you ever want to include me in your personal story. And I'm so thrilled that in your first day as a Christian, you led a friend to eternity."

Baker's eyes were serious when he said, "That's the best feeling in the world. I hope it happens a lot more." His mood suddenly changed, and he grinned charmingly at her. "Maybe I should have reminded you that I write songs—I didn't use your name, but you're already in the one I wrote today. The village asked us to play for all the fans in town for about half an hour tomorrow, and we asked to play at sunset under the lighthouse. 'Inner Light' is about how the Lord used 'a friend'—you—to shine into my darkness. Come and let me introduce you. I'll set the record straight in public about the photos."

Caroline gasped and reached her hand out to his arm. "Did you honestly write a song about this? I'll be in the harbor at sunset, on a yacht for a reception to honor me and my uncle. I won't be able to leave, but surely we'll be able to hear you."

Baker looked thoughtful. "I'll ask around and get the yacht docked near the lighthouse."

The petite girl stepped onto the porch and walked up to Baker's chair. "There you are!"

"I was askin' Caroline to be at the harbor for our performance," Baker said as he smiled up at her. "Caroline, Beth used to be my girl, before me and my mates settled in London."

Caroline smiled and told Beth it was nice to meet again. "Now I know why you looked so comfortable around Baker's family."

Beth laughed. "I go to church with 'em, but had to let Baker go—unequally yoked, you know. I never stopped prayin' for 'im."

The sound of distant thunder sent them into the house, where guests were hoping that the weather would hold out until they got home. Beth gathered her umbrella and an empty platter. Baker brushed her cheek with a light kiss as she walked out the huge front door.

Baker's uncle was in the foyer seeing guests out. He said, "Oh, Mr. Painter, letters came in the post today."

He pulled open a drawer in the foyer desk to take out a bundle of letters tied with a string, handing them to Wyeth. "The phone is disconnected on account of calls about Baker. I'll get it all set for you in case you need it."

"I'll get it, and I'll screen the calls." Baker quickly got down on his knees under the desk and reached for the cord.

Wyeth untied the string on the letters and handed envelopes to Caroline and Natalie, keeping one addressed to him. "Shelly wrote me—this should be interesting." He chuckled to himself.

"I'm ready to turn in," said Natalie as she looked at the letter in her hand. Caroline saw her brother's handwriting on it and smiled to herself. Natalie turned to Caroline and Chrissy. "I'll see everyone at breakfast. We're still just hanging out here tomorrow to rest and get ready for the reception, right?"

Cameron had been looking over her shoulder to see who her letter was from. His eyes met Caroline's when he looked back up.

"Like we can leave?" he said, answering his sister. "We'll need to get creative to even get to the yacht. Looks like the crew and I will get a lot of editing done."

Thunder clapped, and the old house trembled. The phone was already ringing as Caroline ran up the stairs with her letters from home. She could hardly wait to read what her family and Shelly had written, but she'd start with the one from her mom. The lace curtains shivered in the thunder as she cuddled up to her pillow in lamplight to read in bed.

***

Sunflowers were the first thing that Caroline saw when she opened her eyes, and she smiled. On her nightstand were her little travel Bible, opened letters, the florist's card with a message from Chad, and his ring on the chain. For that sweet, quiet moment, life was good. It was calm. It was peaceful.

Sighing, she closed her eyes again and prayed before beginning the day. "Lord, thank You for loving me and for the gift of this day. I hand it back to you as a blank canvas to write or paint on. We both know I'd only make a mess if I tried to do anything on my own."

Peeking out the old French doors, she saw that there was a small crowd of curious people milling around outside. She couldn't paint from the balcony with all the attention, so she decided to stay in her room to paint something from her sketchbook, or perhaps those gorgeous sunflowers. Their soft, dark eyes seemed to look at her solemnly from under their heavy fringes of golden eyelashes.

She stretched through a mini workout routine and showered, her body craving a long walk or jog that couldn't happen. After dressing, she picked up a note slipped into her room under the door. She read her uncle's handwriting. "Last night, bids were coming in on your painting after it was shown on the television news. Decide if you want to sell it. Oh, and you're Baker's grandmother's darling now. She has a special breakfast being kept hot for you."

Mrs. Holmes was in the kitchen kneading dough for some home-baked bread and had a warm, sweet loaf just out of the oven. She wiped flour off her hands and fussed over serving Caroline, chatting about Baker's plans for the day and about the dinner party the evening before. Cornish clotted cream and several homemade berry jams were out on the table beside the loaf, along with boiled eggs. Mrs. Holmes poured some tea in a beautiful porcelain cup for Caroline and indicated for her to sit down while she filled a matching plate.

Caroline paused at the bottom of the stairs on her way back up, noticing the two newspapers in their usual place on the desk. She struggled with her curiosity before walking over.

She was relieved to see that no one she knew was in the headlines of the London paper, but she saw a mention of Public Parking in the Arts and Entertainment section and Gregory Global was referenced in the Financials. She turned to a large concert photo of Public Parking, with Baker at a microphone, his long bangs down over one eye and the other squeezed tightly shut while he sang. The headline announced that the band would not sign the new contract with their record label and was seeking another one.

A smaller sub-headline asked, "What Did She Say?" Underneath, the article stated that she met Baker Holmes and spent an evening with him before she knew who he was. Then it quoted her statement from the harbor interview.

A fan comment caught her eye, and her heart skipped a beat. Someone speculated that her use of the term "friend" for Chad instead of "boyfriend" in the question implied that she had changed her mind about Chad once she met Baker.

She folded the London paper and looked at the local one. Baker was the headline, and his performance tonight was the highlight. It also questioned what she could have possibly said to influence the outcome of his career.

She stood there with a thoughtful look on her face before going upstairs, where she painted her version of the sunflowers on the dresser in the beautiful vase that reminded her of Painter Place. Soon, the sunflowers would be blooming there.

She placed the ship in the bottle close to it, smiling at the memories of Chad's love of tall ships and the adventure stories of the high seas. As a boy, he had been fascinated with how to get them into a bottle. With a little imagination, it was like holding unlimited adventure in your hands. He'd never stopped believing the legends of shipwrecks and lost treasure on the island.

She didn't wrestle with the painting this time, and the work flowed quickly. She noticed that her style was beginning to lean towards bold, modern colors on this trip. As she painted, she listened to music in her headphones and made an important decision.

Chapter Seventeen

*"The depth and strength of a human character are defined by its moral reserves.
People reveal themselves completely
only when they are thrown out of the customary conditions of their life,
for only then do they have to fall back on their reserves."*
—*Leonardo da Vinci*

"Man, oh man," said Jesse with a whistle. "Tell those photographers to bring it on!"

The ladies demurely smiled at the appreciation from the tuxedoed men in their group who waited to put them into limousines.

Chrissy could still have been a model on a runway in her sleek metallic marine blue dress with a slit that reached above her knee and white sequined contrast fabric gathered into a large bow across her shoulder. Her upswept hairstyle highlighted a comb of the same white sequined fabric in the bow, but nestled in a base of blue tulle and white pearls.

Natalie wore a Greek goddess-inspired gold and bronze gown that shimmered when she moved. Long, dangling earrings of laurel leaves swayed from her ears, and her hair was gorgeous—pulled up all around with a French braid that gathered some falling strands wrapped in strings of bronze pearls and crystals.

Caroline felt transformed when she saw herself in a mirror in Juliette's dress with the upswept hairstyle that Chrissy had created. Natalie had smudged a sultry effect in eye shadow and liner, a new trick for Caroline.

She loved the dreamy dress, with its satiny aqua sheen and the slice of sheer back panel embroidered with peacock feather designs. It was much more alluring than if the one strapless shoulder side had only been a low cut back. The best part of the dress, however, was the trim on an otherwise simple affair. A sheer, metallic bronze strip of fabric gathered peacock feathers and ran them diagonally up from the right waist side of the dress to the left shoulder, where peacock feathers sprang up like a corsage. An ornamental flower of deep marine blue feathers formed the base of the shoulder ornament and had a center of sparkling clear crystals. In her hair,

Chrissy set a matching comb with small peacock feathers surrounding a similar feather flower in aqua tulle edging with tiny bronze pearls.

The driver loaded their paintings into the car, and each of the ladies carried a small bag with a change of clothes in case they had difficulty getting back to the inn. Caroline knew she'd never get far from the yacht in the dyed designer sandals decorated with ornamental peacock feathers. She had packed tennis shoes, shorts, and a blouse and had tucked makeup samples into Aunt Juliette's fabulous peacock evening bag for touch-ups.

Their own photographer snapped some shots of the formally dressed group outside the old jade door of the inn and in front of the limousines, letting the crowded street become part of the composition. Some questions were shouted from the street, but the Painter group just smiled and ignored them before getting into the cars as quickly as possible.

***

One look at Dante Kent said volumes. He was one of the most striking men that Caroline had ever seen. It wasn't that he was handsome, but every feature on his face was strong, and every expression was loaded with personality. It didn't surprise her that his voice matched his commanding presence. His accent was like the perfect costume for an aristocrat in a castle in a British horror movie.

She studied Dante during Uncle Wyeth's introductions. In fact, she couldn't drag her eyes away from him. He had piercing, intelligent eyes that were nearly as black as his jet-colored hair. His brows almost met between them. A carefully groomed mustache and goatee contributed to his wolfish appearance. Gray streaks smudged the temples of his combed-back hair. If it had been long, she wondered if she would have been a little frightened.

He turned and smiled graciously at her as if he were used to such a reaction. She blushed. "I'm so sorry to stare. You just—remind me of someone . . ." she finished lamely.

"Like the Big Bad Wolf?" Dante said, amused.

She couldn't help bursting out in laughter and instantly liked Dante's disarming manner. "I hope you've done some self-portraits," she said, hoping to compliment him and cover her awkward moment.

Dante shook his head and smiled wryly. "I'm a landscape artist. Perhaps I'll commission your uncle to paint me someday."

"If you ever come to Painter Place and sit for him, I hope you'll let me share the honor—as his student, of course," Caroline said. "I'm mostly a landscape painter, too, but it would be a great experience."

Dante's look became softer and thoughtful. "Miss Painter, how could I possibly resist such an invitation in such a charming accent? The honor would be mine, I assure you." He made a little bow.

"Dante, I appreciate your willingness to add a few more guests to the list," said her uncle. "They should arrive after dinner."

"We're glad to add to the party tonight. We're short for the reception anyway. When one of our guests' date discovered that we weren't serving alcohol, he said that was no way to spend a Saturday night. I suggested that he'd be happier someplace else, like a pub in the harbor."

Caroline imagined the sight of Dante saying such a thing to someone. She couldn't repress a grin and turned her head away in case she'd meet his eyes and laugh.

"I thought I approved the list," said Wyeth with surprise.

"You approved a museum manager named Holly 'and guest', and her date backed out at the last minute. She got this fellow's name on a gallery list as a recent collector of one of my paintings and saw that he was single. She's regretted the invitation for the last two days," Dante replied ruefully. "She'll be looking for the nearest exit when we arrive back at port late tomorrow."

Dante turned and indicated they should make themselves at home on the yacht and began introductions as they mingled with guests. Caroline marveled at what a good tuxedo and formal dress could do for people you might not notice at all on any given day on the street.

Dinner was sumptuous, and conversation was easy. It was nearly seven when they got up from dinner to move toward the views from the front railing on the lower deck of the yacht.

Cameron made his way over to her when she was alone. "The peacock dress. Another plan that Juliette had for you?"

She smiled and nodded. He laughed, and she suddenly realized she'd never heard him do that.

"On the night she wore it, we attended one of her movie premieres, and we couldn't sit together. I barely saw the movie from watching her across the room. I had to catch the movie later."

Jesse made his way over to Cameron to ask whether he had time to explore the three levels of the yacht. Cameron started to remind him that he needed to be by the cameras when the paintings were unveiled, but stopped in mid-sentence. Jesse visibly flinched and took a step away from Caroline. She turned to see what had gotten their attention and gasped.

Chad was walking purposefully down the harbor wall toward the yacht, reminding her of a man who walks tall, straight, and steady down a dusty street to defend justice in a western town. His straight blonde hair was blowing slightly back from his face and flipped over his collar in a playful way that contradicted his brooding expression. He was wearing a white tux jacket and black pants, both of which looked like they existed just to show him off. The sight took her breath away—or was that the image of a duster flapping in the wind to reveal his gun belt and the long rifle poised in his right hand?

A woman nearby her fanned herself and muttered to another, "Have mercy!"

Conversation around her began to die away as Chad boarded the yacht, his family following. He barely smiled and didn't greet anyone, coming straight to Caroline, who was weak-kneed. After a sister-kiss that barely brushed her cheek, Chad said softly into her ear, "Someday, I'm goin' to kiss you the way I've dreamed of for years, and all this drama will end. When we get home to Painter Place, the press will need a special invitation to get on the island."

Caroline glanced around to see if, by chance, they had any of those fainting couches here to catch belles from the South, who were suddenly overcome. She'd never make fun of those silly characters again. Apparently, it wasn't a British thing, but she did see a chair near the easels. She was pretty sure she couldn't get that far, so she tried a deep breath. But Chad had taken command of her arm, so she leaned on his. She couldn't look him in the eye.

Dante Kent had been an attentive companion to Natalie, and he brought her over with him as he greeted the newcomers, who stood near Chad and Caroline.

"You are just in time, my friends. We are set to unveil paintings by Miss Painter and her uncle during this trip. Please, make yourselves at home tonight."

Wyeth was standing near the easels. He nodded at the Gregory family. Dante made his way over with Natalie on his arm and invited everyone to come closer. He began the presentation with a brief statement about his admiration for his friend Wyeth and welcomed the Americans to his country. Then he turned the floor over to Wyeth, who thanked his host and guests before speaking briefly about his goals in Mevagissey, unveiling each demo painting he'd done for the film, and explaining why he had chosen each subject for a lesson or technique in the series.

The guests clapped, and he motioned for Caroline to come forward to join him. While she came up, Wyeth told everyone that she had mostly been assisting him this week and would be on her own by Monday to choose some plein air sights around the village.

Caroline hoped her voice wouldn't quiver when she spoke, and she wasn't sure now whether she had the courage to go through with her plan. She looked out at some of the people she'd met and began the tribute to her uncle that she had rehearsed in her mind.

"Only a few of you here tonight will be able to truly relate when I tell you that I'm blessed to have been raised as almost a daughter to Wyeth Painter. Some of you know him only by his work and reputation in the art world. But if you know him and can call him friend, you're fortunate. I've studied under him for years as an aspiring artist, and the value of that education expanded far beyond the boundaries of art techniques. Under my uncle's wisdom and teaching, I was able to skip the silly philosophies and empty agendas of an art world that substitutes them for the timeless fundamentals and hard work that makes a painting a masterpiece. While I can't claim to have produced one of those—and may not possess the element of genius to do so—it's not due to lack of knowledge. I haven't yet put in the time it takes for that head knowledge to become something that runs free as I paint. If my uncle has taught me anything, he taught me that it takes years to make an artist, just as it takes years to build character in a person."

She looked at her uncle. "I may never create a priceless painting, but I want to thank you, Uncle Wyeth, for a priceless art education and the experience of a lifetime to study under you."

The guests were clapping and smiling, and there were some comments about how sweet this was as they leaned over to whisper to one another. Caroline could tell that her uncle was very affected by her tribute, and he thanked her before he pulled her into an easy hug.

Wyeth moved a few steps away to the easels to give Caroline the floor again. But she still avoided looking directly at Chad, her eyes only scanning to include his group in a general way with the crowd she was interacting with.

"Most of you here know that an original painting is an interaction with an artist. At any given time on any given day, the same subject matter by the same artist will be portrayed differently according to moods and other influences. Sometimes, we paint a scene simply to share it and get people to look closer. Other times, we're working out something inside of ourselves, the way people might talk things through to see more clearly. And at other times, the subject has special significance on a personal level."

Caroline paused, organizing her thoughts. "One of the terrific things about painting in acrylics is that they are dry enough to handle right after completion. I've painted three canvases in the past three days. Two were plein air views of the sea cliffs around Mevagissey, done as experimental compositions. They fall into the category I mentioned about working things out as if we're talking them through, trying to understand them better. Imagine my surprise when the first one sold from the balcony of my room here on the night I painted it. The other one is titled *Sea Cliffs* and was done for filming here in the harbor yesterday."

She turned as Wyeth pulled the cover from the painting and the guests showed their appreciation. Facing them again, Caroline hesitated. The guests waited on her expectantly. She inhaled and smiled.

"The painting I'm about to show you was painted today. It's an example of an artist choosing a subject for its special significance on a personal level, though it did involve working through some things as the former paintings did. It's full of memories of a girl who likes the sunflowers that grow at her home, and a boy who likes tall ships and is fascinated at how it's possible to get all of that adventure into a bottle. Someone here tonight sent me sunflowers yesterday because they're my favorite flowers and he knew I'd be facing a challenging day. He knew how to show me he understands because he grew up watching me. I daresay he knows things about me that I don't know yet myself."

Her eyes searched to find Chad's. They locked gazes, and his expression almost made her forget she was speaking in front of a crowd. After a moment, she continued. "I painted *Tall Ships and Sunflowers* for my boyfriend, Chad Gregory."

Wyeth unveiled the painting of the sunflowers, different in mood from the cliffs on an easel next to it. It was a still life painting in modern colors featuring the vase of sunflowers and the ship in a bottle that sailed a frothy lace sea in Caroline's room. To complete the composition, she had added the florist's card to look as if it had just been opened and laid down, and Chad's ring on a chain scattered across the top of it.

As the guests clapped enthusiastically, and Jesse and Cole hooted and whooped in a very un-British manner, everyone craned their necks to see how Chad was reacting. He surprised them by coming forward. Everyone whispered and waited to see what he would say.

"I believe she just admitted that I have 'special significance on a personal level,'" he announced to the guests as if they were all in on a secret. Laughter rolled like gentle surf over the group.

In a crowd of British accents, his deep voice and South Carolina drawl made it seem as if he would belt out a country love song any minute. "I'll ask her to translate that for me later, but it sounds promising. Ladies and gentlemen, you're looking at Caroline Painter's first priceless painting," he said, gesturing to the easel.

The crowd cheered and applauded but quickly quieted in expectation when Chad looked into Caroline's eyes for a few moments and put her hand to his lips. "Thank you for the unforgettable gift, Caroline. And I love the painting, too."

A collective sigh came from the ladies in the crowd, and the men applauded Chad's cleverness.

Wyeth and Caroline let everyone know that they'd be hanging around the paintings for a few minutes to answer questions. Their sketchbooks from the trip were displayed nearby on a table.

Caroline answered questions about her work and her goals with filming in Mevagissey. She met some gallery representatives who asked to be contacted when she was ready to show a body of work from the trip.

Chad stayed by her side, getting plenty of attention and some pats on the back for his comments. Something about his intensity and the red rosebud boutonniere on the lapel of his black and white tuxedo made Caroline think of the Phantom of the Opera. She noticed that he drew a lot of covert glances from the ladies. She also saw that he noticed the ladies' attention. He took in all of this and suggested that they try the sundeck for some privacy.

As they slowly made their way up to the second level among other guests, they met Jesse and his crew, who were like kids exploring an amusement park. Cole and his cousin's date were enthralled with the yacht as well. He and Jesse liked one another immediately.

At first, there was another couple on the top deck, but they left soon after Chad and Caroline came to stand by the railing. As they disappeared down the stairs, Chad deftly pulled Caroline around to face him.

"You're breathtaking tonight, and I'm hopelessly wrapped around your finger. How do you keep getting better and better?"

Caught off guard by his directness, she couldn't help glancing away. She smiled slightly. "You're very distracting tonight, too."

Now his voice was teasing. "Tell me what it means that I've become 'significant on a personal level' and moved up from being a friend to being your boyfriend."

Caroline gave a little shrug of her shoulders that drew his attention to the feather corsage. "I worked it out while I was painting," she said, looking out to sea. "The one on Thursday night was when I tried to say goodbye to you before you showed me that I was running away from something else. The painting in the harbor was how I faced reality about Chris, and imagined how it would feel if I'd seen you in photos like the ones of me with Baker."

She paused and glanced at him before looking back out to sea. Her expression was haunted. "Today, I understood that even Painter Place isn't going to be simple anymore. For so long, it was easy to enjoy things like sunflowers and a ship in a bottle together. But that time was interrupted, and I haven't been able to get it back. Seeing the sunflowers and tall ships in Mevagissey made me realize that they could be appreciated in a different place and a different way—it doesn't have to be exactly the same."

She paused a moment, closing her eyes. "You assured me on Thursday night that I'm exclusive, and you said you're waiting for me to make the same commitment. I couldn't do it then."

She opened her eyes and turned to look up at him. "But I'm saying so now."

When Chad had put Caroline on the spot in hopes of bringing her around to the commitment he wanted, he'd expected to get it. But he wasn't prepared for the way she did it. After all these years, he should have known that she'd surprise him. Being around her had always been like an adventure in a tall ship—you could plan your destination, but you never knew what was going to happen along the way.

The explorers in their group suddenly gushed onto the sun deck from the stairs, making witty comments about nautical terms and their definitions. In some cases, Jesse creatively invented meanings for the ones they didn't know, sending the girls into giggling fits and Cole and his cousin's boyfriend into a competition for pithy responses.

Chad winced in resignation at the loss of privacy with Caroline. Some important things would just have to wait.

Chapter Eighteen

"You are the light of the world. A town built on a hill cannot be hidden.
Neither do people light a lamp and put it under a bowl.
Instead they put it on its stand, and it gives light to everyone in the house.
In the same way, let your light shine before others,
that they may see your good deeds and glorify your Father in heaven."
Matthew 5:14-16

As the sun began setting, Public Parking jogged out to an area near the lighthouse—to their drums, a keyboard, guitars, and mysterious boxes housing amplifiers and speakers. Cheers began to rise around the harbor as people realized what was happening.

Caroline, Chad, Cole, and Shannon moved to the front railing along the enormous sun deck of the yacht to get a closer look. Baker Holmes slung a guitar strap over his head and adjusted it before moving close to the microphone, where he tossed his hair and raised his hand. First, there was a surge in the cheers, then quiet so the crowd could hear what he would say.

"Hey, everybody at the artist party—you need a bigger boat!" he exclaimed, pointing and grinning at the group on the yacht. His voice overpowered the din of the harbor gathering.

The crowd roared with laughter before he held up his hand. "I invited the whole town," he shouted and waved his arm as if to sweep them all up. By now, everyone attending the reception had moved to the front railing of the three decks on the yacht to listen and wave.

Baker leaned into the microphone, his mouth almost touching it. "I met a new friend on Thursday evening. She's an artist, and I bought a painting she was finishing. It was a view of the cliffs from the balcony that was once my parents' room." He sighed into the microphone. "That artist, she glows from inside, like the Mevagissey Light." He gestured behind him to the lighthouse. "The difference is, she doesn't need that power station we built back in 1895, 'cause her power's known as the Light of the World. Before she knew who I was, she cared enough about a stranger to listen as he unloaded his conscience. Talking to her, I found out what my real problem was. It wasn't my future in music—it was my future in eternity. Caroline, wave at the crowd!" he shouted, pointing at her.

Taken aback, Caroline gasped before she hesitantly raised her hand and waved shyly from her position at the railing. The metallic threads of the peacock dress trim shimmered in the last colors of the setting sun. Beside her, Chad pushed her hand up high to wave like a beauty queen on a parade float. He joined everyone else as they clapped for her.

"Hey, Caroline, is the chap with you the Gregory with the numbers after his name?" asked Baker into the microphone. She nodded and put her hand through Chad's tuxedo-sleeved arm.

"As of today, my mates and I are unemployed. I hear that guys like you help businesses hire guys like us. If we don't find work 'ere, we're comin' home with you to invade the Continent, okay?" Baker turned to the side, sweeping his hand to include his band. A drum roll, cymbal crash, and guitar riff responded.

Laughter rang out over the water. Chad nodded at Baker and gestured for him to come on.

"Caroline's guy got some bad press this week, and she got caught up in—uh—some argy-bargy with 'im, ya know what I mean? Then some photographers tracked me and Caroline down and created more drama." Laughter and whistling erupted.

"But listen up now, I want to set the record straight," Baker told them. "Her guy never met the other woman, and I'm the one who hugged Caroline on the street. I did it because she had the guts to share Jesus with me. Any of you done that lately?" He shouted the question as a challenge.

There was murmuring and clapping in the crowd. Baker tilted the microphone a little closer to his mouth. "Proverbs 3:5 says, 'In all your ways, acknowledge Him, and He shall direct your paths.' That's how I'm making decisions from now on. To acknowledge Christ, you have to believe in Him for salvation. You have to know Him. My pastor read John 17:1-3 to me. It says that eternal life is *knowing* God, not just believing some true things about Him."

Scattered cheers rose. "Caroline quoted a Bible verse to me that changed my life on Thursday night, sitting at my gram's kitchen table. I memorized it. Zephaniah 3:17. It says, 'The Lord your God is with you, He is mighty to save. He will take great delight in you, He will quiet you with His love, He will rejoice over you with singing.'"

Baker paused and looked out over the harbor. "I know what it is to sing about things I care about, or causes I believe in, or just for fun. But my voice and songs are a shadow in comparison to what God must sound like when He blesses and sings over me now—because I finally told Him that no matter what comes, I'm all His."

The harbor burst into applause. Baker looked out at the yacht, searching for Caroline in the fading twilight. "This is the first of my new songs. It's about meeting Caroline, and it's for Him!" He pointed first at her when he said her name, and then up at the stars.

A memory flashed through Caroline's mind. She heard Chris saying, "When I saw you drive up, it hit me all over again that you are the kind of girl that guys write poems to, sing songs about, and paint pictures of."

This was not Painter Place, and the song was not exactly about her. Still, it was startling to remember. What would Chris say if he saw her mission field?

Baker moved away from the microphone, drew up his knee, and brought down his raised arm to strike the guitar strings in a chord, a signal to the band. Public Parking sprang into action, bobbing their heads and playing music with a jubilant, bouncy, quick rock-and-roll beat. Baker tossed his long bangs aside and leaned into the microphone to sing.

> *"Hear my song about a friend*
> *With a light that shines within—*
> *She glows within*
> *With light used in my soul to mend*
> *She was the one He chose to send*
> *Her Light within.*
> *I was walkin' in the night*
> *When I saw her inner light—*
> *That inner Light*
> *The One who showed me what was right*
> *Changed my blindness into sight*
> *That inner Light.*

Now I have the same Light, too
Light that shines in all I do—
He lights me, too
And it can be the same for you
Eternal light to see you through—
He'll light you, too!
I was walkin' in the night
When I saw her inner light—
That inner Light
The One who showed me what was right
Changed my blindness into sight
That inner Light."

Caroline and Shannon dabbed tears from the corners of their eyes. Natalie found some tissues somewhere to hand out. They all watched the people clapping to the beat and dancing, and many raised their hands in the air.

Public Parking finished the last chords of the new song. The crowded harbor roared. The Mevagissey Light shone overhead, and there were floodlights set up to shine on the band. Baker tossed his hair out of his eyes again, catching his breath and waiting for the clamor to fade.

Chad spoke into Caroline's ear so that she could hear. "You were right—Baker was a direction, not a distraction."

"Thank you for the terrific debut of our song," Baker said a little breathlessly into the microphone. "It's a huge responsibility to know you're watching us in the news and buying our records. We decided this week that we don't care what other bands are doing or what's accepted once they cross the boundaries. We're going to be ourselves, and we don't want to lead anyone down a dangerous road to place called regret."

Before the crowd could respond, he said, "This is one most of you will know. It's not mine, but it's about me. It was written by another Englishman named John Newton." He raised his arms to indicate that they should join him, and he began to sing. Public Parking members ignored their instruments and stood at their microphones.

Ringing out in the harbor, voices rose in harmony to sing "Amazing Grace." Lighters, matches, and flashlights were pulled out in the crowds.

Caroline felt like she was in a dream. It was such a powerful moment, and she knew she'd remember it every time she sang this hymn for the rest of her life.

After the hymn, the band moved back to their instruments while Baker introduced the next song. "I wrote this back when Beth was my girl. She's been prayin' for me, and today, she agreed to be my girl again. Wave at me, Bethy!"

A hand went up to wave wildly, and Beth jumped up and down so Baker would notice. He pointed at her. "That little bit over there is Beth. This is for you!"

He signaled the band and led them into a love ballad that was apparently popular with the fans. Many of the reception guests on the yacht were pairing up and dancing just like the crowds in the harbor.

Caroline took Chad's hand. "I pick you," she said solemnly. "You're the only thing that feels real tonight. I can't imagine doing this without you."

"You'll never have to. Especially if you wear a dress like this," he said.

They listened to the words of the song as they moved to the music, but finally Chad spoke again. "Caroline, will it take a painting for you to work out that you can say you love me?"

The song ended, and he pulled back to search her face. She was glad for the distraction when the band launched into a set of their hit songs.

Baker Holmes finally waved and said goodnight to both the crowd and to Caroline's group on the yacht. It was clear from the uproar of applause that the mini-concert had been a huge success.

A breathless and beaming Cole came over to Chad and suggested that they go down to get something to drink for themselves and the girls. The other men followed.

Shannon, Caroline, Natalie, and Camellia were the only ones left on the sundeck, enjoying a ceiling of stars and the beam of the lighthouse. Natalie and Camellia sat down near the stairway to get off of their feet while Caroline and Shannon continued to watch the harbor view from the railing as the crowds thinned.

Caroline asked Shannon where she was from because she recognized her Georgia accent. Shannon explained that she grew up in Atlanta, living there until her dad was transferred to London two years ago. When she and Cole heard one another's voices in a group at church, they were drawn to the similar sound of home.

Turning their heads briefly, they saw a man they had not met tonight come up onto the deck. They turned back to the view and their conversation. But suddenly, the man was at Caroline's side. He put his shoulder to hers and leered at her. She tried to hold her breath to avoid smelling the liquor on his.

The man was dressed in a black tux and had graying hair that had probably been neatly combed sometime earlier in the evening. He was at least old enough to be her father. Her mind scrambled for a socially graceful way to get away from him.

"It's a hot out tonight," the man said loudly, tugging with one finger at his blue bow tie. "Or is that just the effect you have on me? You look familiar, but I don't think I know you. Don't worry, though. I know what to do about it."

To Caroline's horror, he put his arm around her and moved in as if to kiss her. She protested and tried to push him away.

"That'll only happen when a hotter place than this freezes over!" Chad's deep voice boomed from behind them. "I can send you there right now—or help you overboard to cool off." Chad quickly passed the glasses of Pierre water in his hands to his mother and began walking in the man's direction. His tone left no doubt he preferred the first option. "She's not part of either scenario."

The man stopped trying to kiss her and turned to see who had spoken while Caroline pulled away from his grasp, and Shannon put her arm around her protectively.

Chad stopped when he stood within fighting distance. The man studied Chad before he sneered haughtily. "Who do you think you are, kid?"

"He's my son." Phillip Gregory was instantly beside Chad.

"You!" The man looked surprised before he narrowed his eyes at Phillip. Then he looked at Chad with a challenge in his eyes. "So this is a Gregory whelp." He almost spat the name.

His eyes challenged Chad, and he turned back to Caroline, looking her slowly up and down. "So she's the little prize getting passed around in the news," he slurred.

"Help me not kill him," muttered Chad through clenched teeth as he started forward. Phillip caught his son's arm firmly and pulled him back.

"If I let him go, Wilfred, you'll be the one in the news. Underneath a headline photo of you swimming to the edge of the harbor in of *The Times*, everyone will get to read Chad and Caroline's account of what happened tonight. After that, I'll hold a press conference to talk about something that happened years ago. You'll be ruined."

The man hesitated. Then he shrugged as if they weren't worth his time and began walking with a slight unsteadiness over to the stairs. He stopped when he noticed Camellia. Looking back at Phillip, he laughed before making his way down.

Cole rushed over to his brother, eyes shining with admiration. "Whoa! Good shootin', Tex!" He turned to Phillip. "Dad, who's the drunk? He really hates you! I've never even heard of anyone hating you before."

Phillip let go of Chad's arm, and his son went quickly over to Caroline. Camellia and Natalie also fussed over Caroline, who insisted that she was okay.

Brushing off his tux as if dealing with Wilfred had gotten him dirty, Phillip looked piercingly at Cole. "That's a man who manages people's money and drinks too much, son. He hates me because years ago, I advised some of his prospective investors to find a more responsible person to handle a project. Then he went after your mother—much as he did with Caroline tonight, only he was more her age."

His point wasn't lost on Cole, who flushed under his dad's stern look. Shannon was beside him now. "He did that to Camellia? Did you actually see it happen? What did you do?"

Linking her arm through her husband's, Camellia's eyes showed her relief. "This was like déjà-vu," she said shakily. She looked at Shannon and answered for Phillip. "He did pretty much the same thing Chad did."

Everyone drew closer to hear the story. "Who stopped him from knocking the guy's lights out?" asked Shannon.

Phillip looked over at Chad when he answered, "My dad. Chad may look like his mother, but he thinks like me. I knew exactly what was going to happen if I didn't intervene."

"Did that Wilfred guy lose the project? Who'd the investors go with?" asked Cole.

Phillip looked at him and said simply, "Me."

"We've had enough excitement for one night," said Camellia. "Let's go downstairs. We'll be leaving soon—especially if Wilfred is down there anywhere."

Everyone went downstairs, with Caroline and Chad following last. On the second level, Chad pulled her into a hallway off the deck. He was scowling. "Are you shivering like this because you're upset?"

She nodded and leaned against the wall. "Yes, but don't tell them. I just need a minute. I'll be fine. You're shaking, too."

He hit the palm of one hand hard on the wall beside her, bracing himself on it and boxing her in.   "What if I hadn't come up just then? Seriously—I can't do this anymore this week. I'm fed up with this—" he stretched out his other arm as if searching for the right word to pull out of the air, "this madness! I need to spend time with you, Caroline, relaxing and having fun again. Come with us to St. Austell tonight. We'll come back down to Mevagissey tomorrow in disguise or something so I can sightsee with you. Or we can head out to some trails or a beach."

He paused and waited a moment while she considered, then leaned in closer to her. "Say you will, Caroline." His eyes pleaded. "You can sleep in one of my tee shirts and have my room. Shannon and my mom probably have something you can wear."

"Okay, if you'll really come back with me in disguise. I have a bag with a change of clothes and my tennis shoes."

They looked at one another a few moments before he grabbed her hand and led her to the stairs.

Chapter Nineteen

RAOUL:
"Long ago, it seems so long ago, how young and innocent we were . . .
She may not remember me, but I remember her . . ."
CHRISTINE:
"Flowers fade, the fruits of summer fade,
They have their seasons, so do we
but please promise me, that sometimes, you will think of me!"
— "Think of Me," from Phantom of the Opera

Chad sat close to Caroline in a Mercedes-Benz stretch limousine for the fifteen-minute drive to St. Austell, with Cole and Shannon sitting across from them. The chauffeur maneuvered the winding streets of Mevagissey behind the limo carrying the rest of the Gregory family.

Shannon sighed happily, leaning back into the comfortable seat with her hand in Cole's and looking over at him with a playful look. "I had so much fun! I wish we didn't have to go back tomorrow evening."

Cole glanced at his brother, who looked at him expectantly. He tightened his hold on Shannon's hand and told her it was his fault that they had to get back to London to wait on the results of the investigation at Gregory Global. He haltingly explained why the investigation was happening, and explained that Caroline and Shannon's family accounts were involved in his mistake. He looked at Caroline first, apologizing, and then at his girlfriend.

Shannon looked at him as if he'd just dropped in through the moon roof of the limo from another planet. She pulled her hand out of his with an effort and looked out her window into the darkness. She didn't speak for a full minute.

Cole turned to look out of his window as well. When he looked back at Shannon, he wore the expression of a puppy when he knows he's in trouble.

It took an effort for Caroline to keep from smiling. She had watched his effective use of that look for years, and it had saved him consistently as they had grown up together. She wondered if any girlfriend but Shannon could resist falling helplessly all over him, surrendering any resolve whatsoever.

As she expected, Shannon was steady and her voice firm. "Cole, I appreciate your honesty. But I can't believe you thought any possible good could come from even trying drinking. I hope this experience came with a huge hangover. How can you ever be a leader if you follow stupid people? You need to be clearheaded every minute. And if you'd do something like this behind my back, knowing how I feel about it, where does it end? One of the reasons I started going out with you was because I thought you were different. I'm not looking for just anyone—I can have that any day."

Cole's expression changed to alarm as he glanced at his brother again and began his assurances that he knew he was better than this, and she could trust him that it would never happen again. He told her that he had never dreamed of the cost of getting caught.

"Chad's willing to trust me to try working for him now, but I needed to clean this all up first, apologizing to Caroline and confessing to you. No secrets, even if you change your mind about me. And no secrets from Caroline because—"

Cole stopped when Chad tapped his shoe against his brother's. He chose his words carefully. "Because she's always been basically my sister, and he works closely with the Painter accounts."

The limousine pulled up to the house where the Gregorys were staying. The rest of the family were already inside and saying their goodnights to one another. Shannon went straight to the stairs with a cool attitude toward Cole, who followed her.

Chad led Caroline up to the room that would have been his. Inside the open door, he said, "Looks like he's got to change up his old puppy eyes routine. I hope they save the living room for us if she's going to keep shaking him between her teeth. I'm sleeping there, after all."

"Are you asking me to meet you after I change?"

He was grabbing a carefully folded Carolina blue Nike tee shirt out of his suitcase and glanced up with a grin. "Yes."

He laid the shirt on the bed and closed the suitcase. He pulled back the cover on the top corner of the bed so that it was a triangle with the pillow revealed. He looked down at the lapel of his tuxedo jacket and removed the red rosebud, laying it on the pillow. "A red rose boutonniere—the symbol of passion and love. I wore it for you tonight, and I'm daring to put it on your pillow. Sure hope I'll be the one in your dreams."

Caroline's mouth dropped. "Chad . . ."

Chad headed back to the door, where he paused. He stood with one hand on the doorframe, looking at her as if she might disappear. "I can't believe you're really here." He turned and closed the door.

After Caroline changed and took her hair down, she headed to the living room. Chad wore jeans and the aqua tee shirt and was searching for some soft music on the stereo system. A small lamp created little more than a romantic glow.

He settled into a huge black leather sofa and motioned for her to sit with him. He looked relaxed and younger than twenty-two.

"Do you know what today is?"

She made a couple of witty guesses, but he kept shaking his head. "Admit that you have to give up, and I win."

She groaned and lightly slapped her forehead. "You win."

"This is our one week anniversary," he declared smugly. "By God's grace, we got through a week in which you broke up with me, we only talked once on a call in which you basically hung up on me to be with a rock star, and we were assumed to be in romantic situations with other people—which was all over the news. Yet somehow tonight, you told a crowd of people that I'm significant on a personal level, called me your boyfriend, created a painting that's full of us, and made a commitment not to see anyone but me."

"Wow, I knew it was rough . . ."

From somewhere in the fold of a cushion behind his back, Chad pulled out a long, dark blue velvet box and put it into her hands.

"Open it. It's yours."

Caroline slowly opened the box to find a stunning diamond eternity bracelet. She closed her eyes and bit her lower lip. "I don't know what to say," she whispered.

"Say you love it and ask me to help you put it on," he said. He helped her take it from the box, and then he clasped it around her wrist. He held her arm out and looked satisfied with the small flashes that came from the bracelet when the lamplight was trapped within the diamonds.

"I do love it. Thank you." She settled back against his shoulder. Instrumental music played softly in the background. She kept looking at the bracelet.

"Chad?"

"Umm?"

"How much damage has been done to my reputation over the photos with Baker?"

"None. You've both publicly explained what was really happening, and we were seen as a tight couple at the reception, which should also end my playboy reputation from the photo that triggered all of this. If people didn't see tonight that I only have eyes for you, they're blind. The attention has brought you some professional status though I suspect your dad will be upset, and Wyeth's got some explaining to do. Global's publicity manager and Dad were talking about how poised you are and how much good you've done for us—we're the ones with the questionable reputation right now. Don't worry about what Wilfred said—he was trying to insult me and Dad and used you as his weapon, insinuating that you're—that I'm—"

Chad stopped and groaned, suddenly tense again. He stood up and reached for her hand.

She stood, and he gathered her into a slow swaying dance to the soft music, moving within only a few feet of space.

"That's why you were so angry." Caroline was almost whispering. "He insinuated that I'm easy and beneath your standards."

"Yes. Or that I'm being played. I wasn't in the mood to ask him which, and I wanted to make him pay for both. But it's okay—we know who we are. He could never imagine the price tag on you."

She wasn't sure what he meant by that, and he didn't elaborate. They swayed until the end of the song, and Chad relaxed again. He pulled her back onto the sofa to sit down, sighing deeply and leaning back. "You creative types have all the fun, so tell me about your week in Mevagissey. Start with what happened with Baker."

With her head against his shoulder, she quietly began talking. She stopped when she realized he wasn't responding anymore, his breathing coming in a steady rhythm. He had fallen asleep with his head against the soft leather. Strands of the sun-highlighted hair past his ears and down his neck in back were set off by the contrast of the black sofa cushion. She felt an ache in her heart and raised her hand to touch the ends that sprayed out from where his collar flipped them, but she resisted.

"Finally, I can stare at you as long as I want to without giving you the satisfaction of knowing about it," she whispered.

After a while, she whispered again. "What are you doing, Chad? Why did you leave, and why are you back acting as if we're on a fast track to make up for lost time? You haven't told me everything, and you can't have my heart again until I can trust you."

She stifled a yawn. She wished she could just sleep there against his shoulder. But, however innocent that would be, they'd both be in big trouble with Phillip and her dad if the Gregorys came through the living room and saw them alone at night like that. Chad would get the blame. She smiled to herself. This time, she was going to be the one to protect him.

She carefully got up so that he wouldn't awaken. At the bottom of the stairs, she turned to look longingly at him again. He seemed so young and vulnerable, and yet earlier tonight, he was so strong, in charge, and larger than life.

She tiptoed silently up the stairs. The closer she got to her door, the more distinctly she overheard Shannon and Cole talking. Lamplight stretched itself out into a rectangle on the floor as it escaped from an open area at the end of the hall. Caroline guessed it was an upstairs sitting room.

"Chad told me this week how he and Patrick avoided drinking and parties. He had a condo off campus, and on weekends when he wasn't studying, he or Patrick would travel to see one another to play basketball, golf, go to the movies, and stuff like that. They had some kind of pact about not getting involved with girls until after college, and Chad carried around photos of him and Caroline together in his wallet to prove he had a girl back home, in case girls bothered him—and you can bet they did."

Caroline was rooted and motionless in the doorway to her room.

"Dad was worried sick all the time one summer when Chad took off on his own to work in Hawaii with some of Global's competition. Chad didn't stay in touch or act like himself. By late August, he was back at college but still not in touch often. That was the summer that Caroline and I graduated. I left for London while he was AWOL, so he wasn't around to give me the how-tos on surviving as a Christian in college. My parents thought living with Uncle Justin would keep me straight."

"Obviously, you found a way around that."

"But that's where you come in. I need you, Shannon. I won't let you down anymore."

The conversation was turning more private, and Caroline silently closed her door and leaned back onto it.

She remembered that Chad hadn't attended Cole's graduation because he was in Hawaii. She had thought for sure she'd finally see Chad, after almost two years of hearing nothing and seeing the Gregorys travel on holidays. She was too proud to ask about him when she occasionally saw Patrick, who never mentioned him to her. She knew it was intentional.

It was the day she gave up.

After the ceremony, she had decided at the last minute to jump into Carly's car to head to Myrtle Beach in a caravan of other friends for the weekend. She recklessly gave a long-time wanna-be boyfriend in their group some false hope on a walk on the beach with other friends. The next weekend, Chris showed up with his family at church, where his dad had accepted a call as the new pastor. They kept catching themselves looking at one another.

It had never made sense that Chad just vanished from her life, but it sounded like he did the same with his family that summer. It must have been the tough time he told her about on the beach last Saturday, a time when he was running from becoming his dad and his obsession with Painter Place.

She closed her eyes and rubbed her face with her hands to stop the memories. She walked to the bathroom to wash off her makeup. She put on his tee shirt and smiled faintly at the opening rosebud on the pillow.

***

Chad and Caroline arrived in Mevagissey on the bus from St. Austell as the seabirds were still searching for breakfast. With his Nikon camera and binoculars in a case strapped across his shoulder, Chad was studying a map. Wearing hats and sunglasses, he and Caroline looked like any other tourist or Public Parking fan in town that morning.

Caroline had traipsed some of the narrow and winding streets of Mevagissey with the filming crew to look for painting locations, but she and Chad were going to look for the places that were most likely to have been the inspiration for Susan Cooper's books.

"Looks like we're in for hiking," he mused. "This is definitely not the Lowcountry."

Caroline suddenly took his arm and gently pushed him against the whitewashed wall of a tall but quaint building. She took off her sunglasses and his. Her eyes were sparkling, and he smiled in surprise.

"What did I do to deserve this treatment?" he asked indulgently. "Expect me to do it a lot."

"Do you remember when we were on the pier together last Sunday, and I asked you if you knew what it was like here?"

He just nodded, not wanting to move, still caught up in her excitement and enjoying being the center of her attention.

"You said you were looking forward to seeing it through my paintings. We never dreamed we'd see it together." She paused a moment before adding in a rush, "I can't believe you're here with me."

He was in no hurry to answer. "Me, either. It's a gift, and we should make the most of it." He reached a hand up to trace the curve of her cheek. "I also remember that on the same night and the same pier, I told you that you're beautiful. Your eyes are like the Atlantic on a clear day."

Touched, she reached up to push his long blonde bangs from his brow. Her voice was so soft it was almost a whisper. "And yours are like the cool marsh shadows in summer at Painter Place. You're so impossibly handsome that my heart jumps every time I look at you. How can I ever have any peace of mind with you around?"

Chad had thought he was surprised when she pushed him into the wall—but this was a surprise! She looked at him steadily as if to make sure he understood that she was not kidding, and he forgot to breathe.

"Uh—if I take you somewhere else next weekend, will you do this for our two week anniversary?" he stammered. She smiled. "I'm serious. Stay with us in Charleston next weekend. Dad will drive us home on Sunday night, 'cause Mom might stay for the week."

"I'd love to," she answered. They continued to just look at one another until someone passed near them on the way down the road.

She stood up from leaning on her arm beside him, and he reluctantly straightened up from leaning on the wall. He cleared his throat and tried to focus again on where they were.

Blowing out a deep sigh, he took his sunglasses when she handed them back to him. She put hers back on and looked to see if anything around them was familiar.

"It'll be more crowded in town when churches get out," Chad speculated. "Let's explore the harbor before we head up to the vicarage and rocks on the cliffs."

They enjoyed the personality of the village with all its quirky buildings and doorways perched on the side of the harbor like ever-vigilant birds. Brightly colored boats were strewn across the water like jewelry. The sleek yacht on which Dante Kent had hosted the reception last night was leaving the harbor.

"It's so normal now—last night under the stars and lights, it was magical. Kind of like when the lights decorate the pavilion at Painter Place." Caroline sighed as she looked through the binoculars. She lowered them and turned to him. "You came to the reception!"

"I couldn't stand it any longer." He took his hands off the camera to let it rest on the strap against his dusky purple polo shirt. He reached for her free hand, and the eternity bracelet on her wrist sparkled in the sunlight.

"I was ready for a fight, determined to win you back. Instead, looking so glamorous in that dress, you totally disarmed me with the painting and announcing that I'm your boyfriend. I was the one conquered, without as much as a whimper."

"How could I resist when you showed up looking like a heartthrob with an attitude in that tux? It'll be a long time before I can stop thinking about seeing you coming for me like that."

"Then don't—don't stop thinking about it," he urged.

Someone bumped into Chad. It was getting more crowded. They stopped talking and looked for their next route.

They found a little place for a quick lunch, where Chad saw Stargazy pie on a nearby table. He wrinkled his nose, agreeing with Caroline that it was creepy. Then they enjoyed sightseeing, climbing up to Mevagissey House on Vicarage Hill. Chad got some photos of the boxy structure for her, and they rested before going back by Cliff Road.

They sat on the ground at the cliffs to look over the Channel and the Atlantic. Chad asked another tourist who was taking photos if he would mind using his camera to take one of him and Caroline, and he would do the same for him and the girl with him.

Caroline mused, "We have a new memory now when we sit on the pier." She stretched her long tanned legs out on the grass in front of her and sighed contentedly. "From there, it's only over the horizon to here, where we've enjoyed a day together halfway around the world."

Chad sat up from leaning back on both arms and put one around her shoulder. "It won't be long now until we'll be doing that. Let's get through this week without any misunderstandings. There's no reason to write me off ever again."

He looked at the Submariner on his wrist. "I need to deliver you safely to your uncle and catch the bus back."

He took her hand and put her palm against his face, closing his eyes briefly. "It's so hard to leave. Let's talk on the phone this week as much as we can. When you fly into Charleston on Friday, I'll be waiting at the airport to celebrate our two week anniversary."

They got to the jade green door of the bed and breakfast before anyone realized who they were. Once Caroline was in her room, she took off her hat and stepped out onto the balcony to look at the café sign where Chad told her he'd be waiting to say goodbye. She found him and smiled. He pointed from his heart to hers and waved before walking backward a few steps in his reluctance to stop looking at her. She ducked back into her room to avoid people who were figuring out who she was.

Chapter Twenty

"Say to the righteous that it will go well with them,
For they will eat the fruit of their actions."
Isaiah 3:10 NASB

On Monday morning in London, the photographer with the flat plaid cap sat again in the café on Threadneedle Street. He had hoped to watch for news on Gregory Global but had just heard that there would be no decision announced today. He had failed to get what he'd promised Tippy with such bravado, and his credibility was once again an issue with the papers. He had ended up handing a terrific lead to his competition, and they were profiting from big news in Mevagissey. The best he could hope for was that something interesting would happen with Global this week, and he'd get the shot.

While he sipped his coffee, a boy came in with an envelope, looking around. He spotted the photographer and came to his table. "Sir, do you know a pretty lady named Tippy?" he asked politely.

The photographer nodded. The boy handed him the envelope and said that she'd hired him to deliver it. He stood there waiting for a tip, which the man grudgingly gave him. The boy ran out the door while the man looked at his delivery.

"I'd hand you this myself, but I'm currently packing to leave the country. Enclosed is the retainer fee I agreed to pay for your work on my publicity problem. You did get one good shot. Never say I didn't meet my end of our agreement. Get the rest of your fee from Public Parking and that Pollyanna American. You did a smashing job of making someone else famous. –Tippy."

***

Justin Gregory got an early call that there wouldn't be a decision from the hearing until Tuesday, so Phillip went to tell his sons to sleep in. He and Justin pored over the newspapers, and their publicity manager stopped by for a conference.

When Chad wandered into the kitchen for a late breakfast, he saw the closed door of his uncle's library down the hall and heard voices. He eyed some of the choices being kept warm for him and his brother, then reluctantly tasted something to see what it was. He missed Lowcountry cooking. Whatever he'd just tasted was passable as food, though, so he shrugged and took a serving. He put down a small glass of pineapple juice in one draft and then traded the empty glass for one full of water.

Cole came in looking a little tousled and sleepy but dressed like Chad in a tank-style cotton tee shirt and gym shorts. "We working out in a little while?" he mumbled.

"Yep, if whatever it is that I'm eating has some protein to get me through. We're still not allowed out of the house." Chad nodded in the direction of the library. "What's up?"

Cole looked alarmed and peeked down the hall before he walked over to Chad to get a plate. "Don't know, man, but I sure hope it's not about me. I'm in over my head already."

Chad smiled and swallowed. "Things going okay now with Shannon?"

Cole snorted. "I'm on probation, and there's another guy snooping around, waiting for us to blow up. Seems like the story of my life at the moment. And it's hypocritical that you made me tell her, considering the secret you've kept from Caroline for four years."

Chad nearly choked and had to cough some to recover. "You're just guessing."

"I can't believe she hasn't figured it out. I knew when you left."

Chad coughed again and studied his brother's face. "Let's stick to your own issues, Cole. If you can't be straight up with Shannon, you won't be with me, either. You can't work for me and drink or sneak around—I'm building a reputation in this sideline of young guns. You tested Dad's rule about drinking, but I hope you didn't test the ones about girls. You'll get caught like always, and I can't afford to have you go rogue on me. All you need is a paternity suit or someone blackmailing you with photos. Those things have a way of haunting you and your family for the rest of your life. That goes for any guy—but it's even more serious for a Christian. Just resolve that you're going to live what you believe and follow true north on your moral compass."

Cole sounded frustrated. "I haven't done anything like that, Chad. I know your rules and the family motto—'If you're gonna live like the rest of the world, go work for 'em.' I said I'd be a good little boy."

He downed a small glass of juice like his brother had and took a deep breath. "I don't think it'd matter what I looked like—girls would still come after the money thinking they'll get a chunk when they divorce me. They wouldn't know that Dad's got that sheltered."

Suddenly he grinned, and his voice took on a teasing bravado. "It just so happens that I'm devilishly handsome, though, and when you add that to my charm, I'm a magnet."

"Oh, yeah? You can't come up with an excuse I haven't dealt with. Never be alone with a girl anywhere unless her name is on a marriage license with yours, understand?" Chad took the last bite of his mystery breakfast and chewed it while looking at Cole with raised eyebrows.

Cole nodded impatiently. "Okay, okay, I get the picture. I haven't. I won't. And anyway, I don't want to be with anyone but Shannon, who seems to have been inoculated from charm by a past relationship. She's a Christian, so I can't ask her to do something we both know is wrong, even if I could manage to get her alone. Besides, I don't want to lose the best girl that ever happened to me to someone else over somethin' stupid like that."

"We need to get out of the bachelor market. You can make enough money with me that you wouldn't even have to get your degree first if you play nice and con Shannon into sticking with you for the rest of her life. She's a keeper. Caroline isn't looking for money. She was dating someone who didn't have a dime and went off to have less than that."

Cole chuckled. "Yeah, well, you nailed that one right. If she just wanted money and looks, she'd be with Derrick Wallace, not you. I thought she was going that direction when you went to Hawaii and didn't come to graduation. She broke that day and headed to Myrtle with us, and Derrick was gloating that he had her after two years of relentless chasing. His timing was terrible again, though. He went off to training camp at college just as Chris moved in. He just got drafted to the pros, by the way. Caroline never let him talk to Andy, but they hung out together at school events and when their friends went to movies and stuff. He beat me for prom king, so

I couldn't watch after her for you—she was queen. Did you ever hear how she accidently broke his nose?"

Chad couldn't answer because his mouth was hanging open.

"I'll take that as a no," said Cole smugly. "I saw it happen right in front of me at the bleachers. He was team captain after Patrick graduated. The team told him that he'd never get a kiss from Caroline, but when he tried, he'd have to do it in front of them to prove it. He knew he'd have to trick her. So after the last home game, he came up from behind her to try a sideswipe. She was caught off guard, all right, and he got her left elbow, her right fist, and a mouth full of pom-pom. There may have been a knee involved, but I was too fascinated with the blood to remember."

Cole took a swallow of water and watched his brother's face, delighted to be delivering such interesting news to such a captive audience. "Now I have some life advice for you, big brother. Never try to take anything without permission from a tall girl who works out and can do a cartwheel and a split."

Chad raked his fingers through the back of his hair. "I'm all ears if you're in the mood to fill me in today."

Their dad interrupted at the kitchen door. "Good, both of you are here. Come with me." He turned on his heel without waiting for an answer.

The Gregory brothers tentatively entered the library. Newspapers were opened on Justin's desk and a side table. Chad stopped just inside the door, bracing himself before reluctantly following Cole.

There was a photo of Baker Holmes at the harbor concert on the front of *The Times*, announcing that Public Parking didn't renew their contract over deal-breaking music video content. The article was continued on another page, where there was a photo of Baker pointing to the yacht. Another photo showed Caroline and Chad, with her waving shyly to Baker.

Chad lingered on that one, remembering how she looked and enjoying how great they looked together. Cole was thrilled to see himself and Shannon in the background of something associated with Public Parking.

There was a photo of Chad and Phillip standing side by side in the confrontation with Wilfred. They wore identical expressions, and there was no question they were father and son, despite differences in hair color and features. They had the same jawline, both of which were set in a challenge. Their names were so long that it took the entire space for the caption to mention them and Gregory Global.

The article was continued inside with the one about Baker. There was a photo of Wilfred making his move on Caroline. Chad clenched his fists involuntarily at the memory, then checked himself and relaxed. The caption said he was apparently drunk and not welcomed by Caroline at a reception held in her honor by Dante Kent. Chad and Phillip were mentioned in the article as handling Wilfred both in and out of financial arenas.

The Arts and Entertainment section had a well-done spread of photos at the yacht reception. There was a photo of Chad kissing Caroline's hand in front of the painting she'd given him. He couldn't suppress a satisfied smile.

A couple of the tabloids were next. Baker was given much more coverage, and they were warmer about the faith angle of his concert. They included his direct quotes from scripture and his testimony. There was a terrific photo of the harbor when everyone sang "Amazing Grace."

Phillip saw that they were nearly finished with the pages. "Chad, you and I are being asked to elaborate on or make comments about what happened on the yacht with Wilfred. Do you have anything to say?"

Chad and his father looked steadily at one another for a few moments in silence. "No," Chad finally said flatly. "This photo ought to say it all."

Phillip's smile of pride at Chad's answer was spontaneous. He looked at Justin and Global's publicity manager. "Officially, neither Chad nor I have any further comment. Wilfred will face consequences of his own making."

So that was what the stern attitude was about, thought Chad. His dad wasn't sure he'd pass a test in front of Cole.

Chapter Twenty-One

"The Lord God made clothing out of skins for Adam and his wife,
and He clothed them."
Genesis 3:21

Caroline was excited and rejuvenated on Monday morning, facing a new week of not knowing what would come her way. Her weekend with Chad had moved her significantly from where she was a week ago on the way here, and last night she'd talked with her mom, dad, Patrick, and Marina on the phone. Hearing their voices and all that had been happening at home refreshed her heart. Her dad didn't mind if she waited until Sunday to come in from Charleston, even though it was Father's Day. They would have extra steaks on the grill so that Chad and Phillip could join them.

Wyeth Painter's group looked over the newspapers that morning with Baker. They were relieved that there was nothing outrageous, and Baker was glad to see that some had picked up his testimony. He was spending the day practicing new songs for an album. After all this publicity, the band felt confident that they could get a label to pick them up.

Jesse, Natalie, and Caroline would work near Wyeth's group that day, in case there were any questions. It was a cloudy morning. Caroline set up quickly, hoping to finish before the rain set in. She was disappointed that she wouldn't have good contrast shadows without sunshine. She hadn't yet painted scenes of fishing boats on this trip, so she found a picturesque view to do in watercolor, allowing for some runs and drips in her washes to keep a true feel of water in the painting. She'd have to adjust her presentation to allow for slow dry times in the humidity.

A woman in a broad-brimmed floppy straw hat with pretty gray hair showing underneath, carrying supplies to paint plein air, stood watching her. When Caroline's painting needed another break to dry, she walked over to introduce herself and start a conversation with the artist.

"It's nice to meet you, Miss Painter," said the woman. "My name is Judith, and I wanted to see your group paint while you were here. I saw you on the news." Her accent sounded a bit different from the ones Caroline heard most in Mevagissey, so Caroline asked if she lived locally.

"No, I'm just here for the day. I'm a wildlife artist visiting different places along the coast to paint varieties of birds that are nesting this season on the cliffs. I've already finished studies of sandpipers, turnstone, kittiwake, and herring gulls, but hope to catch some views of the migrant birds that come through."

Judith showed Caroline the studies she had with her. Her paintings were created with pastels and were beautifully realistic and soft.

Caroline was nearly finished with her painting demo of the fishing boats when she noticed that the bystanders looked like they were there to paint in the harbor. More had gathered nearby to watch Uncle Wyeth. She signed her painting and motioned for Natalie, asking her to go check with Cameron to let him know she was finished and ask if her uncle might want to get together to do something to include the crowd.

Natalie talked to her brother while Caroline introduced herself to the artists in the growing group, asking them what kind of paintings they liked to do. Natalie returned to tell her that Wyeth wanted to combine their groups and let the artists ask questions, so Caroline invited them to follow her over to the larger space where her uncle was set up for a session of questions about problems they faced in their paintings.

She went to pack up her equipment. Another fishing boat had pulled up to the ones in her painting, and the men had been listening to her talking to the group. One looked like he was in charge, with boots up to his thighs and a black skipper's cap. Two others seemed to have been mending nets before stopping to listen to her.

She smiled quickly to acknowledge them as she began gathering her things. One of them removed his cap and hit his chest with it. "Te quiero!"

A cheerful, rusty laugh erupted from the man in the skipper's cap. Jesse walked up to see if he could help Caroline, and the man who had his cap on his chest exclaimed, "The way the artist makes the talk—ahhh, so beautiful!" He kissed his fingertips to his mouth and made a gesture to throw it to Caroline.

The artists and bystanders laughed. Jesse looked at her in amusement and said, "I think he means that he has fallen in love with the way you talk."

Caroline laughed. "Gracias, senor! I'm from America's state of South Carolina. Where are you from?"

He looked at his skipper to make sure he understood, and then grinned broadly. "From Spain, senorita. South Spain!" Everyone laughed with him. Jesse explained that Caroline had to go to join the other artists. The fishermen nodded and waved.

Wyeth and Caroline answered questions from their impromptu gathering there in the harbor, and Cameron worked with Jesse and the crew to make sure it was being filmed. Natalie and Chrissy were getting signatures on releases for permission to use the participants in the video. It was a laid-back session that everyone enjoyed until scattered drops of rain began to hint at more to come.

***

Wyeth invited Baker and Beth to meet them for dinner at the same restaurant they'd visited on their first night in Mevagissey, and Patty was working again. It was a dreary, rainy night, and the glow from the little lantern centerpieces were cheerful and homey. Caroline could imagine being in the captain's quarters in a ship on a stormy sea. Cameron asked her to sit with him again, with Beth and Baker on the other side of her.

Patty was happy to see them. She looked at Wyeth and said, "Mr. Painter, ya asked me last week whether the locals would think of artists as being respectable or scallywags."

"And you said we'd have to wait and see!" Wyeth's eyebrows raised as the corners of his mouth turned up. He waited for her to answer. "Have they decided yet?"

"They say you're welcome back anytime," smiled Patty. "You've added color in more ways than just your pretty pictures," she laughed.

***

The rain continued into Tuesday morning, so Caroline worked on her sketchbook, cleaning up some sloppiness from quick notes and making sure her studies would be clear later on when she used them for a reference. Uncle Wyeth came to the door to ask her to come down and talk to Chad while the Gregorys were on the line with news about the investigation at Global.

Cole faced a fine for his association with the young man who had been caught trying to access accounts at Global, but Chad told her that they'd been able to keep their names from being released because Global wasn't pressing charges. The family was relieved that the media would be leaving their stakeouts around his Uncle Justin's home.

Then Chad said that he missed her and that she'd looked great in Dante's press release at the reception.

She told him he looked great in the news this time, too. She observed that all the publicity had taken a toll and had its downside, but good was coming from it. Shelly was having a difficult time back at the gallery handling all the new interest in their work from England and the pre-orders for the videos.

"While we've been imprisoned here, Cole's been sharing some stories about your junior and senior years in Whitehaven with me," Chad said.

She glanced around to make sure no one else was close by, deciding to get some mileage out of this. After all, he should have been checking in on her during those years if it had mattered.

"Oh?"

"Yeah . . ."

"Cole's own stories are much more interesting than mine, in case he left those out. He dealt very creatively with trouble and smiled like an angel."

"Sounds like your own hunk of trouble came in a big package and was incredibly tenacious, and that you were quite creative as you also smiled like an angel," suggested Chad. "Must've been very tempting."

"Some days more than others—especially holidays. But that package was clearly labeled with a big distraction tag," she replied. "Those are best looked at and not opened. They don't fit into Painter Place easily."

Chad sighed. "Well played," he said, not getting what he wanted out of this. He wondered what he'd expected.

"It's not fair that you have Cole's spy stories. I didn't get to hear about your packages of trouble."

"All you need to know is that my packages came with labels, too, and not a single one had 'Caroline Painter' written on it. I wasn't opening anything else."

She was taken aback. "Chad," she breathed. "That was—beautifully done." She closed her eyes.

"It's the truth," he said softly with conviction.

The group was gathering in the foyer to set out now that the rain had stopped. Reluctantly, she told Chad that everyone was waiting, and she'd have to hang up. He said he had some work to get back to anyway and would try to call before he and his parents flew out on Thursday.

"I'm painting in the village," Caroline said. "I'll be thinking of last Sunday when you were here."

Chad chuckled. "Go by the whitewashed building you shoved me into—that was one of my favorite parts. And I can hardly wait until this weekend."

***

Jesse, Natalie, and Caroline struck out on their own to paint in the village. They felt a sense of adventure and looked for a quaint building that they'd seen last week on their scouting trip. The sun was alternately hiding behind and peeking out from clouds. Jesse found a spot where there was some off-street space to set up and the buildings sheltered Caroline's easel, since having a canvas set up on one turned it into a sail in the breeziness.

This painting went quickly and attracted the attention of a group of children. They seemed to range in age from about eight to twelve and were very quiet while they watched her. When she finished, she greeted them and told them her name.

Very politely, they nodded and said hello to her. A little girl with a bright pink triangle scarf holding her hair back asked her why she wanted to paint a picture of that old building. Caroline explained that it was different from the others, and that in America, there weren't many buildings like that.

The little girl asked why the painting was so much prettier, with purple shadows, and Caroline tried to help her see that if she looked closely, the colors were really there, but Caroline had made them stronger. She explained that the little girl just didn't expect to see them, so she hadn't noticed before. She told her that artists were good about looking very closely to find things like that.

The children were enthralled to see what Caroline was talking about. Another little girl asked her to show them what colors she saw in a doorway of another building, where there was a box of flowers. Caroline showed them where she would splash the colors of the flowers onto the wall, where you could look closely and see them in the reflected light.

Baker happened to walk up to the group right then, and he seemed to either know or be recognized by them. He went to stand beside Caroline to face them. After saying hi, the little girl told him that Miss Caroline was showing them the colors on the buildings. She pointed to Caroline's painting and said it looked much prettier than she thought the building was before.

A boy in the group said, "My mum told me to stay away from artists. She said that they're not thinkin' about what Jesus would do when they paint people wearin' nothin' but skin."

Some of the children giggled, Baker was speechless, Natalie gasped, and Jesse almost bent double trying to stifle laughter. The film was rolling.

With an effort, Caroline put on a serious expression and looked right into the boy's eyes.

"Your mum knows her Bible, I can see that. She doesn't have to worry about you being around me. I believe the Bible, too. When people in Bible stories don't have clothes on, it is always shown as shameful, except for when people are married and alone. When the Bible talks about Heaven, everyone is wearing white robes, and that is the place where everything is perfect. Who knows the story of Adam and Eve?"

All the children raised their hands excitedly as if this was a contest. "Good," encouraged Caroline. "And who can tell me what happened when they disobeyed God and suddenly realized they had nothing on?"

The children looked at one another to see if anyone would give them a clue, and after a brief whispered conference, the boy said, "Well, they tried to make clothes with leaves or something," he offered.

Caroline nodded. "So Adam and Eve were alone except for when God came every day to walk and talk with them, and they still didn't think wearing nothing but their skin was a good thing in front of God, did they?"

The children shook their heads to say no. She continued. "So God Himself killed an animal to use the skin to make a covering for them since their leaves weren't good enough. God thought it was so important for them to have clothing that He made the clothes Himself. It was the first time death had happened in the world, all because Adam and Eve disobeyed God and didn't trust Him. Making clothes for them was like a picture that God painted of what He had to do when He would send Jesus. Jesus would be the death that would cover the shame of everyone who would believe and trust Him—like a clean white robe."

The children weren't the only ones captivated by this. Baker wore the same expression as they. The boy asked, "So you wouldn't paint Baker or that guy back there in their birthday suit because of the Bible?"

She heard Jesse and wished she could see what he was doing. She pressed her lips tight to keep control of a grin. "That's right," she answered. "Whose image does God say we are created in?"

"His!" most of them shouted.

"Right! So do you know of anyone who thinks it's alright to paint an image of God with nothing on?" she asked.

"NO!" they shouted together, shaking their heads as if that was ridiculous.

Baker leaned over to her ear. "We're being watched. Sorry—they were tailing me, and I thought I'd come over here to give you some positive press with the children. I might've messed up."

Caroline whispered back. "I saw them. It's not your fault."

The little girl who loved the colors said, "Will you be painting around 'ere tomorrow? Can we come back?"

Another girl asked, "If I bring my paints and paper, would you show me the colors on the wall and the shadows?"

"Me, too," said some of the others in chorus.

Caroline looked at Natalie, who nodded. "Okay, tell me and Baker the best place for us to see some of the colors and old buildings," said Caroline.

The children worked out where to meet, and Baker promised that he would get Miss Caroline there if it weren't raining. They were excited and all started telling one another what they were bringing.

Baker told the children that he needed to help the artist get back to his gram's house, so they scattered. They heard one boy say to another, "I've seen a picture of her boyfriend in the papers, and he'd beat our Baker up if he asked her to paint him like that."

***

The Gregorys expected news coverage and finished dinner early enough to gather in the family room in front of the television. The news started with an overview of the headlines to be featured, but they weren't the first one as they expected.

"In tonight's headlines, Baker Holmes finds out that American artist Caroline Painter won't do a portrait of him in his birthday suit," said the female news anchor with a smile.

"Also coming up, Gregory Global is cleared of any wrongdoing in privacy practices," chimed in a male anchor.

The whole room burst into laughter, and Cole and his cousin fell into the floor in an uncontrollable fit. Chad groaned, sat down hard into a wing chair, and covered his face with both hands.

***

Baker and Beth joined Caroline, Natalie, and Jesse to meet the local children late in the morning on Wednesday. After the photo and news blurb in the morning papers, Beth had agreed to get off from work for part of the day. She thought the news was hilarious and loved the way Caroline handled it.

"It's related to what Baker's problem with the music video was all about," she told Caroline as they followed Baker and Jesse to the chosen spot in the village. "He's learnin' how to defend that decision, and this helps a lot. I'm glad it happened."

The children brought friends, and Caroline's group needed Beth and Baker. Jesse was only filming Caroline's side of the presentation, so they wouldn't need to get permission to include the children. Some simply put their papers down on the pavers in an area they found that was safely away from traffic, sharing paint and water containers with friends. Caroline brought her watercolors so her paint would be similar and showed them how she would draw and paint a picture of an old stucco building with iron-railed balconies and flower-filled window boxes. A lazy cat napped in a window framed by a rickety old shutter that didn't look like it would make it through a storm.

They arrived back at Baker's grandmother's house late that afternoon to find a message from Chad, asking that Baker call as soon as possible. Baker asked Caroline and Beth to be there with him when he called.

"Hullo, Chad." Baker waited and listened. "Sure, everybody in music's heard of 'em." He looked at Beth with raised eyebrows. "I'll call my mates. We can be in London tonight. Do I use this number to call you?" He looked at Caroline. "Okay. I appreciate this. Do you want to talk to your girl? Okay, I'll tell her. Goodbye."

Baker pumped his fist and grabbed Beth in a hug. "Chad might have a record deal arranged for us to consider—some contacts he's made through his uncle. His brother's been workin' on it so he can handle it here after Chad leaves. I need to call the guys to leave right now so we can get to London."

He turned to Caroline and hugged her, too. "Chad's workin' and had a call, but he's goin' to get with you before his flight tomorrow."

Baker turned and picked up the phone, clearly excited. He dialed it and pulled Beth to him with the other arm. Caroline and Natalie smiled and left them together.

***

Thursday was spent packing up to leave Mevagissey. Chad called to say he would be in Charleston that night and would pick her up at the airport the next day when her group arrived. He told her that the meeting with Baker went well, and he thought they'd sign.

"Just one more day, then I can be with you again. We'll stay with my Heyward grandparents instead of the Gregorys since Mom is staying with them next week."

"Montgomery's house? It will be great to see him again," Caroline said.

"You're his favorite Painter," said Chad. She could tell from his voice that he was smiling.

"I'll be praying for you and your parents while you're traveling," Caroline told him. "And I can hardly wait to see you tomorrow."

"Me, too, for you," he answered.

Part Three
Consummation

Chapter Twenty Two

"You may have to fight a battle more than once to win it."
—Margaret Thatcher

It wasn't until Caroline was finally through the whirlwind of luggage, goodbyes, and hellos that she discovered how nervous Chad and her family had been about her plane coming in. TWA Flight 847 had been hijacked by the terrorist group Hezbollah, putting them on edge with "what ifs." When Chad kept looking at Caroline with relief at the airport, she reminded him that she was always ready to leave this world for Heaven or face trouble with the Lord by her side.

"I know," Chad said, taking her arm. "But I've spent four years planning something else."

Camellia and Montgomery came over and hovered around her. Caroline could see that they had been really concerned.

After a Lowcountry meal, she sat on the piazza swing with Chad under a blue-painted ceiling and realized that this evening was really happening. Twilight fell over the hum of people on the Battery. She sighed deeply.

"Your favorite time of day," mused Chad as they sat looking at the evening sky. "And you're almost too tired to appreciate it. It will take a few days to get used to the clock again."

"It only makes this more dreamy—sitting here with you, with nowhere to have to be, no reporters to watch for, relaxing on Charleston time," she answered. "The only place on Earth that's better than this is Painter Place. The moon is a crescent tonight. If only it were on the right side, we'd have palmettos and crescent moons in our own deep blue sky for a flag. We're home."

***

Chad and Caroline were up early on Saturday morning just as his parents were, still on British time. They had breakfast on the piazza, with the beautiful promise of a southern summer day surrounding them. They planned a shopping excursion on King Street so Caroline could pick up a

Father's Day gift and Camellia could look for a birthday gift for their daughter Sandy. Dinner would be at Middleton Place that evening.

King Street wasn't crowded when the stores were opening. The foursome walked together, passing a highly reputable jewelry store. Camellia stopped at the window, telling Phillip that she saw a pair of earrings that Sandy wanted.

Camellia and Caroline went in first while Phillip held the door. Camellia smiled conspiratorially to Caroline and said, "This is where Phillip bought my engagement ring. Have you ever dreamed about what you'd want your engagement ring to be like?"

"Sure. It would be a smaller version of the ring that Prince Rainier gave Grace Kelly. An emerald cut diamond is the shape of a canvas and creates a really artistic effect of play in the light and dark planes. Yet it flashes with fire in the pavilion, and when you look into it, it seems to go on for infinity. That's how I'd like my marriage to be—a smooth blank canvas to paint a lifetime together on, full of fire and flash underneath."

Camellia forgot to hide her surprise, stopping as she looked at Caroline with wide eyes. Behind them, Phillip calmly reached over to Chad's chin to close his mouth for him in case Caroline might turn around.

Seeing Camellia's expression, Caroline blushed. "Sorry, I answered without thinking. I hope I didn't—"

Camellia laughed. "Not at all—you're always refreshing! You've really thought this through."

Caroline followed Camellia over to the case with the display of earrings that Sandy wanted. She agreed that they looked like Sandy. Phillip stepped up beside Camellia while she talked to the jeweler, so Caroline wandered over to see what Chad was looking at. She smiled when he looked up.

"What's so pretty?" she asked.

"You outshine all of it, but this is interesting." He nodded at a dangling spray of tiny diamonds from a single earring, with a photo of a model wearing it from one ear while her hairstyle covered the other. It looked like three tiny eternity bracelet strands of different lengths hanging down in a graceful fall.

"It's gorgeous," she breathed. "When we wear our hair over one ear, a dangling earring tangles, and no one can really see it anyway. We only need to wear one. This is designed for that."

"You only wore one on our first date on the pier two Sunday nights ago."

"You noticed!"

A clerk came over to ask if she could help them, and Chad looked at Caroline before he said that he wanted the earring shown by the model. The clerk smiled at them before wrapping up the velvet box and handing Chad the receipt. "Special occasion?"

"Our two week anniversary," Chad answered, putting his arm around Caroline. He saw the clerk look for a ring on Caroline's hand, but before he could say anything, Caroline did.

"We're dating."

The clerk's eyes widened and she grinned. "You'd better hold on to this one, sweetie!"

***

Dinner was to be a dress-up affair, and Caroline was glad Chrissy had packed one of Juliette's tea-length dresses for her. It was an unusual art-deco inspired style in cobalt blue, with a fringed handkerchief hem and an off-the-shoulder neckline. She had sent along a coordinating collar-style necklace with some sapphire colored stones in it. Caroline created a simple updo that swept over to hide one ear. She put the new earring on the bare ear on the right side. She loved the effect, and it matched the bracelet Chad had given her last weekend.

Chad knocked at her room door to take her downstairs. She opened it, and they both stared at one another. He wore a tailored white dinner jacket and dark gray pants. His tie matched the blue in her dress.

He opened his mouth to say something and then didn't. He closed it and just stood there, then leaned his arm across the doorframe. He reached to touch the earring, creating a gently sparkling pendulum.

"I like that there's only one, like you. And you make me look good," he said, taking his arm off the doorframe and putting it out for her to take.

"Let's get through dinner so that I can take you for a walk alone on the Battery tonight."

***

Back at the Heyward's home later, they changed clothes and went out to walk down the street in White Point Gardens on the Battery. Caroline put on what she'd worn on the night she'd met Baker, but she left her hair up. The wind from the Ashley was strong enough tonight to have blown loose hair into her face all evening anyway. Chad wore jeans and an earthy olive green polo shirt.

Lots of people were walking, laughing, and taking photos. Sails passed by in the harbor, glowing with the first colors of the setting sun. An African American boy came up to Chad to tell him that his pretty girl should have some of the palmetto roses he'd woven. Chad picked out only one, but gave the boy enough money for a dozen.

"Just one, for my only one," Chad told the little boy with a wink. "See—one earring, one rose, and one girl."

The little boy broke into a huge grin. "You just ran outta money for two 'those earrings."

Chad laughed. "I'd run outta money if I had two girls, too!"

The little boy laughed and turned to another couple walking by, trying to sell more palmetto roses.

Chad and Caroline strolled under the oaks, palm trees, and tall sidewalk lanterns until they got close to the raised gazebo. She gently pulled his arm to back him into the foundation. Many other couples were standing around leaning on it, or on the gazebo railing, or sitting on the steps.

Chad relaxed and sighed contentedly as he leaned back and put one Nike running shoe up on the wall behind him. The breeze blew his hair across his brow.

She stood close beside him with her shoulder on the cool stone foundation. Her voice was quiet as if anyone around them might hear her say something she shouldn't. "Thank you," she said, looking up at him. "It's been a dreamy two weeks. This is too good to be real, and I wonder what happens when I wake up."

He lingered in the infinite blue sea of her eyes a while before responding. "You're welcome. I was hoping that you'd thank me like this. You're the one who's made the last two weeks so dreamy, though."

He touched his hand to his heart and then pointed at hers. He reached out to trace the curve of her jaw and chin. His eyes were serious. "This is real, and we're awake."

Someone behind Caroline accidentally backed into her and pushed her into Chad. They apologized, moving away. Caroline settled herself again, moving the rose to her other hand. Chad looked down at it. "Try to imagine that the palmetto rose is red, and put it on your pillow tonight. You never told me how that worked out in St. Austell, by the way."

She teased him with a smile as if she had a secret, twirling the rose before she looked out at the palm trees and oaks.

He took her free hand. "I'm—intrigued. And it looks like you're goin' to leave me that way. In the meantime, each week we get through for a month is a milestone. If I can keep you that long, you might get used to me and stick around."

She traced the palmetto rose on his shoulder, and he watched her face. Suddenly, he saw a struggle in her eyes. Something changed there, and he didn't like it. She impulsively started to stand back up from leaning on the wall, and he quickly pulled her back.

"What just happened?" His voice was still quiet but urgent.

She couldn't bring herself to say that he's the one who didn't stick around before, and that the color of his shirt was the same as Chris' eyes and polo shirt on the night he didn't stick around, either. She heard Chris' voice again. "Caroline, I can't take you where I'm going, and you can't wait for me to return."

She took a gulp of air and avoided his eyes by closing hers. "You might change. How can I trust you?" she whispered.

He groaned and put his head back onto the wall for a moment, looking up into the oaks, palms, and navy blue sky overhead. Then he brought it back up to look into her face, and he put the hand he was holding to his chest over his heart. "I'm not going anywhere, Caroline. I told you—this is real."

Their eyes locked. His were pleading, and hers gave in.

He could tell she was trying to shake something out of her mind as she shook her head. "I'm sorry. I can't believe I did that." She made a weak attempt at a smile. "Please—forget it. Let's talk about what you and Patrick will be doing next week with the Castaway."

He looked around them before making an easy move to stand in front of her. He propped himself with one hand on the wall so that that she would have to look at him. His eyes were serious, and his tone was the same. "I'm goin' to let this go right now. But I made a commitment to you two weeks ago tonight, with my ring on a gold chain. It was about Painter Place, but I thought I was clear that the next day when I talked to your dad, it would become about you, too."

After walking Caroline up to her room later and saying good night, Chad went back downstairs. His parents were watching television with his grandparents. He curtly asked if he could talk to them and headed into the kitchen. His mom stopped at the refrigerator first to get a plate of fruit to set down in front of them.

Phillip sat at the table and waited, studying his son. Chad raked his hand through the back of his hair. His mom ate a grape.

"She's got a serious trust issue with me," Chad said. "It's time for her to know."

Phillip looked down and traced a finger around the circumference of a small plate that Camellia had put in front of him. "Is she asking questions?"

"She's got too much dignity for that, but she's holding me accountable all the same. We're not goin' any further until she trusts me. If you guys thought I could drop into her life again and she'd follow me blindly, you underestimated her. I'm running out of anything to say that doesn't lead back to the reason I left. If that's how you guys want her to find out, I could become a cautionary tale."

Camellia glanced at her husband and back to her son, waiting. Phillip went back to tracing his finger around the plate rim.

Chad blew out a deep breath. "Tonight, I told her that each week for a month is a milestone, and if I could keep her for that long, she might decide to stick around. All of a sudden, I literally watched her go somewhere else through the look in her eyes, and she really tried, but she never came back from wherever that was. She acted like someone had knocked the wind out of her, said I might change, and asked how she could trust me."

"Did you try reminding her of your promise to stay at Painter Place?" asked his dad.

Chad nodded. "She thinks I might change my mind. She's set up a well-guarded boundary, and I'll never break it without an explanation."

He looked steadily and defiantly at his dad, who finally shrugged. "Okay, I'll make the call, but tomorrow's Father's Day, and you can bet it won't happen. Next week we'll be busy catching up from the trip. It might be next weekend."

Chad pursed his lips, sat back, and crossed his arms, feeling very uncooperative. "No promises from me, then."

"Did she look at your shirt when she became distracted?" asked Camellia, picking up an apple slice. She crunched it while she waited for his answer.

Chad was taken aback. "Well—yeah, she was running a palmetto rose along my shoulder. I suppose this is where you tell me she wasn't admiring my muscles."

"You're wearing Chris' color," she said simply. "He wore it a lot, and he left, too. That's two of you. Twice burned, lesson learned."

Chad looked at her in disbelief. An image of Chris in a green polo at the chapel hugging a smiling Caroline flashed into his mind. He leaned up on the table with his hands clasped tightly, narrowing his eyes. His tone was sharp. "If you're saying what I think you're saying, I'm getting really, really tired of this guy hanging around. And I'm planning to get erased from the black list so that he's the only one on it."

He looked down at his sleeve. "Where'd this come from, anyway? It was in my suitcase."

"It's Cole's. Justin's laundress probably mixed them up. You're better with the blue-greens like your eyes, not the earthy yellow ones." Camellia ate another grape and handed one to Phillip. "I'll go through your closet."

"I don't want a trace of this color anywhere near me." He looked at the ceiling. "And I can't believe we're having this conversation."

"Seriously, it's not that hard," said Camellia, handing Chad an apple and cheese wedge with a pretty toothpick in it. "Find out what someone likes or doesn't like, get past good or bad memories, and play up the good stuff. Avoid the bad."

"Do you do that to me?" asked Phillip with a scowl while she put a similar apple wedge on his plate.

"Ever since I've known you."

"You manipulated me?" he asked, choosing his words deliberately. He didn't look sure that he liked knowing about it.

"Sweetie, it's not manipulation if it's done for the right reasons and the other person likes it," she said with exasperation.

Chad rose from the table. "Okay, I feel like I wandered into Wonderland or something. I'm leaving now to change out of Cole's shirt so that I don't look like an ex-boyfriend."

"Lay low this week," his dad said with a warning tone. "We don't know what's going to happen. She's—unpredictable."

"That's one of the things about her that's irresistible to me. I want her trust back, and I'm goin' to make it happen."

Chapter Twenty-Three

"There's a divinity that shapes our ends,
Rough-hew them how we will."
—*Shakespeare, Hamlet, act v, scene ii*

The first week back at Painter Place was a busy one, challenging those who were trying to adjust to island time again. Shelly and the new studio manager Zachary tried to continue on for a few days as if Wyeth and Caroline weren't back, giving them some time to recover and set up a schedule.

Painter Place was hopping with guests. Three writers, ten artists, two solo musicians, and a new Christian rock band on retreat to brainstorm an album were all milling around at various times from the Big House and cottages.

Between his job at Global and his side business, Chad had several projects going on at once, so he and Caroline didn't get to see one another much. He had to catch up with Patrick on getting the Castaway built so Patrick could settle into the job there, and he was helping Cameron get the island involved in a movie as the setting for a spy thriller with a chase scene on the water. Natalie was staying at Painter Place for the summer to handle details, so Patrick was walking on clouds. Juliette would come in at some point, and Cameron would be in as soon as he could.

On Chad's first Friday back at Painter Place, Patrick took him out for a quick lunch at the Sand Dollar drive-in in Whitehaven. They had worked in Chad's office at Global all morning on plans and documents for contractors to begin the restaurant and would spend the afternoon with them getting the schedule underway.

Knowing they'd be playing basketball tonight, they skipped the chili burger and ordered something reasonably healthy. They'd been hydrating all day and ordered more water. Being extremely competitive and being together at lunch was strong motivation to stick to good eating habits.

After Patrick clicked the button on the intercom and ordered, Gloria walked up from behind to Chad's side of the Corvette to talk to him through the open T-top. She placed a beautifully manicured hand on the marine blue metallic paint on the door and said hi. She asked how they were doing, and after some comments back and forth about the beautiful weather, she said she had a job offer in Atlanta but hadn't decided to leave Whitehaven yet.

"You should take it, Gloria," Chad said smoothly. "You'll like Atlanta."

Gloria lowered her voice, but Patrick could easily hear her over the jazz music from someone's car stereo. "I know now the only reason you ever took me to the senior prom was because it was expected for the prom king and queen when they were single. You know I waited four years while both of us were in college, and I even came to some games at your campus to try to see you sometimes. Now you want me out of town."

"I was the envy of every guy at the prom, Gloria. You could've had any guy you wanted," Chad said, taking off his Wayfarers and looking right into her eyes. "Thank you for giving me the honor of being your date that night. But it was only because I couldn't bring a sophomore and had to be there."

"So after all this time, we finally get down to it. It was her even then." It was more of a statement than a question.

He nodded solemnly.

"You could've had both that night, Chad. You never gave me a chance! I expected you to at least try to kiss me." Her voice took on an edge. "Why didn't you even want to kiss me?"

Chad's voice picked up her edge and turned up the volume. "I don't throw them around like horseshoes, Gloria. I only have one first kiss to use in my life. It's always been Caroline's."

Gloria looked as if he'd slapped her. She studied his face. "You still haven't had that kiss." When she recovered, she tossed her head with her chin up. "If you've waited this long, I hope Chris didn't get her first kiss— the one that's supposed to be yours. I guess she told you he's in town today. They're having lunch together on Main Street. Guess he's having a hard time letting go."

Now Chad was the one who looked as if he'd been slapped. He turned a stunned expression in Patrick's direction. A waitress was hanging a tray over Patrick's door, and he turned to hand her the money for lunch.

Gloria took a deep breath. "Oh, I see she didn't tell you. Well, that's not hard to understand." She moved her hand from the car door to his shoulder, and he rudely shrugged it off.

"Take care of yourself, Chad. Maybe I'll see you around sometimes when I'm in town to visit my parents." Gloria turned and walked to her car, which was out of view of the Corvette. Her friend was in the passenger seat finishing a milkshake.

"Well, what happened?" she asked Gloria.

A tear ran down Gloria's face, and she put her hand over her eyes. "I'm taking that job in Atlanta," she said shakily.

***

Chad had changed from his business clothes to a tee shirt and gym shorts when he popped his head into the studio. Caroline was cleaning up to leave for the day.

"There you are," he said. He came in slowly toward the sink where she was standing. "I'm heading over to your house for basketball. Patrick and Natalie will be there soon, and Joey's coming so Marina's goin' to play. Danny's working late but might catch the Tarzan game after dinner."

She glanced over her shoulder at him, nodding and speaking over the running water. "I'm almost ready to leave."

He hesitated. "I heard you went to town for lunch today. Call me next time to let me know, and we'll meet."

He was at the counter now, leaning back onto the edge, when he looked down to see a note in strong masculine handwriting that had a phone number and address. It was signed by Chris Shepherd. He wanted to read it, but he dragged his eyes away and looked at Caroline instead.

She wished she'd put the note away. Turning the water off, she rolled her brushes in a towel, wondering how to talk about lunch.

"Your lunch date?" Chad's tone was even.

"I just ran into him on the street when I went to the post office to get a package for the gallery. We had some ice cream at Millie's on Main. He's on the way to his assignment. He wanted to make sure I'm okay and let me know how to reach him." She smoothed out the hairs of her brushes to dry on the towel.

221

"In case things don't work out with us?" Chad asked, narrowing his eyes. He didn't wait for an answer but abruptly headed for the open door. "It's crowded in here," he muttered.

"Chad," Caroline said. He kept walking.

She stood there for a moment, not believing he'd walked away from her. Then she untied her apron and pulled it over her head, flinging it over the stool, and grabbed her keys. By the time she got to the door, his Porsche was crossing Pavilion Way to go down South Castaway Drive to her house.

Shelly opened the gallery door. "Go after him," she said, tilting her head in that direction. "The way he slammed the door and jerked that car outta here, I knew there was a storm in paradise."

Chad saw Caroline in his rear view mirror, standing in the parking lot looking after him. He felt a rush to see her chase him, but it would take a lot more than that before this was over tonight. His grasp on the steering wheel tightened. He wasn't sure what it would take, exactly, but she'd better come up with it.

It had been a long week of not seeing much of her and being careful what he said, and he still wasn't over being upstaged by Chris in a romantic moment on the Battery last Saturday night. He'd been holding back his imagination about the implications of her seeing him all afternoon while he and Patrick dealt with the contractors. Something snapped at seeing Chris' confident signature and contact info in bold black ink for Caroline to keep, and he desperately wanted to know what else was on that note.

He was steaming with more than the South Carolina summer heat as he was getting a basketball and towel out of his Porsche. Caroline pulled her Mustang into the garage, but he didn't even look her way. About ten minutes later, she came out in gym shorts and a tank top. Without a word, she ran in to rebound the shot he missed and got hers in. Patrick's Corvette slowly pulled in with Natalie in the passenger seat.

Patrick put a hand on Natalie's arm. "Chad's upset with Caroline."

Natalie looked at him blankly. "How do you know?"

"Trust me. It's this thing they do—or used to before he went to college. He wants her attention because she's done something he didn't like and he expects an apology. She'll give him space to blow off steam, but he'll eventually get the puppy dog look that says she's sorry. He'll dangle her around longer until he decides she understands that she can't treat him like that. Then he'll cave. Physical stuff relaxes him, so the issue won't be so important after some basketball. Today's issue is that he found out that Caroline had lunch with Chris and didn't tell him."

"Are you saying they're fighting and will work it out without saying anything?" asked Natalie.

"They'll say a few things in code, but mostly it's intuition and body language. They'll foul one another but won't call it. Chad won't choose her for his team because he wants her on the opposing one, where he can confront her. Joey and Marina will pick up on what's happening, and Joey will jerk him around by guarding Caroline and forcing Chad to handle me. That takes Chad's whole design for her attention away, and worse, he doesn't like any male who's not family to be close to her. Are you up for this?"

"Wild horses—" she began, her eyes wide.

"Couldn't drag you away," he finished along with her. "Good. You won't be sorry." He got out and opened her car door as Joey's motorcycle roared in behind the Corvette.

With his back to the concrete driveway half court where Chad was ignoring Caroline, Joey removed his helmet, brown hair tumbling down, and raised his eyebrows significantly at Patrick while he tilted his head in Chad's direction. Patrick told him under his breath about lunch. Joey grinned, ready to have some fun.

Marina came out, dancing her way down to greet everyone and telling them that her mother was still in her studio and would be calling the pizza order in for seven thirty. Water, tea, and lemonade were on the back porch in pitchers with an ice bucket and paper cups. Salty pretzels, chips, and watermelon chunks were in sealed containers. Lady watched, thumping her tail happily and panting as if she was smiling at them.

Joey set up a compact stereo close to the court to play some cassette tapes with a mix of rock songs he'd recorded on them especially for basketball on Friday nights. The first song out of the speakers was the throbbing sound of "Heard it Through the Grapevine" by Credence Clearwater Revival.

The court was shaded by palms and ancient oaks dripping with Spanish moss. The wind drifting off the water blew softly against gym shorts, tee shirts, and swinging ponytails. Patrick told Chad he could choose his team first, and Chad was making a shot when he said he wanted Joey and Marina. Patrick winked at Natalie as if to say he told her so and handed her and Caroline some bright blue wristbands to identify themselves as his team.

Patrick sent Caroline over to guard Chad, whose team had first possession. He was wearing the Carolina blue tee shirt she had slept in two weeks ago in St. Austell, and she lightly brushed the sleeve with her hand. "Reminding me of good times and good dreams?" she asked softly.

He remained expressionless.

Marina brought the ball in, dribbling slowly to gauge Natalie before she passed to Joey. Patrick got a piece of it and sent it back into the air. The scramble sent the loose ball out to Natalie.

When Marina put on some pressure, Natalie tried to pass, but Caroline had to go up to help her. Chad kept his distance but stood ready. She slowed down the dribble and stood there, unchallenged, to wait things out. Her eyes taunted him to come get the ball. His told her he'd do just that—when he was good and ready.

Caroline looked out to Joey with a shrug as if asking if he wanted to try her. Joey jumped away from Patrick and in front of Chad to get things going. Chad backed away to deal with Patrick, who was heading under the basket to wait on Caroline's pass. But Joey stayed too close to her to work with her brother.

Joey began to sing to her as the song was winding down. "Do you dare let me go for the other guy that you knew before? Ooo . . ."

She grinned back at him as she signaled Natalie, who came in and realized in a flash that the pass would be behind Caroline's back. Caroline kept Joey and Marina from Natalie for the instant it took to get an overhead pass to Patrick, who was barely able to get it past Chad and score.

Both teams reset, and Chad intentionally brushed into Caroline hard. "Behind the back—your blue plate special today?"

Her eyes narrowed. "A guard with that is extra," she shot back on her way over to match up with Joey, who heard Chad. He made the sound of something huge crashing and burning. Patrick and Natalie exchanged glances.

Marina sent a bounce-pass that Chad caught. He evaded Patrick with a double-pivot fake and drove in for an easy shot. He didn't look at Caroline as he walked back into position, so she stayed with Joey. Natalie set up and came in while Patrick and Caroline tried to get open.

Patrick noticed that Joey was getting under Chad's skin by staying closer than he needed to with Caroline. He signaled to her, and she broke away from Joey to take the ball from Natalie. She risked a blind pass to him, and he had to hold back from an urge to dunk the shot.

Natalie's eyes were shining with admiration when she looked at Patrick, who grinned and shrugged. "It happens when you've been playing together for a long time."

Marina passed to Joey, who baited Caroline by turning his dribble into dancing with her.

"Joey!" Chad said sharply. He was free of Patrick in a flash and came by for a bounce pass from Joey to sink a shot.

Patrick groaned and pulled Caroline over to whisper to her. She moved to Natalie's position, standing out of bounds with the ball to catch her breath while Chad huddled briefly with his team. She glanced out over the waterway as a boat passed and another song ended. She brought the ball in toward her little sister as Bonnie Tyler began singing "I Need A Hero."

Marina kept her sister from getting closer to her teammates, but she got distracted when Danny's truck pulled into the driveway. Caroline instantly stepped sideways and drove past her and all the way to the basket for a layup. Natalie cheered and ran under the basket with Caroline, where they sang to each other with fists shaped into imaginary microphones.

> ". . . *Racing on the thunder and rising with the heat,*
> *It's gonna take a superman to sweep me off my feet*
> *I need a hero . . .*"

Patrick broke up the duet when he came up to grab Natalie's arm and swing her around as if he were sweeping her off her feet. Then he huddled her and Caroline together to whisper some plays to them. He sent Natalie out to bring the ball in, and he matched Caroline with Chad again so she would be more open, assuming Chad was keeping his distance. Deep Purple's "Smoke on the Water" came from the stereo.

Chad watched the huddle and guessed what Patrick was planning. He'd be helping Patrick's team if he kept his distance from Caroline so near the basket. He changed tactics, closely screening her. She fought to get open and finally made a frustrated little cry. Chad was relentless, and her hand came down hard on his forearm. He flinched but still didn't give her any space. She was useless to Patrick and Natalie, who had to work together to score.

She was panting and pushed her wet bangs off her forehead as Marina went to the line to check the ball for Chad's team again.

"You wanted a guard," Chad used his steel voice as he caught a pass from Marina over Caroline's head. He sank a long shot before she could stop him.

She looked sullenly over at him. Her eyes said, "I don't like this."

He coolly looked away.

***

Valerie Painter stood looking out the window in her pottery studio at the basketball court with the phone in her hand. "Thought you might be interested in knowing the weather conditions on the court before you come home. We have a dark storm with lightning strikes, but a good chance of starry skies later."

Her husband chuckled. "Should I bring home a big tub of ice cream from Millie's?"

"Only if you enjoy lighting a match to a tanker truck. Joey can't resist, and he's going through a whole box of matches out there right now. I'd stop at the grocery store for Breyers on the way home. Add some chocolate syrup to the list. I just ordered the pizza."

"Anything else I need to know?"

"I'd say Natalie has found a home. We may even have two weddings this year and one next year after Marina graduates."

"That's okay. I have a plan for Chad and Caroline's. I'll just invite the press and charge admission. I know Phillip will love the idea, and he'll wish he'd been the one to come up with it, but Camellia might give us some trouble. We certainly have enough piers around there for Chad to throw someone in the drink."

"Speaking of the kind of guys who throw others off a pier, Phillip should be here by the time you are. Hope you're not too tired to take him on tonight. Camellia comes back from Charleston in the morning."

"As always, you motivate me to dazzle you with my athletic prowess. I've still got a few tricks up my worn-out old sleeves."

"I love being dazzled, and I don't think he can outscore you tonight. He won't have Camellia here to motivate him to show off."

***

On the court, Natalie passed to Patrick. He touch passed instantly to Caroline before Chad could react to block it. In a mood for revenge, she drew contact with a pump-fake and jump toward Chad as she shot. The shot went in. Chad shook his head and smiled despite himself, and her team demanded foul shots.

When she got only one of the free throws, and his team started to check the ball in, she walked back to guard him, brushing against his arm. "I'm not takin' all the blame for this." Her voice was low. "He knows he was just the consolation prize. It's time you figured it out, too."

Chad blinked and swallowed hard before noticing that Marina needed him. She launched a chest pass after faking Natalie, and Chad nimbly sent it to Joey. Caroline bumped into him with her momentum when the ball was gone, and she impatiently spun to see where it was. Joey took a shot that rolled around on the rim. She was unable to stop Chad when he and Patrick went for it, and Chad tipped the ball in.

The goal of twenty-one points was in sight later with Patrick's team still ahead. From the stereo, Bruce Springsteen began singing "Dancing in the Dark." Chad stood dribbling the ball to see where the rest of his team was and who was open. He glanced at Caroline warily before giving Joey a signal. He expected payback, but she was giving him some room.

Caroline was ready to spring, but she was looking at his face instead of the ball. Intrigued by the way she was guarding, he stopped ignoring her and searched to read a strategy in her expression.

"You can't start a fire
You can't start a fire without a spark . . ."

Her eyes glanced down at his mouth, and he caught his breath. He looked at her in surprise but kept dribbling instinctively. A lightning-quick move of her hand brushed a fingertip against the ball. He was just as quick to dribble under his leg to get the ball out of her reach before he drove toward the basket.

It was enough of a distraction for Patrick to get free of Joey to stop Chad's move, so Chad quickly passed to Joey instead. Without Patrick to stop him, Joey scored, and Patrick grunted in frustration.

As they set up again, Chad brushed into Caroline and stayed against the front of her shoulder. "New strategy?" he muttered near her ear.

She turned her head slightly in his direction but kept her eyes on Natalie as she took the ball out. "No. Distraction."

He had to move as the ball came in. The next play ended with Caroline going for a solid jump shot that Chad couldn't guard, and Patrick's team won by a basket. Everyone was panting as they began heading slowly off the half court toward the porch for something to drink.

Chad waited for Caroline to go in front of him, but she stood still, looking at him solemnly. He didn't react, so she turned to follow the others, ponytail swinging with a toss of her head.

Chad reached out and grasped her arm as she was walking away, pulling her back around to look at him. "We need to talk later," he said gruffly.

She nodded. He let her go and walked with her to join everyone else.

***

Valerie, Andy, and Phillip had joined Danny and Lady on the porch to watch the game. Dinner was quick because the guys would eat light and come back for more after their game. The ladies pulled up some lawn chairs to be closer to the court and cheer the guys on. The scent of citronella and herbs came from lanterns nearby.

Valerie looked at Natalie and smiled warmly. "Did Patrick fill you in on the Painter Place summer schedule? It's nice to have you joining us this year."

Natalie used her fingers to account for the schedule. "Let's see," she said as she started with the first finger. "Friday nights usually involve basketball in good weather and board games in bad, with Saturday night around water—like the pool, on a boat, or on the beach. Sunday involves church and dinner at the Big House, and otherwise, anything might happen at any time."

"The guys beat their chests like Tarzan for us on Fridays. Not literally, but you get the idea. They vent the stress of their week, and we just enjoy being the objects of so much effort and bravado."

"Is Joey a friend or family?" asked Natalie.

"He's Chad's sister's husband's brother. Her husband is from Whitehaven, and they live in Charleston, where he works in some kind of intelligence—the kind where he can't tell us what he does or he has to kill us. Joey's always been good friends with the boys anyway. Sandy's husband is older than them and went to the Citadel, but he came home to visit once and met Sandy. Not long after, they got married. So Joey is like family for the Gregorys."

Joey heard his name and looked their way curiously before he flipped the cassette over on the stereo, putting in a collection of older rock and roll songs to fire up Andy and Phillip. He, Phillip, and Chad teamed up against Patrick, Andy, and Danny for a very lively competition, full of jokes, tricks, schemes, shouts, and laughter. Just as Valerie predicted to her husband, he had one basket more than his rival, Phillip. But Chad had more than Patrick, and they both hot dogged around as much as their dads. Natalie fit in just as if she'd always cheered and laughed with the ladies.

When the game was over, everyone gathered back on the porch for more food and ice cream. Chad went up to Patrick's room to take a quick shower and change, and Patrick pulled Caroline aside to briefly tell her about what Gloria did at the Sand Dollar.

"She insinuated I was sneaking around?" Caroline rolled her eyes. "No wonder he's mad at me."

Patrick nodded, swallowing a bite of pizza. "It's more than that— something about Chris and last weekend, but he didn't say what. It was building up, and he hit his limit."

She looked at him thoughtfully. He had to be talking about the Battery. Somehow, Chad figured out what had happened.

"He really said that to Gloria about our kiss—and the prom?"

"You bet," Patrick said between bites. "She tried to touch him, and he jerked away like she'd burned him."

She rushed up to her room to freshen up and change. She brushed her hair into a loose side ponytail with the studded black leather ribbon wrapped around it and put the chain with Chad's ring around her neck.

She saw Chad notice the ring against her sleeveless sweater when she came down. He didn't say anything as he took her hand to walk outside, leading her to the pier in the backyard

The shore of Whitehaven twinkled cheerfully across the Intracoastal Waterway like a strand of Christmas lights, and a few insects were singing to the soft pop music coming from Joey's stereo on the driveway. Caroline could tell Chad was relaxed now as they walked out to the end of the pier and sat down on built-in benches.

"The crescent moon is on the right side this weekend," she said as she looked up at it, hoping to remind him of sitting on the porch swing together in Charleston on the Friday night before. "We have our own state flag tonight."

He looked up at the moon and nodded with a little smile, but he didn't say anything.

"I didn't plan to meet Chris or to hide it from you. I'm surprised you'd think I would have," she began.

She looked over at him, the planes of his face framed by the shadows of the night. He looked like a handsome Greek hero carved into a statue—the moody kind that threw lightning bolts.

"We sat in front of the window at the street so anyone could see us. We weren't sneaking around. He heard about Baker and the children in

Mevagissey and asked to hear the stories. He saw the photos and publicity that Uncle Wyeth put in the Whitehaven Register."

Chad was letting her talk, not saying anything.

"He—uh—well, he did say that if anything ever happened to separate you and me, he'd like for me to tell Sherrie. But the contact info he gave me is for emergencies or to give to friends who want to write to him or send him packages. He doesn't know how long it will be valid, and I can get updates from Sherrie. He wrote a personal message and a quote on it from Jim Elliot, a missionary."

They sat there for a few minutes. Crickets were quite literally chirping.

"I saw him break up with you," Chad confessed, still looking out at the stars reflected on the water.

Caroline was startled. Her mind raced with a lot of things to say, but she was speechless. This explained a lot.

"I'd just come in and was enjoying being home, test driving the new Lamborghini on the island and seeing how many cottages were being used. I stopped and parked at the camping area to walk around and ended up at the chapel. It seemed like a good time to just stop and pray there about—everything." He shrugged. "About you, about my hopes and plans, about my place in regards to the grand scheme of things at Painter Place. I had just gone outside toward the back trail when I heard the little Triumph. I didn't know who the driver was, so I stuck around at the trail to see what he was doing there. He went inside, and he was talking out loud. It sounded like he was praying, too, which made me even more curious. He'd stopped just before you drove up."

Chad showed emotion for the first time. He closed his eyes and ran his hand over his forehead. Then he raked it through his straight blonde hair. He didn't seem to be able to talk, and tears came to her eyes to see his reaction.

"I hadn't seen you in person in so long." His voice broke. "I should've left, but I was totally unable to. When he hit his heart and buckled his knees at seeing you, I was doing the same thing. When you went up to hug him with that smile on your face, I was so unbelievably jealous and wanted to come break it up."

He stopped and swallowed. "By the time you started walking together, I knew he wasn't there for a date. You'd have both seen me if I tried to get away. It would've been too awkward to meet you that way after so long."

He bit his lip and continued to look over the waterway. "I was so glad he was breakin' up with you," he said with intensity, narrowing his eyes and shaking his head. "But at the same time, I felt so bad that you were in that position."

He suddenly smiled faintly into the distance, as if seeing a memory. "You were—amazing, really. That was the one of the classiest things I think I've ever seen you do. Patrick showed up and took you home, but I would have, if it had come down to it. I expected Chris to just drive off into the sunset after you turned your back on him like that. But he sat down and cried his heart out, so I left down the trail to the car."

He paused and nudged her arm. "I admit you picked an exceptional consolation prize."

She didn't say anything. He started talking again in the same quiet, steady tone.

"I went home to call Patrick to see if we could get together that evening, and to see if you were okay. I knew if you were upset, you'd go down by the water after your family was in bed. I parked near the end of Castaway in front of your house. I walked a little on the beach until the lights were off, and sure enough, you finally came out. It was torture to see you cry like that over someone else, but I didn't leave until you went back in."

After a few moments, he cleared his throat and leaned forward with his elbows on the knees of his jeans. His hands were clasped in front of him. He kept looking at the water. "How close were you and Chris?"

"I only have one first kiss, and it's always been yours."

His face showed relief as he turned to look at her. "Patrick told you?"

She nodded, and he sat back, moving closer to rest his arm behind her on the pier railing.

She moved a little closer on the bench. "What you said to me when you got on the yacht in Mevagissey . . . It sounds like a true kiss is dangerous—

not like the easy come, easy go kind of thing in songs. It's hard not to wonder..."

Instantly, Chad's expression changed with a grin so broad that it made the corners of his eyes crinkle. "Miss Caroline Painter, are you sayin' that you've been imagining that kiss? Is that what happened tonight when you were guarding me?"

He groaned and lightly slapped his face with his hand. "Are you doin' this to me on purpose? How many steps up is this from being 'significant on a personal level'?"

Caroline just smiled demurely.

***

Patrick and Natalie walked to the double swing near the pier. "So you've survived a Friday night with my crazy family and gotten a taste of Painter Place," Patrick said as he put his arm around her on the back of the swing. "It's even nuttier when my Uncle Wyeth and Chrissy are here. We kids grew up calling Wyeth, my dad, and Phillip 'The Big Three.'"

Natalie smiled and relaxed in the rocking motion of the swing. She nodded at the pier where Chad and Caroline were talking. "What's next for them?"

"Chad is anxiously waiting for her to tell him she loves him. He does it all the time with that little 'from my heart to yours' thing he does."

She sighed deeply as if the very air was magic. "Everybody else knows she does."

"He knows it, too, but he wants her to give in to it. There's more to this, and it will come out soon. You'll understand that she has reason to hold back. Man, you should have seen her on the Saturday morning of the Island Summer Dance. It was the first time she'd seen him in four years, and it was so electric that it shook even me up. But she didn't know she was doing it!"

Natalie laughed. "She was that obvious? How awkward. What did Chad do?"

"He thought he might have dreamed it. It was definitely his dream to see that reaction from her."

He shifted a little on the swing, animated now that he was telling a story. "This looks like just a fulfilled childhood romance to people from off, but for us, this is history and a lot rides on it. A Gregory has always been a financial guardian of Painter Place. Chad's ancestor liquidated all the nobility assets in England for us and got this island, where both families could escape. I'm named after the original Painter who settled the island, and he launched the Gregorys here so they could do what they do best again. Every generation in both families decides whether to continue the legacy or if those times are over. No Painter ever married a Gregory in those three hundred years—usually the generations weren't timed to match up that closely. It changes the whole financial landscape and inheritance dynamics. As the artist in the family, Caroline gets the mansion and most of the island after Uncle Wyeth, according to how Painter Place is passed on. If she has a child that's the next artist, instead of me having a child who is the next artist, a Gregory will have the mansion for the first time in our history."

Natalie mulled all of this new insight over. The swing swayed as they looked over the water, where stars seemed to have fallen into the current.

"Have you ever told anyone you loved them?" Patrick ventured.

"Na," said Natalie, shaking her head. "I came very close once. But I was forcing things. Have you?"

"Nope. I needed a career plan first so I'd have something to offer whomever I'm supposed to be with—proof that I'm worth having and ready to settle down. But my family and I've been praying for her as long as I can remember."

Natalie took a deep breath. Then she smiled at him. "Guys don't talk like that anymore, you know. Time seems to have stood still on this island when it comes to faith and family."

"I'm glad you like it here."

"I *love* it here. I wish it were my home, and I'd never have to leave." Her voice was full of longing.

The swing moved gently in rhythm. "Does this mean that if you had a reason to stay, you would stick around after Cameron's movie set is over?"

"I would," said Natalie. "I'm hoping you'll give me a reason."

Patrick couldn't help taking a huge gulp of air.

***

Patrick's family was in bed when he called Chad's private line. Chad sounded sleepy when he answered.

"Are you up? I can't go to sleep until I tell you about what happened tonight."

"I was just going to bed. In the morning, I'm going to be feeling the beating you guys gave me tonight."

"Awww, don't be a crybaby. That's what happens when you stay gone too long and hang out with the caviar crowd," taunted Patrick.

"Says the guy whose only paycheck at the moment is from investments I made for him with the caviar crowd," said Chad. "Did you call me for a reason?"

"Natalie told me tonight that she loves it here and never wants to leave. *Loves* it here," he repeated. "I asked her if she'd stay after the movie filming is over if she had a good reason, and guess what she said!"

"There are usually only two responses to that. By the sound of your voice, I'll go with a 'yes'. I'm happy for you, buddy. She's a great girl, and she's beautiful." He yawned.

"Not just a 'yes.' She said she was *hoping* I'd give her a reason to stay!"

"Wow. So—did you?"

"I asked her if I could call Cameron to talk about it. They have no family left but an aunt who is a costume seamstress for the movies. We haven't known each other long, and this is moving fast, but it just feels right. I'll need to get some big questions answered about common goals before I let myself get in any deeper. I'm starting to have to come up for air. At this rate, she'll say she loves me before Caroline tells you."

"Is that—a challenge?" demanded Chad, sounding suddenly very much awake. Patrick could tell from the background sounds that his friend had gotten out of bed. He pictured him looking out the glass doors of his room in the direction of the Patrick's, as if he was talking to him in person.

Patrick's response was a laugh.

"You're on, man," Chad said. "Give me the rules. We start this race first thing in the morning."

Chapter Twenty-Four

"There's a sort of rage a man feels when he's been deceived where he most trusted. It compares to no other anger."
—Orson Scott Card

Saturday would be busy on the island. A crew was coming in to do some preliminary set work for Cameron's spy movie, and Patrick and Chad were going to work to expand the camping area on Dog Head for them to use for a few days. Most of the people associated with the film would stay in Whitehaven, and the residents were excited. Once the schedule was set, some were even planning to stay with friends and rent their homes to any overflow. The movie was going to be a boon to Whitehaven, and they wanted more of this kind of business in the future.

Chad decided to have a short jog on the beach while it was cool that morning, trying to loosen up some sore muscles from the Tarzan game. He slowed when he thought he heard someone talking, but stopped cold when he heard Caroline's voice and tone. He'd be an unwelcome intruder in this conversation, so he went up to stand in a palm tree grove and peeked around one of the trunks.

It looked like Caroline and Andy Painter had been jogging since the sand was scarred with a trail of footprints coming from the direction of their home. Caroline was putting her hands to her forehead, pushing strands of blonde bangs off of her skin. Then she nearly bent double as if someone had kicked her in the stomach.

When she stood up again, she cried, "I can't believe you watched me suffer like that, especially that first year. When every holiday came and went without him coming home, how could you see me so disappointed and never give me a clue? You're supposed to catch me when I fall, not create a cliff to push me from!"

She pivoted away from him when he said her name and tried to reach for her. "Don't touch me!" She shouted with so much venom in her voice that Chad winced for Andy.

She began sobbing, turning her back to him and holding her stomach. Chad closed his eyes and groaned. He desperately wanted to go put his arms around her and assure her that everything was going to be okay.

"Caroline, no one gets my daughter without proving what kind of man he is. And no one gets Painter Place unless he earns my daughter. I'm not perfect, but this was the only way I could see to resolve my concerns at the time. Can't you trust me to always look after your best interest?"

"Not anymore!" Her voice was bordering on hysterical. "Can't you trust me, Dad? Did everyone know except me?"

"No. Obviously Phillip and I knew, and we had to include your mom and Chad's. Patrick, Chad, and Gran Vanna were the only others, unless Phillip told Justin. I think Joey and Cole guessed." Andy's tone was miserable.

"Gran Vanna knew? She thought this was a good idea?" she sobbed, incredulous.

"No, she just agreed not to interfere, like your mom and Chad's mom. No one liked it." He tried to reach for her again.

"What about my feelings?" she wailed, jerking away from him.

"Your feelings were part of the problem, Caroline! They made you unpredictable. Painter Place is about more than anyone's feelings! You needed to learn how to be Caroline Amanda Painter, descendant of generations of talented people with the extraordinary gift of a place to nurture it. You needed to know how to be alone, growing into your own identity, so that you'd know yourself instead of melting into someone else's personality and expectations."

Chad leaned his head against the palm, squeezing his eyes closed with a grimace to fight tears. He remembered how it felt when his dad and Andy had talked to him about this before college.

"It always comes down to preserving Painter Place!" Her voice was intended to be a shout, but it was too ragged from crying. "It owns us. Has any other Painter been treated the way I have?"

Andy didn't answer.

"That's what I thought. I'm the first female to inherit Painter Place, so I'm a problem."

"Only if the man you marry is a problem, Caroline. How can I make you see? If you thought like a man, you'd know exactly what I'm talking about."

Chad couldn't help watching them again. Andy Painter was looking at the cloudless sky and running both hands through his sun-bleached blonde hair. He turned back to his daughter, who was wiping her eyes with her palms.

"Phillip raised his boys on a tight moral ship, hoping for godly men when they left on their own. He knows better than anyone that Chad and Cole have everything it takes to be the perfect storm, a dad's worst nightmare for a daughter."

Andy put both arms out at his sides in a gesture of helplessness. "Cole's been flirting with the extreme edges of what he can get by with ever since Chad left, and unless Chad tamps him down now, God only knows what he's goin' to get into and who will pay for his recklessness. It's already cost Phillip and Justin."

He paused and put his hands on the hips of his running shorts, his eyes and tone pleading with her. "And that newspaper photo I heard about in London with Chad and another woman—baby, can't you see that's just the tip of the iceberg? It was so easy to believe the worst about him for a very clear reason."

His voice became hard. "I swear, if you marry him and he runs around on you, Painter Place will have a worse scandal than his cheating to deal with, 'cause I'll take care of him myself. When the Painter boys are through, his dad gets what's left of him, and he'll still have to face losing Global. He'll have to run a long way, 'cause Charleston wouldn't be far enough."

Andy Painter's voice was shaking. He clenched his hands into fists. Chad blew out a quick intake of breath.

Caroline turned a dragon look on her dad. "But you let me believe the worst about him for four years, when he didn't do anything to deserve it. He was doing all the right things. You let me waste time with Chris because I thought Chad wasn't a choice. What if Chris hadn't left before Chad came back?"

"Give me some credit for a little sense, Caroline! You'd have broken off things with Chris soon, once you realized he wasn't going to fit into Painter Place, so Chad would only have hastened the inevitable. You were smart enough not to fall for Derrick, though I admit you had me going on that one, and I sweated it out. I only agreed to you seeing Chris a few months ago in case Chad fell into the playboy role or didn't come back in the same mindset. It didn't hurt to have some experience with thinking in a new direction with someone from off."

Caroline nearly screamed her words as she balled her fists. "It hurt me, Dad! It hurt me! When Chris left, it was the second time that Painter Place was the reason someone I cared about walked out of my life. Without knowing there was a finish line set up in a plan that involved me, I was blindly headed in a direction that led nowhere. It kept both me and Chris distracted from where we were meant to be going, and it was certainly not fair to Chad. And you knew all the time."

"I couldn't be sure that you wouldn't change your mind about Chad once he was gone, or what kind of man Chad would be. It had to play out."

"Yeah, well, it's all played out now." Her voice was cold. "I don't know what you imagined would happen someday in the future when you told me this. I grew up in a home where there were never supposed to be any secrets. It will never be the same for me again."

She turned and jogged back to the house. Andy Painter called after her, but she ignored him. He collapsed onto his knees into the sand, looking out at the surf. His back was to Chad, but from the way his broad shoulders moved and his hands wiped his face, Chad knew he was crying.

Chad sat down hard on the sand in the palm grove and put his head in his hands. Caroline finally knew. He didn't know if this was a beginning, an ending, or both. But it was finally out. He suspected that the way he handled it now was going to be the key for everyone.

He heard in his mind again Andy's revelation of his wariness about who he'd become. He took a deep breath and rubbed the palms of his hands on the side of his gym shorts to dry them. He knew from his dad in the beginning that this was part of the issue, but actually hearing Andy talk about it to Caroline with so much conviction was startling. After what had just happened in London with Cole, Chad knew he had a point. Things could've gone really wrong there without divine intervention.

Andy Painter wasn't raising a daughter in purity just to turn her over to a guy who played around and could drop scandal down like a bomb onto Painter Place for the first time ever. He wasn't giving his daughter to a guy who was likely to bring chaos to a family with no history of divorce and who could have children that would inherit Painter Place. And Chad realized all over again why this was so important to him, too. It was a mirror image of his own family's history, and why he had to be so incredibly careful of whom he married into the Gregory name and Gregory Global.

He'd passed the test fair and square, and he was feeling more determined than ever. He had the right girl. Now for damage control with Caroline. His dad and Andy were going to have their own challenge in damage control today. When Wyeth Painter found out about this, it was going to be a rough day on the island.

He left the palm grove quietly while Andy Painter was still on his knees in the sand. He went straight back home and was just out of the shower and dressed when Patrick called. He picked up the phone and walked over to look at *Tall Ships and Sunflowers* where it sat propped on his dresser.

"Hey, uh, I'm gonna give you an extra day before we start that competition," said Patrick, tension in his voice. "I'll tell you more when I pick you up. Dad told Caroline what he and Phillip did. She feels betrayed, manipulated, and like Painter Place controls her."

"Don't tell your dad, but I was jogging and heard the end of this between them on the beach. There's no way she's coming through this without some permanent damage. But at least she finally knows I paid a high price to be with her. I've been waiting a long time for this day."

"I want to know what you heard when I pick you up. I've never seen her act like this before."

"Then that makes two of us. I couldn't believe the way she was screaming at your dad—mine would have decked me. But she was thinking with deadly clarity and got right to her point. The cool customer pulled out a shotgun. Did you know she had one of those and knows how to use it? I have a new respect for not crossing the trust line with her. There's steel under that magnolia, and she'll use it on you."

Patrick groaned. "When she came storming in, she grabbed one of Joey's cassettes on her way to her room to get ready to leave the house. I don't know if you can hear it, but at the moment, Black Sabbath's "Iron Man"—about revenge from the guy who doesn't see or feel—is jarring the windows. She called Shelly to say she won't be in the studio today and called Carly to plan a day off the island. She isn't speaking to Mamma or Dad. Marina knows now, too, and that's a whole new can of worms. She's bawling her eyes out."

"Has Caroline said anything about me?"

"No, or me either, so we might both escape the buckshot today. But I wouldn't be looking for an 'I love you' unless she asks you to run away with her. Be ready for anything. Talk to her after she gets to Carly's and calms down."

"Come on and pick me up. Let's finish at Dog's Head as soon as we can. What's Carly's number?"

***

Chad had Patrick stop at the Big House to ask Natalie to go to dinner and the movies with him and Caroline. He needed to keep Caroline off the island tonight. He went into her studio while he waited for Patrick to come back out to the car, urgently wanting a connection with her.

He glanced around at what she'd been working on. He was so full of jealousy yesterday when he'd come in that he had ignored anything else. There were a few paintings from Mevagissey lining the walls as she worked on a series, but she also had a few of the island for the gallery. One was the marsh, and he wondered if she'd thought of what she said about his eyes in Mevagissey. Her style had changed a little since that trip.

That led to remembering the painting of the cliffs, and it crossed his mind that if she had come in today in her current emotional state, he wasn't sure he could handle whatever came out of her feelings about Painter Place on canvas. But he'd bet a rock band would like it.

He almost missed a large one resting on the floor in a corner behind an easel, and he went to look closer. She'd only have put one there if she weren't working on it steadily, which meant it was personal. He pulled it out and squatted down to see it better. He loved what she'd done so far, and his heart ached with sweet memories. It was the night view of the lights of the pavilion at the Island Summer Dance from the front porch of the mansion—the view from the times she'd always picked him to dance there in the dark. He knew she was doing this from years of memories.

He rubbed his face with both hands. "Caroline, you're killin' me. What does this mean?" he muttered.

He remembered Patrick might be waiting and stood back up to leave, sliding the painting back. He saw the note from Chris on the counter where she'd left it when she ran out after him last night. He picked it up with no qualms now about reading it.

"Be who you are and God will open the doors. Baker is only the beginning. As Jim Elliot once said, 'Forgive me for being so ordinary while claiming to know so extraordinary a God.' —Chris Shepherd."

He put the note back the way he'd found it. He felt fortunate that when she had looked for someone to replace him, it was Chris.

***

"You'd have never dared to pull something like this if Dad were still alive. No wonder you two did this behind my back!" Wyeth's voice was just below a shout as he paced in front of the fireplace in the library at the mansion on Saturday afternoon. He looked at Phillip and Andy with contempt. Phillip flinched and bit his lip, but Andy looked defiant.

Memories of little Caroline in her Poppy Noble's art studio flashed through Andy Painter's mind. He knew Wyeth was right, and he hated this confrontation.

"Chad was the wild card," he insisted. "Juliette had left, and Phillip had just gotten through Sandy leaving. In that mindset, I was afraid Caroline might leave if Chad decided to go to Charleston or London. Worse, I was concerned about how Chad would handle being on his own at college. I couldn't let her tie herself to him." He looked haggard from his experience with Caroline this morning. "Phillip couldn't read Chad," he added as an afterthought.

Phillip stood solemnly with his arms crossed and nodded when they all looked at him. "I was—concerned. We say we want our kids to choose their own paths, but what I really wanted was for Chad to be me. I needed to let him be himself. Like Juliette, Painter Place was too confining for Cole, and Cami and I could tell he was going to London or Charleston. The only way I could be sure Chad wasn't just stepping up to please me or to have Caroline was to get him away from Painter Place, and the only way to get him away from Painter Place was to take Caroline off of his list of options until college was over. I feared he'd broken away when he ran off to Hawaii and worked for my competition all summer."

Andy crossed his arms over his chest. "I wanted to make sure that Chad could handle being on his own without all the attention going to his head. I also wanted Caroline to be herself without being influenced by him."

"So this was all about Chad?" Wyeth exclaimed incredulously, his words emphatic and deliberate. He shook his head in disbelief, still reeling from the news. "Are you two seriously telling me that this has always been about Chad, like Caroline only had some supporting role and couldn't be trusted?" He shouted now, hands on his hips. "Andrew, she's the kingpin! Everything hinges on her, and you didn't give her a chance to learn what it is to be a Painter. What do you think you've taught her now?"

Chrissy began crying quietly. Valerie and Camellia looked miserable. Wyeth glanced quickly over at Chrissy before turning back to speak again. He lowered his voice, but it was as hard and sharp as broken glass.

"I never had the privilege of being a dad, but Caroline has always been like my own. Wait until you see what Cameron brings back in the film and photos from our trip—I've never been so proud. Two people more than when we arrived are going to spend eternity in Heaven because of her witness, and who can tell where the ripples from that will lead. Phillip knows that she handled herself graciously and shrewdly with the press in a trying publicity situation."

"A publicity situation she shouldn't have been in if you'd watched after her," growled his brother. "She shouldn't have had her reputation damaged like that."

Phillip quickly put his hand on Andy's crossed arm to stop him from saying anything else. "I was on the phone when it happened, and Wyeth had no reason to suspect that the Holmes' grandson was any trouble. She only went out because he was buying her painting, and she believed Chad was dating the model."

Wyeth's eyes narrowed as he looked at his brother, who still glared at him. "Whatever you think about my negligence, it led to Baker's salvation that night. God Himself set it up, and I don't regret it." His voice choked with emotion and he had to swallow before he continued. "If Chad was only eighteen and was able to handle what you two laid on him, what made you think Caroline couldn't?" He stopped to look at his younger brother and best friend with daggers in his eyes. His tone was menacing. "What made him stronger than her, and who do you think really needed the lesson more?"

"Boys!" said Savanna. Her tone was the one that had always stopped any shenanigans when they were growing up. All eyes moved to the matriarch, who was sitting in a large white wing-backed chair with a luxurious white animal fur throw strewn across one corner of the back.

"Caroline's never leaving because she decided that for herself when she was a little girl. I heard her say it out loud and took it as a promise from the Lord to answer my prayers. She told her doll not to be afraid of a storm because they'd always live at Painter Place, and God was here. That sounds like God's hand on a little girl's life to me."

No one spoke, but Valerie covered her mouth and squeezed her eyes shut.

Savanna continued. "Caroline decided her future at a time when her brother and Chad thought girls had cooties." She waved her hand dismissively. "Charleston is a day trip, and not even Chad could get her to a place like London. Painter Place is in her blood. It's her destiny, and deep down she's always known it."

She glanced at the ladies and sighed. "For Wyeth and Chrissy's benefit, I want to say that like Valerie and Camellia, the only reason I agreed not to interfere with Andy and Phillip's decision was because they are the heads of their own house. There's no way to know if this defined Chad or if he'd have been the same anyway—his character never seemed questionable to me. The gamble seems to have worked for you, Phillip, for he's a fine young man and even more exceptional than his dad and grandfather. But you'll have to live with the damage to your relationship with your future daughter-in-law. I don't even know how you can count the cost of the damage to your relationship with Wyeth, your lifelong best friend. And we'll have to see what happens to Andy's relationship with his brother and daughters."

She paused and looked at Wyeth, who had stopped pacing and was standing tense with his arms crossed tightly. He was sullen and fuming, barely able to stay quiet.

"Since we're throwing around insights and opinions after the fact, I finally get to say I that agree with Wyeth. Caroline was always the point, and she could have been trusted to know what was expected of her without falling apart. She's smart, and she's going to make it through a staggering rite of passage. I think we can expect her to begin re-sorting priorities in light of all this. She will turn to Chad and Wyeth now because trust is her bottom line. I think she'll begin learning how the place works from their perspective and infusing some new life around here, flexing her muscles in a little wholesome payback for what this has cost her. I don't know if any of us can say we have more right to be here than she does."

Chapter Twenty-Five

"The cure for anything is salt water—sweat, tears, or the sea."
—Isak Dinesen

Chad and Patrick finished at the campsites and went to the Gregorys' to hang out around the pool together until the meeting at the Big House was over. Patrick was having a hard time focusing on anything but what must be going on with the Big Three, and Chad wanted to call Cole in London before it was too late there.

Chad caught his brother and Shannon in the middle of a Risk game with Justin's family. They took a break for him to talk, and Chad told him what was unfolding at Painter Place.

Cole whistled low. "Boy, is Dad gonna get it from Wyeth! I wish I were a fly on the wall at the Big House right now. Not many people would dare yell at Phillip Gregory—or get away with it. I bet Wyeth exploded! He'll take this personally, 'cause he thinks of Caroline as his own daughter. Wonder what he and Caroline think now about that little 'trust and integrity' speech she made over here on the news about the Gregorys. Is she all right?"

"No, but I'm working on it. She left the island without talking to me. I caught up with her on the phone at Carly's, and we're all goin' to dinner and the movies tonight. I have a plan to keep her from lumping me into the blame for what she sees as a conspiracy against her."

"Whew, wouldn't wanna be you right now. I knew this was what you were doing for four years, but I didn't know how involved Andy was, or that both of us were on trial. Dad's insulated Global against us until he sees what we're made of, and I blew it in a huge way. I bet we don't know the half of what's even there."

"It didn't hit me how our character was being scrutinized until I heard it out of Andy Painter's mouth this morning. And I may not like the way he separated me and Caroline, but he's right. If he's thinking about how much can change at Painter Place by what he allows Caroline to bring with her into it, you can bet Shannon's dad is thinking through it on a smaller scale. Are you still on probation?"

"Can't get past it right now, but it won't be much longer. I'm doin' everything right, and I'm tenacious. I'm not risking anything except in my world domination on the board tonight. I'm not happy about Mr. Polo player hanging around in the background, but I'm keeping my mouth shut. He wouldn't have a chance if I hadn't been stupid."

"Cole, hiding things, like you did with the drinking, is still deception."

"I know. I wasn't looking at it that way. At the time, it seemed like a personal choice kind of thing—not something serious, like running around on her. I only did it twice and wasn't going to make a habit of it. I was planning to tell you when we talked the next time, but then the trouble started, and you had to come in for the chaos. By the way, I'm changing my major to law."

"So you can see how to get by with things, like that regulation on the accounts you risked?"

"It worked, and it was legal, right? Uncle Justin and Dad agreed. Admit that my brilliance is why you hired me."

"Okay, I admit it. And the Young Guns does need its own lawyer. But I mean it, if you mess up again, I'll be on a plane there with Patrick, and you'll be a spot on that Oriental rug. He's right here beside me, smacking one fist into his hand."

"Tell him I said hi, and I'll see him soon for a wedding. Now let's get down to it—somethin' else is bothering you, and this isn't cheap. You wouldn't call me on a Saturday night just to threaten me."

"Reality hit me. I've realized what Dad and Andy are doin' on a bigger scale, and if my plans work out, I'm goin' to be them. I'll be wondering how to survive, bringing up my kids to take over Painter Place—one of them might even be the next artist at the Big House. I can't do it by myself. I want you and Patrick to help me influence them."

"Me? A role model? That's—disturbing, Chad."

"No kidding. But that's who we are, Cole. Right now, before our kids are even born yet. We can do this the hard way and endure embarrassing stories told about us later, or just get it right from the get-go. You don't sow wild oats and expect to harvest a rose garden. How many times do you think God's goin' to hear your prayers for crop failure? Are you with me?"

Cole exaggerated a sigh for effect. "Okay, but tell Patrick that I'm just doing my part so your kids can have a handsome favorite uncle."

***

With Carly and Cassie as co-conspirators, Chad was able to arrange for their group to have an early dinner in Whitehaven on Saturday evening. Afterward, they went to see *Back to the Future* at Movies on Main, and finished the evening with a walk across the street to Millie's for ice cream. Caroline's mood was pensive, but she seemed to have fun.

They talked about their favorite parts of the movie and what they would go back and change in their own lives if they could. Caroline looked out the window and didn't contribute. They came up with some outrageous outcomes from what might follow a change that would affect their kids and she laughed along with them.

The conversation then turned philosophical. After all, there are ethics involved in changing things to suit your own ends because of knowing how it turned out.

Natalie looked thoughtful. "Everything big that we do in life started with the little things, not with a sudden turn of events. Little things become habits, turning points, or first impressions and how you handle those turns of events influences how everyone sees you afterward."

This led to some more life examples—some of them hilarious—and a flurry of funny quotes from the movie.

"'Whoa, that's heavy,'" commented Cassie's date about her example.

Chad got up from his chair to stand by Caroline. He looked seriously at her, then down at his open hand, from which he read. "I'm Chad—Chad Gregory. I'm your density. I mean—your destiny."

He was rewarded with the same reaction that Marty's mom gave his dad in the movie. Caroline smiled sweetly. "Ohhhh . . ."

Hoots and catcalls followed from their group and people in Millie's before Cassie's date said again, "'Whoa, that's heavy!'"

When Millie's closed, everyone parted on the street. Patrick and Natalie said they were going to sit on the porch at the Big House for a while, and Chad told Carly he'd bring Caroline by after church the next day to get her Mustang.

The red Lamborghini sparkled in the streetlights and was getting a lot of attention from the young crowd cruising downtown. Chad and Caroline smiled and said hello to bystanders who moved aside to let him open the door for her.

"Is it true that you were thinking of Caroline when you picked out this car?" asked a teen girl.

Chad grinned as he closed the door after Caroline and walked around to the driver's side. "Seeing a Lamborghini Countach always makes me feel a little overwhelmed, and it reminds me of how much it's like Caroline—hard to get, creative, exciting, sleek, and gorgeous. I didn't pick this one out, though. It's a trophy from my dad for waiting four years through college to convince Caroline that I'm her prince."

"It sure beats the heck out of a pumpkin carriage," quipped a teen boy.

Chad opened his door and winked at Caroline, letting everyone look inside before he got in. He pulled the car out onto Main Street but didn't turn at the light to follow Patrick across the bridge. A commercial was ending on the Whitehaven radio station before the Shaggin' Pirate introduced "Summer Song" by Chad and Jeremy.

> *"Trees swayin' in the summer breeze*
> *Showin' off their silver leaves*
> *As we walked by.*
> *Soft kisses on a summer's day*
> *Laughing all our cares away,*
> *Just you and I.*
> *Sweet sleepy warmth of summer nights,*
> *Gazing at the distant lights*
> *In the starry sky.*
> *They say that all good things must end someday.*
> *Autumn leaves must fall.*
> *But don't you know that it hurts me so*
> *To say goodbye to you?*

Wish you didn't have to go,
No, no, no, no.
And when the rain
Beats against my window pane,
I'll think of summer days again
And dream of you . . ."

Caroline got tissues out of her purse and started dabbing at tears. But soon she was sobbing. Chad pulled into Whitehaven Point, a public park with a beach that was well-lighted at night for those who wanted to walk or hang out. He leaned over and put his arms around Caroline, just letting her cry and stroking her hair. He closed his eyes and waited. The shoulder of his shirt was wet with her tears.

His voice was gentle when she grew quiet. "Caroline."

She turned swollen, sad blue eyes to his. His throat tightened, his heart flipped over, and he swallowed hard.

She whispered, "That song always hurts."

"I know. But the autumn when I left is over. Now there are only those sunny days, sweet summer nights, and starry skies. We live them every day, and there isn't an autumn anywhere for us."

She didn't say anything and didn't look convinced.

"I never changed my mind about you, Caroline. I went away so I could prove it. Look across the water," he said, tilting his head that direction. She saw the lights of Painter Place and their homes.

"Other people come here and look across, longing to live our lives. If they have broken families, they wish they had ours. They think it must be so easy and wonder why they can't live like that. But ninety-five percent of them couldn't handle it. They can't grasp that it's not easy at all, and they don't know the sacrifices that made Painter Place so different from anywhere else. They don't realize that we can't just do anything we want to, like they do."

He gripped her hand. "But *we* understand, Caroline. We do. If you didn't before, you do now. Painter Place was built on difficult and unselfish choices, pain, and loss. With every generation or wrong decision, Painter Place is a gamble. It would have to be sold off in sections to pay the taxes or put into an historic trust if it weren't dedicated to the same God who provided it in the first place."

Caroline turned from the lights of the island back to his eyes.

"We earned the right to be there together." His voice was full of conviction. "In the end, isn't that the kind of story that everyone wants to believe can still happen? Isn't a fairy tale best when the love story overcame all the impossibilities? There's no story at all if it was easy."

"Are you saying we're like a fairy tale love story?"

A great chance to say he loved her had just been handed to him. It stuck in his throat. He swallowed hard. He didn't want it to happen like this, in the confusion of the emotional day she'd had—and not in a parking lot.

As he had done on their day in Mevagissey, he reached up to trace the curve of her cheek. "It looks like one to me. We've been given the chance of a lifetime. We'll take our best shot, and if we crash and burn, we'll do it together. I have some ideas, and I want you to share yours with me. It's our time. Are you ready to focus?"

She nodded solemnly.

He moved his hand from her face to push a long strand of hair behind her ear. "I don't know how all this will change you, or what it means for me. But your next move is to forgive your dad, okay? We're all on the same side."

***

When Chad pulled into the Painter's driveway to bring Caroline home, they saw her parents' silhouettes as they sat out on the pier. The *Artistic License* was docked there, so some of the family had gone out. He glanced around. There'd be extra security patrol tonight at the pier.

He got out and opened her door. "Everybody sleeps tonight, and everybody goes to church together in the morning, okay? Please? Tomorrow's a big day. Three weeks." He held up three fingers and smiled.

She hesitated, a desperate look in her eyes saying she was ready to bolt. He quickly grasped her hand, leading her out to the end of the pier.

Andy and Valerie slowly stood up as they approached. In the dim light of citronella lanterns, Chad imagined that he could see sparks flying off of Caroline, but she was outwardly calm.

Chad shook Andy's hand and nodded at Valerie. He wanted to get this over with. "Caroline and I have been talking tonight about how what happened is in the past, and that we're all on the same side." He nudged Caroline slightly where his hand rested on the small of her back. "Haven't we, Caroline?"

She nodded, then looked across the water at the lights of Whitehaven Point and tilted her head that way. "From Whitehaven Point, Chad showed me that you can see the island, and he talked about how it's different over here from the way most people live their lives."

Her parents nodded, looking hopeful.

"I'm not a parent yet, so I can't claim to know better than you about how this should've been done," she began. "I'm sorry that my reaction was—over the top. I know you meant well."

"But you're still mad and think I'm wrong," her dad stated matter-of-factly.

"I think you were wrong to deceive me and not trust me, and I'm struggling to get past the anger. It's going to take time, but it won't change the fact that I'm choosing to forgive you. Thinking you were wrong isn't proof that you were. God let this happen to me and Chad for a reason." A three-week-old memory from out here beside the water flashed into her mind. "Nothing is wasted," she said quietly, almost as an afterthought.

"Fair enough," said her dad and reached out his hand to her. She hesitated before slowly putting hers out, and he took it firmly to pull her over to him in a hug that she didn't return. He squeezed his eyes tight. "I'm sorry it hurt you so much, baby. Someday, I want to see what used to be in my little girl's eyes when she looked at me," he choked. "I'll be prayin' it comes back."

Patrick's Corvette pulled into the driveway, and his headlights ran across his family on the pier. He parked, got out, and looked in that direction. Marina's voice startled him. She was sitting on the porch in the dark with Lady. "Chad talked her into forgiving Dad. He really is a prince."

Patrick stood there, torn between whether he should walk out to the pier or talk to Marina. He chose the latter.

"How do you feel about all of this?" he asked as he sat down on the other side of Lady, rubbing her velvety ears.

"Dad should've trusted Caroline. It wasn't right to do that to her," said Marina. "But I love him."

Patrick looked closely at her, disarmed by her conviction. "Marina, do you trust him?"

"No," she answered flatly. "He's not who I thought he was. Caroline feels the same, and that hurts her far more than being kept from Chad. That's why she lost her cool. Maybe you have to be a daughter to understand."

Patrick winced in the darkness. Chad's dad might have gambled and won, but not his.

Chapter Twenty-Six

"How do you go from this tranquility to that violence?" (Brenda)
"I usually take the Ferrari." (Sonny Crockett)
—Miami Vice

The Painters and Gregorys were a somber crowd on Sunday morning as they met to sit together at Danny's church. Patrick followed Chad's lead to separate him and Caroline from their dads, and Marina went to sit with Danny's family.

There were a lot of familiar faces. Shoreline Baptist was a year old and growing steadily. The service was less formal than the Painters and Gregorys were used to, with guitar and contemporary worship songs mixed in with the hymns. Pastor Payne's sermon was based on one of Caroline's favorite Bible passages, Job 38-40. She loved the vivid imagery and intimate references to what God did in creating and caring for the world, and how foolish people are to dismiss or question Him.

Sitting beside Chad, she glanced at his page as he found his place in the Bible first. That was hard to do—she knew exactly where this passage was and had it dog-eared. *Show-off*, she thought. His pages were full of notes everywhere, and when she compared his to hers, his writing was smaller.

She found a blank spot in the margin of her church bulletin. "Tie?" she wrote, looking around to be sure no one was watching as she passed it to him.

He looked at the note and smiled, but shook his head. He found another blank spot and wrote, "No way. I packed more in with smaller notes. I win."

She took a deep breath and looked at the pastor, listening for a few moments before turning the thin page in her Bible to the next one. Chad raised one eyebrow when he looked over at her, turning his page as well. She glanced over and gave a little sigh of resignation. He looked straight ahead but wore a satisfied expression.

In a few more moments, he wrote, "Confession—I knew it was one of your favorites and studied it a lot. You'd beat anyone else. Will you be a good loser and start studying with me sometimes?"

She smiled and nodded slightly.

He bit his lip to keep from grinning and found another blank spot on the bulletin. He waited until no one was looking and passed it to her. "Song of Solomon???"

Caroline coughed as she tried to stifle a gasp and looked up at the pastor as if she was listening. She pressed her lips together tightly. Patrick looked at her and Chad with curiosity. When he looked away again, she shook her head slightly. After a few more moments, she covertly wrote, "You're a distraction today."

In the parking lot, Chad told his parents that he and Caroline would be late for lunch at the Big House while he took her to Carly's to pick up her Mustang. He watched Caroline avoid his dad's eyes, and he caught his dad watching him watch her avoid him. His dad's expression was sad.

Chad moved her quickly away from his parents to his car, but he drove back to the park at Whitehaven Point instead of straight to Carly's house. He parked in the same spot as the night before but left the car running with the air conditioner on in the hot summer afternoon. He turned down the radio.

"Caroline, do you have any issues with me over my leaving?"

He saw a trace of last night's sadness and strain cross her face. She closed her eyes and leaned back against the headrest on the seat. "Not really."

"Convince me."

"How?"

"Look me in the eye. I'll know."

"Chad, I'm—I need some time before I can do that. I'm adjusting my thinking to get used to you not being on the verge of disappearing, like they do on *Star Trek*, only minus the communicator. You just did what you had to do."

"You had the hardest part, not me."

"It's okay. I'm working through it."

He decided this wasn't going anywhere right now, so he asked her if she knew what day it was, and she smiled.

"I do, so you don't get to win this time. It's our three week anniversary. Only one week to go."

"Oh, but I *will* win because I didn't ask the hard question yet. Are you ready for it?"

"Is this like saving the best for last? And why do you get to ask all the hard questions?"

"You're trying to distract me. Here it is—Why do you think I told you in Charleston that you might get used to me and stick around after a month of celebrating anniversaries?"

Caroline was genuinely puzzled. "Hmmm...that's a very good question." She wrinkled her nose for an instant and narrowed her eyes in concentration. "Is it related to the gifts you've given me?"

"You're very warm..."

"Okay—is it related to the fact that there are four weeks in a month?"

"Now you're hot," he said. "And don't say thank you."

With a hint of a smile, she replied, "I wouldn't dream of it. Is it—related to the month of June?"

"Now you're cold. As ice."

"Ouch!" she winced. "Okay...it's about *time.*"

"No kidding!" He burst out laughing and shook his head. "It's about time, all right. Soon you'll know how funny that really is!"

He started laughing again, and she couldn't help joining him. He had tears in his eyes when he finally managed to say, "Give up yet?"

"Yes! You win!" she exclaimed. "But you owe me a ping pong date to rebuild my battered confidence."

He leaned over and reached with his right arm to pop open the glove compartment of the car. There was a beautifully wrapped box sitting in it and nothing else.

"Oh!" She sat there looking at the box. "I'm letting you win more often if this is what happens!"

"You didn't *let* me win," he insisted. "The answer to the question *you couldn't answer* is that every week represents a year that we were apart. Four weeks, four years, four gifts—and it's about time, baby! Open it. It's yours." He settled into his seat to watch her.

"Chad, you've given me so much already!"

His eyes grew serious again, and he reached over to stroke a long strand of her hair behind her ear. His fingertips lingered on her neck. "Because I like decorating the most beautiful young woman on the planet, and I have years of Christmases, birthdays, and expensive dates that I want to catch up on. For the first time in my life, I have the freedom to be extravagant with you."

She reached for the box and gingerly picked it up. She set it in her lap and held it with both hands, then took off the bow and paper. She gasped when she saw the crown emblem on the box.

"Chad! Is this what's really inside? I can't open this!"

"Sure you can," he said firmly.

She remained frozen, so he leaned over the console to gently open the box, his face close to hers. She suddenly put her hand behind his head and leaned her own face onto the side of his, pressing close to his ear. He could feel her warm breath. He took his hand off of the box and did the same, his hand in her hair.

"Does this mean you like it?" he whispered. He could tell that she nodded, her cheek rubbing against his. "Let me put it on."

She slowly moved away, settling back into her seat. He pulled the Rolex Oyster watch out of the box and slid it over her hand, clasping it and turning her wrist over to admire it.

"This is to remind you that it's our time now. See the perpetual date? It's like the eternity bracelet. No autumns of going away are on it. It has a blue dial for the water that surrounds our home. See the little shapes all around the face? They remind me of waves. The two tones of metal work together, making everything more interesting than if they were alike. That's us."

"You were thinking all of this when you picked it out?" she asked.

258

"You bet. In London, after you said I was significant on a personal level—upgraded me to being your boyfriend—and told me that you had no peace of mind because I was impossibly handsome. That was my favorite part, by the way. You also committed to being exclusive to me, so it sounded a lot like you'd give me some time. And as I told you on the yacht, you were breathtaking, and I was hopelessly wrapped around your finger after seeing you in that dress. I didn't stand a chance."

She looked up from the watch, her eyes dancing with the memories.

"We need to go get your car now and arrive fashionably late for a very crowded lunch. Do you want to drive this one and give me the keys to the Mustang?"

"Is that what happens when you put on a Rolex—you get to drive a Countach?"

"Come to think of it, that's exactly how it happened for me, so why not?" He was grinning as he drove out of the parking lot, turning the radio back up. The upbeat song by the Cuff Links fit his mood.

> *"Tracy, you're gonna be*
> *Happy with me*
> *I'll build a world around you*
> *Filled with love everywhere*
> *And when you're there,*
> *You'll be so glad I found you*
> *Come with me, don't say 'No'*
> *Hold me close*
> *Tracy, never, never, ever let me go . . ."*

***

He watched weak-kneed as Caroline pulled out of the mayor's driveway in the red Countach. He would have liked a picture of this moment. He wasn't sure he'd let her be seen driving it alone in a place like Charleston. He was going to have to come to grips with how he handled guys who were just window shopping—through *his* windows.

He decided to put the top down on the Mustang, despite the heat. It had been a while since he'd been in a real convertible.

He slowed when he caught up with Caroline at the intersection to cross the causeway bridge to the island, taking in the situation. "What the . . ." he trailed off.

The light was red, and the passenger door of a yellow Camaro was ajar in the left turn lane beside his car. Someone was almost on their knees beside the driver's door on the Countach, reaching into the open window. Most of his head and an arm were inside.

Instantly, Chad wished he hadn't thought earlier about learning to handle guys who were window shopping through his windows. He groaned. This was shoplifting.

He eased the '65 Mustang up closer to his own red spoiler. The left turn lane arrow turned green, but there wasn't a car waiting behind the Camaro in the intersection. The guy pulled his head out of the Lamborghini's window, and Chad could see sunglasses on top of short black hair. The guy was laughing with Caroline, making some kind of gesture that only someone in the conversation could understand. He noticed the Mustang out of the corner of his eye and waved at it. He did a double take, grinned, and stood up.

It took an effort for Chad to look cool and not drop his mouth open. Derrick Wallace sure had grown up. He seemed to tower over the low profile of the Lamborghini, wearing expensive gym shorts and a tank shirt that showed off very well-worked muscles. He turned back to the open window of Chad's Lamborghini and leaned over to keep talking to Caroline. He had his hand somewhere near her shoulder or her hair.

Chad's mind raced with his choices. At the moment, getting out and standing beside the guy wasn't his first. He didn't want Caroline to see them side by side for a comparison. What would his dad do?

He reached into the pocket of his dress pants for a little case and pulled out a business card. The light turned green, and Caroline's arm was out the window to wave goodbye to Derrick. He grabbed her hand quickly to clasp it, keeping her there an extra couple of seconds. The new watch sparkled, catching the sunlight with a flash that made Chad blink. She eased the Countach forward, pulling her hand away. He let go and waved, watching her drive off.

Now the light wasn't the only thing that had turned green. Chad was almost beside himself, and the rise in his temperature wasn't from sitting in the convertible in the South Carolina sunshine. He imagined that the same heat waves that were shimmering mirages from the surface of the road were coming from his head, which felt like it could explode.

He looked in the rearview mirror. There was predictably still no traffic on this side after church hours on a sleepy Sunday afternoon in Whitehaven, where nothing was open. A car moseyed down Main Street in the other direction. He eased up to the traffic light. It was still green, but he stopped anyway, propping his arm across the top of his driver side door and holding the card inside that hand.

He hadn't been around long enough to recognize the Camaro or its driver. Derrick had sandwiched himself between the car and its still-open passenger door, lounging on it. He smiled at Chad expectantly with a challenge in his eyes and nodded in the direction of the bridge, where Chad's car seemed to be floating over the waterway.

"Nice wheels. Looks like you're doin' well," Derrick drawled.

"Well enough," replied Chad.

"I pictured you in a Ferrari."

"You watch too much TV."

Derrick laughed. "It's my favorite show! You have any of those fancy holsters to wear around your shoulders like his?"

"As a matter of fact, I do, but unfortunately I left them at home today while I went to church. Didn't expect to need 'em."

Derrick laughed again, clearly enjoying this. "His wife's name on the show is Caroline, and that didn't work out."

"Like I said, you watch too much TV."

"You know, I always liked you, Chad. But I liked you most when you left town and stayed gone. When you get bored and ride off into the sunset again soon in that Lambo, I'll be on a plane back. It'll be different now that I'm outta college."

Chad resisted clenching his jaw or his fists and took a deep breath. He forced a smile as he looked at his car disappearing over the causeway bridge to the island. "I'll tell her to be sure and put you down in second place on a waiting list."

Then he turned to look right at Derrick. "It's never gonna happen, pal." He tilted his head toward the island. "It's different now that I'm out of college, too. I'm home for good. You're not."

Before Derrick could say anything, Chad extended his arm from where it rested on the door of the Mustang with a business card held between his first two fingers. "I hear you did pretty well for yourself with the pros recently," he said. "Congratulations. Let's keep some of it in Whitehaven. Call me. You might be interested in some things I've got goin' on with Patrick and Cole. Work with the Young Guns."

Derrick looked at him narrowly. "You got nerve, Gregory."

That was Chad's limit. He slid his Ray Bans up onto his head so Derrick could see the look in his eyes. His steely voice was loaded with meaning when he said, "So do you, Wallace—hangin' all over the side of my Sunday car with a lot of you through the window, touchin' my girl, and darin' me to do anything about it."

Derrick looked at him with a scowl, and they just stared at one another as seconds went by. Suddenly, Derrick smiled and snapped up the card that Chad was still holding out to him. "Fair enough."

"Are we good?" asked Chad.

"We're good," said Derrick.

Chad heard a car drive up behind him and looked at the light. It was green again. He pulled his sunglasses down and eased the little convertible through the intersection, tipping his hand and a thumbs-up sign back at Derrick.

***

Caroline was glad that she and Chad were late for lunch. It meant that everyone would excuse them to go off to themselves with a plate, instead of having to mingle with guests, her parents, and the Gregorys. They went into the library to escape the crowd, and Chad held her hand to say grace. She was unexpectedly deeply moved to be praying with him—not like the countless times they'd been together in the company of people praying, but him being the leader doing it. She impulsively squeezed his hand.

262

As they were finishing, Natalie and Patrick came in, asking them to go out in the boat later while it was at the house. Patrick grabbed his sister's arm and whistled, motioning for Natalie to look. "Is this why you're so late getting here this afternoon?"

"One of the reasons," Chad said.

Patrick looked as if he expected Chad to continue. "I'll tell you about it later," Chad said.

"I need to talk to you, too," said Patrick. "Can we go out on the veranda a few minutes?"

Chad followed him, and Patrick got right to the point. "I have some good news and bad news. Which do you want first?"

"The best for last," said Chad.

"Okay. Marina told me that she doesn't trust my dad now because he's not the guy she thought he was, and that it's the same for Caroline. That's why Caroline pulled out the shotgun we didn't know she carried around. My sisters don't see dad the same way anymore, and things are tense at home. Marina's stayin' gone all day."

He paused and crossed his arms. "After that emergency family meeting here yesterday, Wyeth is still furious. I think we need to leave now and do some things away from everyone until things cool off. Taking the *License* out on the water today won't be seen as too unusual since we didn't go out with them last night, and it's docked at the house. Just don't invite any of them to come with us."

"Okay. Thanks for the heads-up. You could have given me one about Derrick Wallace so I didn't act stupid when Cole told me about him in London. It's a good thing I knew before today when he was all over my car and Caroline."

Patrick hissed. "He's in town? Oh, no! What happened?"

Chad told him, and Patrick laughed so hard that he had to lean against the wall. "Chad, I'm proud of you, man. He's actually a great guy, just unable to grasp that the only girl he ever wanted is the only one he can't have. He was probably just looking at the inside of the car and showing her that he still has a dent in his nose—which he thinks makes it more interesting, and he loves to tell people he got it tryin' to kiss an island girl. I can't believe you invited him to be part of the Young Guns after that."

"If I keep finding out you've been hiding any other huge things like that from me, you and I are going to have a conversation you won't enjoy," Chad said with a threat in his voice. "I already walked onto the island to witness a guy breaking up with your sister, with no idea she had a boyfriend."

"I was keeping you away from guard duty here and on track through college so you could get to this day," Patrick said, emphasizing his words and hoping he was making his point. "And hey, that's some watch—what's next week, a ring?"

Chad cast a faraway gaze out to the beach. "That's not supposed to come before an 'I love you.' I almost tripped myself up and said it last night. But I need to hear it from her first. She needs to give herself permission to feel that way."

Patrick studied his friend's face and then slapped him on the back. "Feel like you're the one doin' all the work, huh? I don't know how you could've handled the situation with her yesterday any better than you did. You held everything together. Marina said you really are a prince." He did a drum roll on the porch railing. "So here's the best for last—Cameron is good with me dating Natalie with serious intentions, and we seem to be on the same page about everything. So now—how are we goin' to get them to say 'it' first?"

"Caroline's thinking about our first kiss because of something I said on the yacht and the way it comes up in love songs," Chad mused. "So—what if we play love songs around them, maybe even plan a night this week around the pool and get in some slow dances? Maybe all they need to say the words is some seriously strong power of suggestion and moonlight."

***

Back in the library, Natalie held out Caroline's arm to admire her watch, and Caroline told her what Chad had said about why he gave it to her.

"Caroline, Patrick told me on Friday night that Chad is desperately waiting for you to say you love him. It sounds like nothing's been easy about the situation with you two, but I can see you feel that way. Don't you think by now he's earned having you say so?"

"Yes, but I didn't know it until yesterday. I thought he'd mysteriously left and never explained, and I wondered if he'd do it again."

"This watch is the kind of gift everyone would expect a Gregory to give if he was sticking around, and Chad obviously knows the level he has to rise to in his position. But he didn't lavish money on just any ladies' Rolex, bracelet, or earring—he went to a lot of trouble to shop for something that was a thoughtful description of your relationship. Even the vase he sent the sunflowers in was a depiction of Painter Place, and he remembered your favorite flower. He's really trying, Caroline. It's safe now for you to show him your feelings and encourage him."

Caroline nodded.

"Would it sound strange if I told you that I suspect that Chad and your brother have a competition going on that concerns me and you?"

Caroline laughed. "No, I'd be surprised if they didn't. It's a lifestyle for them. Maybe we can have some fun!"

Natalie's eyes lit up. "I was hoping you'd say that! I think it's a race to see which of them will get told first that one of us loves them."

"Are you ready to say that to Patrick?" Caroline was surprised.

Natalie laughed. "Yes, but only if I have to. He's what I want, and I'm not going to waste any time. I'm around a lot of men, and I know a rare gem when I meet one. Patrick is refreshing—what you see is what you get—and he's always positive and easygoing. Besides, there aren't many true Christian guys in the world. To find all of that in such a handsome package is really my dream come true! But he won't say he loves me first if he and Chad are flexing muscles in one another's direction."

"So you'd like me to get this done."

Natalie laughed again. "Yes. But we could get a few days of fun out of this if we don't run out of ideas."

The guys came back into the library, explaining their plan for an evening on the boat. Patrick would make a picnic and pick Natalie up. Chad took Caroline's arm, escorting her toward the back door to slip out.

Savanna Painter watched them from where she was talking to a guest artist with Wyeth and Chrissy. She caught Wyeth's eye and tilted her head slightly in her granddaughter's direction as she and Chad made their way to the door, never speaking to her parents or the Gregorys. Wyeth turned slightly to see. "And so it begins," she said to him.

She and Wyeth both looked around to see if Andy and Phillip had noticed. They were looking across the room at one another. Andy looked from Phillip to Wyeth, and the brothers' eyes met. Wyeth's were cool, and Andy's were unreadable.

Chapter Twenty-Seven

". . . I know."
—Han Solo to Princess Leia Organa

"Whoahhhh!" exclaimed Natalie when she got out of Patrick's car at his house. She was gaping at the sporty catamaran that dominated the pier in the warm glow of late afternoon light. "You call this a boat? Isn't it more like a yacht?"

Patrick grinned. "She's a beauty alright," he agreed. "That's the *Artistic License,* and she belongs to my uncle Wyeth. He never had kids to put through college, so he got a boat. She lives up to her name—she's uniquely loaded. Dad and Wyeth keep outfitting her with new stuff and like to take her out for some offshore fishing. Dad keeps her docked at his marina in Whitehaven for security. Come on inside—let's pack up the picnic dinner."

She followed him inside, where two coolers and a picnic basket were waiting to be filled. "Caroline should be coming down soon," he said. "She's emotionally wiped out and took a nap, so she'll be like a new person. Chad's on his way."

"This is the first time you've cooked for me," said Natalie, packing things he handed her for the basket. "I hear you're amazing."

"It's all true," grinned Patrick. "Believe anything good you hear about me, and not a word if it's bad."

"Do you give lessons?" she asked.

Patrick stopped in surprise. "You mean—cooking?"

Natalie gave him a teasing smile. "I did. Were you thinking of giving me lessons in being amazing? Or something else?"

Caroline walked into the kitchen and stopped. Seeing the way her brother and Natalie were looking at one another, she cleared her throat. "Inconvenient sister alert, in case I interrupted something."

Patrick kept his eyes locked on Natalie's. "Natalie's just asking me for cooking lessons. I think we'll start tomorrow."

"Oh. In that case, you're in for a treat, Natalie. He's the coolest teacher you'll ever have. No one else could make cooking so fun and interesting." She walked over to the door to open it for Chad, who brushed her cheek with his.

"What's up?"

"Natalie just asked Patrick for—lessons. They're going to cook something up together," said Caroline sweetly.

Patrick shot Chad a warning look. "If you have something to say, it's the perfect time to keep it to yourself." He started handing wrapped food to Natalie again.

"I'll just choke on it and go put my cooler onto the *License.*"

Chad and Patrick took the boat out of the waterway inlet and kept it near the shoreline to ride for a while, showing Natalie a water's view from the Atlantic of Painter Place. Caroline walked over to Chad's seat and leaned onto it, daring to briefly rub his shoulders around the straps of his tank shirt to get his attention. Surprised, he looked up over his shoulder with raised eyebrows at her.

She ignored the question in his eyes and nodded her head toward the island, speaking close to his ear over the engines. "It looks good from here, doesn't it? Thanks for reminding me what it's all about last night."

He nodded and grasped her hand to keep it on his shoulder. Patrick looked at him sideways, and Chad smiled slyly.

They found a spot to stop the *License* for dinner and a spectacular view of the sunset. Without the engines running, they could put on some music while they were eating. Natalie glanced at Caroline before saying she really loved this first dinner Patrick had cooked for her.

Caroline watched Patrick raise his eyebrows to taunt Chad. So Natalie's instincts were spot on, she thought. This was a race.

Caroline was finishing some of Patrick's chocolate éclair when the song Chad had dedicated to her at the Island Summer Dance came on. She smiled and looked at Chad, who was looking at her. She made his sign, from her heart to his.

At first, he just looked at her as if he didn't trust his own eyes. Then he looked at Patrick to see if he'd been paying attention. Patrick shook his head "no" almost imperceptibly. Chad motioned for her to come to the long seat where he was lounging.

The sunset became the focus of the evening now. They watched it sink over the back of Painter Place. "Sailing" by Christopher Cross was playing, an enchanting melody for an evening on a boat. It was the most romantic and breathtaking view that Caroline could imagine. Her head rested on Chad's shoulder as the catamaran swayed gently on the waves with twilight coming on. She wasn't kidding when she said, "I *love* this. At this moment, there's nowhere else I'd rather be."

Natalie and Patrick were also sitting on a long seat together. No one said anything as if they didn't want to break the spell. The mansion, pavilion, pier, and treeline of the island all slowly lost their colors as they shifted into dark silhouettes.

The cassette in the stereo came to an end. Patrick looked over at Chad. "Let's take her into the waterway for calmer water."

Patrick shut off the engines between Chad and Patrick's family piers, across from Whitehaven Point. It was too far away and too dark for anyone there to actually see them, but they'd see the lights on the *Artistic License* itself. Other boats were out like they were.

Patrick put more music in the stereo, and they all sat back to enjoy the stars.

Natalie asked what constellations were out, and Patrick ran his hand through his hair as looked up and thought about it. She said, "I love the way you do that while you're thinking of what you're going to say." She gave him a winsome smile. He looked at her a few moments before glancing at Chad.

They discussed the outlines in the inky sky overhead, and Chad pointed at Polaris, telling Natalie that it was called the "guiding star," "the sea star," and the "steadfast star."

Caroline caught that arm, lowering it and looking for the bruise she had seen earlier.

She lightly traced around the bruise with her fingertip in the citronella lantern light. She looked up at him. "I did this on Friday night, didn't I?"

He smiled lazily as she continued to trace a finger over the injury. "I deserved worse. I was too aggressive."

"Still, I never want to hurt someone I love," she said.

Chad heard something from Patrick's direction, but couldn't bring himself to take his eyes off Caroline's. His voice was soft. "It feels better already."

"Good. I've been thinking that we need to have another dance here at Painter Place, and it wouldn't be the same if your arm's not up to it. I'll have to get some movie star stunt double on the premises to fill in for you."

His brows shot up. "Not a chance. What do you have in mind?"

"Well, I've been thinking . . . why not have a dance or a concert to welcome the movie crew and the summer guests who happen to be here? It would be smaller than the Island Summer Dance. They could stay on the pier or sit on beach towels and hang out if they don't have their wives or just don't want to dance. We already have some of the crowd facilities on the island anyway for the crews, so there shouldn't be much expense except for music, power, some refreshments, and maybe more security since they won't be used to Painter Place party rules. We could invite a band to play or have Joey to DJ. This crew looks like a rock music crowd, but Joey knows the clean stuff. And Chad, will you start to teach me about how the budget for events works around here?"

"Wow, that's a great idea!" Natalie sat up and leaned forward. "The dance part, I mean. Caroline, the movie crews would love it. It would be good publicity and a goodwill gesture for the cast."

Chad hadn't moved his eyes from Caroline's face or his arm from where her fingertip was still lightly moving over the bruise. His voice was still quiet. "Let's have dinner and a planning session tomorrow in Whitehaven at Dockside when you're finished in the studio. We'll take our plan to Wyeth and see what he thinks. Soon I'll start to teach you everything I know about Painter Place."

When they pulled the *License* up to the pier later and started unloading, Patrick came up close to Chad. In a low voice he said, "I know she said it twice, but she has to actually say the three words straight out and be serious. And either your idea about the music is really working or they're on to us."

***

In the studio on Monday, Caroline kept becoming distracted and tense. It was easier to deal with the shock of Saturday's revelation by her dad when Chad was with her. But now, painful and lonely memories of the past few years kept popping unexpectedly into her head. Sometimes she fought back anger at her dad. She tried listening to some calming music. Finally, she picked up her painting, reference sketch, and brushes and went over to her uncle's studio to ask if she could paint there with him for a while. He didn't seem surprised.

He asked her to tell him about what she was working on.

"I needed to get away from the Mevagissey stuff today. I decided to paint the marsh here at Painter Place from one of my plein air sketches."

He looked at her thoughtfully and said, "Why don't we get out of here for a change of scenery? Let's go out to the marsh and paint plein air."

They were about to leave just as Valerie came looking for them. She had brought some lunch, so they sat down to eat chef salads with her at a studio table.

Caroline noticed some wariness between her mom and uncle, but then they chatted about the crews and Juliette flying in with Cameron by the weekend, and the wariness fell away. As they were nearly finished, Valerie looked at Caroline with pleading eyes and blurted, "Please don't shut me out, baby."

Wyeth stopped chewing his last bite and didn't move. He and Valerie waited on Caroline, who pushed her fork around at the remains of her salad as an excuse to blink away the stinging in her eyes. She looked back up at her mother and nodded.

"I've never doubted you, but the way my dad is made me a wary of what Chad might do once he got off the island, so I went along with your dad's plan to protect you. No mom could ask for a better daughter." Her smile trembled slightly as she looked at Caroline. She reached across the table to touch her hand.

***

On Monday evening, after dinner together in Whitehaven, Chad entered Caroline's house to see how the cooking lesson was going and try some samples. Patrick and Natalie were cleaning up by then and invited them to watch a movie.

"First, I want to give this to Patrick," said Caroline, taking something out of her large bag from the studio. She handed her brother a package wrapped in brown paper and tied with string. It was obvious that he was very affected by the framed drawing of Natalie that Caroline had done in Mevagissey.

"It's a gift to say congratulations to my brother for having such good taste," said Caroline when he hugged her. Still in a bear hug, he swung her around so he could look at Natalie.

"Did you know about this?"

"I saw it for the first time on the yacht with Dante, and it looks even better framed."

Patrick let go of his sister. "Dante? The artist who hosted the yacht reception? He seemed to be hangin' around you a lot. What did he say about you in this?"

"Just some artist language about Caroline's style and skill, and that she had an eye for subject matter."

Chad said quickly, "Hey Patrick, we're inviting the girls to the pool for dinner on Thursday evening, so why don't we ask them to wear what they wore on the yacht? You'll get to see how they looked."

Caroline picked up Chad's lead to change the dangerous subject. "You two are planning a dinner for us? And it's formal?"

Chad and Patrick were looking at one another. Chad said, "Yes, we're having a romantic dinner—moonlight, stars, and music. Is about seven thirty okay?"

Natalie beamed. "Patrick, you really are amazing! What a terrific idea! I can hardly wait to see you dressed up."

Patrick gave her a thin smile and didn't offer a witty comment as usual. Caroline herded everyone to the upstairs den for a movie.

***

On Tuesday, Caroline was back to her struggles with concentration in the studio. She didn't want to be alone with hard feelings and memories of the last four years. She finally went to Wyeth's studio again, this time to see if he wanted her to gesso canvases or do other things around the studio for him before she left for the rest of the day.

He looked at her thoughtfully before asking her if she'd tint some canvases for him—a few in gold for some sunny day paintings and a few in purple for night scenes in Mevagissey. He told her he needed to take care of something at the Big House and would be right back.

Maggie Jane put her head into Wyeth's studio around noon. "There you are, Caroline. I was in the mood for a chicken and dumplin' lunch today and thought you might be, too. I brought a pot over to the gallery stock room so Shelly, Zachary, and Wyeth can join us—if I leave it at the Big House, it'll disappear like a poof of pixie dust. Come on over when ya finish up."

Caroline's face lit up. "Wow, Maggie Jane, you're amazing! That's just what I need. Let me get color on this last canvas and clean up."

Maggie Jane gestured that it was nothing and smiled at Wyeth, who winked at her. "I'll be right there, Maggie Jane."

Maggie went back to the gallery, where Shelly was talking to a man with a little notebook who was asking where the remains of the slave cabins were.

Maggie Jane huffed and answered for Shelly. "Son, you shoulda done your homework before you crossed that bridge. There's never been a slave on this island. People who worked at Painter Place were paid the best wages to get the best work out of 'em, and any whippin' that went on here was given in love in a back room by parents when their kids didn't want to learn the easy way."

The man with the notebook looked surprised. Zachary walked in the door and stopped short, sensing he was interrupting something.

"Here's somethin' to write down in your little notebook. We have an ole chapel here on Painter Place, and some ruins of caretaker cottages that didn't weather some hurricanes, and some legends that might raise your goosebumps 'round a campfire. But we've never had a slave. My family's been in Whitehaven for two hundred years, and a job on this island is considered a gift from God. If ya thought that the name White Island or Whitehaven had something to white skin, Shelly here could tell ya it was

273

named by the Indians. They said good white spirits walked here—and that's close enough to describin' angels to me. The four of us in here might have dark skin on the outside, but I know that for at least three of us, when we're done with our prayers every day, our spirits are as white as snow—like anyone else who lives or walks here. It's what's inside a person that the Painters value."

"Then—how did the Painters and Gregorys feel about the Civil War?"

"They felt like their homeland was bein' invaded by other Americans who raided it and took advantage of them. Hardly anybody actually owned slaves, but they were all punished and ruined as if they did. You'd want to protect your family's generations of hard work, too. Fortunately, the Painters livin' here then had powerful friends in the North who made sure the island was left alone. Those people had fond memories here they wanted to come back to."

The man was speechless.

Maggie Jane continued. "That new restaurant you saw bein' built across the bridge, that'll be named after the first Painter ever to settle here and run by his namesake, Patrick. My family's had a paid cook here at the Big House for generations, and I taught that little boy to cook just as if I was his mama, using only the best stuff from the island's gardens and home-raised meat from Whitehaven farmers. He insisted that I sign a contract with him so when he uses any of my family's recipes instead of his own over there, he'll pay me something for it. It never would have occurred to him that he ever owned a person or their work."

***

Thursday evening finally came. Chad had gone to Charleston on Wednesday for his sister's birthday, so Patrick covered calls and business for him and tried to get the shopping done for Thursday's date. Camellia had once been a designer and gave them ideas from her former pool parties. Both Chad and Patrick were pleased as they looked over the result and waited for their dates to arrive.

The Gregory estate was built in a sprawling Mediterranean Villa style, and the landscaping added to the exotic atmosphere around the pool. A formally set wrought iron table for four was embraced by a tablecloth in the tropical blue color of the pool and showcased a centerpiece of sunflowers and candles. It looked intimate under the ironwork gazebo draped with light sheers that caught the summer breeze. Sculpted plantings and blooming flowers were arranged around it.

An elegant ironwork easel displayed *Tall Ships and Sunflowers*. Tiny white party lights promised to be cheerful once the sun went down, and floating candles and artificial water lilies turned the pool into a waterscape that would be enchanting when night came.

Patrick saw immediately that Chad hadn't been exaggerating when he told him how beautiful the girls looked at the reception. He tried not to stare at Natalie like a smitten schoolboy. She reminded him of those beautiful statues of ancient goddesses, only she lived and breathed.

He could hardly believe the elegance of his sister in the peacock dress with her upswept hairstyle by Chrissy. And if the front of the dress was really something, the back was something more—or less, in this case. It unsettled him a little that she was that grown up. No wonder Chad had created an excuse to see her in the formal attire again.

Camellia and Phillip came out to greet them and took some photos before leaving them to dinner.

The sun set and twilight passed during their meal and conversation, with the soft music of romantic songs coming from the stereo, like "Tangerine" by Herb Albert and the Tijuana Brass. The relaxing instrumental music ended, and the love songs began.

Chad rose from the table first. "Dance with me," he said to Caroline, holding out his hand. Patrick followed his lead but asked Natalie instead of commanding her. The mood was so romantic that neither couple talked while they were slow dancing for the first couple of songs.

Natalie eventually commented softly to Patrick that she was blessed to find a guy who was so good at dancing because she loved to. He smiled and told her that Painter and Gregory offspring learned early how to dance often and well, even a waltz.

"Good breeding," he said playfully, exchanging glances with Chad. "You can take us almost anywhere and make a good impression. We come with exceptional pedigrees. I'm sure we have papers on us somewhere, like racehorses if you'd like to see them."

The Dave Clark Five began singing "Because," and Caroline sighed. It was so perfect that she wished she could applaud Chad. She began singing the words softly.

> *"It's right that I should care about you*
> *And try to make you happy when you're blue.*
> *It's right, it's right to feel the way I do,*
> *Because, because I love you."*

Chad raised an eyebrow and turned enough to see Patrick's face. Patrick was quite content with the impact of the song on Natalie, but he shook his head "no."

> *"Give me, give me a chance to near you,*
> *Because, because I love you*
> *Because, because I love you."*

Caroline said dreamily, "The last time I wore this dress, do you remember asking me a question that I never answered?" They continued to dance slowly around the enchanted pool.

"Countless times every day. It's a wonder I get anything worthwhile done. You can put me out of my misery any time now."

She pulled her head back to see if he was teasing.

He grinned down at her. "Is that the best you can do at coming up with a hard question?"

She laughed shortly. "Don't get me started with you trying to win, or I'm not goin' to say it."

"Say what?"

"That I love you!"

Chad stopped dancing, gripping her hand tightly. They locked eyes. "Say it the right way."

"What's the right way?"

"The way you want me to say it."

"Oh. That way . . ."

He nodded slowly.

"I can't do that here. My big brother is around somewhere."

Chad lightly slapped his forehead with his hand in frustration.

Patrick and Natalie weren't dancing anymore, captivated by Chad and Caroline.

"Just pretend I'm not here," chimed in Patrick. "I won't look."

Natalie said they were going inside for a break. She took Patrick's arm roughly and pulled him toward a wall of glass doors, ignoring his teasing protests.

Caroline was obviously struggling not to lose control and burst out laughing.

Chad turned away to look out at the pier, taking a few deep breaths to reset his mood. When he turned around, Caroline was standing at the table sipping some water from her glass. Like him, she was also taking a few deep breaths, and her gaze was past the gazebo at the next building. He stood admiring the back of the stunning dress on her before he slowly walked over.

"What's going on at the guest house?" she asked unexpectedly.

"Remodeling."

"Show me."

He hesitated but then took her hand and led her through the gate in the wall.

Once they walked through the gate onto a path of pavers, she pulled him off into the grass toward the side of the wall closest to the water. Boat lights passed, and the Beatles sang "Here, There, and Everywhere" on the pool stereo, joining the sounds of the island evening that surrounded them.

Caroline led Chad into the shadows, where the wall was cool when his back and head rested against it. She leaned into his side and tiptoed so her face would be close to his ear.

She spoke with intensity. "I love you, Chad. I always have. I never got over you, and never can. No one is going to keep me from you ever again. It's our time, and I trust you to decide what's next for us."

She lightly brushed a kiss on his neck above his collar before lowering from her tiptoes. He quickly reached around her to keep her close.

"I need a minute," he said hoarsely.

She put her palm on his chest to rest her face against so she wouldn't get makeup on his white jacket. She closed her eyes, hardly believing the day had come when she'd said this. She felt peaceful as they stood there enveloped in shadows and the summer night. It was as if something she had always needed to do had finally been done. She felt free.

"*. . . Each one believing that love never dies, watching her eyes and hoping I'm always there,*" sang the Beatles.

They heard Patrick and Natalie come back out by the pool on the other side of the wall. Patrick teased her about how intimidating it was to dance with a Greek goddess statue.

"Can you wait for me to get back with you on this?" Chad whispered into her hair, running his palm lightly down her arm from her shoulder to wrist before taking her hand.

"Not any longer than our four weeks anniversary," she whispered firmly. She held up four slender fingers on the other hand.

"That's my girl," he whispered, kissing her temple.

Chapter Twenty-Eight

*"He created them male and female and blessed them.
And he named them 'Mankind' when they were created."*
Genesis 5:2

The Tarzan game was bigger than usual the next evening. Cameron, Juliette, and Jesse had flown into Whitehaven in Cameron's 1975 Cessna Golden Eagle, and Wyeth and Chrissy came over to Andy Painter's house with them. Having some visitors pushed the tension in the family dynamics down into an undercurrent, but Wyeth was cool to his brother and Phillip even in the heat of the game. His eyes and manner were aloof, but he played with even more drive to win than he usually did.

Cameron and Jesse took turns of time in, not used to the grueling pace in the island humidity. An overnight storm was brewing in the sky. Jesse was delighted with the games and a chance to see Painter Place. He sat with Caroline and Juliette during one of his off times to catch his breath.

"I love the feeling of Painter Place," Jesse told them. "It's as if I walked into the things that are good and wholesome about life when I stepped out of the plane into Whitehaven, and especially when I crossed the bridge to the island—almost like I'm suddenly drinking pure water instead of a glass dipped into the marsh."

Juliette smiled at him. "At Painter Place, men are men, women are cherished, and kids are brought up to know that right and wrong aren't about our opinions, but written by God in His word and on our hearts."

***

Everyone noticed that something important had changed between Chad and Caroline. Overnight, Chad had lost his restless, sometimes brooding look. Caroline lost the guarded distance she had around him. Andy Painter watched closely when they interacted and finally looked at Phillip with raised eyebrows and a tilt of his head in their direction.

Phillip came over for a brief discussion and ended by saying, "We need to tell Wyeth." He looked in Wyeth's direction. "I can't live with being his ex-best friend or the way he looks at me now. I miss him. Besides, if he

279

keeps up this smoldering mood, we'll never win another basketball game or anything else. It's on you and me to ask him to forgive us and work to make things the way they were. It's not about whether we were right or wrong."

"I don't know the answer to that one myself. It's a good day now if either of my daughters glances my way," Andy said. He followed Phillip's eyes and saw Wyeth look away from him dismissively. He snorted. "Have fun making the first move. We'll just replace your hand with a hook when he bites it off and spits it out."

To his surprise, Phillip caught Wyeth's eye again and motioned for him to come over. He watched Wyeth look away and hesitate as if deciding whether to ignore Phillip. Then he seemed to change his mind and joined them.

***

Chad led Caroline away from the bonfire group to sit on the pier. She loved the way he was always so relaxed and conversational after the Tarzan games.

"I haven't told you yet about Hawaii," he began after they settled into the bench. "You interested?"

Caroline nodded, trying not to look too eager. "Sure. I guess you're goin' to tell me about more than the views and the Arizona Memorial. Do I need to brace myself?"

He laughed easily and put his arm on the pier railing behind her. "No worries. I told you when I gave you my ring that I hadn't done anything immoral or illegal. I tried being open-minded about ladies my age there for about a week, but it was more frightening than fun. Imagine a million females like Wilfred in a place where no one knows you and doesn't expect to. Some seemed beautiful until they opened their mouth or I watched their actions for a few minutes. The ones behaving like ladies were with guys who were treating them as such. I finally met some Christians doing beach ministries with a local Baptist church, and I went there for the summer and made friends. They took me to see places only the locals know about."

Chad's expression changed, and he paused for a few moments rather than trying to speak over the motor of a passing boat. "I resented not being able to come home for Cole's graduation without breaking my deal about staying away from you. I got worse as the date got closer, and I thought about just coming in anyway, standing at the door, and leaving as soon as it was over. But I knew I couldn't hide my feelings when you'd certainly see me, and Patrick warned me not to waste two years of staying away."

He paused, pushing hair back from his forehead. "I felt desperate, trapped by Painter Place and Global. Out of the blue, I got an internship offer at a firm in Hawaii on Oahu, and it included a place to stay in Honolulu near the office. It was the perfect chance to just escape and have a good excuse for not being at graduation. I basically worked against Global with Dad's competition all summer. I wanted some control over hurting him like I thought he was controlling and hurting me, so I just left and sent a postcard. I think that's when he started protecting Global from me and Cole. Cole was pushing all Dad's buttons after guessing what happened when I left for college and now was going to be unleashed in London."

He swallowed hard. Caroline nodded but didn't say anything. She watched the backlit clouds as lightning flashed in the distance, where a storm was more than a threat.

"When I came back for my junior year and Dad could reach me at my condo again, he asked if anything had happened to void our agreement or ruin my chances with you, and I said no. But taking off like that was a huge strike against me, and he's watching me. He's curious about my side business—he knows I started it in college as an option to Global if things didn't work out. So I protected myself from him, and he protected himself from me. See why I can relate to your meltdown last Saturday?"

"Did you sketch anything?"

He smiled and shook his head. "It's just like you to think of art when I'm spilling my guts. No, that would've reminded me of Wyeth's classes and Painter Place. I practiced what I learned in photography class. I have photos in an envelope somewhere in my closet."

He glanced at her before looking over the water again. "Only my boss knew who I was, so no one expected me to act like a spoiled brat. As I got to know some of the guys at church, I shared a little about you and Painter Place. It helped to talk about it, and they prayed with me about the situation. By the time I went back to school, I was past a lot of the resentment. The rest worked out back on campus when I realized I needed to just be who I am and stop fighting it."

Caroline turned from another blink of lightning behind clouds in the night sky. "Did you totally get past being mad at your dad?"

Chad looked over to the beach at his parents.

"I think so. When I watched him in action in London, I remembered that I'd always admired him and wanted to be like him. I don't think I'd have been the risk he and your dad thought, and I believe you and Wyeth should've been included in knowing their plan. But that's from hindsight, which is always 20/20. They're facing something no dad at Painter Place has ever faced before. I haven't told you everything yet—I overheard the end of what happened between you and your dad on the beach."

Caroline brought both hands to her face and groaned. "Ouch—I'm embarrassed. That wasn't my best moment, and Dad was brutally honest about you and Cole."

He nodded and rubbed her shoulder as if to reassure her. "Don't worry. Now I'll always behave myself because I'm scared of you and your family."

She burst out laughing, and he joined her. The group on the beach looked over at them and smiled before getting up to put out the fire before the storm blew in.

Chad sobered and looked at her thoughtfully, reaching to toy with her hair. "It feels good to finally tell you what happened. Running away to Hawaii wasn't my shining moment, either. I'm disappointed at the immature way I handled it. At least you screamed at your dad and got it over with."

"I ran away for a day, remember? And you came to get me, straighten me out, and bring me back. So you learned something in your experience that made you the only person who could help me. Nothing is wasted."

They looked at one another for a few moments before she spoke. "Will you show me your photos? Maybe we can see some of those out-of-the-way places on Oahu together sometime. I can paint plein air, and you can sketch. I guess you've noticed my sketches are still often unfinished and loose, really just a thought to get me to a painting. You'll win because yours are art."

282

He sighed contentedly "I'm working on a way for us to get there. But right now, we should get back to the house."

She walked with Chad to his Porsche. He leaned back onto his door and took her hands into his.

"I asked you last Sunday to convince me you don't have any issues with me anymore over leaving. Can you?"

This time she met his eyes. "Last night wouldn't have happened if I did." She started swinging their joined hands and smiled up at him. "Tomorrow, you're going to say something important for our four week anniversary, and we're going to Rock the Island!"

He laughed at her unexpected response. He'd laughed a lot tonight, and it felt good. He brushed a kiss on her temple and opened his car door as thunder rumbled closer.

Wait until you see how funny that really is, he thought as he closed his door. He pointed from his heart to hers before he backed out and headed home.

***

It rained overnight, but Saturday morning dawned with clear skies and cooler readings on the thermometers. Journalists for two art magazines came in and were getting settled for a weekend of interviews with Wyeth and Caroline. There would be a presentation on the Mevagissey trip in the afternoon at the Big House, with dinner for family, friends, and the journalists afterward. The journalists were invited to Rock the Island that evening, and would finish the weekend with an interview on the *Artistic License* on Sunday.

Chad came into the hall of the gallery complex from outside with a bouquet of sunflowers and a steaming cup of chocolate-flavored coffee for Caroline. He was hoping to catch her in her studio, working on the painting of the scene of the Island Summer Dance from the porch of the mansion. He'd been keeping sunflowers fresh in the vase he'd given her in Mevagissey ever since they'd returned.

"Cameron and I can't believe they did this to you!" he heard Juliette say vehemently. He stopped instantly, only a few steps from the open studio door.

"You haven't heard Dad's side of the story," said Caroline. "Talk to him. I never wanted to be a divisive issue in my family."

"I've called him and he promised to make time for me for lunch. I'm taking him something to the marina to eat—maybe a crow." Juliette huffed.

"He said he's sorry that his decision hurt me so much. But he's apparently not sorry that he didn't trust me. He's not sorry that he deceived me. Those were the things that hurt the most, and I have to let them go and forgive him. But forgiveness hasn't put back the indefinable 'something' that simply vanished, as if I suddenly saw Dad for the first time, and he isn't a hero after all."

"You and Chad were both young. Andy wanted you to know yourselves and have a backup plan if Chad was reckless with women or chose another career path. Would you have done that if you'd known?"

"That's one-sided, Juliette. I'd have been alone more to work on knowing myself anyway. Why did Chad get to know what was going on, when I didn't? Just because he was the one being vetted for a career here? I'd have cooperated with the plan by going out to please Dad, but I admit I'd only have given someone a real chance if I knew Chad was doing the same. Dad knew that and had to keep me in the dark to get what he wanted. With his way, I'd assume Chad was enjoying freedom from me and Painter Place. Real or imagined, rejection felt the same, so why not let me experience the real thing?"

Chad was getting uncomfortable now. He glanced in the other direction at the door to the gallery, where he could leave the coffee and flowers with Shelly to give Caroline.

Caroline continued. "It was obvious from the moment I first saw Chad again that what had gone to sleep inside me for him was suddenly wide awake. He couldn't have come back here with someone else and lived on the island to work with me. My status here trumps his, and I'd have sent him packing. I couldn't have hidden my feelings from anyone if Chad came near me, least of all him."

Chad's mouth dropped open, and he heard her take a deep breath. "Knowing that he knew and still chose someone else would have been too humiliating to imagine. I'd have had to be notified and off the island if he visited. I planned this in Mevagissey when I saw him with the model and was goin' to call my dad the next day to put it into action. Chad would've lost his dream to be at Painter Place merely by not choosing me. I'd have been single all my life—what guy would knowingly live with that situation? I can't even comprehend such a disaster. Yet now I know my own dad and Phillip could have set me up for it."

There was no way he was leaving now. He hoped no one else came in to interrupt or let them know he was there.

Juliette spoke next. "Derrick would gratefully take any bit of your love if it came to that. He's a confident competitor who doesn't want the easy path because the hardest way is fun. He'd assume you'd get over Chad once you'd been with him. He'd have wanted you to be here with him at least once when Chad visited just so he could show off that he got you and Painter Place after you made Chad leave."

Chad leaned back against the hallway wall, remembering his little business meeting with Derrick last Sunday. If the guy was anything, he was confident, likable—and incredibly patient. A stab of real pain hit his heart when an image of Derrick with Caroline came to mind.

Juliette continued. "My friends in Whitehaven told me he came in last weekend just to see you. He found out Chris left and you were back from England. But Chad told him you were his and he wasn't leaving anymore. So Derrick has a friend here watching what happens. I'm sure he's not spending time alone, but he's focused on his career. He doesn't know yet that Chad was forced to stay away in college, so he's hoping he'll get bored and leave soon. Derrick would have to be gone a lot, but you wouldn't have to be home all the time, either. God always provides a way around here, Caroline. He wouldn't leave you with no one to carry on at Painter Place."

"I'm just saying that so many things could've gone wrong with Dad and Phillip's plan by not including me and Uncle Wyeth. With Dad, it's the trust issue that gets me the most, not whether the means justified the ends. I see Phillip differently, too, and it's awkward to know that the ladies around here knew. I feel like everyone was watching, as if I might do something stupid to bring down Painter Place. I think the stress within the family will heal with time, but I don't see how I'll be the same."

"Caroline, are you hoping to marry Chad?"

Chad stood back up, perfectly still.

"Now that I know what happened and that I can trust him, yes. But I'm not ready to have my dad or Phillip involved in all the warm fuzziness of a wedding for a while, or to be part of paying for mine as their victory trophy. I don't want to be married in the chapel as tradition dictates. Chad saw Chris break up with me there. I want something new, all our own. I'd rather that we just eloped to Charleston one day and came back as Mr. and Mrs."

"What if I could help you find another way that included the family?"

"I'm intrigued, but Chad hasn't asked. He's only been back a month, Juliette. I still find myself thinking this can't be happening—it's too perfect to be reality, and I'm not used to it yet."

"Let's switch gears. Can you take a break and come over to my cottage with me? I'll have you back in time for the first studio interview with the journalists. Having them here is making my staging instincts for you and Painter Place work overtime. Humor me and give me something to do as your publicity agent. I know you've probably planned what you'll wear tonight, but I want you to see something that would look great on you if you like it better."

Chad silently took a few steps back to the outside door, leaning on it and slipping through. His mind was overwhelmed with all the new food for thought.

They came through the door together, assuming he'd just walked up. They fussed over the gifts he'd brought Caroline. The look in her eyes the instant she saw him confirmed why she'd made the plan to send him away from Painter Place if he wasn't there for her. She was right—it would've been the only way unless Derrick made her get over him. But still, there'd always be the memories . . . and neither of them could escape those.

She handed the covered coffee mug to Juliette so that she could hug him without spilling the hot liquid. He closed his eyes with her arms around his neck. He remembered the day he'd told her dad he still wanted to see her and had done all he asked. He had gone home realizing that there'd never been a Plan B for him, where he and Caroline merely worked together. There'd only ever been Plan A.

Chad walked them over to Juliette's cottage, then over to where Patrick stood near the pavilion. Some of the crew was hanging the lights and doing the work he and Patrick had meant to do. Patrick told him that Cameron insisted that he'd worked things out with Mr. Paul as a gesture of appreciation for tonight.

"Let's head over to the pool and relax a while," suggested Patrick. "I could use some laps."

Chad nodded and turned to walk to their cars. "Me, too. But first, my dad and I are goin' to have a serious conversation. You don't want to be there. Just go out to the pool after you change."

***

The ballroom at the Big House was lined with some easels of paintings that Wyeth and Caroline had created from their trip to Mevagissey, and albums of photos and boards of photo montages were on tables. A screen was set up in the front.

Every chair had a good view of the screen for a couple dozen family and friends. The two art magazine representatives sat on the front row with Wyeth and Chrissy, but Caroline sat with Chad on the third and last row. They weren't looking forward to the newspaper segment of the presentation.

"I'd like to meet Jesse," whispered Carly to Caroline. "Will he be at the dance tonight?"

"Yes, and he's been looking over here at you."

Cameron and Natalie did most of the presentation, with comments on quick slideshows of photos, leaving out the newspaper accounts. Jesse played "Dirty Laundry" by Don Henley in the background as he clipped on Cameron's microphone and they whispered together before changing places. He took the remote control for the slideshow and opened a box of newspapers, which he placed out on a table.

"When I took the job to work on the Painter trip to Mevagissey with Cameron a few weeks ago, I honestly expected it to be boring. Instead, it's become one of the most rewarding jobs I've had, and I can't imagine never having met Caroline, Chad, or Baker Holmes. I can't understate how much impact the press had on our group almost every day for a week. You'd

287

miss so much if you looked at the newspapers without a timeline and personal insights."

Jesse's presentation was full of reactions from and interactions in the audience before he ended it with a newspaper photo of the harbor full of people singing "Amazing Grace." Everyone clapped, and once again he switched places with Cameron.

Cameron continued the presentation with the harbor concert and wrapped up with the speeches and photos from the yacht reception. Patrick became tense. Every time a photo came up with Natalie on Dante's arm, he narrowed his eyes, ran his hand through his hair, or squirmed.

Caroline saw that Chad noticed Patrick's reactions, too. She leaned to whisper, "He's jealous. I hope he won't turn this into their first fight tonight."

Chad nodded before he leaned close to her ear. "Now I see what he's watched me do for years."

After the presentations, Caroline introduced Carly to Jesse, and he asked her to sit with him at the early dinner party and be his date for the dance that night.

Patrick was subdued, but Natalie acted as if nothing was wrong. As soon as dinner was over, Juliette gathered the young ladies, saying they were all getting dressed for the dance at her cottage, and they would see the guys there at around eight.

Cameron emptied the last of his glass of sweet tea and looked at Chad. He shrugged. "Juliette has something special in mind for Caroline, so you should practice breathing. Can I talk to you about something—in private?"

"Sure. I'll meet you in the library. I just need to speak to Patrick a minute."

Cameron nodded and headed in that direction. Chad turned to his best friend. "Want to talk about it? I was there."

"No, I know what you'll say. She didn't do anything. We weren't even dating yet. I just can't bear to see her with such an obviously more sophisticated older guy. The wolf man really enjoyed being with her. I'm trying to get a grip on being a guppy in the big pond."

"Now I see what you've watched me do around Caroline, and you see what I was feeling when you watched. It just took you longer to get here because it's the first time it's mattered. Don't let it become a fight tonight at the dance. You won't win, and you'll end up feeling stupid. Turn it into a positive."

"A positive? You're kidding," scoffed Patrick.

"Talk to her about it."

Patrick rubbed both hands over his face. "I don't think I'm ready for that."

"Well, while you think about it, keep Joey here for a few minutes 'til I get back. We need to check his music list."

***

Chad had a preoccupied look on his face when he found Joey and Patrick about fifteen minutes later. "Patrick, can you and Natalie come over to the pool tonight to talk about something?"

Patrick raised his brow and nodded while Joey unfolded a paper from his pocket, stepping closer to Chad. "For the slower choices, I have some things I know she likes. For the more rowdy tunes, I have songs from our Friday night collections for basketball—the Big Three haven't complained about any of these. I'll be sure to make our girl's idea look good, and maybe we can do this more often. I haven't gotten anything from Public Parking yet, but I'm working on it for the future." He pointed to the top of the list. "We can use a couple of the clean Foreigner songs, like 'Juke Box Hero.' Do you mind if I get that dance early while you keep an eye on the booth? It's our song, and I never get to dance with her anymore since you came home."

Chad rolled his eyes good-naturedly and nodded. Joey said, "Trust me, you won't be sorry. Keep your eyes open. Oh, and I have two songs ready in case something special happens tonight. You're never gonna catch me off guard, man." He slapped Chad on the back. "By the way, here's a heads up. The Big Three requested the opening song, but I promised not to tell you what it is, and I honestly have no idea what they're up to."

Chad and Patrick looked at Joey with wide eyes before looking at one another. Patrick exclaimed, "I thought it was too good to be true that they were on speaking terms last night after basketball!"

"They're planning something, like the old days," Chad muttered, narrowing his eyes.

Joey grinned. "Be ready for anything. We're set for the first Rock the Island event at Painter Place!"

Chapter Twenty-Nine

"I know it's only Rock and Roll, but I like it."
— The Rolling Stones

The guys decided to arrive at Juliette's cottage at the same time. Cameron arranged for a photographer for the group photo of them walking up the stairs to her porch. The setting sun was already sending flickers of warm yellow light.

Chad saw Caroline, the center of his universe, wearing a little black dress that was at once both demure and exciting, just like Caroline herself. Now he knew what Cameron meant when he told him to practice breathing. The dress fitted into a v-shaped seamed yoke in a flattering way before flaring out into a short skirt that would flutter in dance moves but stay modest with black Capri leggings. It was strapless with a small two-inch slit from the top in the center. Feminine ankle boots with a bow-tie, buckle, and low heels would be comfortable to dance in and easy to kick off in the sand.

But what made the whole outfit was a slender fitted little shrug that opened around her neck before it ran across both shoulders. It encased her upper arms almost to the elbows, where little zippers created a slit on each arm up from the edge. It was a light material that mimicked leather and had some dainty buckles and metal rings. A sprinkle of black sequins in a spray design scattered across the fabric, shimmering in a play of light. There was no question the dress was inspired by rock and roll, but it didn't come across as a statement.

Her hair was styled in a version of the fascinating waterfall hairstyle Chad had liked from the Island Summer Dance. The French braid ran from one side to fall over to her left ear into the rest of her hair. On the other side, she wore the one earring Chad had given her, as well as the eternity bracelet and watch.

Cassie was beside herself when Chad arrived. She whispered to Marina, "I told you! In that jacket and aqua Henley shirt, he could jump over the rail in one sweep and grab Caroline to whisk her outta here!"

Juliette's cottage was across from the Big House, the first one by the gardens and on the beach closest to the pier. The couples walked from there to the pavilion, passing tables being set up for snacks. Many volunteers from Whitehaven wanted to help, and some young people planned a party in a parking lot across the bridge where they hoped to hear the music.

A crowd was gathering, their voices blending into the swishing surf sounds. Twilight was deep enough for the glowing lanterns to flutter gaily in the breeze.

Chad kept looking at Caroline appreciatively as they reached the sand around the pavilion. She took a deep breath and looked up at him. "Now that this is happening, I'm a little nervous."

Shelly walked up with Zachary. She wasn't looking at him as a rival anymore. In fact, Caroline had never seen her wear this expression. Like Shelly's dad, Zachary was from Jamaica, and they'd apparently found a lot in common.

"Shelly, you look beautiful!" exclaimed Caroline, hugging her friend. Shelly was wearing a hot pink outfit set off by her bronze skin. Seeing Shelly in that much pink was a new experience for Caroline, and she knew instantly that it was intended to attract Zachary—like a butterfly to a flower.

"And look at you!" exclaimed Shelly, beaming at her. "Have mercy on poor Chad!" She hugged him, too.

Chad laughed as he let her go. "It's no use, Shelly. I'm done for."

"Well, you two are gonna give everyone somethin' to talk about, that's for sure. You lookin' like you came off the set of Miami Vice to take care of business, and her stirrin' things up around here like a rock star."

Andy Painter came from behind Caroline and grabbed her hand. "Honor me with the first dance on the island tonight?"

Caroline was totally taken aback. Chad managed to nod, and she followed her dad onto the empty pavilion floor.

The first notes of "Let the Good Times Roll" by the Cars stirred the night air at Painter Place. The insects and wildlife grew quiet to listen. The crowd moved closer to watch, assuming this was a solo moment for father and daughter.

Caroline's dad had been her first dance partner as a little girl, picking her up and holding her while she giggled and he did the steps. As she grew tall enough for her feet to reach the floor, he'd helped her learn the steps. She thought she knew all his moves, but he'd added some new ones tonight.

"I was impressed by the presentation this afternoon. I couldn't be more proud of how you handled yourself in Mevagissey. You're quite a poised young lady."

"Thanks," she said, concentrating on following him. Cameras were flashing around them.

> *"Let the good times roll*
> *Let the stories be told*
> *Let them say what they want*
> *Let the photos be bold*
> *Let them show what they want . . ."*

"I wish I had trusted you about Chad. I was afraid you'd act like me when I was your age."

She came out of a turn to look up at his face, startled, and missed a step. It didn't matter because Phillip was suddenly there to take her away from her dad in one swift movement as if it were choreographed. Her dad winked at her and reached for her mom, who came up to dance with him.

"Let the good times roll . . ." sang the Cars.

It had been a while since she'd danced with Phillip, and after the revelation that he'd been part of Chad's absence for four years, she felt awkward. He was a dashing dance partner, as strong and suave as he was at any other time. She'd always felt a little like she was dancing with James Bond when she danced with Phillip. She followed him in some quick turns that left her breathless before he spoke to her.

"I never told you how impressed I was at how you handled yourself in Mevagissey," he said. "You saved the Gregorys' reputation and represented Painter Place well. There's no one in the world I'd rather see with my son. He chose well."

Wyeth took her away from Phillip in another smooth transition with his own little creative flair.

"Let the good times roll . . ." sang the Cars.

Wyeth grinned at her. "Havin' fun yet?"

"This has to be a dream. I'm totally flustered inside, hoping the lessons in ladylike demeanor from Gran Vanna are hiding it."

Wyeth laughed out loud in his jovial manner, and everyone watching smiled. "Then we're all in the same dream, and you learned well from the grand lady. We wanted to show that we like what you're adding to Painter Place, and we wanted to rile up the competition again with Chad and Patrick now that they're home. Our journalist friends are eating this up, and I'm lookin' forward to your interview on the *License* tomorrow."

He swept her into a dramatic dip as the song ended, and he, Andy, and Phillip all pointed to her and encouraged the crowd to applaud.

Patrick shook his head and grinned at Chad as they joined the applause. "Did you see the new moves? They just put on a show to let us know they won't be outdone by our rock 'n' roll party. We'll have to come up with another challenge for the old guard."

Joey pushed through the crowd to go up the steps to replace Wyeth, taking Caroline's hand and whispering something to her. Everyone poured onto the floor as "Juke Box Hero" began. Caroline quickly glanced around for Chad and didn't see him.

Chad smiled when he saw her looking for him. He was still reeling from the little show during the first song, and wondered what the Big Three had said to her. After his conversation with his dad and listening to his dad call Andy this morning at the marina, it would've been encouraging.

There were two guys standing in front of him in jeans and sleeveless tee shirts. One was burly and was wearing a ball cap, and the other had a ponytail. The burly guy pointed at Caroline and made a comment close to the ponytailed man's ear. Then he crossed his big arms over his chest. Chad couldn't make out what the guy said, but the music transitioned to a quieter pulse and he heard the ponytailed man respond.

"You'd better watch it. She ain't no six-pack-by-the-river-on-Friday-night kinda girl. Talk around here is that she has a boyfriend who walks tall and carries a big stick—and acts like he owns the place. They say he threw a guy off a yacht for messin' with 'er."

"Yeah, well maybe he wrestles 'gators, too," growled the other man with a snicker.

"Problem is, you look like a gator and he don't, so which one ya think she'd be running from if she's got any sense a'tall?"

Chad turned away to laugh and couldn't wait to tell Patrick. Still grinning, he looked back at the dance floor. Joey came down to one knee to play a strong air guitar with a force that threw his long hair over his face.

Unfazed, Caroline twirled around, her long hair in motion, and pulled out her own air guitar. She put her boot on Joey's knee to play with a swaying motion that shook the metal rings on her shoulders. Chad let this burn into his memory as another one of those surprising things she came up with that delighted him. She and Joey had obviously practiced, and Chad realized with a pang that he'd missed years of this in her life. Joey had undoubtedly logged in lots of time dancing with her while Big Mike had been the usual DJ. Good thing he thought of her as his sister and considered her Chad's territory. Chad smiled as he wondered how Caroline had looked dancing with Cole those first two years after he left. That would definitely be a show worth watching.

The song ended, and the distinctive riffs of the beginning of a Kinks song sliced out of the speakers. Chad passed Joey at the steps coming off the floor. "I'll go shine up a trophy," he said sarcastically.

Joey laughed. "Told ya it'd be worth it. Thanks for sharing."

"Don't get used to it."

Caroline pushed her way through the crowd on the floor to meet him. He stopped, waiting for her. He liked having her come after him and rewarded her with a look that said so.

"Have I told you how gorgeous and unpredictable you are tonight?" he asked when she came up and put her hand on his sleeve.

"Only with your eyes. Did you hear mine?"

"Loud and clear, but do you mind saying it with your voice?" He took her arm to dance, making space for them.

"You're still impossibly handsome and slightly dangerous, and it took my breath away when I saw you come to pick me up tonight."

> *"See, don't ever set me free*
> *I always want to be by your side . . ."*

sang the Kinks.

He searched her face. "I'm glad I asked. I didn't catch all that in the look. I guess my mind was—wandering." He impulsively pulled her close to him as they came out of a turn. Her arm crossed the front of the slit in her dress with her hand in his at her shoulder, where he was behind her against the soft black material. He felt the cool metal rings on his chest through his shirt. He closed his eyes for the moment it took before she turned again.

> *". . . Yeah, you really got me now*
> *You got me so I don't know what I'm doin' now . . ."*

When the song was over, Joey let everyone catch their breath. "Hold On" by Kansas enveloped the crowd in the signature haunting sound swelling from the speakers. Kerry Livgren sang the words he'd written to his wife. The sand around the pavilion filled with slow-dancing couples who couldn't find a place on the floor.

> *". . . Hold on, baby hold on, 'cause it's closer than you think*
> *And you're standing on the brink*
> *Hold on, baby hold on, 'cause there's something on the way*
> *Your tomorrow's not the same as today . . ."*

Jesse and Carly danced next to Chad and Caroline on the crowded pavilion floor. "They don't act like they've ever kissed," said Jesse.

Carly raised her eyebrows. "They haven't. Come back on their wedding day."

"Are you serious?" asked Jesse incredulously. "Why not?"

Carly glanced over at them before she looked back at Jesse, her dark eyes serious. She was disappointed that he didn't know the answer, and she had to think about her response for a minute as the song played and they slow danced.

"Outside your door He is waiting, waiting for you
Sooner or later you know He's got to come through
No hesitation and no holding back
Let it all go and you'll know you're on the right track.
Hold on, baby hold on, 'cause it's closer than you think
And you're standing on the brink
Hold on, baby hold on, 'cause there's something on the way
Your tomorrow's not the same . . ."

Carly moved to talk closer to Jesse's ear in the loud music. "Think about how you noticed that they'd never kissed. Couples act differently when they've crossed that line. It's like sneaking open the tape on a gift to see what it is, then trying to wrap it back up even though you know it can never be exactly the same. A true kiss isn't supposed to be harmless—if it was, what's the attraction? A real kiss is a really big deal, which is why it comes after your wedding vows in the ceremony—you know, when the preacher says 'you may kiss your bride.' It's a sneak peek at the gift. Often, couples can't resist and just tear the paper off and open it. Then they change their mind, and there's no commitment to keep what they thought they wanted. What's so special about re-gifting? Isn't that a white elephant? Why spread something so important all over the place? It would lose its value and be worn out, like the tape on the package when you tried to seal it back."

Jesse didn't say anything for a moment as the song changed. "What about people who've already had a first kiss with someone else?"

"Everyone gets a second chance if they change their mind and do it right the next time," she said.

Led Zeppelin's "When the Levee Breaks" began throbbing through the speakers, and the beat vibrated through the very boards of the pavilion. It was their cue to gather with the others in their group in a circle to switch partners during the lengthy song, ending up with their date again. Caroline had fun dancing with her brother, Danny, Jesse, and Cassie's date, but kept exchanging glances and smiles with Chad.

As the throb of Neil Young's "Hey, Hey, My, My" made the pavilion boards tremble again, Caroline breathlessly reminded Chad that they were hosts. They took a break to get something to drink and join Cameron and

Juliette, who were mingling with the cast, stunt actors, and crew around the pavilion.

"... *Hey, hey, my, my*
Rock and roll can never die.
There's more to the picture
Than meets the eye.
Hey, hey, my, my ..."

Caroline whispered to Juliette. "Is the secret out? You and Cameron are obviously a couple to all these people now."

Juliette whispered back. "We've decided that we're ready to deal with it. The worst that can happen is that he has to marry me to defend my honor. I can live with that."

Chad was questioning the stunt actors about some of the water vehicles being used around the pier for a chase scene. They explained that no one on the pier could be hurt, but it was possible that one of the drivers could be. They invited him to come out during practice and try them out off the set.

"We aren't going as fast as it will look on film. It's just that some tricks are involved," explained one stunt actor. "The best scene of all is around sunset, so we'll be practicing many evenings. Hope it won't disrupt the peaceful setting here for all of you."

"Since it's a spy thriller, will there be an Aston Martin used anywhere?" asked Caroline.

Cameron looked delighted. "You know what an Aston Martin is?"

Juliette, Caroline, and Chad all laughed. "The men at Painter Place like cars," Chad explained. "She grew up with car magazines and NASCAR."

"I could see about working something in," said Cameron. "Maybe a scene where we have one parked on the beach with something happening over the sand dunes, or a scene racing across the causeway bridge. I can't guarantee the scenes would make the cut. I'll be sure to let you sit in it and take a photo."

"I have a bigger request, but I want to talk to you about it with Patrick," said Chad.

Eventually, Chad saw the two men he'd heard earlier talking about Caroline. They were looking at him and her together, and the one with the ponytail jabbed the other in the ribs with his elbow. Chad put his arm around Caroline and pulled her closer, enjoying his reputation as bad news. Maybe looking like Sonny Crockett would help. It could come in handy sometime.

They went back up onto the dance floor for a few songs, and then Chad glanced at the front porch of the mansion. "Remember how we always end dances?" he asked near her ear.

"I get to pick you," she answered. "But we still have a little time tonight."

"Let's go," he said, ignoring the question in her eyes as he took her arm. He led her off the dance floor just as Jan Hammer's theme song for *Miami Vice* began. People smiled and turned to look at him. Chad rolled his eyes.

They walked away from the crowded pavilion, across Pavilion Way, and up to the Big House, where they climbed the many stairs to the veranda. The metal on Caroline's dress jumped with her steps, throwing off reflected beams from a moon that was almost full. They paused to catch their breath at the top, leaning against the railing to look out over the always-enchanting sight of the lights, crowd, and ocean.

Whatever Joey was thinking when he'd played the *Miami Vice* song as Chad left with Caroline, he was right on cue now. The guy was really paying attention. Chad made a mental note to reward him for this one.

"I pick you," Caroline said, and Chad reached for her in the shadows to dance.

> *". . . I can't see me lovin' nobody but you*
> *For all my life*
> *When you're with me, baby the skies'll be blue*
> *For all my life*
> *Me and you and you and me*
> *No matter how they toss the dice, it has to be*
> *The only one for me is you, and you for me*
> *So happy together . . ."*
> sang the Turtles.

Before the song ended, he had deftly reached into his pocket and placed something in her hand, just as he had at the Island Summer Dance. Just as she did then, she blinked but didn't stop to look at it. "Another promise?" she whispered near his ear.

"The ultimate promise," he whispered back. "I'll always love you."

He stopped dancing, pulling her arm to take her over to the wall of the porch near the library window so that her back rested on the cool surface.

He cleared his throat. "You know, something's just not right when you can consistently beat your prince at ping pong."

Caroline was only taken aback for a moment. "My prince? As in a fairy tale love story?"

Chad nodded. "The same. Exactly four weeks ago, the youngest of the sisters of the Painter Dynasty sent me on a great quest to prove I'm a prince and not a frog, worthy of a kiss from her sister that will transform me forever."

Just as he did on the beach four weeks ago at the Island Summer Dance, he reached down to her hand, turning the palm up and opening her fist at her pinky finger. She didn't open the next one, so he pried it up, too.

Caroline was pressing her lips together in a line, trying not to smile at making him work for this. She didn't open any other fingers. He exaggerated a sigh and played along until her palm was open.

She kept her eyes on his, not willing to look down at what was revealed in her hand. Her eyes held a hint of panic, and he felt that inconvenient fluttering sensation in that indescribable location somewhere in his middle as he picked up the ring and slid it onto her finger.

"It's a ring from a prince. An emerald cut diamond, the shape of a smooth blank canvas to paint a lifetime together on. When you look into it, it seems to go on for infinity. But underneath, it's full of fire and flash, like me and you. Don't take my word for it—look at it."

He extended her arm so that her hand was in the light from the window. She tore her eyes from his and gasped when she saw that it was exactly what she'd dreamed of. The fire and flash exploded in bursts, trapped in the diamond from the sideways lamplight of the library.

When she could speak, she said, "Is this—real?"

"If it isn't, I have a serious problem with the bill."

"I mean—is this really happening?" She tore her eyes from the ring to look at him hopefully.

"If it isn't, at least we're in the same dream. That's fine for the moment, but if you can work that kind of magic more often, it's goin' to be a problem."

She smiled now but didn't seem to be able to say anything. She just looked at him with a bewildered expression that said this was not sinking in.

"Did—did your mom tell you what kind of ring I wanted?"

"No, I overheard you and memorized it. It's not the kind of statement a guy gets over."

She smiled and bit her lower lip gently. Then she looked at the ring again as if it would disappear.

"This is the only way I can say that I love you that tops the way you said it to me. And the only way I can get that kiss that'll rock my world is if you'll marry me."

She looked up at him with a challenge in her eyes. Now he had the normal Caroline back. He grinned.

"Okay, I admit, this is better than my way of saying I love you. But I haven't said yes, so you haven't won yet," she reminded him.

"Oh, but I have. Are you really goin' to give me that rock back?"

She sighed and groaned, pretending she was indecisive. "You're a genius at planning for me to win if I lose, so I'll let you win again. My answer is yes."

He was leaning on his shoulder against the wall, looking at her intently. He reached up to trace the line of her cheek and jaw. "I dreamed you'd say yes out here when we were kids. You just made my lifelong dream come true."

"Then we wandered into the same dream again. It's becoming dangerous. We have to do something about that."

"Like get married—soon?" He grinned and held up her hand closer, kissing it near the ring. "Let's go tell everyone, then go to the pool to talk about plans." He took a step away to lead her to the pavilion.

"Chad," she blurted out, not moving from where she stood. He looked back and saw the expression in her eyes. His own expression softened, and he stepped closer to her. He should just savor the moment, enjoying a dream come true right where he'd imagined it for years.

"I know," he said as he settled back against the wall beside her.

***

The crowd was enjoying "Magic Carpet Ride" by Steppenwolf as Chad searched for his parents.

The Big Three, their wives, and Savanna were standing in the sand. He went straight for them, his arm around the soft black material on Caroline's shoulders. The waterfall strands of blonde hair cascaded over his sleeve.

Phillip saw movement from the Big House in the corner of his eye and turned his head to see them coming. He reached over to slap Andy's arm.

Chad took a deep breath and held Caroline's hand up for them to see. It would be hard to talk over the music, so he went for the visual effect. Besides, it would announce their engagement to them all at the same moment.

Chrissy was gawking at the ring with her mouth open, keeping Caroline's hand in hers while Valerie hugged her daughter and Savanna waited to do the same. "It's about time," she said with a smile and a kiss for her granddaughter.

Joey was playing the next to the last song as Chad and Caroline finally reached the pavilion floor. Chad made his way to where Joey could see him, holding out Caroline's hand. Joey's mouth fell open before he recovered and laughed. He held up his hand in Spock's Vulcan "V" to say "Live long and prosper." Others saw the gesture and started smiling and pointing.

Patrick worked his way over with Natalie. Caroline smiled and held out her hand, which her brother grabbed quickly to gape at before he swung her around. He pumped Chad's hand vigorously, telling him they were finally officially going to be brothers. Natalie's hands flew to her mouth before she reached out to hug Caroline, making it obvious something exciting was happening.

Marina, Danny, Juliette, and Cameron had reached them, and Marina let out a squeal of delight before hugging her sister and Chad. Shelly and Zachary pushed through the crowd to get to them and joined the excitement. Now everyone on the dance floor was watching and laughing. Carly, Jesse, Cassie, and her date walked up from the beach to see what was going on.

Andy and Valerie were standing with Phillip and Camellia in the sand near the pavilion, enjoying the view of their children revealing their engagement. Wyeth, Chrissy, and Savannah were nearby, explaining the impact of the engagement on Painter Place to the journalists and the local reporter from Whitehaven.

Joey used his microphone to announce that Chad Gregory had just made history at Painter Place during Rock the Island by giving a rock to Caroline Painter, and that the last dance would be on the sand for everyone but them.

The crowd poured down the steps, circling the pavilion for the best view. Chad and Caroline beamed at one another, standing alone face to face.

"You know, you never actually ask me to dance. You just tell me to and whisk me away, all strong and in charge and everything," Caroline said.

"You never ask me, either. You just say, 'I pick you,' looking at me with eyes that go on into infinity, blue as the Atlantic, flipping things over inside me and leaving me dazed."

Orleans began the first notes of the last song. Chad reached for her to slow dance.

"So dance with me," he said.

"I pick you," she answered.

They began to sway to the beat of the song, singing the words to one another.

> *"Dance with me, I want to be your partner.*
> *Can't you see the music is just starting?*
> *Night is falling, and I am calling*
> *Dance with me.*
> *Fantasy could never be so killing.*

I feel free, I hope that you are willing
Pick the beat up, and kick your feet up
Dance with me.
Let it lift you off the ground
Starry eyes, and love is all around
I can take you where you want to go . . ."

When the song was over, Chad and Caroline spun around in the pavilion together while everyone applauded, whistled, and hooted congratulations.

***

Later, Patrick and Natalie went to spend time around the pool with Chad and Caroline, having some sandwiches and talking about wedding plans. The music for the formal date night with the girls two nights ago played on the stereo.

Chad told them what he'd talked to Cameron about that afternoon. Patrick and Natalie loved the idea, and they all waited on Caroline's reaction.

"We'd need to keep it a secret until we're closer to the time, but six of us already know about it. Can we get by with that?"

Patrick and Chad shrugged almost at the same time and nodded at one another.

Natalie's eyes danced. "I think the secrecy will build up a lot of expectation, yet they'll still have no way of anticipating the reality when it happens. They could never imagine it."

Caroline looked at Chad. "I told you that I trust you to know what's next for us. Is this what you want?"

"Now that I've had time to think about it, I'd be disappointed if we didn't."

Caroline laughed. "It's settled, then."

Chad stood up, holding Caroline's hand and motioning for them to follow.

The gate Chad and Caroline had gone through on Thursday night was open. He smiled at her and glanced over at the shadows on the wall. They reached the beautiful new door of the remodeled guest house, and he

304

pulled a key out of his pocket to put in her hand. It had a ribbon and a tag on it. It said, "Direction."

She just stood there for a moment, letting this sink in. Natalie laughed, delighted at how Chad was telling Caroline where they would live.

"Open it, it's yours," he said. "No more distractions. This is our direction."

***

When Patrick took Natalie back to the Big House, he pulled in the front circle drive and walked her up to the porch. The lights and torches from the party had gone out when most of the cleanup had been done, but a few people still milled around on the pier and beach.

Patrick hesitated at the top of the steps. A few cheerful lights were still lit inside the front rooms of windows.

"Patrick, something has been on your mind all day. I don't like the way it's distracting you and keeping me from getting your undivided attention."

He ran his hand through his hair, looked up at the huge light fixture on the high ceiling overhead, and then looked directly into her eyes.

Natalie waited, her dark eyes never leaving his face.

"I don't like seein' or thinkin' of you with Dante Kent. He's way out of my league, and it makes me question what possessed me to imagine that someone like you would be interested in a guy like me."

He blew out a deep intake of breath. Good or bad, it was finally out.

Her hand flew to her mouth, and she closed her eyes.

Patrick just stood there a moment, not sure what to say or do. Impulsively, he reached out to pull her to him.

"Did you just say that you love me?" she whispered.

He laughed shortly and whispered back, "Yes, I did."

Chapter Thirty

"Let him kiss me with the kisses of his mouth."
Song of Solomon 1:2, KJV

Chad stopped by the studio again with coffee for Caroline on Monday morning as he left to work at Global's offices in Whitehaven. He hoped she'd be working on that painting he wanted to see. If there was any time when the subject matter would be on her mind, it should be today.

He knocked lightly on the doorframe and peeked in. She turned from her work, and her face lit up in that way that made his heart jump. She walked toward him as he came in, with President Reagan speaking in the news on the Whitehaven radio station.

He brushed a kiss on her temple and handed her the coffee. "Seen the morning paper yet?"

She took the sealed coffee mug and said thanks with her eyes. Then she looked at the paper in his hands. "No—is Rock the Island in it?"

Chad laughed. "I'll say! And a whole lot about us. This should put to rest any question in Whitehaven as to whether I'm back to stay."

He opened the paper to the right section and put it on a table nearby, where she looked at it while sipping her coffee. He walked over to her easel, on which the canvas was sideways to him. He stopped in front of it, speechless.

Caroline came up beside him. At first they just stood there together, transported to the moment of the view. She put her hand around his dress shirt sleeve. "Like it?" she asked softly.

He blew out his breath before answering, not taking his eyes off the painting. "Love it. Love you."

"You weren't supposed to see it yet, but now that you've asked me to marry you there, it'll be an engagement gift from me to you. I wasn't sure where I was going with it when I started."

She turned from the painting to look at him. "Chad."

He reluctantly turned his head to her, wearing a faraway look.

"I never took anyone else onto the veranda like that—or anywhere else where I had special, secret memories of you. If anyone was ever here on the island with me, I kept them on the well-worn paths. It hurt during the Island Summer Dances when you were gone. I'd look over at the Big House as I danced with someone else. I'd imagine us there, looking out at the pavilion and pier or dancing together."

His eyes stung, and he wrapped his arms around her. Someday, he hoped all these bittersweet memories would fade as they replaced them with happy ones.

***

The events of the month of June eclipsed the rest of the summer of 1985 for the young generation at Painter Place, but they set the stage for it. An important change had come over the island. Every day brought a feeling of excitement and anticipation as if Painter Place had re-charged and taken a fresh direction. The Big Three kept expecting a payback from Chad and Patrick after the surprise kick-off to Rock the Island, but it was slow in coming.

Shelly and Zachary were a formidable team in the gallery and studios, and Wyeth couldn't have been more pleased with his assistants and the success of his matchmaking. With a lot of the business side of things handled now by them and the gallery flourishing from all the summer publicity and videos, he was getting more painting and speaking done.

Caroline and Chad worked on furnishing what would be their first home. He designed one room into a home studio for her, with skylights and a wall of glass overlooking the Intracoastal Waterway, opening to the balcony. She could sometimes escape the busy and often distracting traffic at the gallery studios. Caroline invited Valerie, Camellia, and Chrissy to have dinner at Dockside in Whitehaven one night in July to talk about gift registry decisions and shopping for decor.

After they ordered, Valerie looked at Caroline. "Now tell us how to help with your reception and what your wish list for the house is. Can we plan a shower?"

"I'll leave it up to all of you how to handle the bridal shower, but make sure everyone understands that the date and setting are a secret. The theme is Painter Place. We'd like a small reception at the Big House, with only the family and a few friends. Here's a list to plan food for. It will be late at night, so keep the food light and simple. Wear something classy yet comfortable to be outdoors in."

The waitress brought their food, and Valerie said a blessing while they held hands.

Caroline swallowed her first bite. "As for the house, I love Camellia's remodeling design and hope that we can plan around a few inspiration pieces. Chad and I want to include the vase he sent to me in Mevagissey and two paintings, *Tall Ships and Sunflowers* and *Island Summer Evening*. I took these pictures for you to carry if you want to spend some time shopping for ideas for us." She handed the three of them some photos.

Caroline had hoped that inviting Chrissy to help her mom and Camellia would heal the undercurrent that could sometimes still be felt about her and Wyeth being kept in the dark in the plan for Chad and Caroline. When it became obvious that little things could still be awkward, her mom sighed and stepped up to handle it.

"Look, I'm goin' to be the one to mention the elephant in the room. Let's all talk about it and move past this. I'll go first."

The ladies walked out the door of Dockside without the distances between them that they'd walked in with.

***

Friday evening Tarzan games and volleyball nights on the beach were favorite gatherings that summer, but rainy nights with board games were no less competitive. Occasionally, there was a hint of tension within the Big Three though only family would have noticed the difference in how things used to be and how they now were. Caroline understood the cool look in her uncle's eyes sometimes when he looked at her dad and Phillip. Even when something was forgiven, it changed your reality. It took time to rebuild damaged relationships.

Savanna Painter began a new book. She said it was from her journals and told everyone who asked about it that it was called *Painter Place*. Wolf Lyons returned to Painter Place for a brief publicity trip for the book he'd written in the setting of the island and revealed that the murder in his story took place on the bridge crossing over from Whitehaven. Once this news was out to the public, it would be another one of the stories and legends told around the campfires on dark nights by the local campers on Dog's Head.

***

Near the end of July, Marina dropped by the studio with a letter from Sherrie Shepherd. "This came in the mail today, and I thought I'd bring it by instead of letting everyone look through the mail at home and see it. You might not like all the inconvenient questions."

Caroline put down her paintbrush and wiped her hands on a towel. "How thoughtful, Marina—thanks! Stay here while I read it. You can see it if you want to."

She opened the seal and read her friend's beautiful cursive handwriting on pale yellow paper that looked like someone had pressed sunshine into it.

"Dearest Caroline," the letter began. "Chris and I want to join our parents in congratulating you on your engagement to Chad Gregory. He sounds like a perfect match for you. We know God will bless your marriage to His own purposes under Heaven.

"I won't be coming back home at the end of the summer as planned. I've met a young man here on staff that has gotten me a full-time position because he wants me to stay. I'm daring to think that all the pain of giving up my brother led me here to my future. Time will tell.

"Friends tell me that Patrick is very happy. Please tell him I wish him well and that the Castaway is a great idea that I know will be successful in Whitehaven.

"Chris is doing as well as can be expected for someone new in the field. Being on staff, I get to know more about the inside workings of his position and don't dare tell my parents. He's seeing spiritual warfare like he's never imagined and needs prayer.

"I'll try to stay in touch and should be home for Christmas. Maybe we can get together for lunch? Friends always, Sherrie."

Caroline looked thoughtful as she handed the letter to Marina.

Marina studied her face without looking at the letter. "Sometimes it still hurts a little, doesn't it?"

310

Caroline nodded. "But it's not the same as what I have with Chad. It's like missing a friend that I can't talk to anymore."

She wiped tears that unexpectedly stung her eyes, and her sister hugged her.

***

In early August, Caroline asked Chad to take a day to go with her to Charleston to pick out his wedding band.

"Let's make it two days," he said. "The first day, we'll shop for my ring and a dress for you to wear to Middleton Place for an engagement dinner with my family. We'll stay at Montgomery's that night."

Chad planned to reset the memory on the Battery when Caroline had questioned his trustworthiness and brought Chris between them. He wore a shirt the color of twilight, her favorite time of day. The only earthy green anywhere was on the palm trees and grass.

Even on a hot August weeknight in Charleston, lots of people were walking on the Battery—laughing, taking photos, and having fun together. The same little boy came up to Chad to tell him that his pretty girl should have some palmetto roses and recognized him.

"You still spendin' all your money on one girl?" he asked with a big grin. "She got two earrings on this time. You must've got a night job or somethin'."

Chad winked and picked out only one rose but gave the boy enough money for a dozen. He handed the rose to Caroline.

"She's still my only one," explained Chad. He took her hand and showed the boy her engagement ring. "See—one ring, one rose, and one girl. And that ring took all my money. I work nights and Saturdays now."

The little boy whistled at the ring and broke into a huge grin. "She must be somethin' else! She gonna make you work like that the rest o' ya life?"

Chad laughed. He leaned forward conspiratorially with his hand beside his mouth as if to keep Caroline from hearing a secret. "I'm the one who makes her do what I want. It just takes a lot of work."

The little boy was the one who laughed now. "Gonna remember that when I grow up," he said.

311

Another couple walked by, and he was off, trying to sell more palmetto roses. Chad and Caroline strolled slowly under the oaks, palmettos, and tall sidewalk lanterns until they got close to the raised gazebo. Caroline gently pulled his arm to back him into the foundation, heading to the only available spot among the other couples.

"This is my favorite habit," Chad said lazily. "Promise me you'll keep pushing me around after we're married."

She was close beside him with her shoulder on the wall, tilting her head to rest against it and holding the palmetto rose in that hand. "I will. It's one of those times when I win." She traced the rose over his shoulder.

He chuckled. "Ohhh no, you don't. It's rigged. I win."

They were quiet for a few moments, listening to the night sounds on the Battery and enjoying being close to one another.

"You know why I bought you the rose?" Chad said eventually.

"So I'd imagine it's red and put it on my pillow tonight?"

"You still haven't told me how that worked out in St. Austell."

As she did the last time he mentioned that here, she teased him with a smile, as if she had a secret, twirling the rose before she looked out at the palm trees and oaks.

"Okay, I'm more intrigued than ever, and it looks like you're still plannin' to leave me that way. What's it goin' to take to get what I want this time?"

"Marry me."

"Ohhhh, I get it—if you tell me, you have to own me or kill me, right?"

"That's my price. Take it or leave it."

"I'll take it! At what point in this deal will you stop dangling me around?"

She smiled as she leaned closer and looked him right in the eye. "Since our wedding is a special occasion, we'll be leaving in the Lamborghini. Before we get out at our house, I'll tell you."

Chad blinked and swallowed. "You're obviously doin' this to me on purpose, Caroline. And I bet it's always goin' to be this way. You win."

312

She laughed—that sound like cool water that he loved. He exaggerated a deep sigh and put her hand up to his heart, his eyes never leaving hers.

"Thanks for giving me those first four crazy weeks to prove you can trust me. Let's make a new memory here." He kissed her hand near her engagement ring. "My love for you isn't just the kind that keeps me distracted or something I fell into like a klutz. It's about a lifetime. I love you, I'll be faithful to you, and I'll never leave you, no matter what."

***

Chad made a long distance call to Cole during the last week of August to get an update on how things were going with Baker's new situation.

"Public Parking is doing great and will be coming to America for a tour eventually. Baker said to tell you he'll be sending a package your way soon with the new releases and some tee shirts. The album includes Caroline's song, and he's recorded a Christian project on the side he'd like to see if we can find backers for. He wants to do a concert at Painter Place for Whitehaven, so I'll get some dates to think about."

"Good to hear. I think I have some ideas of who to call, and if you want this one, I'll turn it over to you. Stayin' off probation with Shannon and Dad?"

"Yep. She and I went to the summer Bible study for the college group at church. God really worked on me with your point about praying for crop failure."

"He has a way of keepin' a theme goin' until you catch on. Can Shannon make a trip with you with Uncle Justin's family?"

Cole drew a quick breath. "Is it time?"

"No one here will know until Monday, so tell Justin to plan the travel, but not to say anything to Dad yet. Granddad and Dad already planned to have everyone in at a moment's notice. The wedding is the end of next week, but we don't know what day. Your tux is ready."

"Are you?"

Chad grinned at the phone. "Can't wait. Get in here to make me nervous."

Caroline called their family and friends on the first Monday in September to tell them they'd be married on one of the three last days of the week, depending on weather. They asked that everyone plan to be at the pier an hour before sunset on the first clear day, dressed for their wedding. The family was in a state of excitement, wondering what was going to happen and when.

Extra crews came rolling onto the island the same day. A covered trailer parked off the road near the pavilion, which aroused a lot of curiosity. Andy, Wyeth, and Phillip gathered at the Big House after dinner to watch all the activity, standing at the base of the steps to the veranda. The ladies sat in rocking chairs on the porch with cameras, ready for anything.

A crew walked up to the trailer and began the process of unloading it. A vehicle was rolled down the ramp, and men began working on pulling back the cover. A silver Aston Martin gleamed in the late afternoon sunlight. The Big Three looked at one another in disbelief.

Someone dressed as a stunt driver walked up to them. "Are you the Painter brothers and Phillip Gregory?"

They nodded mutely.

He handed Andy the keys. "You have an hour to drive around the island before I need it, compliments of Chad Gregory, Patrick Painter, and Cameron Fisher. They said to tell you that this puts them one up, and they'd like to see the Big Three top this."

***

A rehearsal for the wedding ceremony was planned on Friday after dinner at the Big House. Cameron and Juliette thought they'd have to set up for a practice run on the veranda, but there was a break in the otherwise rainy day, and the group went to the end of the pier. Juliette put down strips of tape with names on them so they'd know where to stand and what signals they were waiting for. A four-man band of actors gathered over to the side of the pier on the beach but didn't take out their instruments in the damp weather.

Chad and Caroline practiced their vows with the actor who was also a pastor. The wedding party had scripts in hand, and Cameron addressed them all afterward.

"If you haven't guessed already, Caroline and Chad's wedding is part of the movie I'm filming, though the ceremony will be official. All of the attendants know about the plan and have agreed to be extras. By participating, you're also serving as extras, but only in a crowd situation, as a background. Don't act—just forget about the cameras and be yourself. You won't be in the movie except possibly as a shape from a distance. If you don't want to do this, stay near the beginning of the pier by the sand, and you can still be part of the event without worrying about the film. Everybody understand?"

There was a buzz of excitement, which he let die before he continued.

"The band will play instrumental music, but they will become part of the activities here on the beach. Ignore them after the processional, which will be the end of the music for the wedding. I'll be down on the beach directing, and Juliette will help me with signals from the ceremony. Cameras and distractions will be around, so just focus on what you're here for—to see Chad and Caroline tie the knot."

The group clapped, and Cole and Joey whistled.

"After the ceremony, the wedding will clear the pier and go over to the reception. We will continue with the filming in the twilight for a little longer, with lights underneath the pier and on the water with the *Artistic License.* It's such a hot boat I had to use it in the movie. We'll have fireworks from the beach to celebrate when the shooting is over, and if you want some music in the pavilion, feel free to do that while we clean up. Chad will eventually take Caroline to their house in the Lamborghini because it's a special occasion. It will be too late for them to travel, so they'll take a plane to Hawaii the next day."

***

On Saturday, shortly before sunset, Caroline arrived with her dad in the Aston Martin in the parking lot near the pavilion, where Marina, Natalie, Carly, and Valerie waited. They all grasped hands, and Andy prayed with them, asking for the Lord to bless this day for His glory at Painter Place and in Chad and Caroline's new life. They kept Caroline hidden behind the pavilion as a photographer took their photos with the Aston Martin. They watched for the signal to walk to the pier.

Chad was waiting in his white tails and bow tie near the end of the pier, with Cole beside him in a dove gray tuxedo and an ultramarine bow tie.

Cole looked at Chad and spoke low so that only he could hear. "I'm goin' to propose to Shannon after this tonight on the beach. It's a great place for a memory, and besides, we'll end up living here eventually unless Dad relents on something for me at Global in London."

Chad looked at Shannon, who was sitting with his family. "Long engagement?"

"Not too long, if things keep goin' this good with the Young Guns," Cole answered.

"Got a ring yet?"

"No, promising her a shopping trip in Charleston or London."

The acting pastor asked Chad to turn and look out at the water until Caroline and her dad could get to the pier. The band was playing instrumental love songs along with the swish of gentle surf for the prelude.

Now Chad felt the butterflies, and he tried to focus on a very real-looking fight taking place on board the *Artistic License*. A boat with cameras was in place to film the wedding and a chase scene from nearby. They'd get a great view of the sunset behind Painter Place.

And he was getting married. Right here, on the spot where he'd had his first official date with Caroline, the night after the Island Summer Dance. The spot where she'd asked him what his weakness was because he couldn't be a golden boy, and they'd agreed to tell one another when something was a distraction or a direction. It was the spot where they'd looked up at Polaris—the "guiding star," the "steadfast star." It was the spot where they'd wondered whether the English Channel was this beautiful, and the spot they'd thought of when they were on the cliffs of Mevagissey over the English Channel, looking at the horizon.

The pastor broke into Chad's memories, saying he could turn around. Chad hesitated. The day was finally here. A Painter and a Gregory were going to be married for the first time in the history of Painter Place—over three hundred years. And his wedding was going to be part of a movie.

Beside him, Cole cleared his throat. "Come on, brother," he said, trying not to be obvious. "You're up."

Chad slowly turned around. The wedding attendants stood in front of Caroline to hide her until they came down. They were wearing stunning ultramarine blue dresses that blended with the gray tuxedos to look like flowing water.

Once Patrick had escorted Natalie down, Chad let his eyes rest only on Joey and Carly coming down, not daring to look at Caroline yet.

But then, there was only Caroline. She was on her dad's arm, and Marina walked behind her to watch after the train of her dress. He was glad he remembered it was not in the script or appropriate to say, "Wow." But seeing her soothed his nerves. He could face anything if she were with him.

The band's instruments played the processional, "Here, There, and Everywhere" by the Beatles, and he remembered how it was playing when she told him she loved him for the first time ever.

Caroline walked slowly toward him past their guests, who were lined up along the pier railing. She didn't seem nervous at all. She was smiling at everyone but had a special smile for him. It reminded him that she had something to tell him later in the Lamborghini.

Her brilliantly white dress was inspired by an island theme, very classy and simple but dramatic. He knew she'd worked with Juliette's designer to create it herself as if it were one of her paintings. It was fitted to her all the way to her knees, where it began to flare out softly, reminding him of a fashion doll's dress. But by the time she faced him, he could tell that there was something alluring going on in the back of it, where the cameras would be.

After her dad gave Chad his blessing and her hand, she stepped closer, and he could see more of the dress. When she turned to hand her bouquet of sunflowers and palmetto roses to Marina, he was stunned at the genius of this little number. Strips of silky scarf material pulled the halter neckline across her bare shoulders, lacing up into loops on either side of a backless cutout that formed a point near her waist. A huge gathered bow of the same fabric was attached at the point to form an airy short train of silky sheer scarf fabric behind her.

317

Her hair was pulled up in a design that looked like a seashell, draping enticingly over her left ear. Her right ear was left bare by upswept hair that seemed to flirt with the breeze, and on that ear she wore the earring he'd bought her in Charleston. The diamonds sparkled with all the colors of the ever-changing sunset surrounding them. Besides the earring, the eternity bracelet he'd bought in London and her engagement ring was the only jewelry she wore.

As everyone was appreciating Caroline's dress and watching her settle in beside Chad, Patrick looked over at Natalie. She smiled. Keeping his hand in front of him so the guests couldn't see, he pointed to Caroline and Chad, then at himself and her. Her lips parted in surprise.

With a coy expression, she tried to be unobtrusive as she pointed to her ring finger.

Smugly, he reached into his pocket and revealed a ring near the end of his little finger.

She couldn't help it. Her mouth fell open and her eyes widened.

The pastor was beginning the brief ceremony. The sound of jet skis fired up in the distance, joining the hum of the boats involved in activity surrounding the *Artistic License*.

Patrick watched a series of expressions cross Natalie's face before she nodded slightly. He smiled and put the ring back into his pocket.

When the pastor asked Chad and Caroline to exchange rings, Chad added a slender wedding band to her ring finger to join her engagement ring. She placed a platinum band with a brushed stripe onto the ring finger of his left hand. Then she took his right hand, putting the ring he'd given her with his family crest and Bible verse onto his finger.

She kept holding his right hand and looked up at him solemnly. "To remind you that you have two promises to keep and that if you're going to be my leader, you have to be a follower—always seeking the Lord's path for us."

Chad, the pastor, the wedding party, and family near them were taken aback, but the pastor smiled as if this was planned. The microphones were on.

Chad recovered and nodded at Caroline. "I promise. Always."

Andy Painter leaned back slightly and looked in Phillip's direction. Their eyes met. Andy's expression said, "Here we go. Warned ya."

Juliette motioned frantically to get Cameron's attention on the beach. She made their sign of wild horses running free. He grabbed some headphones from a person next to him.

Juliette turned back to the wedding. "That's my girl," she said to herself. "Don't let them box you in with a script."

The pastor moved on with the ceremony, finally looking at Chad and saying, "I now pronounce you man and wife. You may kiss your bride."

Chad and Caroline faced one another as jet skis and a power boat thundered under the pier. He hesitated.

"No pressure," Caroline teased.

"This is for the cameras. It's not the dangerous kiss."

"Can't you make it a little dangerous?" Her eyes were laughing as she waited. "After all, a spy underneath our feet is risking his life to save the world. Those aren't bad guys—they're worse guys. Show some courage."

Cole coughed, giving himself an excuse to put his fist to his mouth. This was like the torture of thinking something funny in church, when everyone else was serious and you couldn't laugh. He risked a glance back at Joey, whose grin stretched from ear to ear.

The pastor and Patrick were twitching in the struggle for a straight face. Marina pressed her lips together, breathing deeply. When this was over, she was going to be hysterical.

Savanna pressed her fingertips to her lips. Her shoulders were shaking with suppressed laughter, just as Wyeth beside her. Valerie's mother cleared her throat to cover a giggle.

Guests who weren't close enough to hear over the boats waited and looked at one another, wondering what the conversation was about. Chad and Caroline were supposed to have their first kiss. Cameras were rolling, and the pier was rumbling.

Cameron looked up to Juliette, his demeanor urgent and his hands spread out as if to ask what was going on. Chad had to do something, quick.

Chad shook his head slightly and groaned. "You're really asking for it."

"You bet I am. And it's about time, baby."

Cameron held on to the headset at his ears, overcome with laughter. He hoped the stunts were going as planned without him. Jesse had the main camera on Chad and Caroline and watched in fascination. This seemed to be a standoff, and she seemed to be daring him to kiss her! He'd seen some actors go off script in his time, but nothing like this.

Chad glanced out at the chase scene, churning the last sunset colors on the water. He made a decision, quickly reaching out to take Caroline's face into both his hands. For an instant, he just let himself get lost in those blue depths, shutting out anything around them. The pier trembled with the roaring motors around the pilings. Or was that the earth moving?

He closed his eyes and barely let his lips touch hers in a shy kiss that quickly became a hungry one, the one he'd dreamed of, for only an instant before the applause reminded him that they weren't alone. He reluctantly pulled away. He didn't take his eyes from hers and decided he wanted to kiss her again, so he put his arms around the back of that amazing dress. This time, he kissed her during a dramatic dip, and then again when he was swinging her around as if they were on the veranda on a night when she'd picked him to dance in the shadows. They were in a movie, after all. Anything could happen.

Epilogue
Hawaii, Honeymoon Week Two of Three

Chad was rubbing sunscreen on Caroline's back as she lay with her eyes closed, relaxing on the sugary sands of a beach in Hawaii during the second week of their honeymoon. Next to them, Juliette and Cameron, newlyweds themselves, were lounging with music on a portable radio. Chad glanced their way and wondered if they were asleep behind their sunglasses, then remembered that he could kiss his wife any time he wanted to, even if Cameron and Juliette's eyes weren't closed.

He gently put his lips on the back of Caroline's neck where he'd pushed her hair aside for sunscreen, intending only to brush a kiss and then get into his own chair. But she smiled and made a warning sound in her throat that he'd better stop. It was too much like a dare. He couldn't resist getting closer, this time on her ear, and then quickly caught the side of her smile before she could do anything about it. He considered it a win. After all, Derrick got a broken nose for trying that.

Feeling very satisfied with himself, he athletically dodged her arm as she tried to slap his leg. He settled into his own chair as the weather report was just coming over Cameron's radio.

"Hurricane Gloria is barreling toward the Carolinas and is already being called the storm of the century."

Caroline rose up on her elbows and looked at Chad. "They named the hurricane of the century 'Gloria'? And it happens right after you marry me?"

Juliette didn't open her eyes as she said, "Sometimes a girl just has to vent."

Beneath the Surface

Painter Place is a fictional island, but it represents family and what that stands for in any person's life. When did you last think about your ideals for your family? Are they worth the extra personal cost and sacrifice as you struggle to uphold them?

How can your commitment to live on a higher plane than the world affect your family? Your search for a spouse? Your dating habits?

No one lives without consequences to themselves and everyone around them. Have you ever considered the collateral damage that your bad choices have had on your family, friends, and career, or do you feel your choices are your own business?

Was Andy Painter right or wrong in his choice of how to handle his beloved daughter's future? His scope of reference was Painter Place as a whole. Have you ever had to choose to handle a situation in light of the broader implications, rather than personal feelings?

If a situation like the one with Baker Holmes was suddenly plopped into your day, are you prepared to handle it? If not, what steps can you take to be ready?

How does recognizing the source of someone's authority for their morals help you communicate with them?

Take time to write down the scripture references throughout the book. Consider how the meaning was applied in the story and then apply them to your own life. Is there a similarity?

Do you actually know what you believe and why?

Themes in Painter Place

If you want to live on a higher plane that the world, you have to commit to doing what it takes to make it a reality instead of doing whatever pleases you.

The source of authority for the morality in your life determines many of your decisions.

Parents and other relatives in a child's life should be mindful of their role in the outlook of the next generation. Parents should closely emulate behavior that is humble, yet heroic.

Christians live in the world, and interacting with the world requires discernment. We are salt and light to freely mingle into the world, not to be hidden under a basket in fear.

Goals of the Author

To show that living a life committed to righteousness is not boring, sterile, or bondage. Christians have joyous victory and freedom in their salvation.

To show that people with wealth and responsibility have inroads to be greatly used by God. The body of believers has been uniquely gifted in many ways to work together for the same goal in their own spheres of influence. If all believers lived in poverty, who would be the salt and light to the rich and famous?

To show that there is another option to the endless pain of shallow dating. When being with someone is a means of feeling worthy or for something to do, the relationship's purpose has already failed.

To reveal the reality of how much a potential spouse affects family dynamics and direction, and to show that one does not "fall" into romantic love. Falling is considered an accident anywhere else.

To remind Christians that marriage between men and women is intended to bring glory to God. It is NOT ultimately about personal satisfaction and the fulfillment of unrealistic dreams. It should include a like-minded, exclusive partner for life's main goals for couples—provision and support, safe haven for physical relationships, and a nurturing environment for children.

Made in the USA
Charleston, SC
29 July 2015